THE NEXUS HAS FALLEN

DUSTIN A. FIFE

Books by Dustin Fife

Love the Unloved

Eloq's Lightning (December 2018)

Death by Gravity (2019)

Forgotten Again (2020)

Keep up to date on publication announcements at www.dustinfife.net

This is a work of fiction. All the characters, organizations, and events portrayed in this novel are either products of the author's imagination or are used fictitiously.

THE NEXUS HAS FALLEN

Cover art by tatline.net

ISBN-13: 978-1986476676
ISBN-10: 1986476677

FOR MY GRANDPARENTS

Whose colorful personalities inspired so many of the characters in this book.

Acknowledgments

Writing a novel is a *massive* undertaking. I thought I had completed this project in the fall of 2012 and was ready to submit my baby to editors and agents everywhere.

I was wrong.

I am *deeply* indebted to the many, *many* readers who were kind enough to not be kind to my manuscript. You all have turned a terrible novel into one that, I hope, is excellent.

First, let me thank my first line of defense against embarrassment, my alpha readers. These include Michael Mohon, David Lyon, Laurel Cunningham, and Roger Colby. I am deeply sorry you had all to deal with such a despicable mess, but I thank you for your valuable feedback.

My list of beta readers is long and incomplete, and include Laura Reynolds, Jerry Quinn, Cormac O'Hugh, Derek Cummings, Jason Robert Smith, Jeffry Smith, Michaël Wertenberg, Victoria Smith, Mildred Gable, Dave Cushing, Catherine Michelle, Brandy Smith, Ashley Searcy, and Shannon Pierce. My deepest apologies if I have missed anyone.

Finally, to my last line of defense, my "post-beta" readers, which include Aleesha Carother, Aria Clawson, Rebecca Lewis, Lori Garman, Gregg Platt, Chris Banford, Amber Fife, and Lindsay Hiller.

To those whose names who fill this page, and to those whose names I have forgotten, I thank you.

See you in the next book, my friends.

Chapter 1

Quincy Sturgess—dead. My family—gone. Humanity is without intellect. What else must I suffer to atone for my careless comment? But I can't give up. Quincy died for this.

Journal Entry from Gene "the Ancient," dated four years after the Genetic Apocalypse.

July 12th, 2246

President Akram of the Malkum marched down the hallway, traveling with the vitality of a much younger man. People would guess him to be half his age. Or less, for the man was 243 years old. Frozen in time. An immortal among mortals.

He grazed the concrete walls with his fingertips. The florescent lights flickered and buzzed, flickered and buzzed, like a dumb firefly. Spencer Burton sat in a chair in front of a door, munching on potato chips. Akram cleared his throat.

Spencer flinched and spilled his chips. Akram tightened his fist. After centuries, he grew tired of people like Spencer—men who coasted, waited, *reacted.* Centuries ago, while nations warred, Akram *acted.* To prevent nuclear winter, he released the virus that crippled 99.99% of human intellect.

Sometimes, he wished the other .01% would shut up.

The man stood with a grunt. "Morning, President. Good morning. How are you today?"

Akram looked at Spencer in silence.

"Right, right. No time for pleasantries. Follow me." Spencer removed a keycard from his pocket.

"Custodial closet?"

"Yes, sir."

"I assume you didn't summon me to inspect maintenance records."

"No, sir."

Spencer waddled into the room. Akram followed, brushing aside cobwebs.

"Sorry about the dust." Spencer hacked. "This room hasn't been touched for centuries."

Akram side-stepped a toppled shelf, empty cleaning bottles, and a wiry mop. The air smelled of molding carpet and insect carcasses, garnished with a dash of mouse crap.

"I hope this has a point."

"Yes, of course. You'll want to see this, sir." Spencer pointed.

"A vent?"

"Well, it's what's *behind* it that's interesting."

Spencer fumbled with the gridded cover before dropping it with a clank. "Sorry," he muttered under his breath. Wiping his face with his shoulder, he shone a flashlight down a dirt tunnel.

Akram crouched and cocked his head. The light disappeared into darkness.

"It's about, oh, I'd say 100 yards long or so. And there's a room at the end with computers, electrical cords, blueprints," Spencer wheezed, "journal entries. But the strangest thing was the newspaper clippings. These clippings—they're centuries old."

Akram raised an eyebrow.

"And..." Spencer grabbed a spiral-bound notebook. "We found this inside." The wires were bent, and the cover hung weakly from the binding. The faded ink bled into the yellowed pages. Spencer thumbed through the book and pointed to text.

April 18th, 2042. The rebellion begins.

Akram blinked. Sergeant Drakes—had he *actually* been right about the rebellion?

No. It didn't make sense. The man's...*evidence* was...just strange. And for weeks, Malkum soldiers had combed the planet for these rebels, based on nothing more than this man's far-fetched testimony.

But this tunnel changed everything.

"It seems that Sergeant Drakes was right," said Spencer. "After his...you know...we started searching the compound and found this."

Akram shook his head. It couldn't be. The whole story was too unlikely. And he'd worked too hard to see the world fall to ruins again. Another rebellion meant more war, and more war meant death.

He'd already seen too many die. Over centuries, the sting of their deaths hadn't diminished—his cousin, his neighbor, half his classmates.

His twin.

Ancient friends and family members who had died in the war—killed by weapons developed using *his* research.

War wouldn't come again.

But if there was a rebellion...

His mobile rang. Akram looked at his watch. 8:05. He cursed.

"Hello?" he said.

"Mr. President, it's your secretary. I'm calling to remind you—"

"Yes, I know." Akram rubbed his eyes. "Cancel my meeting with the council. Apologize for my absence."

His secretary paused. "Uh...sir?"

"Something urgent has come up." Akram hung up. He'd pay later. His relationship with the council was already precarious. But *this* was more important than petty politics.

Akram stood. "How long have you known about this?"

"Couple days."

"Why haven't I heard anything before?"

"We..." Spencer rubbed the back of his neck. "We wanted to be sure."

Akram's eye twitched. Spencer shifted his weight, resembling an elephant side-stepping a rodent.

"Where is this rebellion?" Akram asked.

"The rebel...well, um...he doesn't know. It seems he remembers two different pasts...a-and doesn't know which is real."

"I want to talk to this defector." Akram charged toward the hallway. "Where is he?"

Spencer trailed behind. "H-he's been detained. At level one, sir."

"I want to see him. Now."

"Yes, sir."

"In the mean time, search the tunnel for anything that will help us find this rebel group. Do a background check on everyone who worked here 200 years ago. Search security personnel, scientists, janitors, everything. And double the number of men searching for this rebel group."

"Um sir, I believe we've exhausted recruits from Fahrquan."

"Then recruit outside Fahrquan." Akram stopped walking, bending toward Spencer. "I want a hundred choppers in the sky in *one hour*."

Akram turned and marched down the hallway.

"President?"

Akram stopped and lifted his head without turning to face him.

"Sir, did you want us to destroy the tunnel?"

"No. Let them think their secret is safe."

Cole lay on the grass, gazing at the rising sun. Orange light peaked over the evergreens, casting shadows across the meadow. He inhaled the crisp morning air.

Suta jumped on his belly. "Get up, Coe."

Cole grinned. "It's Cole. Collllllllla."

"Coe...la."

"No. Colllll."

"Coe...el."

"Close enough." Cole lifted the boy, who giggled.

"Wets count."

Cole chuckled. "You wanna count, huh?"

"Yup."

Suta hovered above him. Sunlight reflected off his green eyes and bathed his olive skin in warm light. Like the rest of the villagers, dirt caked his tattered clothes.

"Alright," Cole turned face-down. "Let's count."

The boy climbed his back. Not for the first time, Cole half-regretted teaching him to count this way. It had been fine when he could only count to ten.

But now?

"You ready?" Cole asked.

The boy wrapped his arms around Cole's neck.

"Not too tight," Cole said, sounding like a frog with a cold.

"Go!"

Cole began doing pushups.

"One. Two. Free." Suta giggled. "Faster, faster!"

"I'm getting tired, buddy."

"Seven. No yer not. Eight. Nine."

"It hurts!" Cole said.

The boy giggled. "Tenty. Tenty one. Tenty two."

"Twenty," Cole shouted.

"Tee-wenty free. Tee-wenty four."

Never once had Cole failed the boy—as high as he could count, that's the number of pushups he did. But Suta was learning to count faster than Cole could keep up.

"Fody-free. Fody-four. Fody-five."

Cole paused.

"Go wazy bones. Jump it!"

Cole leapt with his hands, clapping between pushups.

"Seventy-nine..." The boy paused. "Ummm..."

"You can do it, buddy."

"Eight-deeeeeeeee."

Cole laughed. The boy knew the pattern—another ten pushups would be guaranteed.

"Eighty-nine!" Suta clapped. "You take a break now."

Cole collapsed. It was quite a milestone. None of the adult villagers made it past five, and even then they were probably guessing.

But Suta was different. Somehow he'd escaped the effects of the Genetic Apocalypse. They'd have to start hiding him from the Malkum raids. His intelligence was too visible—dangerously so.

The boy skipped toward the village. Cole lifted his bag over his shoulder and followed.

Tall fir trees framed the trail to the village. He watched the placement of his feet, careful to sidestep spiders, ants, and grasshoppers. They passed makeshift dwellings constructed of logs, old cloth, and crumbling concrete. The homes circled an opening large enough for the hundred or so villagers to gather.

"Is Coe, is Coe." The villagers ran toward him. With calloused hands they patted his shoulders, greeting him as if he'd been absent for weeks.

Huka approached. The man's girth rivaled a tree, though most his mass settled in his midsection. By weight, Cole and Huka were about even, though Huka was a half-head shorter.

"Coe fight Huka," he said, his voice deep and throaty. He bumped Cole's shoulder with a dirt-stained fist.

"Didn't I fight you last week?"

Huka laughed. "I beat you."

"That's right." Cole rubbed his chin. He'd let Huka win, of course. The man was predictable, as all villagers were. But he didn't want to humiliate the man. Yet of all the villagers, Huka was the only one sizable enough to present a challenge.

"Maybe next week," Cole said.

"Coe scared." Huka side-hugged him.

Cole coughed at Huka's body odor. "I'm terrified." He grinned.

"I go easy on you."

Cole sighed. "All right, Huka."

The villagers cheered, clearing a circle. The two men circled one another, kicking up dirt. Cole searched Huka's green eyes. Huka tucked his body behind his shoulder and charged. Cole jumped to the balls of his feet while Huka pushed.

Cole jumped back and pretended to trip, landing hard. He coughed at the cloud of dirt. The 230-pound Indignis man leaped on top of him. Cole struggled to breathe. Some in the crowd cheered. Huka smirked.

But it wasn't over yet. Cole arched his back. Nothing gave. Again.

But maybe he could distract him. As Cole looked at Huka, he smiled. Huka cocked his head. Cole felt the weight on his body decrease almost imperceptibly.

Cole threw his weight to one side, tossing Huka. Before the man could scramble, Cole leaped, pinning his shoulders. Huka stared at Cole, stunned. The villagers remained silent.

Cole beamed. "Yeah!" He pumped his fist in the air. The villagers cheered.

Cole stood and extended his hand to Huka.

"You fight good this time," Huka said. Cole grunted as he lifted Huka's massive frame.

The villagers pumped their fists. "Coe best! Coe best! Coe best!"

They continued chanting as Cole climbed a granite boulder. He gazed over the tops of the heads of the villagers. Huka stood alone, several paces from the crowd. He smiled, but his eyes gradually broke contact with Cole's, sinking to the ground.

"Coe best, Coe best, Coe best."

Cole's smile faded. "Come, Huka." He extended his hand. The burly man trudged toward the rock, his eyes still lowered.

"Huka's best!" Cole shouted. "Huka's best! Huka's best!"

Seemingly forgetting who bested whom, the crowd repeated Cole's chant. Huka lifted his chin and smiled as he joined Cole on the boulder.

"Huka." Cole wrapped his arm around the man's thick shoulders. "You did well, *brother*."

The crowd quieted. Huka wiped his eyes with dirt-stained palms. "No, Coe best!" he said, his voice cracking. Huka—an only child, fatherless. To be named brother must have meant more than winning a thousand fights. All traces of disappointment vanished, replaced with a grin. He was happy to be second best to his brother.

Cole's smile faded, but why? Was it guilt? Was he being manipulative—winning their affection so that they would do as he asked?

It's for their good, he thought, unconvinced. In reality, Cole and his mother's efforts to improve things had already cost one his life.

Rook.

But that wasn't the reason for his sadness. Cole too had no brother, no father.

The villagers grew silent. Cole shook his head, forcing a smile.

"You all know what today is. It's gathering day!"

The villagers cheered.

"Remember, it's going to get cold pretty soon. Brrrrrr!" He hugged himself with an exaggerated shiver. The crowd laughed. "We need to gather enough to get us through the winter. You all remember what to do?"

The villagers smiled.

"Ready? Go!"

The crowd dispersed.

Aumora walked toward Cole. The placement of his mother's feet was as precise as a dancer's. She smiled, though her eyebrows furrowed as they often did, as if she were computing the favorability of a thousand decisions. Cole smiled under her scrutiny—there was no need to feel unnerved under her gaze. Her silent probing more often led to a new jacket or an increase in food rations than a reprimand.

"I don't know how you do it," she said.

"Do what?"

"What you did with Huka. 'Tis a mystery, my boy."

Cole chuckled. "Boy?"

Aumora grinned. "Until you're thirty-five."

"I thought it was eighteen." Cole lifted an eyebrow.

"Yes, but then you had a birthday."

"And..."

"And you're still my boy." She grinned. "I'm not ready to give up the label. Now quit distracting me."

Cole chuckled.

"About Huka," she said.

"What? You couldn't see his sadness? He looked like he'd lost a puppy."

"I could see it. But Huka." She rubbed her chin. "Yes, Huka. The man's stubborn. It takes a lot to pull him out of it."

Cole shrugged. "I just called him brother."

"Brother." Aumora studied the sky. "Clever strategy."

Cole shook his head. "It wasn't a strategy."

"And that, my boy, is why it worked." Aumora lifted her elbow. "Shall we go?"

He extended his arm, his mind lingering on his exchange with Huka. "We shall." He smiled, then linked arms.

They walked the well-worn path between the pine trees. A comfortable silence fell between them. Beams of sunlight filtered through the branches, warming his skin in patches. The random pattern of tree trunks seemed to extend for miles in all directions.

He savored these moments—silent walks to the river, or even the not-so quiet ones. She was the only person with whom he could have an intelligent discussion, whether talking philosophy, history, or religion. Sometimes she'd favor him with impromptu riddles and puzzles difficult enough to keep him awake at night. Though he loved the villagers, his affection resembled a parent's feelings toward a child. Even parents needed confidants.

Aumora was his only confidant.

"Mom...why are we different?" he asked. "Why didn't the pandemic affect us?"

"Not different, my boy, just blessed."

Cole frowned. Aumora—calculating, compassionate, and *secretive.* What lie within the nooks of their shared history was a mystery—one she was intent on hiding. And it was frustrating. Her vague responses created an invisible barrier.

Companionship—that's what he wanted. He'd seen it among the Indignis. Years ago, at a feast to celebrate the wedding of Silke and Goth, Cole sat at a long table, surrounded by villagers. As they guzzled the ale, the mood grew festive, their jokes more absurd, and their laughter grew louder. Cole sat with a smile plastered on his face, but his happiness was not genuine. He felt as out of place as an adult at a child's birthday party.

Instead of companionship, he had settled for something much less.

Cole breathed in the scent of the pine needles. Snapping twigs punctuated the silence. They exited the forest north of the riverbank and walked several paces to the river. Full from the spring rain, the water rushed past. A large felled tree bridged both shores. The path of the river carved, snake-like, through the evergreen forest. Trees blanketed the rolling hills. East of the river, at its origin, jagged mountains pierced the heavens. He smiled. Despite his frustration, his pulse slowed and his shoulders relaxed.

Breathing the scent of the fresh mountain water, he removed the fishing net from his bag.

"Can I cross the river this time?" asked Cole, elevating his voice above the churning water.

"Sorry, my boy," she said.

"You keep saying 'boy' and I'll call you 'old lady!'"

Aumora laughed. "Sorry, manly manly man." She winked at him. "I'll be crossing the river this time. Too dangerous—can't afford to lose you."

"We can't afford to lose *you.*"

"You're far more important than I."

Cole shook his head. Crouching, he untangled the net. It was *his mother* who had transformed the pack of brawlers into a peaceful community. *She* organized the gatherings.

"You made the rules," said Cole, "not me."

"Yes, but they follow *your* leadership. They *love* you. They tolerate me."

"They love you too."

Aumora raised an eyebrow. "They hardly remember my name."

Cole shrugged. "They still love you. I just...your humor is too sophisticated for them."

Cole looked at the sky, squinting. "I think they could survive without me. Maybe not as well, but they could survive."

"Perhaps. But you are destined for greater things."

She sucked in a breath. Her smile faded, and her eyes widened almost imperceptibly.

Destined for greater things. Cole scrutinized her face. What was that supposed to mean?

"Cole, will you pass me that bag?" She feigned a smile.

Aumora avoided his gaze. After grabbing one end of a fishing net, she crossed the mossy log. He watched, his mind lingering on what she had said—

destined for greater things.

A deep hum sounded in the distance.

She lifted her head like an alert deer. Cole sucked in a breath.

"Do you hear something?" she asked, her voice trembling.

He strained to hear above the roar of the river. Suta entered the clearing, his eyes wide.

"Air-pane, Air-pane!"

Cole looked up, but the trees blocked his view. Aumora dropped the net and bolted toward Cole. She grabbed his hand and ran, pulling him beneath the trees. Cole reached for Suta.

"He'll be fine. Let's go!"

"Mom!"

"They're not after him!"

Chop, chop, chop, chop.

"A helicopter!" they said simultaneously.

It was happening again. The Malkum were coming. Just as they had when they killed Rook.

"To the hatch!" Aumora shouted.

Cole's pulse matched the pace of his legs.

They'd never sent helicopters.

His feet quickened.

It had always been airplanes. Helicopters wouldn't pass in an instant like the airplanes. No, a helicopter could hover, could search, could fine things—the farm plots, the animal traps, the tools.

But the villagers *had* been trained—training they had taken much more seriously since Rook's death.

He tried to relax. Yes, they would know what to do.

He pressed against Aumora's back, urging her forward.

He stopped as his stomach tightened. The villagers knew what to do when they heard an airplane. But a helicopter? Would their training generalize?

"Let's go!" Aumora pulled his arm.

Cole regarded her, before turning the opposite direction.

She screamed.

Chop, chop, chop, chop.

The sound was louder, closer.

Cole entered a clearing. Laki and Madi stood, carrots in hand, watching the sky.

"Hey!" he shouted.

No response. He rushed toward the camouflage blanket.

"Airplanes!" he shouted. The women spun, dropping their carrots.

Aumora entered the clearing, panting. "Let's go!"

Cole, Laki, and Madi finished covering the plots.

Cole and Aumora ran toward the village. The thunderous rudders drowned out Cole's gasping breaths. Ducking beneath bushes, he looked skyward. Nothing but blue skies. Silke stood by the open hatch, beckoning.

"Now!" Aumora shouted.

He ran. Sound waves crashed against his chest. He jumped from the grass and fell through the hatch, landing hard in the concrete bunker. Aumora followed and Silke closed the hatch.

Would she remember to conceal it?

He cursed. The sound grew louder—nearer.

She'd forgotten. He groped for Aumora's shoulder. The sweat of his hand seeped through her shirt. Cole closed his eyes and counted backward from thirty.

30, 29, 28... The chopper wailed overhead. *20, 19, 18...* Was it happening? *10, 9, 8...* Yes, the sound was fading. Then, as if on cue, *3, 2, 1, 0.*

Chapter 2

International Think-tank Created to Tackle World Problems

New York Times

The United Nations announced plans to organize a think-tank of the most prominent scientists. All major disciplines will be represented, including biology, physics, and chemistry. Hans Malkum, Austrian UN representative, will chair the committee. "We're trying to put the brightest men and women to the task of solving world problems. I think it's a step in the right direction," said Malkum.

Newspaper article extracted from the Archive, dated seventeen years before the Genetic Apocalypse

---

Spencer's mobile rang. "Hello?...uh huh...wow...okay, just a minute."

Spencer lowered his phone. "We found something."

"What?" asked President Akram.

"I don't know, sir. But a helicopter was dropping off recruits and...saw something."

"What?"

"There was..." He cleared his throat, "a grassy clearing with a hatch. The helicopter came closer, then one of them stupid people—the Indignis—

covered it with some sort of grassy thing."

Akram furrowed his eyebrows. Were the rebels consorting with the Indignis?

Spencer lifted the phone to his ear. "Just a minute." He looked at Akram. "What do you want to do, sir?"

"How long ago?"

"Forty minutes."

"How far is the closest chopper?"

"Well, the closest one is the one that discovered it, so forty minutes."

Akram smiled. *You're dead!*

"Bomb the village."

Tonight, Elsa Alsvik would be alone. She exhaled, slowing her heart, trying to hide her excitement.

Alone, a nomad.

A traitor.

It was the only way to escape the Malkum—join the military, then run. And not get caught. And hope the devils die.

Through her rectangular glasses, she stared ahead at the empty seatbelt. The thumping of the helicopter gave her a sense of isolation, as it muffled the chatter of the men in the aircraft.

The sergeant approached. *Emotions can be felt, not shown.* Her heart quickened again, but not from excitement. This man made her efforts to conceal her annoyance exhausting.

Emotions can be felt, not shown.

"We're about there, Elsa." He sighed. "Now, I know yer a girl and used to being pampered, but this is the military. You get no special privileges and if you fail, you're dead just like the other half-dozen divas who showed their face in my army."

She tightened her jaw, but not enough to be visible. The sergeant scrutinized her, apparently waiting for any indication that she was unnerved, or afraid, or shocked. She regarded the red-faced man, her face placid.

"Yes, sir." As intended, her tone was emotionless.

His stern face softened and he searched Elsa's expression.

"Ahh, you'll be all right, kid. Just don't get yerself killed. I'd hate to lose you, pretty as you are." He tucked a strand of her red hair behind her ear.

She imagined strangling him. Yet she showed nothing. His affection was a lie, of course. Nobody cared.

The man broke his gaze as the aircraft began descending.

Elsa stole as smile as if the curtains closed after a performance. *Alone.* Her anticipation made her heart flutter. She stopped her breath until her heart returned to normal.

Elsa—the master of her own physiology.

Cole sat on the concrete floor, elbows on his knees, pulling his hair. It was just like last time—when Rook had died. Cole had donated his jacket to the old villager, who never stopped shivering, despite the many layers of clothes he wore. The following day the Malkum raided their village, searching for intelligence. The black jacket—still clean from Cole's safekeeping—had stood out among the filthy villagers. They had mistaken cleanliness for intellect.

And they had murdered him.

And like then, Cole waited. How long ago had the helicopter left? Half an hour? An hour? He stood, pacing in the humid room.

"I gotta go back up," said Cole.

"No. They could be out there. Wait 'til someone lets us out."

"This can't go on."

"They'll be fine." Aumora sighed. Yet there was a tremble in her voice—just like before.

"You said that last time."

Silence.

Images flashed into his mind—Rook's half-closed eyes, his broken arm, the burial. It couldn't happen again.

"Let's move the villagers," Cole said, "find a cave."

Aumora's mouth clicked, but she said nothing.

"We've gotta do something!" Cole said.

"So we leave. Then what? What about the other villages?"

Cole stopped pacing. He hadn't thought of it—all the other villages. He'd been so caught up in *his* people. The Indignis were terrorized the world over.

He sunk to the ground. "We can't hide."

"No."

"We have to...stop them."

"We do."

Silence.

"But how?" he asked.

Aumora left the question unanswered. A village of Indignis, one middle-aged woman, and one man against an entire army. The task was daunting—impossible.

"We can't do it," he said.

"Not alone."

Light flooded the room along with the scent of pine trees. Cole's chest tightened. Silka stood above the opened hatch. She smiled and said something unintelligible.

Cole exhaled, letting the light warm his body like the relief he felt.

Like a field sergeant leading an ambush, Aumora raised her head above the bunker, scanning the meadow. She studied the scenery—calculating and emotionless. She beckoned with a finger. "Let's go."

She leapt from the bunker. "Gather the nets. I'll find out what happened."

"We can get them later."

"No. Now. If the Malkum see them, they'll know something's up."

Cole stared at her. Her ever-present smirk was gone as was the light tone in her voice. Something was really wrong.

She grabbed his shoulders. "Go!"

He blinked, then ran. He couldn't shake the rumbling in his stomach. Why had she been so afraid? He reviewed the possibilities, none of them likely, all terrifying. Suta emerged from behind a tree, skipping toward Cole, grinning.

Cole relaxed.

"You okay!" Suta said. "Air-pane scawy."

"I'm okay, buddy."

"I miss you first, then you miss me?" He tilted his head and raised an eyebrow.

Cole shook his head, brushing aside a host of unsettling thoughts. He smiled.

"Nope. I missed you before I even left." He poked at Suta as if to tickle him. The boy jumped, laughing, before narrowing his attention to something behind Cole. He squinted, lowering his eyebrows.

"I be back," he said, his gaze intense.

The boy bolted into the forest. Cole waited on the trail, smiling. Suta returned a minute later, holding something behind his back.

"Is a peasant. Cose yo eyes."

Cole closed his eyes, extending his hands.

"Open," said Suta.

Cole opened his eyes and looked at the boy, who beamed. A smooth crescent-shaped river rock rested in his hands.

"Is a dinosar. Rarrrr!"

Cole laughed and inspected the rock, trying to see how Suta found a dinosaur in its odd shape.

"I'll treasure it forever." Cole kissed his head. The boy blushed then skipped toward the river. Cole placed the dinosaur rock in his pocket. It would soon make its home among other rocks, twigs, desiccated bugs, flowers, and leaves—all "peasants" Cole had collected from Suta.

"I race you," said Suta. He bolted down the trail.

"I'll win."

Cole followed. As they entered the riverbed, Cole froze, his eyes widening. He frantically reached for Suta, but was too late. The boy stopped half the distance to the net of fish. Perched over the net was a young woman, pointing a gun at the Indignis boy.

Chapter 3

War Breaks, Malkum Remains Neutral

CNN

China launched a series of attacks on India today after a mysterious plague ravaged China's western border. Xu Zhao, China's President, placed blame for the plague on India after recent land and trade disputes. China's attacks targeted Mumbai and Delhi, India's two most populated cities. Initial mortality estimates reach into the millions, most of which are civilians. Leaders from the UN condemned the attack and promised retribution if the attacks continued. Russian president Sergei Demodiv, however, voiced his support of the Chinese attacks. "I would not remain idle and allow cowardly attacks on my people." The Malkum, on the other hand, expressed sorrow over the attacks but restated its position of neutrality. "We will not direct any of our resources, intellectual or otherwise, to helping or hindering any side of any war. Our position has been, and always will be, complete neutrality," said Malkum spokesman Halek Stagnot.

Newspaper article extracted from the Archive, dated four years before the Genetic Apocalypse

---

The girl crouched in front of the net. She was thin but looked deadly, with muscular arms, crimson curls, and a penetrating gaze behind rectangular glasses. Her clothes were unblemished except for the mud that creeped up the sides of her boots, making her cleanliness as out of place as freshly folded laundry in a sewer.

Cole lifted his trembling hands. She moved her revolver from Suta to Cole. Cole closed his eyes, then exhaled. *Run Suta!*

The boy remained, his face contorted.

She said nothing.

Cole swallowed, his pulse rocketing. He looked down the dark barrel, tracing it to her whitened knuckles and her...quivering fingers?

Her face remained placid.

"Let the boy go," Cole said.

She looked at Suta, then flicked the gun's barrel toward the forest. Suta backed away, wide eyes fixed on the girl. He dropped from the periphery of Cole's vision.

A breeze blew, bringing with it the scent of the girl's natural smell, sending an unfamiliar thrill through Cole.

She was beautiful. Having lived among Indignis, he'd never experienced such a feeling, one heightened by terror.

He coughed. "Hi."

The girl made no move.

As the minutes lengthened, his tremble lessened, but his heart rate did not.

"Good, um...good afternoon," he said, his voice cracking.

She looked at him, her face absent of emotion.

"My name's..." His voice cracked again. He cleared his throat, deepening his voice. "My name's Cole."

He searched her expression, struggling to focus. Her deep red hair, her blue eyes, her smooth skin all muddled his concentration.

He blinked, then searched again. It was strange. Never before did he need to *search* for signs of emotion—reading others was intuitive, even with Aumora. This girl was different.

"What's your name?" he asked.

Why wouldn't she do something? Or at least say something.

"...You, uh, gonna rob me or something?" he asked with a nervous chuckle.

The girl said nothing.

"...What's the plan?"

Several more minutes passed, it seemed, and still nothing happened. There was no *immediate* danger. He searched her face for *something*. But the girl was like a book with blank pages.

She wouldn't kill him, would she? If that was the plan, wouldn't she have done it already? And why did her fingers tremble? He thought he saw something hidden behind her eyes—a concealed softness.

She was obviously Malkum—that much was certain. It couldn't be coincidental that she arrived shortly after the helicopters circled his village.

But Aumora said they'd kill him. Why hadn't this girl?

"Can I guess what this is about?" he said, feigning calm. "You're Malkum. Are you more interested in capture than execution? Have you contacted the boss?"

No reaction.

"Ok, so you're not interested in capture."

Her face remained placid. Would she even react to a correct guess?

"So why would a Malkum assassin—"

Her lip twitched into a snarl, right as he said *Malkum*. He almost missed it.

She hates them.

He opened his mouth to speak, but stopped. Was he reading her correctly? If he was wrong...

Well, he might be dead anyway.

"You hate the Malkum," he said.

Her ears reddened.

"You're a traitor. But you found me...and that's thwarted your plans. Now you don't know whether to let me go, or kill me, to hide your treason."

The girl's eye twitched.

"But *why do* you try to conceal it?" he asked, his steadiness increasing. "I can guess, but if you just told me..."

She remained silent.

"All right." He sighed, feeling more confident. "I've got two guesses. Maybe they train you all to suppress emotions."

The girl began lowering the weapon, unconsciously, it seemed. Cole inched closer, his heart beating frantically.

"But I don't think that's it." He inched closer, his fingers trembling. "You don't look like an assassin."

He inched another half step.

"So why would you choose this? Escape, maybe? Was there something you were trying to escape from? Something so traumatic, it taught you to hide all emotions."

The girl's lips parted slightly as she inhaled—a gasp.

He was right. He had read the unreadable. Close enough to make a move, he lunged.

"Are you seriously that stupid?" Elsa said.

Her indecisiveness and indifference faded. What was the point of hiding anymore?

She sat atop the man—Cole, was it?—digging her knee between his shoulder blades. She pinned his arms behind his back and shoved her elbow into his sweaty neck, pushing his face into the dirt. Like the men in her training group, he had assumed he could overtake her. Well he was wrong. Elsa Alsvik was an unyielding boulder.

Cole winced. "Nice to see you talking now."

Elsa flipped him around and sat on his chest. She held the gun to his head and gripped his throat. "How did you know?"

He had guessed everything—her treason against the Malkum, her indecisiveness, and the reason for it. She had been exposed.

Cole shifted his gaze to the boy, who emerged from the forest. His grimace framed bloodshot eyes. He held trembling fingers in his mouth. She sighed. It wasn't supposed to happen like this. Like a poison, the compassion she'd long tried to repress returned.

He was just a boy—not much older than Celso had been. Guilt turned her stomach in knots. What was she doing? What was she *not* doing? She cursed.

Cole threw his weight, launching her. She landed hard on the dirt then gasped. Cole jumped on top of her, pinning her, gun held in his hand. She thrashed, but he was too strong and too heavy.

She cursed.

Cole shifted his knees, pinning Elsa's arms. With one hand, he opened the cylinder of the revolver and ejected the bullets before putting them in his pocket.

"How did you know?" she asked.

She smelled his scent—repulsive. She swallowed bile like the flood of memories threatening to break through.

"Promise not to kill me," he said.

She looked away.

"Promise me." He paused. She returned his gaze. His expression softened.

"I promise," she muttered.

"How do I know you're not going to break that promise?"

He shifted, lifting pressure off her shoulders. She threw her weight to her left. Cole yelped. She pushed again, throwing him onto his back. She jumped to her feet before walking toward him. He scrambled backward. Elsa pulled the knife from her belt.

"I *never* break a promise." Her voice cracked.

She felt naked in front of him. No matter the mask she attempted to wear, he pierced it.

She returned the knife to her belt pocket. He stretched his hand toward her. She folded her arms. Cole shrugged, stood, and brushed himself off.

He searched her face, and his brown eyes softened. "Whatever happened to you, I'm sorry."

Silence.

Another lie. Why would he care? Nobody *really* cared. Her breath quickened. The wind carried his scent again. She nearly wrinkled her nose. She tightened her jaw, before freezing her expression.

"You owe me an explanation," she said. "How did you know?"

"Tell me your name first."

She narrowed her eyes. She owed him nothing.

He waited, raising an eyebrow.

Whatever. It didn't matter.

"Elsa," she grumbled.

"Nice to meet you Elsa. I—"

"'Mora, 'Mora," said the boy.

Chop, chop, chop, chop.

Two people approached, a woman and an old man. The woman marched with the commanding presence of a general while the old man hobbled, though with no less confidence. Each held branches in each hand.

"Mom, what's going on?" asked Cole.

"There's no time." She handed him several branches. "Hold onto them. They'll keep you buoyant." She turned toward Elsa, then blinked, though her expression remained as emotionless as Elsa's.

"Where are we going?" Cole asked.

She continued staring at Elsa.

"Mom!"

"What?"

"What's going on?"

Chop, chop, chop, chop.

The Malkum were returning. Had they known she hadn't killed Cole?

"We're leaving," Aumora said, eyes lingering on Elsa—eyes that studied her as a father might a boy for his daughter's first date. Aumora nodded. She bent toward Cole, grabbing his arm. "We're going to stop this."

Elsa's eyes widened. Great. Of all people, why did *she* have to find the not-so-mythical rebellion?

Chop, chop, chop.

It was nearing.

"Go 'Mora!" the old man yelled.

The woman dropped a stack of branches and turned to Cole. "Jump into the river. Don't let go of the branches. Luther?"

His mother looked to the old man. He passed branches to the boy and guided him to the water. They approached the riverbank. Cole stopped, looked at Elsa, and beckoned.

Elsa shook her head. She'd planned a life of seclusion— a home in the wilderness—listening to the calling of birds and watching the sun set over the river. Alone. By herself. She couldn't go with them.

But what of Mother? What of Celso? Could she allow their killers to remain unpunished? No. If they had a plan—if there was a rebellion...

Elsa cursed and leapt into the water.

They had come back. Why?

The current buried Cole's head. He gasped, sucking water as he tried to breathe. Gagging, he kicked, pulling against the branches. His head emerged, then the river dropped, submerging him again.

His throat tightened. He kicked. With one final thrust, his head emerged.

To his left, Suta floated on his back, his feet facing downstream. The boy looked at Cole, grinning. Cole smiled. His heart slowed as he shifted to his back, dividing the branches between his arms.

The current massaged his back and legs. His shoulders would have relaxed had the water not felt like icy needles. He coughed several more times at the burning in the back of his throat.

The old man floated behind him. Who was he? And his mother had said something about stopping *this*. Did she mean the Malkum? And what did this man have to do with it?

He had a bald head with liver spots, a potbelly, and a large nose above his scowling mouth. His mother had called him Luther. His eyes suggested he had intellect, but beyond that Cole knew nothing. She must have known him before. But how? And how would he help stop the Malkum?

As questions accumulated, his frustration deepened. Aumora wouldn't tell him.

Elsa's chest rose and fell with each breath. Her body trembled, whether from cold or memories of her past, he did not know. Either way, He wanted to reach for her, still her trembling hands, rescue her from...whatever it was she tried to hide.

The river carried them further from the helicopters.

An explosion. Cole's eyes jolted open. He turned his head. Fire billowed above the trees. Black smoke filled the sky.

Oh God no. His stomach tightened. It couldn't be his village. The smoke—it was too far away.

Yet as Cole noticed the blur of the trees, he felt sick—they were moving fast.

"*NO!*" he screamed. He thrashed, driving toward the shore. The water plunged his head under. He coughed, emerging from the water. "No!" He kicked, pulling against the branches, trying to lift himself above the surface.

Icy water lodged in his nose. "Huka! Steep!"

Legs weakening, he coughed, ejecting water from his mouth. He kicked and thrashed. The river sloped downward, submerging him again. His lungs burned. Like a man buried alive, he reached for the surface, coughing more water from his lungs.

His strength weakened. His throat ached and his legs burned. He quit fighting, laying on his back as he willed the current to swallow him and spit him out dead.

When the current slowed, he languidly kicked. Cole dropped the branches, which the current swept away. He stood. His rubbery legs nearly collapsed beneath the weight of soaked clothes. Sand clutched his feet as if to pull him under.

Gone. He looked at the smoky horizon, feeling his throat tighten.

No! He fought for another step, eyes fixed on the billowing plume.

"Cole." Aumora grabbed his arm.

"I've gotta..." Cole trailed off, then vomited. The contents of his stomach splashed on the river rocks. The water diluted the bitterness of the bile, yet it still stunk like rotten flesh. He wiped his mouth, then marched toward his village.

Aumora followed. "Cole! You can't—"

"I'm going home!" Cole spun, glaring at Aumora. "And you can come with me, or stay here. But I'm going."

Her eyes glistened. "But." She blinked. "There is no home."

He stopped. He'd never seen her cry—not even when they killed Rook.

"You go back, you die." Aumora sniffed.

He shook his head, then headed toward the village. "I don't care."

And he didn't. If they were really gone, did it even matter? Did anything matter?

"If you stay," Aumora said, her voice cracking. She cleared her throat. "If you stay—if you're *alive...*"

Her unfinished phrased echoed in his mind. *If you're alive...*Cole stopped. What had she said earlier? *We're going to stop this.* He looked again at the billowing smoke—a black marker of a distant grave.

But maybe somebody survived. Maybe Arg or Luka or Sal. He couldn't leave them alone.

Yet she was right. If he went back, he'd be hunted. If he were dead, he couldn't fight back. This had to end. No more raids. Nor more hiding in bunkers. No more cowering before the Malkum. He tightened his jaw, then spun to face the old man.

"Son." The old man grinned. "Let's destroy *their* village."

Cole nodded, allowing his anger to boil just above the surface of his grief.

Then he heard the helicopter.

Chapter 4

Cyber-attacks Cripple Internet, Malkum Safeguards Only Known Copy

The Daily Mail

The global war, led by China and India, has extended into the digital medium. The Internet has been paralyzed by the attacks. Users dropped from billions to thousands in only a few years as both sides have released debilitating viruses that attack both data and hardware. Analysts predict that within six weeks, the Internet will be completely destroyed. Anonymous sources within the Malkum confirm that a complete copy of the World Wide Web is secure in Fahrquan. When asked about the backup, Malkum officials refused to comment.

Newspaper article extracted from the Archive, dated eighteen months before the Genetic Apocalypse

---

President Akram marched down the hallway. A rebellion? It was impossible. The entire world was dead of intellect. But if it began from within? And they escaped unnoticed?

But how?

He stopped. The faint outline of a memory tugged at his awareness—an event, long forgotten. Escaped unnoticed. Yes, there was a man once—a man who had died trying to escape, or so they had thought. Weeks later, he returned, only to die again. What was his name?

He shut his eyes, focusing on the thought. Two hundred years of memories flitted through his mind, like a swarm of bacteria-infested flies. Attempting to retrieve one thought among the billions was—

His breath caught. He smiled. "Quincy Sturgess!"

"Pardon, sir," Spencer asked.

"Quincy Sturgess. He's our dissenter." Akram marched toward the door that incarcerated Jason Drakes—the defector. For centuries, the rebels had metastasized and somehow had planted one of their own within the Malkum—a sergeant too.

But whatever trick they had used to bring Drakes here, it had failed. And today, Akram would get some answers.

He stepped inside the metal door. Chipped white paint covered the walls and two folding chairs occupied the center of the room. A muscular man stood in the center—as motionless as a corpse. Sweat stained his armpits and collar, filling the room with the stench of body odor. His buzzed hair surrounded an island of baldness on the top of his head.

Sergeant Jason Drakes—the man who had spoken of the rebellion.

"Spencer, I'll take it from here." The president sat in a chair opposite Drakes. The sergeant stood at attention while Spencer exited, leaving the two men alone.

Akram leaned back in his creaking metal chair. "You're a sergeant?"

"Yes, sir."

"How long have you been in the Malkum army?"

"Sixteen years, sir."

"And how old were you when you joined?"

"Twenty-two, sir."

"Most recruits join when they're eighteen. Why did you wait four years?"

"Honestly, I'm not—"

"And reports say that you took to your new profession like a bird to flight."

The man cleared his throat and shifted his weight. "That's correct, sir."

"It's almost as if you were trained by another army before you came here."

Drakes lowered his eyebrows and continued to focus on the wall before him. "Seems that way."

"So what? Were you planted by the enemy? As a spy? As a saboteur?"

"I honestly don't know, sir."

"Well, what *do* you know?" Akram stood. "Your story's a bit hard to believe. You claim you spent twenty-two years with the rebellion, forget about them, then spontaneously remember everything."

"Like I said to Spencer—"

"I don't care what you said to Spencer. You tell me everything." Akram returned to his seat.

Drakes nodded. "Sixteen years ago, I arrived as a recruit, just like all the rest of 'em. My parents had just died. Or maybe they didn't. See, I don't know."

Akram rubbed his forehead. "Tell me what happened two weeks ago."

Drakes sighed. "I wake up, like any other day. I look at the calendar and something happens." He shook his head. "Something about that day...I don't know. Suddenly my head feels like it's going to explode and I remember." He shrugged.

"*What* do you remember?"

"I spent the first twenty-two years of my life living with the rebels. But I also remember spending the first twenty-two years of my life with my parents on a farm. I got two lives, sir. Both as real as the other and I don't know what's true and what's false."

"I can tell you what's true. The rebellion is real. You didn't make that up."

Drakes lowered his eyes to the floor.

The two men sat in silence for several moments. Akram rubbed his eyes. It didn't make sense.

Akram sighed. "Do you know the name Quincy Sturgess?"

Drakes went rigid, his eyes widening. He panted before a shrill scream escaped his mouth.

Akram stood and backed into an empty corner. His pulse quickened as he stared at the soldier. Drakes grabbed his head, howling. The door swung open. Spencer entered, his gun at the ready.

"It's happening *again*!" Drakes yelled.

His screams died suddenly, replaced by labored breaths.

Akram exhaled. "What is going on?"

Spencer lifted the soldier by the arm. Akram kicked a chair in the soldier's direction.

"Y—you ok?" asked Spencer.

Drakes's gaze bored into the president. Akram's throat tightened, but he forced his breath to slow.

Drakes's eyes unfocused. He grinned, as if a cacophony of memories finally came into focus. "Quincy Sturgess—yeah, I know the name. He and the Ancient formed the rebellion 200 years ago. Quincy's dead, but the Ancient lives."

Drakes's eyes rolled to the back of his head and his body fell limp to the floor.

What had happened? How could a man forget living with the rebellion? And who was the Ancient?

Akram tapped his finger on his ebony desk—waiting, as he'd done all afternoon. He stared at his mobile, then picked it up and dialed.

"Sir?" Spencer said.

"What's the status on the bombing?"

Spencer cleared his throat. "Let's see..."

"I don't have all day."

"Yes, of course. It looks like...they won't be able to search the ground until tomorrow. But they've got helicopters circling the area."

Akram rubbed his forehead. It was taking too long. "Fine. What's the status on Drakes?"

"He's been transferred to a locked hospital room."

"And?"

"Uh...I. He's being checked in, I think."

Akram growled. "Find out."

"Yes, sir."

"And what have you found about Quincy?"

"Just looking into it." A keyboard clicked in the background. "Yeah, I can't find anything, sir."

"What do you mean?"

"I mean, there's no record. Seems the twin strikes deleted his records."

Akram cursed. That lightning strike had caused no end of grief. Personnel records, global histories, centuries of research—the entire Archive, gone in an instant, fried by a freakishly coincidental act of God.

Akram ground his teeth. He'd long suspected that the strike was too coincidental—the probabilities so minute it didn't require a statistician to conclude it was impossible. Until now, the evidence hadn't existed.

The rebellion—*they* had destroyed the Archive, and probably stole a copy for themselves.

"Where are the hard copies kept?" Akram asked.

"73004."

"Meet me there."

Spencer arrived, panting. Sweat dripped from his fat head and pit stains crept toward his oversized stomach.

"Sorry...I'm late."

Spencer opened the door and flipped the lightswitch. Florescent tubes hummed and flickered. Some turned on, though a third of them remained black. The room was hot and muggy and smelled of dead rodents. Dust covered rows upon rows of filing cabinets of various colors—camouflage green, off-white, and puke brown.

"Took some time to figure out the RFID for this room," Spencer said. "Seems nobody's been here in a *long* time."

Akram scanned the room. Each filing cabinet nearly reached the ceiling. Each row extended about 100 yards. And there were dozens upon dozens of rows.

"Where is it?"

"Pardon?"

Akram clenched his jaw. "Where's. Quincy's. File?"

"Oh yes." Spencer rubbed the back of his neck. "Honestly, I don't know, sir. As I said, nobody's been here in decades, at least."

Akram approached the first row of filing cabinets. "Have several dozen men sent here. We're finding this file today."

Spencer stared at the immense room and frowned. "Today, huh?"

"Today."

Akram swiped away a cob web, then opened the top shelf of a filing cabinet.

Chapter 5

To: Keston@Malkum.net

From: Gene@Malkum.net

Re: Nexus

I've been thinking about what you said. It's brilliant—keeping one's memories hidden from even one's self. Do your models suggest anyone can form a Nexus? Or just the impressionable? Do you think one can alter one's beliefs or even someone's physiology?

Email conversation extracted from the Archive four years before the Genetic Apocalypse.

"Under the trees. Now!" Luther yelled.

Cole grabbed Suta's hand and ran toward the trees.

Chop, chop, chop.

His legs quickened, but Suta's did not. Cole bent, scooping the boy into his arms.

Chop, chop, chop.

The sound neared.

Aumora pressed against his back. Gritting his teeth, he ducked into his run.

Luther beckoned from within the cover of the trees. Elsa searched the sky.

Cole leaped toward the two.

Chop, chop, chop.

"I think you made it." Elsa scanned the blue skies. She nodded as the sound faded. "I think you made it."

Cole lifted his hands above his head, gasping. He leaned against a pine tree. It vibrated from the noise of the fading chopper.

"I don't like the sound of this." Luther frowned, scanning the sky. "They'll be on our tail." He cursed, striking a tree trunk with his palm. "Why now?"

Yes, why now? For years Cole had wished for a chance to take down the Malkum. Now his mother had hinted at a plan. And Luther must be a part of that plan, maybe even central to it. But first, they had to escape.

Someone shouted. Luther held Elsa in a headlock, thrusting a knife toward her neck. Cole leaped to his feet.

"You do this?" Luther asked. "You bring the Malkum?"

Cole's throat tightened. "What's going on?"

"She's Malkum, Cole," Luther said.

"I know." Cole held his hands toward Luther. "But who are you?"

Luther gave a half-grin. Elsa's gasps filled the silence.

Luther inched the knife toward her throat. "She brought them." Luther pointed with his eyes to the sky.

Elsa looked at Cole, eyes wide.

"She didn't." Cole lifted his palms to the air, taking a step toward Luther. "It's got nothing to do with her."

"Luther." Aumora too held her hands up. Her face was calm, but her fingers shook. "I don't think that's a good idea. Let's talk about this."

Suta's eyes darted from Luther, to Cole, to Aumora. Cole watched Elsa try and fail to freeze her expression into one of indifference.

"You're both siding with the enemy." His eyes shifted between the two.

"Knife down." Aumora took another step. "There's better ways to do this."

Cole's wet clothes clung to his body, chafing his skin. He shifted his weight, feeling Elsa's gun in his waistband. The hard cylinder pressed against his back.

He'd removed the bullets, but Luther wouldn't know that. Should Cole threaten him? No. Not a good idea. It'd probably only make things worse.

"She's not worth the risk." Luther tightened his jaw. Elsa let out a gasp.

"No!" Aumora shouted.

Cole pulled the revolver from his belt. Luther froze just as his knife broke the surface of Elsa's skin. Blood oozed down the slit.

Luther snarled. "You threatening me, boy?"

Cole said nothing. Instead, he focused on calming his trembling hands.

"You gonna kill me?" His eyes darted to the gun and back to Cole. "For her?"

Cole remained silent, but his heart raced.

"Put it down, Luther," Aumora said.

"What's wrong with you people?"

Aumora stepped toward Luther, extending her hand. "You do that, you've lost him." She glanced from Luther to Cole.

Luther gritted his teeth. He sighed as he shoved Elsa. She stumbled, wiping the blood from her neck. Cole reached for her but she slapped his hands away.

"You may have cost us, 'Mora." Luther shook his head, frowning.

"You might have too." Aumora looked at Cole.

Elsa left the cover of the woods. Though her face was expressionless, her march toward the river was as devoid of emotion as a rattling snake.

"Just who do you think you are?" Cole asked.

Luther's face reddened. He opened his mouth to speak.

"Enough," Aumora said. "Everyone." She looked at Cole. "Hand me the gun."

Cole shook his head. He motioned toward Luther's blood-dripped knife.

Aumora nodded. "Luther. Your knife."

The old man glared. "I'm not—"

"It wasn't a request!" She glared at him. Luther glared back. Aumora advanced. Though half a head shorter than the old man, she made Luther look like a cadet in bootcamp. He broke his gaze and surrendered his knife.

She extended her hand to Cole. "Gun?"

He muttered a curse, but handed her the revolver. He spun and marched toward the river.

"Where you going?" Aumora asked.

"To find Elsa."

Elsa paced beside the river. She kicked the dirt, hoping to expend some anger and still her trembling hands. Her facial muscles hurt, unaccustomed to displaying so much fear, so much anger. She removed the knife from her sheath and threw it. The point stuck into a log. Elsa smiled with satisfaction. She exhaled one last time before freezing her expression. She sauntered to the log, retrieved her knife, then put it back in her sheath.

That coward. The old man didn't have the balls to challenge her in a real fight. Never again would he catch her by surprise.

This was why it was best to be alone. She sat on a nearby boulder, closed her eyes, and allowed the sounds of the environment to soothe her. The wind rustled leaves. The rumbling of the river vibrated against her chest. *This* was what she wanted—solitude. It was stupid—following a group of strangers with a faint hope that somehow they might take down the Malkum.

But seclusion—she could have it *now.*

The knot in her stomach tightened—ever her companion, a constant reminder of what she'd lost—Celso, Mother, Father. And so much more. That knot was like kindling, always ready to ignite the anger. Her heart drummed, pumping rage through her veins, channeling her focus on one goal—a goal that was once impossible, but now within her reach.

The Malkum would die. And if that meant following a testy old man, she'd do it. But never again would he catch her unprepared.

Footsteps crunched against the river rocks. "You okay?" Cole asked.

Elsa remained silent.

"I'm sorry," he said.

He gently squeezed her shoulder, causing an unwelcome warmth that spread through her body. Again, the yearning came.

"Touch me again, and I'll break your hand," she said, but immediately regretted it. Was that how to thank someone who saved your life? She opened her mouth to apologize, but remained silent.

She expected some retort, but Cole said nothing.

"I'm sorry," she said.

Cole shook his head, gazing at the horizon. He shivered when his eyes met the smoky plume. His gaze fell to the ground and his shoulders sunk. Grief radiated from him like heat from a fire.

"I have nothing to do with this," she said.

"I know." He forced a smile. "And I think he knows it now."

Silence.

"Thanks." Unconsciously, she half-smiled.

"We should get back," said Cole.

She looked at the river. The white bubbles flowed over concealed rocks. The breeze blew, cooling her skin. The scent of the river mingled with wildflowers. Was it so wrong if she remained alone?

Elsa sighed. "Fine. Let's go."

Night had fallen. Elsa and Cole arrived at camp. Cole hugged himself as a breeze iced his skin. Luther and Aumora sat before a campfire. Orange light flickered off their faces and the scent of burning wood wafted through the air. Suta slept. Luther and Aumora's lips moved, though nothing was audible above the roar of the river. Aumora laughed, touching Luther's shoulder. His mouth lifted slightly, going from a scowl to a slight smile, before returning again to his resting face.

Aumora turned. "We saved some food for you." She pointed to a blackened piece of meat. Cole sat, then broke it in two and gave half to Elsa. When she lifted it to her mouth, Luther scowled.

She handed the meat back to Cole. "I'm not hungry." Her stomach rumbled.

Apparently Aumora hadn't convinced Luther Elsa was harmless. Cole yawned. It was late. And he was tired. And a *lot* had happened today. He didn't have the time, or the energy to deal with this cantankerous old man. Perhaps tomorrow he'd find a way to convince him.

Elsa's stomach rumbled again. Cole sighed. "Come on, Elsa. Don't insult the man by refusing his food."

He returned the chunk of meat. She snarled, but grabbed the meat. It was cold, overcooked, and bland. Squirrel meat. He hadn't had that since—

Cole shook his head. He couldn't let his mind go there.

"So where are we going?" Cole asked

"We're—"

"Don't say a thing, 'Mora," said Luther. "Not in front of that dirty traitor."

Cole tightened his jaw. "You—"

"Enough," Aumora said. "Honestly, Luther, you're acting like a spoiled toddler."

"I'm not—"

"Lose your favorite toy?" she said.

"Mora!"

"Need a diaper change?"

He shook his head, but a hint of a smile pulled his lips.

"How about a binki?" Aumora asked.

"That would be nice." Luther grinned. "Maybe warm milk and a nap."

Aumora pushed Luther with a chuckle. "Then go to bed, you old grouch."

The fire crackled, filling the silence.

"So where *are* we going?" Cole asked.

Aumora studied Elsa, who stared at the embers of the fire.

"It's late," Aumora said. "We've been through a lot. We'll talk tomorrow."

"Fine." Cole sighed. "Good night."

Elsa sat cross-legged, resting her chin on her palms. The smell of the dying coals filled the air. Those around her slept, including Luther who had volunteered for the first watch.

Dirty traitor, Luther had said. If he only knew how true that statement was, but not in the way he had supposed.

Elsa's mind drifted. An owl hooted, waking her. *Gotta stay awake.* She fought to keep her eyes open, but her lids became heavier with each blink.

Elsa sat on a microfiber couch inside her living room in Fahrquan. She held a book resting her feet atop the coffee table. The diffused sunlight lit the pages, and vanilla incense filled the air. Someone whistled outside the window.

Father was home. She smiled and closed a ribbon in her book. She scurried around the couch. After opening the front door, she raised her hands in the air. "Father!"

"Hi, princess." He embraced her, kissing her cheek.

"I missed you sooo much!" She squeezed him.

"I've missed you too." He pulled from the hug and searched her eyes. "Why are you crying?"

"I haven't seen you in two years, silly." She wiped her tears with the sleeve of her shirt, laughing. It was so good to see him after all these years. Father raised an eyebrow, then faded from view.

She sat in front of the river, but this time with Cole. She wrapped her arm around his, nestling in his neck. For the first time in years, she relaxed in a man's embrace. Comfortable. Happy. She felt her chest rise and fall with his. She tried to time her breath with his, but couldn't inhale when he inhaled. And she couldn't exhale when he did. She couldn't breathe at all.

Her eyes jolted open. She tried to gasp, but an old hand with thick fingers and liver spots blocked her mouth. The smoldering coals of the fire reflected in Luther's malicious irises.

"Listen, missy. You—"

She grabbed his wrist and yanked. He spun. She kicked, landing a foot in his back. He staggered, then fell forward. She jumped on his back and pushed his face in the dirt.

"Just wanna talk," Luther said.

She pressed her knee against his spine. He yelped.

"Stop it!" Aumora shouted.

Elsa turned. Luther thrashed, throwing Elsa. She landed hard, wind escaping her lungs. Luther charged. Her muscles tightened. Aumora continued shouting.

Cole shoved the old man to the ground. "What is wrong with you?"

Luther wheezed. He grunted as he stumbled to his feet. "She's..." He panted. "She's..."

"Enough!" Aumora approached. Her sleep-mangled hair tossed with the wind and her clothes were wrinkled. Despite that, she silenced everyone.

Luther tightened his jaw, but remained quiet.

Aumora lowered her gaze on the old man. "I thought I said enough, Luther."

He opened his mouth, yet seemed to think better of it. He sighed. The rigidity in his body leaked from his muscles.

"I said enough, Luther," Aumora said again.

"I heard ya."

"I. Said. Enough."

"I heard ya!" His voice echoed through the trees, silencing the cicadas.

"That's what you said last time." Aumora crossed her arms. "And here I find you sneaking up on the girl."

Luther shook his head. "She's Malkum."

"We've established that! She's not the first to escape the Malkum, or have you forgotten?"

The old man chewed his lip, then nodded. "Yer right."

"Apologize."

He tightened his jaw. "Fine."

The cicadas called.

"Fine?"

"I'm sorry!" His jowls shook, but then his shoulders sunk. "I'm sorry. It won't happen again."

The scowl in Aumora's face faded. "Thank you."

Aumora turned her gaze to Elsa. "For what it's worth, I'm sorry this happened."

Elsa regarded her.

"And I understand if you want to leave," Aumora said.

"No!" Cole said.

"Cole."

"It's her choice. Not yours." Aumora's gaze returned to Elsa. "So...what'll it be?"

Elsa looked from the river, to Cole, to Aumora, then to the old man. He thought he could hurt her. She'd faced tougher men than this old grump.

"I'll take next watch," Elsa said.

Aumora nodded. Luther gazed at the ground as he trudged toward the remains of the campfire. Suta remained asleep. Cole's arms remained crossed in front of his chest, jaw tight.

"I'm sorry," Cole said.

Elsa shook her head. "Don't be."

"I'm sorry."

"Relax. I've dealt with worse. Go get some rest."

Cole searched Elsa's face. She went rigid.

"I'm glad you're okay," he said. "G'night."

Elsa nodded.

Chapter 6

Malkum Accused of Nefarious Solution to Arms Race.

Fox News

Several months after the Malkum announced their intent to address the nuclear threat, Malkum spokespersons have been suspiciously silent. In the three press conferences since January, Malkum spokesperson Helen Kunitz has refused to offer details about the Malkum's solution to the nuclear threat. However, an anonymous tip reported that Fahrquan's plan will have devastating consequences. The tipster failed to arrive at a predetermined appointment where exact details would be forthcoming. Malkum officials deny any wrongdoing and have refused to comment.

Newspaper article extracted from the Archive, dated thirteen months before the Genetic Apocalypse

---

Akram looked at his watch. 2:15 A.M. He could hardly see. The shuffling of papers and erratic footsteps filled the silence. For hours they'd scoured the filing cabinets. And he *still* hadn't acclimated to the horrid stench, like the dirty bath water of molding rodents and ancient books.

He wiped sweat from his forehead. Whoever had organized this place was an idiot—obviously they'd relied on computers for too long. There was no order—the files hadn't been sorted by last name, first name, date, or anything. Except maybe in how *not* related to Quincy they were. Nothing. Nothing. Nothing. And they weren't even a quarter of the way through.

Akram rubbed his eyes. They stung from sleep deprivation and deciphering bad handwriting. But what else would he do? Sleep? The thought was laughable.

Spencer rushed toward Akram, leaving a trail of dust behind. His bulbous belly jiggled. "Sir?"

Akram turned.

"I think we've found it."

Spencer opened a manilla dossier, revealing a photograph of Quincy Sturgess. The image conjured a cascade of memories. The man in the image smiled, his eyes squinting and his lips reaching to the edge of his cheeks. He had short dreadlocks and wore a Hawaiian shirt and a beaded necklace. Yes, he remembered him. Quincy was a brilliant engineer and had masterminded the security system they *still* used today.

Akram let out a breath. *Finally.*

"Is that Quincy, sir?" Spencer asked.

Akram raised an eyebrow. "You didn't know it was him?"

Spencer flipped through the pages—nothing. The multitude of forms appeared to be empty.

"Bruce Hinkley found a stack of seemingly blank records," Spencer said.

Akram angled his flashlight. Whoever had organized this room may also have been dumb enough to use pencil. In this humidity, it was surprising the filing cabinets hadn't buckled.

He adjusted the angle until...

Akram grinned. Light skidded off the paper, casting tiny shadows in the imprints where the pencil marks had been.

"Got it," Akram said. He closed the file, then marched toward the exit.

"Sir?"

"To my office. Now."

Minutes later, they arrive. Spencer wheezed and dabbed sweat from his forehead. He collapsed into a folding chair.

Akram flipped through the pages—medical records, employment history, insurance information

Incarceration.

He grinned, then read the text.

May 11th, 2036. Alicia Dawn Oliver, daughter of psychologist Keston Thomas Oliver, was sentenced to death for sedition and malfeasance by the council. Dr. Quincy Malcolm Sturgess was called as a character witness. During his remarks, Dr. Sturgess testified he had known the Oliver family for years, had been college roommates with Dr. Keston Oliver, and was Alicia's godfather. He testified of her brilliance, good nature, and honesty. Had his statement ended there, the court may have excused Dr. Sturgess's remarks. However, he proceeded to accuse the council of nefarious activities. In order to protect the integrity of the Malkum and to prevent an uprising, Alicia was quietly sentenced to death. Because Dr. Sturgess limited his remarks to the council, he was given a lesser punishment of 15 years in prison.

Akram squinted. Keston Oliver. He could vaguely recall the man—short, stocky, quiet. Yes, he remembered the psychologist, though he couldn't recall what his research was about.

He turned the page. Death and police report.

July 17th, 2040. During his forth year in prison, Sturgess attempted to escape. The guard on duty, Jerry Quinn shot and killed Sturgess outside his prison cell. He then deposited his body in the incendiary room before an autopsy could be performed.

Akram turned the page again. Second Death and police report. He read the text and froze. The man had been killed within *one hour* of the lightning strike. One. Hour! Yet the official story was that it was an "act of God." Any link between Quincy and the strike had been dismissed—they searched the building for co-conspirators and found nothing, concluding there was no evidence it had been caused by anything other than the storm. They also concluded that, with the assistance of the man who had "shot" Quincy, his death had been faked, and Quincy attempted to capitalize on the electrical disruption to escape.

Jerry Quinn disappeared and was never found.

It was a shoddy investigation. The man invented the security system. This rebellion could have been squelched centuries ago. Instead, they had survived and festered.

But he had a name—Keston Oliver.

Spencer's snores filled the room. Akram slapped his desk. Spencer woke with a snort.

"We've got work to do," Akram said.

"Huh?"

"Keston Oliver—find his file."

"Who?"

"Keston Oliver. He's a co-conspirator." Akram leaned back, rubbing his chin. Could this be the Ancient—the only other man in the world who had succeeded in conquering death? A psychologist-gone-geneticist?

Akram shook his head. It couldn't be. Discovering the Death Antidote required more than know-how—it required brilliance—as Einstein was to physics, Akram was to genetics. One couldn't simply switch expertise willy nilly and make the most difficult, most brilliant, most stunning discovery of human history. No, his rival *had* to have been a geneticist, and a brilliant one.

But what was Keston's role? A psychologist? Psychologists were as useful as ants on a battlefield. It didn't take a PhD to know—

Akram's eyes widened. Drakes—the man's own memories had somehow been replaced. Had Keston been behind whatever voodoo had tampered with his mind?

Spencer resumed snoring.

"Wake up!"

Again, Spencer woke with a snort.

"Locate Keston's file. And find out whatever you can about his research."

Akram lifted his glasses and rubbed his eyes. Sleep eluded him. He had spent the night reviewing faded personnel records, written by imbeciles who couldn't function without computers.

But worst of all, Keston Oliver had no file. They'd scoured every record, checking, rechecking, and checking their rechecking of the faded personnel records.

Nothing.

That lightning storm. The only reason Quincy had a file was because his death occurred *after* the attack. Apparently the report was made retroactively, or so it seemed.

He flung the dossier across the room. Sunlight blared through his window, sending shards of pain to his temples. At 200 stories high, his office overlooked the black clouds that shrouded the landscape.

He'd never decipher anything useful in these records. He marched to his desk before picking up the phone.

"Hello," said Spencer. He sounded as if he had just awaken.

"Is there any news on the rebel hideout we bombed?" asked Akram.

Spencer muffled a yawn. "I was just about to call you, sir. It's not a hideout."

Akram cursed. "And what makes you say that?"

"Well, it was a hatch, but it covered a tiny room, no more than seven foot by five foot. Hardly enough room for rebel headquarters."

"Any evidence they had access to the Archive?"

"Well...not really, but we did find something. The room had a large collection of books, so there was *something* going on. Whether it was related to the rebellion, we can't be sure."

"Did any of the Indignis survive?"

"It was pretty extensive, but one person did. His name is Huka, a burly idiot, if you ask me." Spencer chuckled.

"And what have you learned from this Huka?"

"He's undergoing a genetic scan. We should have results shortly."

"No, I mean, does he have any information? About the rebellion? About the books? What does he know, Spencer?"

"My apologies. He hasn't said a word, not of significance anyway."

"I'll be the judge of what's significant. What has he said?"

Spencer shuffled through papers. "Ah, here it is. Yes, he just keeps repeating the same phrase. 'My brother is dead. My brother is dead. My brother is dead.'"

Chapter 7

Malkum Spokesman's Death Raises Suspicion

New York Times

Sources within the Malkum report that Nikolas Kostas, Malkum scientist and Internal Disease specialist is dead. Little is known about how Kostas died and Malkum officials refuse to allow an investigation. Galina Itsov, Malkum spokesperson stated, "We are fully competent in conducting our own investigation. Any additional investigation would place an undue burden on the victim's family." Kostas's death raises suspicion about Malkum involvement.

Newspaper article extracted from the Archive, dated thirteen months before the Genetic Apocalypse

---

Aumora approached from the river. Like Elsa, she was expressionless, yet the expression looked foreign on her. The vitality of her gait was gone. Instead, she plodded.

"Morning," she muttered.

Cole nodded.

Suta slept by the remains of the fire. Elsa returned from the river carrying several canteens of water. Luther emerged from the woods, carrying a bag of fruits and berries. Cole suppressed a scowl.

"No time for meat this morning," he said. "We'd best get moving."

"Where?" Cole asked.

Luther looked from Cole to Elsa, then back to Cole. Shaking his head, he bent to pick up his canteen.

"Where?" Cole asked again. "Where are we going?"

Luther looked up. "There's an Indignis village nearby. I reckon we can stay there 'til we figure what we're gonna do about the enemy."

"What *are* we going to do about the enemy?"

"You hear what I said, boy?" Luther lifted his chest, but his posture withered when he regarded Aumora. "We gonna rest, then figure it out."

Cole gritted his teeth. It was secrets all over again. He opened his mouth to speak.

"Please, Cole," said Aumora. "Luther knows what he's doing."

"Luther, huh? A man I've never met, never *heard* of."

"I had reason to—"

"I know," said Cole. "Another secret." He shook his head. Like the secrets that kept him locked in the dungeon while the Malkum murdered Rook.

Whatever. What did it matter? The villagers were dead. There was no reason to care about secrets anymore. He looked to Elsa, who shifted her gaze, feigning disinterest.

"Fine," he said. "Let's go."

Luther shook Suta's shoulders. "Wake up, little guy. Time to go. We've lots of cool things to see today."

Suta stretched, grinning. At least someone would have fun. The boy had once spent several days with Aumora making a coat. When finished, Suta insisted they, "Do again. Do again." The next day Aumora saw another villager wearing it. When asked about his coat, Suta said, "I think it's gone, a little bit."

Suta stretched and gazed from person to person. "Loofer sweep good?"

"I slept good, youngen'."

"Coe sweep good?"

Cole nodded.

"'Mora sweep good."

"Yup."

He raised an eyebrow at Elsa. "Ahh...pwetty girl sweep good?"

Silence followed, long and awkward. Cole looked at Elsa, who forced a smile. Hesitantly, she extended her hand to Suta's. "My name's Elsa." She bent at the waist making her eyes level with his.

He smiled, shaking her hand. "Elsa...pwetty name, pwetty girl."

Elsa released some tension in her shoulders and her smile reached her eyes. Cole too smiled.

"All right, 'nough spittin' around." Luther stood. "It's time to get, b'fore Malkum start tracking us. Normally, I'd say we follow the river on down east then turn north in 'bout two days' time. But, seeing as how 'princess Elsa' may have given us away to the Malkum, I'd say we use a different strategy."

Cole shook his head, glaring at Luther, but the old man continued, "If we head northeast now, we might could avoid any unexpected rendezvous with the enemy. But we'll be without a water source for nigh on a day, so I'd suggest we stock up."

"Elsa already filled the canteens," said Aumora.

Luther pressed his lips together. "Then let's go."

Cole watched him walk, but hesitated. This man could bring him to the Malkum, but he'd also tried to kill Elsa.

It didn't matter. What else could Cole do? Wander in the forest alone, hiding from the Malkum? And besides, if this man had a plan, Cole had to come.

Luther led the way through the underbrush, hacking at branches and bushes with his knife. The snapping of sticks and rustling of bushes filled the silence, leaving Cole's mind to wander.

All dead.

He shivered, trying to push the thought from his mind.

After several hours, hot sweat stuck to Cole's skin. His stomach rumbled from the paltry meal of berries and nuts. Yet Elsa's rumbled louder, despite her insistence she wasn't hungry.

Suta stopped. He lowered his gaze, peering into the forest with the intensity of a stalking lion. Cole arched his back, smiling.

Luther stiffened and he searched the forest. "What is it?"

"I be back!" The boy sprinted toward the evergreens. Luther lunged, but Aumora grabbed his arm.

"Everything's fine." She smiled. "He'll be back."

They waited while Suta disappeared. He returned smiling as wide as the river.

"I got peasants." He beamed. "For you." He handed Luther a smooth black river-rock. "Is a hewicopter."

"Would ya look at that?" Luther inspected the rock. "Always wanted one of these."

Suta grinned, before looking at Elsa. "And for you." He handed her a withering piece of bark. "Is a dog. Watch out. He bites!"

Elsa smiled, then took the object. "Ouch."

Suta laughed. Cole regarded Elsa. A gust of wind whipped her red hair over her shoulders. She smiled to herself, turning the bark in her hand.

What was it about Suta that removed her defenses? Like Aumora, she carried secrets with her, mysteries Cole yearned to uncover. Yet she was more impenetrable than his mother.

"Best gift anyone's given me, son," said Luther. "Sure is, best gift ever."

Elsa tousled the boy's hair.

The boy beat his fist into his palm, imitating Luther. "Times-a wastin'."

Even Luther laughed, then they continued their walk.

Elsa listened for Luther's steady breath. When his snoring began, her shoulders relaxed, yet her stomach rumbled. Only Cole remained awake. The orange fire light reflected in his morose eyes.

Was it all an act? He had saved her life, sought her out when she stormed off, and defended her from Luther. Either he was a talented and persistent actor, or it wasn't an act at all. She wanted to believe he was sincere, but each time she had trusted in the past...

Cole stood. "I'm gonna go for a quick walk."

Elsa looked at Cole, but he didn't return her gaze. Instead, he stared vacantly in the direction of the forest and began walking.

Her instincts prodded her to follow. He disappeared beneath the shadows of the trees. She removed her shoes and placed them on a log by the campfire. Her calloused feet glided silently on the rocky dirt. The last two years had been harrowing, but at least she had learned one thing—to move fast and silent. It was as if her feet had foresight into every uneven bump and desiccated twig. Her toes were like a tactile magnifying glass, and her foot and ankle muscles adjusted with the precision of a guided missile.

Elsa entered the dark forest, following the sound of crushed leaves and snapping twigs. Eventually, she focused on another sound—Cole's ragged breaths.

He entered a clearing. Moonlight outlined his figure. He looked toward the stars before collapsing onto his knees. His cry broke the silence, dispersing birds. He buried his head in his hands.

A lump formed in Elsa's throat.

He's toying with you.

Such thoughts had kept her safe, warning of danger and placing armor around her sympathetic emotions. She resisted the onslaught of empathy. As her armor took effect, she scowled, then turned.

But who would he deceive, alone in the forest?

She pushed the thought aside and the empathy from her heart. She welcomed the tension back into her shoulders and focused on the sound of the wind whistling through the trees. She returned to camp and waited for the deceiver to return.

She plopped a log into the fire, before sitting on the ground. The wind shifted directions, blowing smoke into her eyes. She waved it away with one hand and rubbed her eyes with the other.

She struggled to open her eyes.

Despite her efforts, she sunk to the ground and drifted into sleep.

Elsa sat before a computer in a cubicle. She tapped her fingernail on the laminate desk as she waited for the translation to fail, as it always did. And as it likely always would.

It was a difficult task, no, an impossible task that her father had undertaken. Since his abandonment, she was the only employee with enough expertise to continue the work of translation. A small collection of hard drives remained alive—barely. Their pulse was so faint it was uncertain if their data could be revived.

Whether this tiny section of hidden data contained anything useful was a gamble. The timeline icon read 47%. It had been stuck there for over an hour, a sure sign that the translation had failed again. She reached for the power button, then froze. The timeline flashed all numbers between 47% and 100% before disappearing.

She smiled. The screen displayed hundreds of files. Most looked the same —a file name preceded by a red X. But four files looked different.

She opened the first, revealing hundreds of lines of text. She lowered her eyebrows and leaned closer to the screen.

She swallowed a gasp, but she could not stop the sweat that streaked down her temples.

Footsteps approached. She closed the file. The footsteps neared, but sounded different. A hand brushed her hair behind her back.

She jolted awake, jumping to her feet. Cole remained crouched where she had been laying.

"What are you doing?" She blinked against the light from the glowing coals.

"I found these plants." He cleared his throat. "They're an antiseptic. I was hoping to treat your..." Cole pointed at Elsa's neck. "But I didn't want to wake you. Sorry."

She straightened her spine, freezing her expression. "I'm fine."

Cole sighed. "What are you afraid of, Elsa? You think I'm going to hurt you? Look, I'm sorry for whatever happened to you. But that cut's going to infect if you don't do something about it."

"I'm not afraid of you."

"Prove it."

She glared at him, then sat, pulling her hair behind her back. She reached for the pile of leaves in Cole's hand.

"It's better if I do it," said Cole. "We had to do this kind of thing a lot in my..." Cole's voice cracked.

With a sigh, she lowered her hand.

He popped his canteen. Water splashed against the dirt. His warm wet hands gently touched her neck. She resisted the temptation to recoil. So many memories had begun similarly—a gentle touch and a promise. And then...

She shivered.

"Sorry." He caressed the wound. "This next part might hurt. I've got to clean it first."

He wet his hands again, then rubbed her neck. They were gentle and soothing. Her shoulders relaxed.

No, she couldn't relax. She tensed again.

"Sorry. Didn't mean to hurt you," Cole said. "Almost done."

She felt the texture of the wet leaves on her neck. The pain of her injury dulled. Deceiver or not, he had lifted a burden.

"Thanks," she said under her breath.

He walked in front of her. "My pleasure." He smiled, studying her face. "I'm glad you're here."

Despite her best efforts, Elsa smiled.

Cole's chest rose and fell. She couldn't remember how long she'd watched, nor did she immediately realize she was smiling as she recalled the feel of his hands on her neck and the warmth it brought.

Snap out of it.

She tiptoed toward Aumora who held Luther's knife in a holster on her hip. Elsa hesitated, then approached.

It was risky. If she were caught, she'd lose whatever trust she'd gained with the woman. Aumora might even let Luther kill her. But she was sick of being nothing more than another mouth to feed.

She reached toward Aumora's belt buckle. Aumora coughed. Elsa froze, staring at the woman's half-opened eyes. Her pupils moved back and forth before her deep breaths continued.

Elsa froze, poised to flee. When Aumora's breathing steadied, she reached for the handle of the knife. Aumora turned her body, rolling to her back. Using her momentum, she removed the knife.

She removed her shoes and tied the laces around her belt loop. Again she fell into the familiar pattern of walking barefooted.

Luther would discover what a 'helpless girl' she was.

She sat on a large boulder just inside the forest. She waited for her eyes to adjust. Crickets chirped. A icy breeze chilled her skin. She closed her eyes and hugged her torso, trying to focus on the scent of the pine trees.

The boulder numbed her butt. As the tingling traveled down her legs, she stood and opened her eyes. Moonlight skimmed off the leaves and needles. The underbrush resembled small mountains of shadow.

Who was she kidding? She'd never see game in such darkness. She looked toward the river. Perhaps she'd arrive by the afternoon if she left now. No more drama. No more death threats. Just solitude.

But if she left, she'd leave a smug old man. And Cole. Her pulse quickened.

She shook her head. No, she wouldn't leave. There were more important reasons to stay. Celso and Mother counted on her.

She gripped the handle of the knife—cool, yet familiar. She closed her eyes, rehearsing the motion in her mind. She sighted a tree trunk, pulled the handle back, then flicked her wrist. The knife shot forward, disappearing into the darkness, before landing with a thud.

She smiled with satisfaction, then weaved between underbrush and fallen branches, gauging her surroundings by feel more than sight. After retrieving her dagger, she sat on a log and unfocused her eyes, watching for movement.

She waited.

A deer would be nice. She'd had venison once. Saliva filled her parched mouth and her stomach rumbled. Venison. Maybe they could find some sage or rosemary. She'd even take it raw.

Her stomach hurt. Like a spoiled child, it seemed to lash out against her.

She waited.

She'd even take a squirrel. It wasn't much to brag about, but it was *something*.

She waited.

Even a bird. Just one stupid bird.

Nothing. The sky turned dark purple. She dropped her head with a sigh. Her stomach rumbled. There was *nothing* here. But she couldn't go back—helpless and hungry *still*. No, she'd either go back with game, or not go back at all. And if she abandoned them, someone would discover the missing knife. Then what? Her "dirty traitor" brand would stick with *two* companies.

She popped her knuckles.

Movement in the corner of her eye. Elsa froze, then shifted her head.

A boar. A small one, but it was a lot bigger than a squirrel. She grinned, cocked the knife, stilled her breath, then threw.

The knife stuck in the animal's fur, between its forelegs.

The boar turned its head in her direction, then grunted.

It charged. *Thump-thump, thump-thump.*

She gasped, frantically sprinting. The beast neared. *Thump-thump, thump-thump.*

She cursed. Her blood pumped faster. Tiny sticks and pebbles stabbed her bare feet. She could hear grunts closing behind her.

I can't escape. She spun, poised to fight. The boar paused, grunted, then roared.

She lunged sideways, reaching for the knife. She missed, but so did the boar. Its fur grazed her arm.

It turned, beginning another charge.

Thump-thump, thump-thump.

Can't miss. The knife protruded from the boar's fur. It ducked its head. She lunged again, reaching for the knife. Wind whipped past her and her finger grazed the knife's blade. She gasped, grabbing her hand.

She spun. The dagger had fallen. The boar turned, barreling toward her. Where was the knife?

It balanced sideways on a rock between her and the boar.

She set her jaw, then leaped.

Thump-thump, thump-thump. The boar aimed its tusks. She grabbed the handle then stabbed upward.

Hot blood spurt from the beast's neck, spilling onto her jacket. It's body relaxed with a final grunt.

Silence.

She panted. Her heart thudded against her ribcage. She stood, placing her hands behind her head.

She laughed. She'd done it—faced a boar and killed it. She hadn't run, hadn't hid behind a mask of indifference. She'd stuck a knife in its brain.

Beaming, she reached for the tusks and heaved. Nothing moved. She pushed against a tree trunk for leverage. Still, nothing. She cursed. Blood dripped from her fingers. Her empty stomach and blood-loss made her head spin.

The sun was rising fast. If she didn't return soon, someone might discover the missing knife. Better to explain after showing him the boar. She'd have to come back later.

She jogged, the sun growing dangerously bright. Wind tossed her hair, icing her wet clothes. Twigs snapped beneath her feet. Her head swirled.

The clearing lay just ahead. She stopped, then returned to her silent walk.

She grabbed her jacket, attempting to wring the remaining blood. Tears lined the fabric and the blood oozed into the white padding.

She tossed her jacket aside, but not before the blood had seeped into her shirt. How would she explain it? A missing knife, a bloody shirt? She may never even convince Luther to follow her to the boar, she'd have to—

She stopped.

There was a noise—the rustling of leaves. She grinned. Maybe Luther wouldn't have to follow her anywhere. She held the knife next to her ear, then looked toward the source of the sound. She saw faint movement.

A Malkum soldier pointed a rifle toward camp. Her eyes widened. He moved his finger over the trigger and took a deep breath and slowly began to exhale. She'd be too late. She fixed her eyes on the rear of his neck, then hurled the dagger.

The knife thudded and the rifle fired. Which noise came first? Did it matter? Yes, it mattered. If the shot came first, she was too late. But if the shot came second, maybe she altered the trajectory. The man gasped before collapsing. He fell forward, grunting his final breath.

The blood from her hand continued to drip. She heard screams near camp.

She fainted.

Chapter 8

Virus Plagues North America

USA Today

A debilitating virus has begun spreading through North America. The first victims were reported near Atlanta last week and within three days, symptoms were discovered as far as Paraguay. Epidemiologists estimate that 90% of Americans have been affected. The virus targets the frontal lobe of the brain, which is responsible for planning, impulse control, and higher order functioning. So far, no victims have recovered from the virus and no deaths have been reported.

Newspaper article extracted from the Archive, dated one week after the Genetic Apocalypse

---

"Elsa, wake up." Someone shook her. "Elsa, Elsa!"

Her eyes flickered. Two people stood over her—Aumora and Suta. The scent of blood filled her nose. Her hand stung.

Where was Cole? Her pulse quickened. *Oh no, oh no, oh no.* Had she been too late?

She bolted upright, nearly fainting again. She tried to stand, feeling woozy. A cold breeze blew. She looked toward the campfire. Shapes moved in the distance, but only one.

Her throat tightened.

“Did he hurt you?” Aumora looked at Elsa’s blood-stained shirt. "Where's your jacket?"

Elsa squinted. Still, only one shape moved.

“Did the soldier hurt you?” Aumora asked again.

“Where’s Cole?”

“He’s fine. Are you ok? What happened?”

“I’m fine.” Everything spun and she grabbed Aumora’s hand.

“But you’re all bloody. Your hand is cut. You don’t look well. What happened?”

She shook her head, fighting the dizziness. She ran.

When Cole came into view, she pressed her palm to her chest. *Thank God.* He stood over Luther, who lay with one elbow on the ground.

Suta caught up. “Loofer bweed bad.”

Elsa sucked in a breath.

“Cole!” the old man said, “I’ll give you about a hair-split of a second to let me go b’fore I give you some hemmhoragin’ to cry about.”

“Ahhh, quit your whining, ya old grump,” said Cole. “I’m almost done.”

Elsa smiled and she peered over Cole’s shoulder. Blood stained Luther’s plaid shirt, but he was alive.

But why would she care if Luther was okay? The jerk had tried to kill her.

She shook her head. It didn’t matter. Maybe he’d finally trust her.

Blood dripped from a long gash on the left side of his neck. Her hand reflexively reached for the cut on the right side of her own.

Luther looked at Elsa’s neck, then reached for his own. He grinned. “It seems the Good Lord’s got quite a sense of humor, doesn’t he?”

Elsa regarded him. “He made you, didn’t he?” Wind whistled between the nearby trees. She smiled.

Luther barked a laugh, which turned into gasping guffaws. His face turned red and he fought for breath.

"He made you, she says."

Cole chuckled. Her forced smile turned genuine. She rolled her eyes.

Cole finished the bandage and the old man turned to lie on his back, still recovering from the laughing spell.

"It's a good thing yer not a doctor." Luther reached for his bandage. "You got all the tenderness of a porcupine, and half the brains."

"Elsa, next time someone's aiming a gun at Luther, do us all a favor. Make sure they get a solid hit."

"Didn't know where he was aiming." She shrugged. "Should have waited for the next shot. Sorry."

"Ahhh, I'd a caught the bullet with my teeth," said Luther, showing his off-white fangs. "You aint gettin' rid o' me that easy."

Cole laughed. "We'll work together next time, Elsa."

Cole proposed several ways they could eliminate Luther, while the old man invented absurd ways to avoid an untimely death.

Aumora arrived, panting. She scanned the scenery, Elsa's revolver in hand. "Time to go."

Cole raised an eyebrow.

"If we found one, chances are—"

"No," Elsa said. "We travel alone."

Aumora gazed at Elsa.

"We...They cover more ground that way."

"Alone?" Aumora asked.

"Alone. We're probably safer now than before. Here."

Aumora nodded hesitantly. "You sure."

"I'm sure."

Aumora let out a breath before tucking the revolver behind her belt. "So what happened, Elsa?" Aumora pointed to her bloody shirt. "You're not a walking corpse, are you? And where's your jacket?"

"Not my blood." She coughed, then crossed her arms, trying to hide her laceration. Aumora raised an eyebrow.

"Well, what happened?" Cole asked again.

"I." She coughed again. "I went to pee." She shrugged.

"Dangerous bathroom break," Cole said. "And last I heard, it doesn't take a knife to pee, but I'm not all too familiar with feminine anatomy."

Out of habit, Elsa tried to suppress her smile, but a laugh escaped her mouth. Cole leaned back, eyes wide.

"Really, though. What *did* happen?" Cole asked.

Elsa hesitated. "Couldn't sleep. I decided to hunt, so I...*borrowed* Luther's knife."

She looked at Luther out of the corner of her eye. He said nothing, but his grin faded.

Her face turned placid. She erected the emotional barriers. Hadn't they passed a milestone? She'd saved his stupid life. Wasn't that enough?

So I stole your knife, she thought, trying not to care how he felt.

Silence lingered. The old man looked at her. "Well, go on. What happened next?"

She regarded him, unsure what to make of the armor she had erected. Cole reached to touch her hand, but hesitated. For once, she didn't cringe. Rather, she thought of the night before—Cole's soothing hands on her neck—and fought a smile.

"I spent some time hunting," she said in a guarded tone. "When I came back the soldier was there. I threw the knife. Lucky shot."

Silence.

"You kill any...ah, cats?" Suta asked.

They laughed.

"No." She pointed to her blood-stained shirt. "But I did kill a boar."

Aumora cocked her head. Luther's eyes widened.

"Couldn't carry it back. It's somewhere over there...along with my jacket." She pointed toward the forest.

Their eyes followed her hand before resting again on Elsa. Cole gradually smiled. "Bacon for breakfast?"

"I hear Luther's got a great recipe," she said.

Aumora tended Elsa's wound as Cole, Luther, and Suta dressed the boar on site. They returned, hefting chunks of meat in a blanket, then cooked it in the fire.

Luther poked a piece with a stick and handed it to Elsa.

"No thanks, I'm not hungry," she said.

"It's like ya said, I got a mean recipe. Don't go insulting me by refusing ma food."

Elsa accepted the meat. The old man watched as she took a bite. She let the juices linger in her mouth. Hunger got the best of her and she inhaled the rest.

"Now that's better," Luther said with a wink.

Elsa held her breath, trying to ignore the metallic stench of the sniper's blood. She shivered as she stripped him of his gear. The man deserved it. She wished she could put a knife in every one of their throats. Yet her stomach still twisted. She killed a man, and it may not be the last time.

"What do you think?" Aumora asked.

Elsa grabbed the soldier's phone and popped the lid of her black canteen. "Don't think he targeted us specifically."

"So he doesn't know who we are?" Cole asked.

Elsa shook her head. She pushed the phone into the canteen and motioned the way they had traveled. "Let's walk that way."

"Why?" Cole asked.

Luther nodded toward the canteen. "Solar powered?"

Elsa nodded.

"Clever," said Luther.

Suta drew pictures in the dirt with a stick while Aumora and Cole raised their eyebrows at Elsa.

"The phone tracks his movement," Elsa said. "If we shut it off, they'll know something's up. But if the signal gradually stops transmitting, they'll think it's a faulty solar cell."

Aumora nodded. "So we walk in the opposite direction."

"Keep the phone in darkness." Luther pointed at the canteen. "'Til the batteries go out."

"Ah," Cole said, nodding.

They walked. Suta stood, his eyes lingering on the stick figures he had drawn. The crunching of their feet filled the silence.

"Why do you think the soldier tried to kill us?" Aumora asked.

"He probably only intended to kill off those he assumed posed a threat—Cole and Luther."

Aumora smirked. "He'd have guessed wrong."

Elsa grinned.

"You said they were searching for something?" Cole asked.

As they entered a grassy clearing, their footsteps quieted. Elsa studied the ground. Should she tell them? Aumora and Luther already seemed to know. But what if they didn't?

She sighed. "They're looking for the rebellion."

Cole cocked his head. "The rebellion?"

Elsa peered at Luther. The old man frowned, then nodded.

"The rebellion," Elsa said. "The Malkum used to send soldiers to search for intelligence among the Indignis. Once they learned about the rebellion, they began fanning out in singles, combing the planet. It looks like he," she pointed toward the dead body, "was one of the many searching. Unlucky for him, he actually found what he was looking for."

She turned her head to Luther. He squinted into the horizon, but made no comment.

"What rebellion?" Cole asked.

Elsa cocked her head. He returned the gaze.

"Luther?" Elsa asked. "You want to tell him?"

"Tell me what?" Cole asked.

Luther looked at Elsa, biting his cheek. His labored breaths and the impact of his walking stick filled the silence.

"The rebellion," Luther said. His gaze pierced hers, as if still uncertain.

I saved your life! And *still* he didn't trust her.

Luther winked. "Yes, Cole. There's a rebellion."

There was a rebellion. Cole's heart fluttered, and he quickened his pace.

"The rebellion." Luther breathed deeply, as if preparing to tell the entire story in one breath. Cole felt like a dog waiting for a scrap of meat. *Finally,* answers would come.

"'Bout 200 years ago, countries was fightin' with one another. When they started threatening nuclear weapons...well, that's when the Malkum stepped in. Now, I'm not all that sure if they was bad before or started getting bad then, but some moron proposed they cripple the world's intellect."

"Why?"

Luther shook his head. "They says they wanted to make sure nobody never have the brains to build weapons again. Well, if you ask me, it was an excuse. They make everybody dumb, who can oppose them?"

Cole shook his head.

"Anyhow, the Malkum vaccinated themselves and let the world go to hell. That's how the Indignis came to be. They're humans, like you and I, just dumber."

"So what does that make us?" he gazed at Luther. "Are we some accident of evolution? Is that how the rebellion began?"

"'Mora...you wanna take this one?" asked Luther.

Aumora smiled. "After the change, the Malkum took natural selection into their own hands. For the last two hundred years, they've hunted the 'Mutations' as we call them—individuals who were born with a flipped switch." Aumora glanced at Suta. The boy's eyes were thoughtful, apparently contemplating Aumora's words.

Suta had always been different—the counting, his understanding of subtle social cues, the quiet way he listened to conversations. *He* was a mutation. Had he not belonged to their village, he would have died a martyr at the hands of the Malkum.

"They don't want anybody to challenge them," Aumora continued, "so they kill those who develop intellect. They call it the 'NSI,' or the Natural Selection Initiative. They raid villages, looking for Mutations. And no doubt there are *others.*"

Cole furrowed his brow. "So am I a...Mutation?"

Aumora shook her head. "Like Elsa, I was once Malkum."

"What happened?" Cole asked.

"My parents were researchers, and they trained me. I did research in immunology. I did well for myself, professionally and politically, and was invited into certain circles of influence."

She looked at Cole. "You see, son, most Malkum have no idea about the NSI—most have no idea what's going on outside Fahrquan. I climbed the political ladder high enough that I learned about it. So I left."

"You just...left?" asked Cole.

"I had a little help." She smiled, slapping Luther's shoulder.

The old man studied the trees. Again, their footsteps filled the silence.

"You too?" Cole asked.

Luther shook his head. "Nah. I'm a rebel—born and raised. 'Bout Two hundred years ago, a man we call 'The Ancient' formed a group of rebels."

"The Ancient?" asked Cole. "Is that his...name?"

Luther chuckled. "I know some dumb parents, but not any dumb enough to name a newborn 'Ancient.' If I had to take a leak-in-the-dark kinda guess, I'd say it's a nickname. I mean, the man is over 200 years old."

Cole laughed. *Right.* "So what does that make you? 202?"

Luther's smile faded. He pressed his lips together. "The Ancient...he really is over 200."

Cole stopped walking. *200 years?* He inspected the grass near his feet before gazing at Luther. "So he's...immortal?"

"So far," said Luther.

"Magic?"

"Magic to me. Although, the Ancient would claim it's 'simple genetics.' Well, if you ask me, it ain't simple if only one other man in the world has discovered the secret to livin' forever."

"There's another?"

"Yep. There's the problem...The other immortal is President Akram of the Malkum."

Cole's mouth went dry. "How can we defeat an immortal?"

Luther snarled. "A bullet to his head."

"But...I thought—"

"He can die," Luther said. "Just not a natural death. And that's what this is all about. We've gotta bust his brain with bullets, son. But we got help. Two-hundred-years ago, the Ancient formed the rebellion. He used to be a part of the Malkum, see, but when he found they was as well intentioned as a rattlesnake, he started pulling people out of Fahrquan. Eventually, he left the Malkum and has been preparing near 200 years to overthrow them."

Cole's grin widened. He'd always assumed it was he and Aumora, that they alone had to overthrow the Malkum. But with the rebellion, they could do it.

"So why wait 200 years?" asked Cole.

"We had to wait 'til the rebellion grew large enough. Two-hundred years ago, it was Gene and a handful of others. Now, they've grown big 'nough to do something."

"And what's the plan?" Cole asked. His fingers tingled.

Luther sighed. "I tell you what the plan *was*. We was gonna invade Fahrquan, execute the council, put a dagger through Akram's heart."

"*Was*?"

Luther nodded solemnly. "We've got two problems, Cole. First, them rebels been cowering like timid dogs for two centuries. They never seen so much as a skirmish, and you think them kinda people just gonna leave their cozy homes and march into death's kitchen with an apple in their mouth? And all for a race of humans they never seen b'fore?"

"Okay."

"And second," Luther sighed, "is General Mason."

Cole bent toward Luther.

"'bout 40 years ago, the Ancient starts pressuring the council to prepare fer an invasion. But they don't wanna do nothing. They never even seen Indignis." Luther spat. "They don't care. We'll the Ancient tried fer 20 years to get them to invade. Nothing. Nothing, nothing. Then General Mason comes along. He starts spreading rumors 'bout the Ancient—says the man's lost his mind. But suddenly, at the council meetings, he starts backing the Ancient—says we need to save the Indignis, invade Fahrquan."

Cole furrowed his brow. "Why?"

"Cuz he plans to replace Akram—swap one dictator for another. So Gene quit pressuring the council to war and started tryin' ta oust Mason."

"And?"

"And nothin'. No matter what the Ancient tried, Mason won. The devil's still there. The council won't sanction an invasion. The army's too timid to overthrow the general. And it seems Mason's preparing to make a ploy for more power—overthrow the council, sack the Ancient, set himself up as dictator."

Cole's stomach dropped.

"We can't invade until we topple Mason," Luther said. "Not an easy task."

Cole raked his hands through his hair. "So how we gonna do that?"

"What we need," Aumora began, "is someone who's seen the suffering of the Indignis—someone who cares."

"Okay."

"Someone who hasn't been paralyzed by the system," Luther said. "Who's not been trained ta be afraid of Mason. We need someone on the inside. One who can win the trust of the army from within—inspire them to fight back."

Cole struggled to swallow.

Aumora's face went somber. "Someone who's been kept in the dark their entire life. Someone who came to love the Indignis, not because they had to or because they were told to."

"But because they chose to," Luther said.

Cole felt cold, as if his stomach were surrounded by ice. "Okay."

"Them devils killed yer people," Luther said. "And I ain't gonna let that pass. But first, yer gonna have ta topple Mason."

The revelation hit his gut like a baseball bat. "I-I-I." Cole shook his head. "I can't."

"Think about it," Luther said, then he turned to walk.

I don't have to think about it. Cole trudged behind Luther. *I won't do it.*

Chapter 9

The world is quiet now. I feel sick that peace cost such a high price. The only way I can live with myself is by ensuring this never happens again.

Journal Entry of President Akram dated two weeks after the Genetic Apocalypse, extracted from the Archive.

The smell of disinfectant hung in the air. In the center of the room, Sergeant Drakes lay motionless on a gurney. Electrodes surrounded his head, feeding results into a monitor. *Beep...beep...beep.* A spotlight glowed with orange light.

Akram stood over the unconscious soldier. The monitor displayed wavy lines of green, blue, and black.

He rubbed his bloodshot eyes. "So?"

Dr. Beatriz Perrot looked at the monitor. She was a lean woman with dyed brunette hair, puffy eyes, and cherry lipstick painted beyond the boundaries of her thin lips. Her ring finger was bare of any wedding band and she reeked of strong perfume.

She furrowed her brow. "Dr. Wang sent him to me because he didn't display some of the symptoms common among those in a coma."

Her voice had a nasally whine, like a bike horn that had learned to speak.

"Such as...?"

"For one thing, patients in a coma frequently have reduced blood flow to the brain, but his is normal."

"And what have *you* found?" asked Akram.

"I'm not entirely sure. You see, the brain displays different patterns of electrical activity, depending on the degree of arousal. Beta waves occur when one is awake. Alpha waves occur when one is relaxed, but *not* asleep. Theta and delta waves occur when one is sleeping. For those in a coma, they tend to have low brain activity, such as that which is characteristic of delta waves. But Drakes is different."

"What kind of waves does he have?"

"These are definitely alpha waves." Dr. Perrot turned to look at Akram. "Almost a textbook case."

"I thought you said—"

"Exactly! Alpha waves only occur when one is awake."

"So, he's awake."

Beep...beep...beep.

Dr. Perrot shrugged her shoulders.

"Here's the other interesting thing." She pointed to a rotating three-dimensional projection of the brain.

"This shows the results of an fMRI, or a *functional* brain scan. When a patient uses a certain part of the brain, the fMRI will 'light up.' The parts that are activated pulse in red."

She pressed a button which paused the rotation. She pointed to the left side of the brain. "Watch this." She lifted a finger to her lips, while pointing at the image with the other.

Beep...beep...beep.

The image remained unchanged.

"And now this."

The area near her finger pulsed.

"Now watch this." She bent toward Drakes's ear. "Mocknehemo."

The image did not light up.

"AL-68 Grenade Launcher and Assault Rifle."

The image flashed.

"Huh." The president lifted a finger to lips. "Language comprehension, I assume?"

"Precisely," said Dr. Perrot. "Because he was unfamiliar with the first word, his brain failed to activate. But when I mentioned the grenade launcher, it lit up."

"So he can hear *and* understand everything we're saying," said Akram.

Dr. Perrot nodded her head.

"So is he faking it?" asked Akram.

"Not at all." She bent and tapped the soldier's right arm. The image remained unchanged.

"The man is paralyzed," she said. "Or at least temporarily."

Her bike horn voice echoed in the room. The president lowered his stubbled chin, then smiled as an idea formed. "What happens if I say the name of someone he knows?"

"It depends on how common the name. Suppose he knows someone by the name of Jack Casey and one by the name of Daniel Hobbs. If you say the name 'Jack Hobbs,' his brain will light up. But rather than activating because of someone named Jack Hobbs, it will be because he knows someone named Jack and someone with the last name of Hobbs."

Akram frowned. "But if I find someone with unusual first and last names, it would only light up if he knew that individual?"

"Most likely," said Perrot. "Although, you must remember this is patient zero, so everything we do is guesswork."

He grinned. Finally a lead. They had failed to gain any information on the identity of the Ancient and they still had no idea where to find the rebels.

He considered several names he could vocalize. After centuries, they became jumbled in his mind. And to have to narrow it down to the unusual ones was even more difficult.

He bent toward Drakes. "Wilhelm Reffold."

Nothing pulsed.

"Eckehard Billigins." Again, nothing lit up.

"Amaliricus Roser." Nothing.

Who was he kidding? It was useless. His memory stored centuries of information and having to recall a narrow sliver of that on demand was unrealistic. He needed to go back to the original personnel files.

Before he got to the door, a thought occurred to him. Though Akram had caused many of the Malkum to 'go missing' over the last 200 years, there were few who had *truly* disappeared.

Akram bent toward Drakes's ear. "Aumora Brooks."

The monitor flashed.

The following day Akram stood in a small, white-painted room. Cages lined the walls, each containing a mouse. The room reeked of animal litter. In his hand, he held a syringe. He pressed the bottom, releasing a purple-tinged liquid.

A clank sounded from the metal door.

"Come." Akram lifted his glasses from the vinyl table and rested them on his nose.

"Sorry to interrupt, President." Spencer entered, panting. "Your secretary. She said I might find you here."

"So you have." Akram opened a cage, removing a hairless mouse from inside. Its skin felt like smooth leather and its tiny feet tickled his palm.

Spencer stepped forward and sat on a three-legged stool.

"This mouse," said Akram, "is very young—only five days old."

Spencer tilted his head, creating large folds of skin around his neck. "Sir?"

"Watch."

Akram pressed the needle into the mouse's abdomen then cradled it so Spencer could see. "Tell me if you see anything change."

Spencer peered at the mouse. It grew in size. Spencer's eyes widened. Within a few minutes, the radius of its belly doubled and a full coat of white hair hid its pink skin.

"Amazing." Spencer beamed.

Akram too smiled. *I should have been a teacher.* And he might have pursued teaching, had not a more lucrative offer come.

"Not all that amazing." Akram threw the mouse. It's body thudded against a metal container. Spencer gasped and he rushed toward the trash.

"It's simple genetics," Akram continued. "It works with humans too. With only a slight modification in one's genetic makeup, an individual will age at an accelerated rate. And I can control not only the rate of aging, but also whether that rate continues until death. This is what made me famous, you know. This is what brought me to the Malkum. And by the time the virus hit, what I just demonstrated to you was common knowledge.

"But nobody cares about aging quickly. Save for little children who want to 'grow up' like mommy and daddy, no one wants to accelerate aging. They want to slow it down."

Akram paused. Spencer stared vacantly at the garbage can, his body rigid. Mouse cages rattled, filling the silence. Spencer shivered, turning his attention to Akram.

"Ok," said Spencer. "So what?"

"*This*," Akram pointed to the serum, "is the first step toward eternal life. Anyone who understands *this* is 90% of the way to discovering the secret of the Death Antidote."

"So why are you...a-and the Ancient the only ones who have discovered it?"

"Because that 10% was a massive pain."

Spencer chuckled, then rubbed the back of his neck.

"That 10% requires a whole lot of work, and a lot more brains. Whoever this Ancient is...he's brilliant, you can count on that."

Spencer nodded.

"Listen. Things are getting more complicated, more urgent. We *must* find the Ancient, and soon. So what can you tell me that I don't already know?"

"I'm not sure, sir. We have no records of anyone named 'Ancient' or any variant of that."

Akram stared at Spencer. He shook his head. "Of course you don't. It's obviously a nickname." The president leaned forward. "Unveiling his identity is essential to discovering the rebel hideout, which is how we will recover the Archive."

"I understand, sir."

"I don't think you do. Think hard—who else could have developed the Death Antidote?"

"That's why I've come, sir. Was there anyone else on your research team? Did anyone assist with developing the Antidote? Where did you store your research? Maybe someone hacked into your files."

Akram had already asked these very questions. He'd worked alone, behind layers of locked doors. He stored nothing digitally—it couldn't be hacked. He recorded his notes in ink on a notebook stored in a safe within a safe within a safe. And those safes were built into the wall of his office, hidden between studs and drywall. It was both concealed and protected. No, it was impossible to steal. Someone else must have developed the Antidote independent of him, somebody brilliant.

He shook his head. "This Ancient developed it. I need to know who he is. I want you to find the name of every geneticist within a hundred years of the origin of this rebellion. He has to be a geneticist, and a brilliant one at that."

It seemed fitting his rival would be a fellow geneticist. The Ancient may have been smart enough to develop the Antidote, but he hadn't conquered the world.

"I'll do my best, sir. But the storm—"

"It wasn't a storm!"

"Right." Spencer bowed his head. "Well, the...destruction of the hard drives. It, uh, well, as you know, records before the storm are sketchy at best. If he's not Malkum—"

"He *must* be Malkum. He's too brilliant to have been overlooked. *And*, the virus would have crippled him if he weren't."

"Yes, sir. We'll keep looking. And one more thing, sir."

"Yes?"

He fidgeted with his wedding ring, and rubbed his sweaty, pock-marked face. "Two of our soldiers recently...dropped off the radar."

"Is that unusual?"

He shrugged. "No. S-sometimes our tracking devices short out, weather damage and such. It's rare. They're pretty robust, b-but it happens."

"So why should I care?"

"Because one of them was dropped off near the hatch we blew up. I mean, i-it's rare to lose track of someone, but to lose track only an hour after w-we drop them off? And to have it happen right near the hatch, then have another vanish only a few days later. It seems too coincidental."

Spencer bounced his knee with his foot on the rung of the stool. "And..." he cleared his throat. "...one of them is Alfred Alsvik's daughter."

Akram's eyes widened. "She's the physicist's daughter?"

"Yes sir."

Akram's skin went cold. Elsa Alsvik—daughter of Alfred. These two had shown the most promise in recovering the Archive. He clenched his fists then leapt to his feet. "Why is she tromping through the forest?"

"She slipped through the cracks. We-we've been disorganized since we've increased recruiting."

Akram slammed his goggles on the table. "Follow me." He marched toward the door.

Spencer stood, adjusting his pants. "S-sir? Where we going?"

"To find out why she left!"

"Where did she work?" Akram asked.

Spencer jogged to keep up with Akram, wheezing. "Elsa?"

"Yes, Elsa."

"Twenty." A labored breath. "First floor."

The pitter-patter of keyboards quieted, replaced with whispers and squeaking chairs as people stood. Heads popped out of rows of cubicles. Spencer leaned against the wall, his body odor masking the scent of printer paper and fresh ink.

"Elsa Alsvik. Where did she work?" Akram asked.

The air conditioner engaged, punctuated by Spencer's rasping breaths. The people's gaze shifted to the back left corner.

Akram nodded and followed their silent directions.

Simon Stanton, Chief Research Officer, exited his office. He had an island of baldness on the crown of his black head and a rotund belly. The large man waddled like a penguin as he approached.

"Dr. Stanton."

"Oh no need for formalities, President. Call me Simon. Pleasant surprise, pleasant surprise. 'Afternoon Spense. Anything I can help you with?"

Akram turned, looking behind a white panel. A black computer monitor sat atop a stark desk—no pictures, no potted plants, no cheesy quotes.

"You cleared her desk?" Akram dug his nails into his palms.

"No, sir," Simon said. "Elsa. She was an oddity. Closer to a hermit than a human, at times, I fear. No, that's how she kept her desk—nothing but the computer and her stoned faced expression, I say."

Akram sat in the chair. His knees touched the underside of the short desk.

He powered on the computer and entered his login credentials.

"Might I ask, Mr. President, what it is you seek?" Simon asked.

"Elsa left suddenly and without notice." Akram spun around in his chair. "Nobody knows where she's at. She won't respond to her radio and her tracking unit has dropped off the radar. Does *any* of this sound suspicious to you?"

Simon pulled a seat from an empty cubicle. The chair protested his weight with a squeal. "Absolutely, I fear. All of it, every last bit of it sounds suspicious, Mr. President. I mean no disrespect sir, but my men have already combed her hard drive—there were no photographs, no suspicious searches in her history, no secret diary of Elsa Alsvik, I fear. Mr. President, she may have been planning months, years, or decades, for all I know."

Akram frowned. "Nothing."

"Nothing, I fear." Simon sighed. "Good worker. Dedicated as I'll get, just like her father was. Work, work, work. All she ever did."

Akram sunk deeper into his chair. Could it all be coincidental? He'd had a hunch there was a connection, or *thought* he'd had one. Why else would she leave? But if all she did was work...

Akram lifted his head. "What's the status with her work on the Archive?"

"Same as always—nothing, I fear," Simon said.

"You're sure?"

Akram faced the computer, before typing. If all she did was work, then whatever caused this must be related to her work. He browsed her file structure and naming conventions. All files were contained with a deeply nested folder structure, and each document had been duplicated so it could be found by date, category, or size. Each duplicate was synchronized with a sophisticated version control. A gradient of colors illustrated the level of activity for each folder. And within each deeply nested directory was a copy of a log file, one that had been duplicated for each nested folder—a master log file.

The girl was organized.

Akram grinned. "Spencer. When did Elsa join the military?"

"Three months ago, give or take."

"What is the exact date?"

Spencer fumbled with a portable computer. "Ah, here it is. April 17th."

Akram nodded. He scrolled down the log file. "That." Akram pointed at the entry for April 17th. "That is where we begin, Simon."

"Pardon?" Simon asked.

"On April 17th, Elsa joined the military. If she's anything like her father, she's not one to dawdle. Whatever happened occurred right before the 17th. Search her files, search her timestamps. She found something on the Archive and I want you to find it."

Simon's lips parted as he lifted his head. "I see. Yes, of course, of course. I'll do my best." Simon pulled his phone from his pocket. "Now if you'll excuse me, I've—"

"Tonight," Akram said. He began marching toward the exit. "On my desk," he shouted over his shoulder. "By tomorrow morning."

Akram sat in his office, holding a personnel file and tapping a pen on the surface of his desk.

The Ancient—he had stolen the Archive and taken Aumora. Now, their only other hope of recovering it—Elsa Alsvik—was gone. The rebellion must be involved. Every blow—a calculated plan to cripple the Malkum.

His fatigue fled. He closed the folder, rubbed his stinging eyes, then reached for a binder. He scratched another name at the bottom of a Malkum stationery.

Vincent Eugene Howley.

Dr. Howley wasn't Malkum, but showed up as a personal reference for one of the geneticists. The list of names before him was useless. All of them failed to activate any part of Drakes's brain.

And what did Aumora have to do with this?

A knock echoed in the room.

"Come." He tossed his pen on the Ebony desk.

Simon Stanton entered, carrying a folder.

"What have you found, Simon?"

"You don't look well, sir. I can come back later." Simon backpedaled. "I'll just—"

"No," said Akram. "What have you got?"

"I think I know why she left." Simon sat. He bent forward, lips pressed together.

Akram smiled. "Go on."

"We found something. Cracked some encryption, so to speak. There were two documents. One mentioned what I assume is an ancient policy of the Malkum—the Natural Selection Initiative."

Akram folded his arms, furrowing his eyebrows. Elsa Alsvik had discovered the NSI, and so had Aumora. Both left suddenly after learning of it, though Aumora truly vanished while Elsa had left on her own. Did the rebels have something to do with it?

Simon lifted his chin, raising his eyebrows.

"You say something?" Akram asked.

"The NSI, ancient policy, right?"

Akram's expression remain placid. "Yes...an ancient policy."

Simon's shoulders relaxed. "So I assumed...so I assumed."

"There was another document?"

"Yes sir. Now you may already know this. The other document's 200 years old and I know that...you, uh...well you were there. Back then, I mean.

So...what I'm trying to say is this may be stuff you already know, but I thought I'd share it anyway."

Simon handed Akram a stapled document.

"Seems it's a detailed plan," Simon continued. "A proposal if you will, for how to stop the war. Dated eighteen months before the virus was released. Now we all know the virus was indeed released, but one thing on that list did *not* happen. If you'll turn your attention to part four."

Akram turned the page and read the section title. He furrowed his brow. "Mortem Bacillus?"

"Yes sir," said Simon. "Or the MB virus. Now technically, it's not a virus, it's a bacterium and—"

Akram cleared his throat.

"Yes. Seems someone intended to destroy the Indignis permanently. I deduce from your reaction, this is all new to you?"

"It is," said Akram. "Back then, every board member submitted a proposal. I submitted one myself, but no. I've never seen *this* one."

Simon handed Akram another document. "Here's the details on how to create the infection and a detailed report on it's effects in primates."

"Good. Thank you, Simon."

"My pleasure, sir." Simon grunted as he stood.

"And be sure to keep this," Akram pointed to the document, "between us."

"Of course, of course. Only you and the corporate board know."

Akram's eyes widened. "You told the counsel?"

"Uh." Simon fidgeted with his wristwatch. "I-I thought I was doing my duty, sir."

Idiot! Akram rubbed his forehead. Simon just handed the council a deadly weapon, one they were all-too-willing to use.

Akram smiled. "That's exactly what you should have done."

And now the Indignis would die at half the price of bombs.

Akram paced his office. The Ancient was a threat—a threat to Akram, a threat to the Malkum, but more importantly he was a threat to the world. Akram had brought peace to a war-torn planet. The existence of the Ancient meant the wars would begin anew.

A war like the one that killed Adam Gianni. For 40 weeks, Akram had shared a womb with Adam. The two had spent their childhood in poverty and had remained unseparated until the Malkum invited Akram to work with them. He joined, promising a better life for Mom and Dad.

And Adam Gianni.

But his twin was called to war and killed through biological warfare. One minor alteration in Adam Gianni's allele was all that was required—an alteration made possible through Akram's own research.

Time hadn't yet healed that wound, and perhaps it never would.

Two hundred years ago, the Malkum had remained neutral until the virus was released. Not this time.

Their armies would be ready.

A knock echoed in the room, sending shards of pain to Akram's temples.

"Come," he said.

A short man entered, dressed in camouflage. He was thin, with the build of a distance runner and short-cropped hair. He saluted. The gesture was precise, coming from years of practice. Yet something about the man's salute wreaked of contempt, of sarcasm.

Akram repressed a scowl. *I should kill you.* Akram had seen many generals come and go. But Scott Chambers had political ambitions unmatched by any of his predecessors—dangerous ambitions.

"General." Akram nodded.

"You wished to see me," said Chambers in a tired, sarcastic voice.

Akram scowled. "Have a seat."

"I prefer to stand."

"Suit yourself." Akram walked around his desk, facing the window. "What's the status?"

General Chambers sighed. "Thanks to your dedicated leadership, recruiting has skyrocketed, our army has quadrupled in size, the rebellion shall be defeated, etcetera, etcetera."

Fatigue fled. The president spun and closed the distance to the general in three strides, towering over him. "I. Could. Kill. You."

"No. You. Can't," the general said. "Need I remind you that you preside under the direction and permission of the council? Any harm caused to me would be considered treason and grounds for removal and death."

"It might be worth it," Akram said with a sadistic smile.

The general smirked. "You wished to see me."

Akram began pacing again. "General Chambers. We have an enemy of unknown size and unknown whereabouts. What is our strategy?"

"I think you know my strategy."

Akram nodded, then sunk his chin to his chest. He had hoped otherwise, but he did know. "I do."

The general had long advocated genocide. No more searching for Mutations among the Indignis.

"As you're aware," said Chambers, "the council has heretofore agreed with you. Destroying each village would be too costly—more costly than searching these forsaken colonies year after year. But now that we know of the MB infection..."

"You know very well that I cannot vote," snapped Akram. "As the President—"

"I am aware of the bylaws. But you *can* influence those who are undecided. Many on the council look up to you. If you recommend genocide—"

"I won't—"

"We have no choice. Now that we know of the rebellion, We. Must. Act."

"They have the Archive! If we release the virus, we've lost it forever."

"Perhaps." The general shrugged. "A compromise, then? What I suggest is that we draw the enemy out—begin a bombing campaign of the Indignis villages."

Akram sighed, shaking his head. What he had done 200 years ago, creating and releasing the virus, was repulsive but necessary. He hadn't taken the decision lightly then, and he wouldn't take this decision lightly either.

"Not yet," he said. "But if it comes to that, I will do my duty to the Malkum. But in the mean time..."

"Very well." The general saluted. "We will continue our hunt for fish in an ocean of black water. Good day, sir."

Chapter 10

My twin is dead.

Journal Entry of President Akram dated two years before the Genetic Apocalypse, extracted from the Archive. Historical commentary: After this entry, President Akram's journal remained blank until after the Genetic Apocalypse.

Elsa fell into a comfortable routine—traveling by day, and sleeping on the hard ground at night. At first, she slept shallow. Discomfort and mistrust kept her on edge. But as days turned into weeks, she relaxed, the ground seemed to soften, and her sleep deepened. She felt comfortable, something she hadn't felt for two years.

Cole had also changed since learning about the rebellion. It was strange—she had to cajole *him* into conversation. Yet he remained lost in thought—distracted. The new burden he carried showed on the way he trudged through the wilderness, his eyes downcast. Whatever battle he waged, he chose to do it alone.

Elsa looked to Luther, who held his hand on his back, wincing with every misstep. He was too old for this sort of journey, but refused to slow on his own behalf.

"What exactly do you do for the rebellion?" she asked, intending to distract him.

"Oh, nothing that requires more than half a brain." Luther grinned. "Fortunately for me."

Their footsteps thumped along the dirt. He grimaced after another misstep, grabbing his lower back. Elsa winced.

"What do you do for the rebellion?" she asked again.

Luther's perpetual frown faded, and he chuckled. "Persistent one, aren't ya?" He opened his mouth. Elsa stepped closer to him, perking her ears, then held her breath. Luther's mouth remained open, but the edges of his lips curled into a smile.

"Well?" she blurted.

Luther laughed, squeezing her shoulder gently.

"Just toying with ya," Luther said.

Her face warmed and she averted her gaze. Yet asking the question had the desired effect, Luther's wheezing lessened.

"I was in charge of communications. Any mission that took the rebellion outside Azkus City, well it took me too."

Elsa furrowed her brow. She'd always assumed the rebellion remained locked in some underground cavern. "What kind of missions?"

"All kinds." Luther sipped from his canteen. "Sometimes we'd be getting low on supplies. Missions like the one to get Aumora. Other rescue missions. Surveillance missions."

"Do you often go near Fahrquan?"

"Near Fahrquan? You mean *in* Fahrquan?" He grinned. "More times than I can count on all my fingers 'n toes."

Elsa lowered her eyebrows. "That's impossible."

"Fooled even you, did we?" he asked.

Cole raised an eyebrow.

"The Malkum are paranoid," Elsa said. "Akram in particular. He worries the surrounding cities might start a war. So he's got an entire team of technicians who constantly monitor radio activity, making radio communication ineffective, unless you want to be detected."

"So how'd you do it?" she asked, turning to Luther. "Some sort of encryption?"

Luther raised his eyebrows and nodded. "Something like that."

"Encryption?" Cole asked.

"I don't know how it works with radios," Elsa began, "but in computer programming, a cryptographic hash is an algorithm that takes something like a password and converts it into nonsense."

"So why would that be beneficial?" asked Cole.

"It's dangerous to store passwords, for example, as plain text. If your password was 'ilovedogs,' and you stored it as that, it would be easy to steal. But, if you run it through an algorithm, it could store it as something that doesn't make sense. Then if someone hacked into the database, all they would read is nonsense."

"Ok," said Cole. "But if it's converted into nonsense, how does that help?"

"Well," said Elsa. "Some algorithms can be inverted. The algorithm that converted the password into nonsense can be reversed so it is turned back into the password."

"Ok...and how does that relate to communication?" asked Cole.

"When signals is sent, it's scrambled inta static noise," Luther said. "Then on the other end, it's converted back inta the signal."

"So, if someone was monitoring radio signals," continued Elsa. "All they would hear was static noise."

"Interesting," Cole said.

The old man continued limping, but his wheezing lessened. She watched him limp, then traced the path from Luther's feet to his hip. She stared at the radio, mentally dissecting the engineering behind it, then looked at the digital display, which read 26.98 megahertz.

The scent of the extinguished coals lingered in the air, mingling with the crisp smell of the coming fall. The wind rustled the leaves and Luther snored gently.

A gust of wind blew and Elsa shivered. The temperature dropped each night. Aumora and Cole shared one of the two blankets while Luther and Suta shared the other. Elsa had, more than once, insisted her sleeveless jacket was enough, but it wouldn't be for much longer.

Cole sat up, resting his elbow on his knee, head buried in his palm. He'd become so distant of late. She half-longed for more difficult times—times when Luther had threatened her and Malkum soldiers hunted them—times before Cole had become a silent traveler—a stranger.

Elsa sat up too.

He turned. "Hey."

"Hey."

"Can't sleep?" she asked.

He shook his head. "I've slept outside almost my whole life. You'd think I'd be used to this."

"Circumstances are different."

Cole nodded.

Another gust of wind stirred the branches of the trees.

"You okay?" she asked.

"Yeah."

Silence.

He stretched, then lay back down. "Night."

"Good Night."

Elsa remained sitting, listening to Cole's breaths. They remained steady, though not deep enough for sleep. She opened her mouth to speak, but what could she say? How could she comfort a man with such a weighty responsibility?

Elsa sighed. "I'm sorry."

Her ears acclimated to Aumora's deep breaths, punctuated by Luther's guttural snores.

"Sorry for what?"

"What Luther said. The general thing." She pressed her lips together. "I'm sorry."

"Thanks."

"You wanna talk about it?"

Cole chuckled. "I'm afraid talking won't change things."

"True." Elsa leaned back onto her palms, stretching her legs in front. "It may not change things, but it still might help...you know, lift a burden."

Cole chuckled. "What about you?"

"What about me?" Elsa asked.

"Your burdens. The ones you carry. You never did tell me if I was right."

"About what?"

"About..." Cole gazed upward, watching the stars in the cloudless sky. "...about whatever happened to you, that made you leave the Malkum."

Elsa tensed. Cole regarded her, his face concealed in darkness. She could almost feel his eyes detecting every tense muscle in her body, from her tightened jaw to her stiff shoulders. How did he do that? It was black as crows, yet he still seemed to sense her change in mood. The man had enough talent at reading people, he could make a living impersonating a psychic.

He returned his gaze to the stars. "Touchy subject."

"For both of us," she said.

Cole laughed. "A less weighty topic then?"

Elsa grinned. She couldn't see his smile, but could hear it in his voice. The sound was relaxing—deep and soothing, like the rumbling of the river.

"Sure. A less weighty topic."

"What's your favorite color?" he asked.

"White."

"Huh." She envisioned the curiosity in his expression—the furrowing of his brows, the nodding of his head.

"Why's that?" he asked.

"It's pure. Clouds. A baby's teeth. A blank canvas. White."

"I like that. Kinda like a blank slate."

Elsa nodded. "How about you? What's your favorite color?"

"White."

She rolled her eyes, which he probably detected even in the dark.

"Really," he said. "Two minutes ago, it became my favorite color."

"What was it before then?"

"Black."

She punched him. He laughed.

"Fine. I've always liked blue—like the water or the sky."

Cole lay on his back, resting his head on his laced fingers. "Next question."

"Okay."

"Favorite sight?" he asked.

"Sunsets."

"Wow," Cole said. "You didn't even have to think about that."

"Never have. I've always loved sunsets."

"Why's that?"

"No matter where you are. No matter what's going on." She hesitated, pressing her lips together. "No matter how difficult things are." Did her voice just catch? "—there's always beauty."

She paused. Had she revealed too much? Her breath quickened. But she wanted it—to tell Cole everything, to hear him tell her things will work out, tell her that she mattered and that *someone* cared about more than the two mounds surrounding her heart.

Silence.

"I really am sorry," he said. "Whatever it was, *who*ever it was...I wouldn't."

Roddick's face flashed in her mind. "It's fine."

"If you ever need anything."

She shivered. "It's fine."

"Just ask."

"I'm fine." She exhaled. "Can we talk about something else?"

"Favorite smell?" he asked without hesitation.

Luther grunted a snore.

"Smell..." Memories flitted across her mind—roses before they'd fully bloomed, cow dung in the suburbs of Fahrquan, crisp paper from a freshly printed book, the innards of a pumpkin.

"Rosemary," she said.

"Rosemary?"

"Yeah."

"Why?" he asked.

She hesitated, her breath quickening. "My mother."

Cole said nothing.

"It was her favorite spice. She used it for everything—roast, lamb chops, vegetable salads."

"Rosemary."

"Yup."

That hadn't been so bad. She'd succeeded at separating the pleasant memories of mother from—

"Rosemary," she said again. "How about you?"

"Rosemary."

She raised an eyebrow. Again he seemed to understand her invisible cues.

"Maybe not my *favorite* favorite, but it's one of the few spices that grows natively."

She grinned. "Glad we share a common interest."

She didn't know how long they talked—of scents and sounds and tastes—of favorite past-times and future plans. Nor was she sure of when she fell asleep. Yet when she woke, a blanket wrapped her body and a branch of

Rosemary lay at her side.

She smiled, touching her cheek, wondering if the moisture she felt was from a real or a dreamt kiss.

The fire sizzled as Aumora poured water over the embers. Darkness enveloped the camp and steamy smoke wafted into Elsa's eyes and nose. She coughed, and attempted to shield Suta, who slept in her lap. His lips relaxed as they always did when he slept—the only time he didn't smile.

It had been a long day and fatigue penetrated her bones. The longer she stayed awake, the harder it would be to rise in the morning.

Aumora whispered goodnight. Crickets filled the silence.

She should rest. Yet she couldn't stop stroking the boy's black hair and humming, savoring the surge of memories and emotions. In fear she had shielded herself, but it had come at a cost. This. To feel *this* again was overpowering and invigorating.

In so many ways, he was like Celso—no more than nine-years-old, perpetually dirty, and ever smiling. At least until Mother's death. A lump formed in her throat as she focused on a memory. It was four years ago. Her little brother had awakened from another nightmare. He cried in vain for Mother. Father had stopped trying to comfort the boy, but not Elsa.

Just as she did with Celso, Elsa stroked Suta's hair with her fingernails, humming as she rehearsed the words to a song.

I know you're scared and frightened,
That I can't deny.
But I'll always protect you,
So you need not cry.

She stopped humming.

I'll always protect you, she thought bitterly. She was only fourteen, how could she have protected him? Yet she failed.

She would *not* fail again.

Chapter 11

I wish today had never happened.

Journal Entry of Gene The Ancient dated 212 years after the Genetic Apocalypse, extracted from the Archive.

Sergeant Roddick Maleen kicked another rock. The smell of this placed was repugnant—deer crap and rotting carcasses. And it was so hot—not an air conditioner in sight.

It wasn't a reassignment. It was punishment. For fifteen years he had ascended the ranks until becoming a sergeant. And that's where he stopped. He should be general of the whole army. None had his strength, his intellect, his military prowess, and his decisiveness.

Insubordination! He spat. Is it insubordination when your superior's an idiot? Captain Kliv had refused to promote Roddick, so he backhanded the old man. His punishment? A career of solitude, hiking these forsaken forests, looking for a mythical rebellion, or even better, Alfred Alsvik's daughter.

But Roddick knew better. The rebellion didn't exist and Elsa was dead. Last he bedded the obnoxious brat, he knew she was stupid. Most women pretended to resist at first, until succumbing. But Elsa's stone-faced resistance was genuine. Her placid expressions had deterred others. But not Roddick.

Yes, she was stupid. He knew it was only a matter of time before she was dead. Sure, he missed her body, but didn't regret her death. People with that much blackness between their ears deserved to die.

Roddick wandered the forest. The trees blocked the evening light and the air finally cooled. The thought of napping beneath branches and between rocks pissed him off. Maybe he'd find an Indignis village he could terrorize.

Something caught his eye. Warm light flickered. That was unusual. Scouting reports hadn't shown any nearby villages.

Instinct moved his feet with silent precision. He withdrew his black pistol, but he didn't need it. His hand-to-hand combat skills excelled all others.

He entered a clearing. Surrounding a dying campfire were two women, two men, and a little boy. They spoke in quiet tones. The men and the boy could be killed easily, of course, if it was worth his time. But the women...He had only been gone from Fahrquan a few hours and he already missed the...luxuries. His heart raced.

The group slept. He waited over an hour before he began moving, silent as a stalking snake. One woman was older—perhaps Roddick's age, but firm enough to do. But the other, now she was someone he could have fun with. Her shape seemed familiar.

No. It couldn't be.

He froze. He recognized that shape. A shape he had missed, but from a girl who was too stupid to appreciate his body. Yes, it was Elsa. So she wasn't dead. He wondered whether the Malkum were right about the rebellion, but that would be too far-fetched.

He smiled. Captain Kliv would soon be taking orders from him. If he were the one to bring in Alsvik's daughter, they'd have to promote him. And the rebellion? He didn't believe for a minute they were real, but he could claim they were. If they said otherwise, he'd say they were trying to protect their group's identity.

He smiled. He could be back in Fahrquan tomorrow.

He could take them now. Kill the men, capture the woman. But no. Most people were asleep. When he arrived in Fahrquan, he wanted to make an entrance. He returned to the forest, deep enough that his call to Fahrquan could not be heard.

Akram trudged down the hallway on the 200th floor of Malkum headquarters. He stroked his face, feeling the stubble on his cheeks. Rubbing his bloodshot eyes, he opened the door.

An oval table dominated the center of the room. Moonlight spilled in from the windows, and the dimmed recessed lights cast shadows over the aged faces of the fifteen members of the Malkum counsel. The smell of expired aftershave filled the room.

"Sit," said Director Mikhal Raine in his deep raspy voice. Moonlight reflected off his glasses, concealing his dark eyes.

Akram closed the door behind him, before sitting in the at the rear of the table. Chilled air from a nearby vent blew.

"You don't look well," said the director.

"What you see is the evidence of my tireless efforts on the part of the counsel."

"Some within the counsel argue otherwise. Your position is tenuous, President."

The clock ticked. The counsel members' gaze pierced Akram like a firing squad. Yet he said nothing.

Director Raine bent forward. The overhead light cast a shadow across his shaven skin, skidding across a deep scar on his chin and further concealing his eyes.

"As you are aware, there has been a shift in opinion," said the director. "We opposed the annihilation of the Indignis because the cost was too great. Then we discovered the MB infection. Many who were most opposed to destroying the Indignis have become the most vocal proponents at our counsel meetings."

Akram's stomach turned. "You can't." He shook his head. "The Archive is out there. The rebels have it. If we release the virus, we lose the Archive."

"You forget, president, that all of us have lived without the Archive for our entire lives. I don't doubt that recovering it would be beneficial to our noble society. However, is it worth the risk?"

"Yes!"

"Mr. President!" Raine slapped the table. The sound blended with the ticking of the clock. "They could attack at any minute. We don't know how large their army is, we don't know what strategy they will use, and we haven't a clue about what kind of weapons they have. If they have the Archive as you say, then they may be in this room with jackets of invisibility for all we know. Some would argue that the only sure course of action is to release the virus."

Akram scowled and watched as several within the counsel frowned back, many reflecting hatred in their wrinkled faces.

"Fortunately for you," continued Director Raine, "it seems that it is particularly difficult to immunize our own people against the virus' effects. Our most optimistic projections estimate that it will be at least three months before the antidote is ready."

Akram's shoulders relaxed and a smile formed on his face.

"Furthermore," said Raine. "One of our foot soldiers has discovered Elsa Alsvik and the rebels. Within thirty-six hours, they will be in our custody."

A large grin formed on Akram's face. "That is excellent news."

"It is. However, do not mistake this news as a sign of leniency. Your position at this point is very tenuous."

Akram clenched his jaw, hoping the low light would mask his anger. "Yes sir."

Cole woke late. He struggled to stand.

Overthrow the general? It was ridiculous. He couldn't do it—wouldn't. What did the Ancient know about him? And how? What could he see that Cole could not? He had to know something, of his father perhaps. But even then...

Cole shook his head. He stretched. Joints popped and cracked, but the stiffness in his back never left. Rubbing his eyes, he inhaled the scent of the dew. Across a clearing, Luther wore only an undershirt. He bent behind Suta, one hand on the boy's wrist and the other pointing to a tree dripping with exposed sap. Suta held Luther's knife.

"Now, now, lil' one. Don't look away from the mark," Luther said, "'Member to take it slow, breathe as you throw it, and I'm betting my jacket that you make it."

Luther winked at Elsa, who wore an oversized flannel coat. She smiled.

Cole cocked his head. *That must have taken some convincing.*

Since she lost her jacket in the boar hunt, the nights had become increasingly cold. Aparently cold enough that she was willing to accept help from Luther.

She bunched the oversized sleeves and folded her arms. Her blue lips shivered.

"You can do it!" She tucked a strand of her red hair behind her ear.

Suta smiled at Elsa.

At least one thing had changed for the better—Elsa had become a different person. She had dropped her barriers and had found happiness in return. Or so it seemed.

"All right, youngen'," said Luther. "On three. One. Two. Three!"

Suta flung the knife. It thudded into the tree, several inches from its mark. Luther and Elsa roared. Aumora gave him a high five. Suta bounced on the balls of his feet, laughing. Elsa hugged him and Luther tousled his hair.

As Cole approached, Elsa began removing the jacket, her teeth still chattering.

Luther squeezed her shoulder. "I'm a man of ma' word. I lost myself a bet."

Elsa raised an eyebrow. "But...the knife missed."

"Technicalities. The jacket's yours." He lifted his finger to her chattering chin. "I'm bettin' you need it a bit more than I. Keep that pretty face of yers from shaking like an earthquake."

Elsa regarded him. Her chin quivered, though Cole suspected it wasn't from the cold. She nodded, biting her bottom lip. "Thank you."

"Time to invent new methods of warmin' up." Luther winked. He reached toward Suta, lifting him onto his shoulders. Luther began a shuffling jog, yelling an impromptu rhyme, "Suta, better watch where you put your foot-a, else Mr. Suta will use his knife and cut short your life."

Suta laughed.

"He'll throw it like a soldier-a, right into your shoulder-a. Suta, Suta, Suta."

Luther began wheezing. He set Suta down, before sprawling on the ground. "Ya wear me down, lil' one."

The boy extended a hand to Luther. "More. More."

Luther yanked the boy's arm, tickling him. Suta's voice pitched high with his laughs and he squirmed.

Cole watched, grinning. Then his smile faded. They'd soon be there. He hadn't realized how simple his life had been—surrounded by adult children, spending his days collecting food and water, teaching the Indignis. But now? Everything would change. The weight of his responsibility would multiply and bury him beneath his own inadequacies. It was an impossible and unrealistic responsibility, one he was certain he was unqualified to do.

I can't do it, he thought, as he had so many times before. The thought became a mantra—replaying over and over in his mind.

"All right, folks, listen up," Luther said. "If we push ourselves like a momma goat in labor, I'm betting we can reach the city b'for sunset."

Cole felt queasy. It couldn't be so soon.

"B'fore we go, we best stock up," said Luther. "We're running mighty low on fruits, so get movin'."

Luther clapped to dismiss the group. Aumora wrapped an arm around Elsa and led her into the forest. Suta bounded toward Luther.

"Not this time, youngen'," said the old man. "I aint gatherin' today. Got to make sure I've got my bearings straight."

Luther drew map-like images on the dirt, studying how the shadows fell on his watch. Suta watched, his head cocked.

"Now, Sut, you best get gathering. The way you throw that knife, that makes you a man now! So you best be a man and go get some food for us."

"Come on, bud," Cole said. "You can come collecting with me."

Suta tilted his head. "I'ma man now. I go by self."

The boy reached for Luther's knife. Cole opened his mouth to protest, but Luther interrupted, "Atta boy! That's a real man right there."

Cole shrugged and watched the boy trot toward the forest.

"Don't run with the knife, Sut," said Cole. Suta slowed, then started skipping. The boy had a knack for carelessness. The first time Suta met people from another village, they came with sticks and rocks, ready to kill for whatever reason. Suta was so fascinated, Cole nearly had to pin him to prevent him from meeting his 'new fends.'

Cole walked tangential to Suta, crossing into a dense deciduous forest. The trunks of the trees were wide and the underbrush thick. He hacked with a stick to clear a path. As he delved further in, everything darkened. The tree leaves covered the landscape in shadow. He shivered as a sudden breeze iced the morning air.

He trudged through the underbrush. The dark green landscape seemed to stretch for miles. In the eerie silence, Cole began to feel uneasy.

A crack filled the air.

Birds scattered. Cole stopped. His heart rattled his ribcage. A sickening dread filled his stomach. He exhaled, closing his eyes.

A scream.

"No!" another voice screamed, a female voice.

Cole's heart raced. He bolted toward the sound. Protruding branches sliced his exposed arms. The wind howled, like the final cries of a dying man. His vision blurred.

More screams that turned to whimpers.

Oh no no no no.

Bile climbed his throat and Cole's legs weakened. He approached the edge of the clearing, but couldn't see...

Cole's body went limp and he dropped to his knees. Suta lay crumpled on the ground near a man holding a gun. Crimson stained the front of the boy's shirt, and his right hand dangled over his wound.

Oh God no. He blinked, certain his vision deceived him. *Oh no no no no no.*

Tears burned his eyes. He howled, then leapt to his feet, his eyes trained on Suta.

"Don't move, or I shoot them," said the man. Sweat matted his hair. Dark circles surrounded his eyes and a thick mustache hovered above his scowling lips.

Cole stopped. The soldier trained his gun on Aumora and Elsa, who stood next to each other. Elsa whispered as she stared vacantly at the ground. Aumora stared at Cole, her face contorted.

No. This couldn't be happening.

"Now I need you all to come with me," said the man, "or you die right now."

Cole trembled. He couldn't pull his eyes from the boy. But he didn't move. He couldn't. The shock, the fear, the grief. The *anger*. It all paralyzed him, seizing his muscles, freezing his legs.

A cough.

Cole sucked in a breath. Suta twitched. His chest rose, his breath wheezing. Suta lifted his head as he coughed again, ejecting blood from his mouth. He looked at Cole. His face trembled and paled as blood dripped from his lips, which whispered.

There was still time.

Cole prepared to run.

"Stop or you die!" screamed the man, his cheeks bouncing up and down. Corded veins formed on his neck and his face reddened.

Cole clenched his jaw. "Then kill me!" He walked toward Suta, his eyes trained on the soldier.

"It's not you I'm going to kill." The man moved his gun from Cole to Elsa and Aumora.

Cole froze. His body trembled. His eyes darted from the man to the boy, to Aumora and Elsa. The soldier was too far away to make a move, but not Suta. He was only a few paces. His instincts shouted at him to run and save Suta. But they also screamed for him to stop.

One life or two?

Another gargled cough.

Another wheeze.

Another whispered sentence.

Cole stepped toward Suta, but the man flexed his hand.

"No!"

Silence.

Cole panted, again looking from Suta to the man. Aumora motioned to the gun behind her back. The gun with an empty cylinder. Cole padded his leg, feeling the weight of the bullets in his pocket.

It was hopeless.

"Please...I....don't...." Cole raked his hands through his hair.

He fell to his knees, howling.

"Just let him go!" Cole whimpered. "Just—"

Thump-thump...thump-thump...thump-thump...thump-thump.

A pair of footsteps, like the rapid heartbeat of a dying man.

Luther emerged from the clearing, opposite Cole. Aumora threw the gun. Cole leaped, catching the revolver. He fumbled with the bullets, placing one in the cylinder.

Bang!

The sound wave of the man's gunshot crashed into Cole's chest, sending a tremble through his body.

Cole lifted the weapon and pulled the trigger.

Click, click. Nothing.

Luther's footsteps continued, much slower. *Thump-thump...thump-thump.*

Click.

The soldier turned his attention to Cole, leveling his weapon.

Bang.

The soldier screamed, dropping his gun. He clutched his arm, which cascaded with blood.

Luther charged, shoving a crimson-stained shoulder into the man. The soldier sailed through the air, landing hard on the grass. Cole still couldn't move.

The soldier raised himself to his hands and knees. Luther kicked his jaw, sending the man sprawling on his back. He jumped onto the soldier's stomach. The old man pounded his fists in rapid succession into the man's face. The soldier screamed.

When the man fell unconscious, Luther rushed toward Suta, who fought to keep his eyes open.

Yet Cole remained paralyzed. "Oh no no no no. Oh no no no."

"Hey, lil' guy, it's no big deal. Nothin' more than a bee sting," said Luther. His voice trembled. "Aumora, I need you!"

Aumora stared vacantly at the boy.

"Now, 'Mora!"

She blinked, then focused on Suta. She tore the bottom of her shirt. She crumbled a piece of fabric and pressed it into the wound. Reaching into the boy's mouth, she scooped out blood. Suta coughed, his eyes jolting open.

And Cole remained paralyzed, still weeping.

"Just keep breathing, Suta." Aumora stroked his hair. "Just keep breathing."

The boy coughed, ejecting blood. "C-C-C-C." He reached out his hand.

Cole crawled, unable to stand. He grabbed the boy's fingers.

"C-C-C-C." Suta's eyes widened.

"Keep breathing buddy, keep breathing."

Suta coughed again, ejecting more blood. He wheezed. Aumora pulled more blood from his mouth and Luther held the cloth in the wound. Elsa sat on the ground, whispering a song. Suta looked at Elsa, pointing.

Cole looked from Suta to Elsa.

"Louder," Cole said.

Elsa stared vacantly at the dirt.

"Louder!"

Elsa sucked in a breath. She sung, her voice trembling.

"I know you're scared and frightened,
That I can't deny.
But I'll always protect you,
So you need not cry."

Suta relaxed and his eyes half-closed.

Elsa quieted. Suta's eyes went wide.

"Keep going," Cole said.

"I know you're scared and frightened,
That I can't deny.
But I'll always protect you,
So you need not cry."

Cole combed his fingernails through the boy's hair. Suta closed his eyes and his skin paled. The boy's breaths became more infrequent. Cole held Suta's face. The boy's eyes opened, but immediately began closing again.

"Suta!" He shook him.

"I know you're scared and frightened,"

Another cough. Another wheeze.

"That I can't deny."

The boy stopped breathing, and his body relaxed. Cole felt Suta's neck for a pulse. He felt a low throb and held his breath for the next.

But the next never came.

"But I'll always protect you,
So you need not cry."

Cole stared at Suta's neck.

"Move!" Luther pushed Cole and Aumora aside. He pumped the boy's chest with his hands.

Oh God, no.

Aumora blew into his mouth.

Cole paced. *Oh no no no no.*

"Live!" Luther struck the boy's chest with his fist. "Live!"

A strange howl came from Luther's mouth. The old man stood. He approached the soldier, whose chest rose and fell, his eyes half-opened. The man mouthed something.

"What did he ever do to you?" Luther kicked the man in his side. "He's nine. Years. Old!" He kicked again. "You murdered a child!" He kicked his ribs.

"Nine." he kicked his hip. "Years." He kicked his neck. "Old." He kicked his head.

The soldier lost consciousness, but Luther continued kicking. He jumped on the man, landing blow after blow in the man's face and neck. He reached for the gun, firing at the man.

Bang. Bang. Bang.

He fired seven rounds, beginning at his gut and moving toward his head.

Elsa and Aumora flinched with each shot. Cole remained silent, his hand still on Suta's neck. This couldn't be happening. It was a dream. He would soon wake, screaming.

Bang. Bang. Bang.

The gun clicked empty.

Cole's shoulders relaxed. Luther leaned over the dead body and searched the man's clothes. He soon found another magazine, then replaced the empty one with another.

"That's enough!" Cole screamed. "He's dead!"

"Not dead enough." Luther clenched his teeth. His voice cracked and tears streamed down his eyes as he fired two more rounds.

"No! That's enough. Gun down."

He ignored Cole. *Bang. Bang. Bang.*

Cole jumped, grabbing his shoulders.

"That's *enough*! He's dead, *dead*! And shooting him won't bring Suta back!"

Luther twisted Cole's arm behind his back and pushed his face into the ground. Pain shot through Cole's arm.

"Listen, boy," Luther said, his voice malicious. "You know nothing! *Nothing!* I'll do whatever I want and no one's tellin' me otherwise."

The old man pushed Cole's face into the ground.

Cole stood, spitting dirt from his mouth. "No, you listen! No one loved Suta more than I." His voice cracked. "If anyone has a right to kill him, it should be *me*. But even *I* understand how pointless it is to waste all this ammo on a soldier who was dead thirty bullets ago!"

"*It's not just about him!*" said Luther, his voice rising an octave. Tears cascaded down his wrinkled face. "They killed her too! They killed my wife."

Cole blinked.

Tears dripped down the old man's cheeks. He threw the gun across the clearing. Cole reached, but Luther batted his hand away. Blood oozed from the shoulder that had born the bullet wound. His shuffle returned and he reached his hand to his back, before disappearing under the cover of the trees.

A cold, dead silence fell. Silent sobs shook Aumora's body. She collapsed next to Suta and clutched his lifeless hands. Elsa sat with a stone-faced expression, whispering a mantra.

The noises—the gunshots, the sobs, Elsa's whispered mantra. Cole wanted to escape reality, but each sound forced him to accost the waking nightmare. He wanted to run, but grief sapped his strength.

Instead, he crawled toward the boy, the small rocks on the ground digging into his hands and knees. He made it halfway before his strength failed and he fell to his side, lying in a fetal position. He sobbed in silence, waiting for his strength to return. When it did, he crawled to Suta's body and joined Aumora as they embraced the dead boy, his quiet cries mingling with hers. And off in the distance, Luther's cry echoed in the air.

Eventually they sat in silence, too enervated to weep. The emptiness deepened when he could no longer exert the strength to release his cries.

"I know you're scared and frightened," Elsa chanted in a monotonous whisper. "That I can't deny, but I'll always protect you, So you need not cry."

She repeated the words, staring at the dead soldier. She erected the concrete walls, but they failed to numb the grief, the guilt, and the anger.

Roddick Maleen—dead. She'd hated him long before. He was one of many who raped her. But her former hatred paled in comparison.

She raged.

Because of Roddick, she'd broken another promise. *I'll always protect you.*

Everything had happened so fast. When Roddick had threatened Elsa and Aumora, Suta had launched into the clearing and threw the knife. The weapon dropped dozens of feet from the soldier. Suta ran for a second throw, but the soldier shot him, his face an indifferent mask.

The boy died trying to protect her.

I *should have protected* him, she thought bitterly. The boy was dead. And the love she felt was poisoning her.

It always happened like this. Each time she loved.

It would never happen again.

She crouched and began digging at the dirt with her fingernails. The dirt lodged beneath the nails that hadn't broken. Her knuckles chafed against the soil, causing abrasions. But the physical pain took her mind off of the emotional. She dug faster, all the while remaining expressionless, as if she wouldn't feel it if she didn't show it.

Cole too crouched and dug. Aumora's face remained as vacant as a corpse and just as pale. The woman, always so stoic, was broken.

And she wasn't the only one.

Hours later, the stench of dirt covered the metallic scent of Suta's blood. Elsa's blistered and sunburned fingers throbbed, but the shallow grave was finished. She stood. Aumora carried the boy toward the grave. As she passed his body to Cole, Elsa reached one last time to stroke his matted hair with her broken fingernails, humming as she did.

Then she wept.

Chapter 12

It's a shame our forefathers lacked foresight in forming this government. Choosing the president based on seniority may have seemed reasonable back then. If only they had known one of their own council members was immortal. Yet if the opinion of the council sways in my favor, I believe I may have found a loophole.

Email communication intercepted from Councilman Clyde Marks, 106 years after the Genetic Apocalypse

---

Cole, Aumora, and Elsa trudged back to camp. They gathered kindling and built a fire.

The crackle of the logs filled the silence. They stared vacantly at the orange embers.

"I should've done something," Cole whispered. "My little brother was dying, and I fell on my knees and wept."

"There was nothing you could do," Aumora said.

"Luther did something." Cole clenched his jaw.

General, he thought bitterly. What general falls to his knees and cries?

Aumora and Elsa fell asleep. Cole watched the fire. Footsteps approached.

Luther emerged from the darkness. Amber flames illuminated his sunken eyes. The dancing flames cast moving shadows across his weathered cheeks. He looked like death.

"You ok?" asked Cole.

"Yeah. You?"

"Enough."

Silence fell. Luther put a withered hand atop Cole's shoulder and squeezed. The gesture pinched an emotional nerve, and Cole's throat bubbled. Tears spilled from his eyes. Luther squeezed again and Cole gasped.

The crackle of the fire ceased. Crickets called.

"I'm sorry about your wife," Cole said. "I didn't know."

"That's ok, son."

"Did you want to talk about it?"

Luther tightened his lips. "Nah."

"I'm here if you need me."

Silence grew, as did the vividness of Cole's memory. The gunshot, Suta's blood-stained shirt, Cole's knees falling to the ground, the crippling indecision.

"Her name was Helena," Luther said. "Boy, she was radiant. Like a fine wine, just got better with age. Oh, Lord, I miss her. Ya never realize how someone becomes a part of you 'til you lose 'em. When I lost her, was like I lost ma arm."

Cole nodded.

"Always so good to the bone, she was. I mean, she was patient enough to live with me for forty years." Luther chuckled.

"How did they get her?"

"They put me in charge of surveillance. Helena always got a kick out of tagging along. She liked the fresh air, and all that, I s'pose. Well, one day five of us get sent out to an area, oh I can't remember the name of the place, to collect some copper. You see, some of them uppity engineers got to thinkin' that we need to rewire the place. I thought it was just fine, but they weren't too keen on being told where they could put their copper, if you know what I mean.

"Well, we was far from Fahrquan, so I let things get a little lax. It happened to be that there was a group of fifty Malkum, armed to the teeth, doing routine searches for mutations. Helena and Kat, a lady friend of hers, realized too late what was happening and..."

Luther paused and gritted his teeth. He closed his eyes. "I heard a scream, then pop pop pop." Luther pointed his finger like a gun. "And that was the end of her. I tell you, I'll never forget the sound of that scream. I'd never been more terrified. I was so mad and panicked at the same time. I just didn't care what happened next. I ran as fast as ma ole legs could carry me, wishing to save my bride or die trying. Well, you know how that turned out. They'd already left by the time I got there."

Luther rocked back and forth on the mossy log.

"Not a day goes by I don't curse ma-self for being so stupid and careless." Luther's voice became an intense whisper, speaking through tightened lips. "*I* was in charge of the mission. *I* was in charge of their safety. And *I* failed them. And I'll never forgive myself for it."

Luther's shoulders sagged. He dropped his battered and bruised hands in his lap. Only hours ago, they were weapons that had viciously killed the Malkum soldier. Yet they'd also caressed Elsa's chin, and affectionately squeezed Cole's shoulder. How was it that this tender, empathetic, and patriarchal man could have been capable of such violence?

"Did it make it go away?" Cole asked. "The anger?"

"No," said Luther. He dropped his gaze, his posture sinking. "I thought it'd go away, hoped it would. But no."

He sniffed, pressing his palms to his moistened eyes. "I'm sorry ya had ta see that, Cole. I'm sorry."

Cole squeezed the old man's shoulder.

"It's ok," Cole said. "I understand."

"I killed a man, Cole. I didn't have to kill him. But I did. I wanted to."

The old man gazed at Cole. "That man didn't kill Helena. But even if he did, I can't hide the fact that *I* killed him. I *enjoyed* killing him. If I enjoy killing, am I any better than the Malkum?"

Luther's eyes glistened in the fire light. "Son, I've looked forward to this day for a long time—the day I finally meet one of them blasted Malkum...And I tell you what..." He shook his head. "It ain't worth it."

Luther stood. "I've had 'nough killing for one lifetime."

He approached Aumora. After pulling a blanket to her shoulders, he kissed her on the cheek, then lay down to sleep.

Silence returned as did the images of Suta's death. He shook his head and walked toward Suta's grave, following the light of the moon. He entered the clearing and knelt before the grave, grabbing a handful of the dirt that covered his body. He poured the dirt into his canteen before lifting it to his lips.

I. Did. Nothing.

Never *again will I do nothing!*

The crimson sun loomed over the mountains surrounding Fahrquan. An icy breeze blew, sending leaves scampering across the pale sidewalk.

Akram had another sleepless night. Never had his position been so delicate. If he did not produce results soon, no telling what the council would do. They might even surrender any chance of recovering the Archive, the fools. The thought turned his stomach in knots.

All night, he'd waited for word about the rebels, tossing in bed. Fortunately, his sleeplessness had yielded a critical realization.

He walked the meandering path west of Fahrquan. Tony Chrishelm studied the ground, hugging his torso. His faced was patched with red, highlighting a landscape dotted with acne.

"Good morning, President," said Chrishelm, his voice cracking. He pushed his thick glasses higher on his nose.

Akram nodded.

"I must say, I'm a little surprised," said Chrishelm. "This is a most unusual meeting location."

"I was thinking," Akram pressed his lips together, "my initial impressions of the Ancient may have been incorrect."

Akram walked. Chrishelm followed.

"I assumed," Akram continued, "he was a brilliant geneticist, yet I have combed the personnel files, speaking name after name to Jason Drakes. Not one of them had the expertise, nor did any activate Drakes's brain. I even searched outside the Malkum."

"Ok..."

"And then I remembered that Drakes had known Aumora Brooks, despite the fact that Drakes entered Fahrquan years after Aumora left. So how could he have known Aumora unless they knew each other while residing with the rebels?"

Chrishelm wrinkled his forehead, stroking his chin. "Good question."

"Therefore, Aumora was taken by the rebels. But why? What about *her* did they find valuable?"

"Another good question."

"Ah, but there's an even better question than *why* they found her valuable." Akram stopped walking, peering at Chrishelm. "How did they *know* she was valuable?"

Chrishelm's eyes widened. "They've been spying on us."

Akram nodded. "If I were smart enough to escape the Malkum, start a rebellion, and keep it secret for centuries, I'd find some way to spy on my enemy."

"And if he spied on us, the Ancient might have watched you develop the Death Antidote."

"Exactly," said Akram. "Perhaps our foe is not as brilliant as we once thought."

Chrishelm grinned.

"Oh don't get me wrong," said Akram, "he is clever. And we're blind, while he's not. But still."

"It's something," said Chrishelm.

"Here's what I want you to do." Akram faced Chrishelm. "I want you to determine their method of espionage, but do it discreetly. I don't want the rebels to know that we're on to them."

"Ok." Chrishelm looked sideways, shifting his feet. "But...Spencer. Does he know about this?"

"No," said Akram. "Spencer's a bumbling idiot with the grace of a drunken elephant. He was fine as Chief of Security when the position didn't matter. But now...No, Tony. I need you."

"Yes sir." He lifted a scrawny hand to salute and smiled.

Black clouds blocked the sun. It looked closer to twilight than noon. Save for the distant rumbling of thunder, all remained quiet. Not even the birds called. The air still smelled of Suta's blood.

Suta—Cole's brother. Though not by blood, the ever-present lump in his throat didn't know. For all the times he'd worried about the energetic, careless, wonderful boy...all his worry was for naught.

"Wouldn't be surprised if we saw a storm b'fore long," said Luther. "We'd best pay our last..." Luther cleared his throat. "Last respects b'fore we go. Lord knows I'm hankering to confront the Malkum, but I'd rather have an army behind me when I do."

Luther stood, wearing his white undershirt. Loose skin jiggled as he walked toward the clearing. The remainder of the camp followed, walking into the darkness of the trees' shadows, sticks stabbing their legs.

Luther limped toward Suta's grave. The moist dirt contrasted with the surrounding soil. The old man knelt on one knee before the gravesite, holding sticks in each hand, fashioned into a cross.

Cole approached the gravesite. Luther planted the sticks, which contained an inscription, carved with Aumora's hands—*Here lies God's greatest angel, whom He called home.*

Luther stood, pressing against his knee with his left hand. His right shoulder dangled limply, caked with blood that had dried black. The old man opened his mouth, but shook his head. "Words can't express."

He faced the group. "We'd better—"

Static cackled from near the body of the dead soldier.

"Boston Eagle Seven Niner, do you copy?...Boston Eagle Seven Niner, send your traffic...Boston Eagle Seven Niner, give us the go-ahead on the rebel wanderers. Have you made contact with the enemy?...Boston Eagle Seven Niner, are the rebels in custody?"

Luther rushed toward the body and pulled a phone from the ground.

"We've been discovered." Luther cursed, his face turning red.

Cole's heart raced. "What do we do?"

Luther frowned, lowering his eyebrows. He lifted the device up and down, then up and down. He raised the radio to his mouth. He pushed a button, before pausing.

"Wait." Aumora turned to Elsa. "Did you know him?"

The radio crackled. "Boston Eagle Seven Niner."

Elsa stared at the mutilated corpse.

Aumora grabbed Elsa's shoulder. "Did you know him?"

Elsa turned her gaze. "Yes."

"Does he sound like Luther? Or Cole?"

Elsa shivered. "Neither."

Aumora shook Elsa's shoulders. "Who sounds more like him? Luther, or Cole?"

Elsa again stared at the corpse. "Luther, but more nasally."

Aumora regarded the old man and nodded.

"This is Boston Eagle Seven Niner," Luther said in a nasally voice. "Do you copy?"

"Boston Eagle Seven Niner?" the man on the radio said.

"Roger."

"Roddick?"

Luther cleared his throat. "Roger."

"Who is this?" the man on the radio said.

Cole's throat tightened. The old man cursed.

"What do we do?" Luther asked Aumora.

She said nothing.

Luther lifted the radio. "I want you to relay a message to President Akram." Luther narrowed his gaze on Cole, his eyes penetrating. He pressed the button. "Tell that child murderer his immortality will soon expire. Our new general is going to send him and his army to Hell. End transmission."

Luther ripped the battery from the rear of the phone. Everyone looked at Cole. He tried to smile, tried to show strength. The drumming of his heart, *thump, thump, thump,* steadied his nerves, building resolve with each echo through his bloodstream. This had to be stopped. No more waiting for attacks. No more deaths. No more grief. And if it meant he had to lead, he'd do it.

Cole smirked. "Let's go send them to Hell."

Chapter 13

Councilman Marks went missing today. Quite a shame. I enjoyed his politicking and the subtle way he maneuvered for my position. Though his insight and counsel will be missed, I fear it is for the better. There is only one who sits on this counsel who has seen what war is like.

Intercepted journal entry of President Akram, dated 106 years after the Genetic Apocalypse

---

Spencer Burton stood before the communications room and gazed at the rows of computers.

The previous day Spencer had witnessed a private meeting between President Akram and Tony Chrishelm on a security feed. When he confronted Tony about the meeting, the lad had sidestepped the question.

Thirty years he'd worked here. And for thirty years, his performance had been exceptional. *He* had discovered the underground tunnel. If it weren't for *him*, Akram wouldn't know about the rebels!

As he entered the room, he caught the tail end of a transmission. He'd heard it several minutes before from his own computer. The transmission came from Roddick Maleen's radio. Only it wasn't Roddick Maleen who spoke.

It was, most likely, a member of the rebellion.

A woman picked up a phone.

"What are you doing?" Spencer asked. Several communications personnel turned to look at him.

She rolled her eyes. "Dialing the president."

"No," he said. "That's not necessary. The president wishes not to be bothered."

"But—"

"For anything." Spencer adjusted his glasses. "He's left me in charge until he's available."

The woman shrugged, before hanging up the phone. "What would you like us to do?"

Everyone's eyes turned to him. His face warmed. "Do we have a location?"

A man at a computer typed several keystrokes. "Yeah, it's about a three-hour chopper ride from here."

"Do we have any aircraft any nearer than that?"

"Nope. They're all outsourced elsewhere."

"So the fastest we can get there is three hours?"

"I didn't say that." The man leaned back with one arm over the rear of the chair, his gum smacking.

"Then how fast *can* we get there?" asked Spencer.

"If we send the Rockshot, it will be there in thirty minutes, including takeoff."

"Help me out. What's a Rockshot?"

"Bomber plane." The man twirled a pencil over his thumb. "The thing can go many times over the speed of sound. It can put a bomb half an inch from its target. Or so I've been told. But I'm only a communications guy."

"That doesn't help us," said Spencer. "If they're smart, they'll be far from that target by then. What else you got?"

"Cluster bombs." He spun in his chair. "We use those, they'd be hard-pressed to escape in fifteen."

"And what's a cluster bomb?"

"Think of a shotgun, inside a missile. There's a big bomb, but inside is lots of baby bombs. Drop the bomb, seconds later, momma bomb gives birth, baby bombs spread out, and light the world on fire."

"And how big an area can they cover?"

"They say it's got a radius of four miles. That what you wanna do, boss?"

"Yes!" said Spencer. "Make sure it hits at the very center of where the signal is coming from."

"What about Alsvik's daughter?" asked the woman. "I thought Akram wanted her alive."

Silence filled the room. The gum-smacking man's chair squeaked as he rotated back and forth. Spencer's forehead began to sweat. "What's the probability of being hit directly, given that someone's in the center?"

Someone in the back typed. "If we assume a maximum radius, the probability of death is..." More typing. "...only 26%. But there's a 95% probability of severe burns."

"I'll take my chances. Send it. And send a cargo plane of soldiers to make sure they don't escape. Have them surround the perimeter of the blast radius."

The rain fell like waterfalls. "We need to do something about this," Cole shouted, pointing to the phone.

"Under the trees," Aumora said.

Elsa grabbed the phone. "We don't have enough time."

"How much time do we have?" asked Aumora.

"Depends," said Elsa. "If they send helicopters, two to three hours. If they send planes, much less."

Elsa's monotonous tone had returned, as had her indifferent expression.

"So what do we do?" he asked.

"Chances are, they're going to target the location of the signal and blanket it with bombs."

"Ok, so let's turn it off and run," said Cole. "Or not turn it off, but let's go!"

"Too risky." Elsa shook her head. She removed another phone from her pocket. "They might just bomb everything within three miles. Unless we can move more than three miles really fast..." Elsa began typing commands in the phone.

"What are you doing?" asked Cole.

"Shhhh," she said. "I've got to think. Get everything ready to move. Luther? Which direction will we be heading?"

"That way." He pointed west.

"Ok," she said. "I want you all to run that direction. I'll redirect the signal east. If you can travel two miles west, and if I can gradually direct the signal two miles east, you should be outside the bombing radius."

No one spoke.

"Now!" she yelled.

"But what about you?" asked Cole.

"I'll come after I redirect it. But it won't work with you all here. The static from your bodies interferes with the signal. So you need to run, now! I'll be there in ten minutes."

Cole scrutinized her face, searching for any indication of a bluff. Elsa's stone face revealed nothing.

"Promise me," he said.

"Yes, I promise." She returned her gaze to the phone. "I wrote the algorithms before I left the Malkum in case something like this happened. All I need to do is execute the program. I'll catch up in ten minutes!"

"Luther?" Cole asked. "What do you think?"

The old man focused on the ground. "It's a good plan." He nodded, looking west.

She said she never breaks a promise, Cole thought. "Ok." Cole nodded. Though a deep uneasiness settled in his stomach, he turned to run.

Elsa ran.

Another lie. Another broken promise.

There was no algorithm. If she'd had weeks, she might have been able to develop something.

She had lied.

"The static from your bodies interferes with the electrical signal," she had said. It was preposterous, of course. But Cole wouldn't know.

As for Luther, there was something about his expression. He knew she was lying, but thankfully he didn't say anything.

Elsa ran, not west as she promised, but east. At her best, she could run a mile in under six minutes and two under thirteen. If she pushed herself, she'd be five miles from the others in under twenty minutes. No bomb had a five mile radius.

This was the solution. Despite the exertion sapping her lungs of air, a sense of contentment filled her. She'd always tried to escape the agonies of life by building barriers. They had protected her emotions, but prevented her from feeling love.

Now she could have both. She could escape heartache by choosing death, doing so for those she loved. And perhaps they would overthrow the Malkum and Celso and Mother's murderers would be punished. She smiled.

The sonic boom announced the planes, followed by explosions. *No matter,* she thought as she began to form her next thought. But that next thought didn't come.

Cole dodged protruding rocks. His lungs wheezed. Luther and Aumora struggled to keep up. Jagged branches grazed his arms.

Something gnawed at him, but he'd been too distracted by the tortuous path to think. Something about his conversation with Elsa.

Had she lied?

No. She promised. And she never broke promises. Besides, her face held no deception.

But her expressions showed nothing—completely emotionless. Why would she hide her emotions?

"Oh no." Cole's eyes unfocused.

"What?" Luther panted. "What's wrong?"

"She lied." Cole turned. "She *lied*!"

Jets passed. Cole leapt toward Elsa.

Luther tackled Cole, slamming his body to the ground. Wind rushed from his lungs. With the old man still holding his legs, Cole grabbed a boulder. Luther pulled him to the ground.

An explosion sounded. Fire consumed the leaves and needles of the surrounding trees. He ducked behind a rock, as the heat grew around them.

All went silent.

"You knew," Cole said in a whisper.

"It was the only way, son." Silence. "But God bless that girl."

Chapter 14

Should I rejoice? Should I weep? I find myself doing both. Today I finally made a breakthrough, saw the step that I had hitherto missed. I have finally discovered how to conquer death. My heart has never drummed so vigorously. I shall see this plan through to its end, which makes me shout with joy and cry in misery.

Journal Entry of Gene The Ancient dated forty-three years after the Genetic Apocalypse, extracted from the Archive.

Rebellion headquarters was situated inside a mountain covered by evergreens. Glaciers blanketed its top. A lake reflected the setting sun as waterfalls and streams emptied into it.

Cole, Aumora, and Luther entered a cave, traveling several paces in darkness. Motion-sensing lights flickered on, revealing a granite corridor. The metal walls and ceiling reflected light onto the path. Shiny pipes hung on the ceiling, welded into abstract shapes. Along the walls hung paintings placed at even intervals, illuminated by track lights.

Cole studied the paintings, trying to think of anything but Elsa, of Suta, of his village.

"It's dangerous to go wanderin' outside," Luther said, "so we take our beauty inside."

They entered an elevator. Luther punched in a series of numbers on a keypad. The screen flashed.

"Ninety-seven numbers, ninety-seven levels," Luther said. "Two-hundred years of nothing to do but make babies will make a colony grow."

Cole forced a smile.

"Best hold on." Luther smiled. Cole grabbed the railing. The elevator rocketed downward. His stomach lurched into his chest. Almost immediately after it started, the elevator came to an abrupt but gentle halt.

"I'm guessin' yer in need of some rest," Luther said. "So let me show you to your—"

"No." He shook his head. "I want to meet the Ancient."

Luther lifted his chin. "I'll tell him we've arrived. Wait here." He pointed to a bench opposite the elevators before disappearing down the corridor.

"Nice place," said Cole.

Aumora said nothing. She did nothing. Did she not feel anything? Did she not care? No, she did as she always had—ever stoic, ever distant.

She reached toward Cole's arm and hesitated, before pulling him close. With the other hand she grabbed his head and pulled it to her collar. For the first time since toddlerhood, Cole wept in Mother's arms.

"Go on in," said Luther. "The Ancient'll be right in."

The Ancient's office was cylindrical, with rust-colored walls. The room was tall, the height of at least two men and wide enough to fit a young pine tree. Ivy decorated sections of the room, surrounding paintings illuminated by recessed lights.

Cole entered, stepping onto transparent glass. Beneath, an underground river passed, illuminated by colored lights. The glass path terminated at a black marble slab. Water trickled down its front, the sound mingling with meditative instrumental music.

The Ancient's glass desk dominated the center of the room with two marble pillars on either side. Each pillar held an intricate wooden maze that rolled two steel balls through the labyrinth of wood. As one ball thudded against the end of the maze, its weight lifted the other to the start where the process seemed to repeat indefinitely.

"Welcome," said a weathered voice.

Cole spun. A lanky old man entered. In one hand, he held a cane. With the other, he held his lower back.

"I see you've discovered my labyrinth." The Ancient smiled.

"It's nice."

"Brazilian Rosewood," the Ancient said. "Quite an exercise in patience to shape, yet well worth it, I'd say."

Several days of stubble marked the Ancient's chin and disheveled gray hair covered his head. His knitted vest was large for his emaciated frame. He wore sandals, exposing varicose veins and discolored toenails.

Cole stared at the old man's feet, until he noticed the silence. "Sorry." He cleared his throat. "I should have dressed more formally."

The Ancient laughed, slapping Cole's shoulder. "Take a seat, son." He pointed to a leather chair.

The old man pulled his chair close enough that their knees almost touched. The Ancient leaned forward, squeezing Cole's shoulder. The man held his mouth open, his lips forming a circle as if preparing to whistle. It was a strange expression, yet the Ancient held it in such a way that it seemed to be his resting face.

The Ancient scrutinized Cole—as if he knew all his secrets yet passed no judgment. A contentment filled Cole's chest.

"Yes." The Ancient nodded. "I was right about you."

"About what?" asked Cole. "Sir, uh Ancient."

The old man laughed. "Ancient's just a nickname. Please, call me Gene."

"All right." Cole sighed. "Luther tells me you have big plans for me."

"I do."

"Why me?"

Gene chuckled. "Do you want the scientific answer, or the real one?"

"Whichever will help me understand why I'm here."

"Let me start with the scientific answer then," the Ancient said, adopting a less casual, more erudite tone. "It is commonly believed that individuals are composed of two parts—one part genetics and one part environment, though not necessarily in equal amounts. I knew that I needed a revolutionary—someone very different from Mason—one the soldiers could look up to. However, unlike chemistry, the proper 'formula' for genetically creating a mutineer is far less deterministic than in chemistry. Yet despite that, it always involves altering these two elements: environment and genetics.

"Fortunately, we have computer models of human outcomes. I simply input two people's genetics, specify an outcome or outcomes of interest, then the computer calculates the favorability of the outcome. So the scientific answer to your question is this—I asked the computer to pair your mother's genes with your father's."

"Oh." Cole lowered his head. "I always assumed." He cleared his throat. "I assumed my parents loved each other."

Gene patted Cole's knee. "I understand." He stood, pacing. "You see, Cole, for generations, every man within our colony has donated his sperm, and every female has donated an egg. The donor that brought about your existence lived generations ago."

Cole frowned.

"But," the Ancient continued, "I knew him. And I know your mother. Both are the best of people. Surely that's enough."

But was it? Or was he nothing more than a man-made creation—a puppet in the hands of the Ancient? One that had already sacrificed countless friends for this war that hadn't even begun.

But would he do any different? After watching so many die—Rook, Jud,

Kel...Suta and Elsa—what else mattered but stopping the Malkum?

What of Huka? His burly Indignis brother—would he be willing to forfeit Huka's life to stop the Malkum? Or what of Steep? Or Arg?

The Ancient cleared his throat. "When the computer paired your mother's genetics with your father's, it predicted you would excel in all relevant traits. However, there is one caveat, and this is where the environment comes in. Most of your abilities would lie dormant until motivated to blossom. We sent you away to give you reason to fight—so you could grow to love those that most don't consider worthy of their notice, let alone their lives. We sent you away, so the system didn't corrupt you as it has so many others."

"You mentioned there was another answer," said Cole.

Gene returned to his seat, crossing his legs. "There is another reason." Gene dropped his erudite tone. "I believe scientists die before making their greatest discoveries. They learn enough to become arrogant. Then they believe that their particular dogma or paradigm can explain everything that's explainable, and even those things that are not. And then they die without learning that which is truly remarkable."

Gene paused with a contented smile. He nodded his head as if his statement was a sufficient answer.

Cole raised an eyebrow. "And what is that discovery?"

The Ancient leaned forward. "That some things can't be explained, not now, not ever. I looked at the computer models, performed the comparisons, and altered hundreds of variables in an effort to find you before you were born. But I didn't need that. The moment I met your mother, I knew—calculating and commanding, yet compassionate and empathetic. Distant, perhaps, but ever calibrated to the needs and emotions of others—the antithesis of Mason. I knew she would raise the one with the capacity to lead us out of this mess. I knew you had to live among the Indignis. And I know..." His eyes narrowed on Cole, "that you will succeed. You will topple Mason. Then you will lead the men into Fahrquan."

"But...you don't even know me."

"True. But I know your genetics. I know your potential."

"And what of my father?"

"Your father." Gene smiled, lifting his eyes as if to gaze upon the memory. "The best soldier we've had. Talented in ways that cannot be measured. Your mother—the strategist. Your father—the terminal soldier. They passed these traits to you. These predispositions have sat dormant, doubtless waiting for a time such as this. But most important of all, you are blessed with an empathy unmatched by any but Aumora herself."

Cole scoffed. *My empathy.* That same empathy that weakened his knees at Suta's death? He'd frozen, unable to devise a strategy. What commander weeps when his men are attacked?

"Empathy." Cole sighed. "My empathy makes me unfit for command. My *empathy* wouldn't allow me to send soldiers to die."

"Then you must learn to temper your empathy. You must not let your empathy for one soldier or squadron or army overpower your empathy for the Indignis, for the rebels, or even for the entire world. The enemy, the Malkum, *must* be stopped. And it is your empathy for the world that will do it. You must learn to sacrifice the *one* for the *many.*"

The trickle of the water fountain filled the silence. Warmth settled in his chest. A certainty overshadowed his mind that what the Ancient said was true. He would succeed. The grief and anxiety of the preceding weeks melted as peace circulated his body like his pumping blood. Cole smiled, sinking deeper into the couch.

"There is much we must cover in a short amount of time," Gene said. "I'm sure you have many questions. What can I answer for you?"

"Luther mentioned a Nexus. What is it?"

"Ah, yes," said Gene, resuming the erudite tone. "A colleague of mine, Dr. Keston Oliver, proposed the theory of a Nexus many years before the Genetic Apocalypse. You see, memories are stored in neurons in the brain. These memories tend to cluster together. For example, if I say the word 'bed,' your mind will likely conjure other words related to bed, such as blanket and pillow. Now, although memories tend to cluster together, there's a high degree of overlap between clusters as well. Let's do a demonstration, shall we?"

Cole cocked his head, then nodded.

"Beginning with the word 'bed,' by the process of association, I want you to get to the word 'shovel.'"

"Okay." Cole studied the ceiling. "Bed, home, underground, dig, shovel."

"Very good. Now, memories have multiple pathways. For example, you might have used 'Bed, blanket, sew, needle, tool, shovel,' or countless other associative chains. Now, before I said the word 'shovel,' were you thinking about a shovel?"

Cole shook his head.

"Precisely. So in a sense, you had 'forgotten' the word. Now, suppose we could shape memories such that that an entire cluster had only *one* single connection—or *one* associative chain. That collection of memories would remain forgotten until that single chain was activated."

"Okay..."

"Suppose we shaped your memories such that the only way you could remember 'shovel,' was to first remember your underground home. You would forget that word 'shovel.' We might even say 'garden tools,' and if your memories have been shaped accordingly, you will be unable to recall the word 'shovel.'

"A Nexus is that single memory which connects the memories for which you are aware with those you are not. So in our example, the memory of your underground home is the Nexus."

"Ok," said Cole. "So how is that helpful?"

"Espionage, for one."

"Espionage?"

"The best spies are those who are unaware of their purpose. They can take detector tests, they can be tortured, they can be hypnotized, and yet they will reveal nothing. The only way they can be 'broken' is if the Nexus has been activated."

"So we have men on the inside?"

"We *had* two. One, Jason Drakes, was under the influence of a Nexus. We gave him a collection of false memories and hid the real ones about our rebellion and hideout. The other spy was fully aware of his rebellion."

"You *had* two? What happened?"

"Drakes's Nexus was activated shortly before Luther found you. Under the circumstances, our other spy fled. Unfortunately, I don't know what the Malkum are doing with Drakes. My guess is that he's being detained somewhere."

"What was Drakes's Nexus?" asked Cole.

"A date."

"A date?"

"Yes. July 12th, 2484 if I remember correctly."

"His Nexus...was a date?"

"It was. Drakes was like a hidden time bomb, just waiting until his clock ran out, at which time his mind exploded with memories."

"So the activation of his Nexus was intentional?"

"Quite so," said Gene.

"Why?"

"Certain elements of the plan required it. I do wish I could give you full details, but when I finally tell you, you will understand the wisdom in withholding that information. In all likelihood, Drakes woke up one morning with an enormous headache as the previously hidden memories activated. If things went as planned, a second Nexus induced a coma. My hope is that he is being detained until we can rescue and wake him."

"Aren't you worried they'll kill him?" asked Cole.

"Of course. But you must remember, he has information they are desperate to have. They will keep him alive until they either find no use for him or they believe he will never wake. I do fear that time is rapidly approaching, which makes your assignment all the more urgent."

"Are we safe here?"

"Yes. Very few within our company know where we're located, including Drakes."

"How is a Nexus formed?"

The old man stood and walked to his desk. He pushed several buttons, revealing a holo display. Cole circled the desk, allowing himself a 360-degree view of the live image.

The image showed a young man. He was naked and his body was shaved of all hair. The man stared at a screen that appeared to give text prompts.

"Forming a Nexus is strictly a behavioral and cognitive exercise," the Ancient began. "There's no secret surgery, no pill. It requires a disciplined mind and years of training." He pointed to the display. "The screen instructs him on what to think about and when. As they follow the prompts, it shapes their memory in minuscule degrees, without their awareness. Those who volunteer to form a Nexus do so in solitude, otherwise it would be impossible to create. They typically begin when they're sixteen-years-old and their solitude lasts approximately ten years before the Nexus is formed, although Drakes was a notable exception."

Cole bent closer to the display, squinting his eyes. "You must have difficulty recruiting."

The Ancient grinned. The camera panned out, revealing the room in which the man sat. As it continued to zoom out, the screen revealed several more rooms, each occupied by more individuals, all naked and shaved. It panned until the distance was too great to see any level of detail. It must have been thousands of rooms.

Cole's jaw dropped. "How did you convince all those people?"

"We have our incentives," said the Ancient. "Though I do wish it were easier. Forming a Nexus is time-consuming and difficult. It would be quite convenient if we could simply copy the memories from one person's Nexus to another. But our attempts at that failed."

"You actually tried?"

"We did, and unfortunately succeeded a measure. You see, Cole, we have the technology to *replace* another person's memories in whole—wiping their mental hard drive so to speak. But how could we justify that? A person who knew themselves as Robert would suddenly become Julie or Thomas. For all intents and purposes, Robert as an *individual* would cease to exist. It would be nothing short of mental murder."

"And you cannot copy just a part?"

"Sadly no. The mess of memory neurons is so convoluted that separating what identifies us as unique from the part that forms the Nexus is impossible."

"But, you said you had two men on the inside. Why train a whole army if it only requires one or two to spy on the Malkum?"

"There's other applications of a Nexus aside from espionage."

"Such as?" asked Cole.

The Ancient remained silent.

"Another secret," Cole said.

The Ancient chuckled. "In time you will discover all secrets and the reason behind those secrets."

Cole nodded before looking at the holo display of the Nexus army—no, the prisoners. What sort of incentives could they possibly offer?

The camera panned in and out, side to side. Countless men and women stood before a computer, like robots.

He furrowed his brow and bent forward. Something was different about the image. A section of rooms held a half-dozen individuals, lying on the floor with cords attached to their heads.

"What's with them?" Cole asked.

"They're under a simulation," the Ancient said.

"What kind of simulation?"

"An important one. You see, the Nexus takes *time—years*. Too much time, it seems, especially considering the present circumstances. The simulation aids our efforts. By connecting an individual's brain to a computer, so to speak, we can create an alternate reality—one free of the present associations that are so difficult to negate. One where they can feel a breeze just as tangibly as if we stood atop a mountain. One where they can peruse the halls of Malkum headquarters as if they were really there, when in fact they are not. In this reality, they can interact with the enemy as friends and know no different."

"Then why don't you place *all* of them under the simulation? It seems infinitely more humane than incarcerating them in a...closet like you do."

"In time we hope to," the Ancient said. "But, you see, the simulation is experimental. Without the proper precautions, we may inadvertently expose thousands of individuals to devastating side-effects."

Cole nodded.

The Ancient smiled before pressing another button on his desk. A clock appeared. "I do wish I had more time to converse with you, Cole. But we have more important things to discuss."

Cole raised an eyebrow.

"How you'll topple Mason."

Cole laughed. "About that." His smile faded.

"I know. You're under-qualified, you've never so much as held a rifle, you've never led non-Indignis, etcetera, etcetera."

"And yet . . ."

"And yet you will be the general. You *must* be the general. But unfortunately, I cannot just give the position to you. Though at one time, I ruled this colony as a benevolent dictator, things have gradually changed such that I am little more than a figurehead. I have desperately tried to prepare the way for your military leadership. But alas, my efforts have been futile."

"Ok." Cole sighed, raking his fingers through his hair. "So how..."

"You see the problem," said Gene. "Though I need you to be the general, I cannot give the position to you. You must acquire it through your own means."

"And what means are those?"

"I don't know. Perhaps you can convince him to retire and give the position to you willingly, though I doubt it. I'm betting your best approach will be a carefully planned coup d'état—you join the military, secure the trust of the men through your military excellence and charismatic leadership, and through some pivotal contest of wills, you overthrow his leadership. It's been known to happen—Napoleon climbed the ranks in eight years. All you must do is be as charismatic as Napoleon and in a fraction of the time."

"Is that all?" Cole chuckled. Though his tone was jovial, he sunk into his chair. "Luther said you planned for every contingency. It seems there's a lot of gaps in this plan."

"Plan? It's more of a rough outline." The Ancient winked. He stood and paced. "Rest assured, I've watched the soldiers from a distance. They're anxious for change. There's been a drought for many years and the desiccated desert has waited for the consuming spark. You are that spark, Cole."

Cole shook his head. There had to be another way.

"Forget about Mason," Cole said. "Why not just assassinate President Akram? Seems it would be a lot easier."

"Unfortunately not." Gene sighed. "Although Akram sits at the top of Malkum authority, and has done so for over a century, the chain of command is still a chain. If he is eliminated, another dastardly villain will take his place. All things considering, we could do worse than Akram. But even if you crippled Malkum leadership, there is still a vast army in Fahrquan with an ambitious general that would continue to fight in the name of the Malkum for years to come. No, we must neutralize both the chain of command and the military in a single deadly blow, or I'm afraid we will simply be scratching an eternal itch. And before we do that..."

"Mason."

Gene nodded. The old man grabbed Cole's palm. The man's hands felt like cold leather. "There is only one way. You will lead this army, but the general will not forfeit his position graciously. He's going to try to undermine you in whatever way he can. You don't let him. You're better than him, and you will come to see that."

Cole exhaled and straightened his spine. "It has to be done, right?"

Gene nodded.

"Okay."

A knock echoed in the room. A uniformed soldier entered. "Lieutenant Briggs, here to escort Cole to General Ulysses Mason's office."

Chapter 15

Though it tears me apart, I cannot in good conscience keep my sweet wife and beautiful daughter by my side. They are too free-spirited and never meant to live in a prison-cave. So I quietly exited their lives, trusting their care to God above, if such a being exists. Had I known beforehand my soul would feel so broken, I may not have fled. I'm glad I hadn't made that realization before I left, or I never would have done it and the world would forever lie in ruins.

Journal Entry of Gene the Ancient dated six months before the Genetic Apocalypse, extracted from the Archive.

Akram paced. Soon their soldiers would capture the rebels. Soon Elsa would arrive in Fahrquan. Soon.

But what was taking so long?

For the fifth time, he called Spencer. With each previous attempt, the phone rang endlessly, boring into his ear and splitting his head.

"Hello?"

"Spencer?"

"No, sir. This is Tony Chrishelm. He left his phone in the security office."

Akram tightened his jaw. "What's the status on Elsa and the rebels?"

"Ummm..." Chrishelm cleared his throat. "Y-you haven't heard?"

Akram tightened his jaw. "Heard what?"

Silence.

Chrishelm coughed. "Ummm...well. They're either dead or they've escaped."

"What?"

"Dead. Or escaped. We're not sure which."

Akram slapped his desk. "How. Did. This. Happen."

"T-this morning—w-when the rebels answered Roddick's radio—"

"This morning? Why haven't I heard about this?"

"Uh-uh-uh...It was Spencer. He said not to bother you."

Akram flinched. "Spencer said not to bother me?"

"Yes sir. Apparently he came to the control room this morning. He authorized carpet bombs to keep the rebels in place. The men are searching the bomb site, but so far haven't found anything."

He struck the desk again. Spencer would pay for this.

Akram sat at his desk. Spencer fidgeted with his wedding ring, bouncing his foot on the rung of his chair.

"You don't look well, Spencer." Akram leaned back in his seat.

"My apologies, sir. Like you, I have labored tirelessly to find the rebels." The man's voice wavered.

"I understand." Akram smiled, struggling to hide his rage. "Fortunately, we have made great progress today."

Spencer's shoulders relaxed.

"Have a drink, please," Akram said.

"Uh...thank you, sir." Spencer cocked his head.

"I haven't been able to sleep of late."

"I understand." Spencer chuckled. "More than most, I understand."

Akram repressed a scowl. "I ignored my insomnia, at first. I thought I might be more productive if I didn't spend so many hours unconscious. But it began to affect my cognitive functioning. I could not think clearly, I missed connections I otherwise would have seen."

"An unfortunate side-effect."

Akram nodded. "So I developed my own drug—one that would help me relax, not worry so much. Since then I am a changed man."

"Very good, sir."

"Would you like to try it?"

"No thank you, sir."

"Please, I insist. It works at the genetic level, inhibiting a man's tendency toward anxiety. Think of it as natural medicine."

He handed Spencer a capsule, who accepted it with a shrug.

Spencer downed the capsule. His shoulders relaxed. "Much better, sir."

"Genetic alterations don't take place instantly. Several days, at least. What you're feeling is only a placebo. But, in the next few weeks you will become a changed man."

Spencer smiled. "Once again, thank you, sir. Your kindness is undeserved."

"It is!" Akram slammed his hands against the desk, bending toward Spencer. "Thanks to you, Elsa and the rebels are probably dead. Thanks to you, we may have lost any chance of finding the Archive. You'd better hope they'll be found. Because if they are not..."

Akram removed a rectangular device from his drawer. "That pill will not alter your genetics. It holds an explosive I can trigger with this remote. It's large enough to destroy your internal organs without piercing your skin. So, I can kill you without making a mess."

Spencer bent over, sticking his finger in his throat. The man gagged. Traces of bile escaped his mouth, but the pill remained inside his body.

"Within minutes, the outer coating will dissolve and the miniature bomb will begin its way to your intestines."

Spencer shook and sweat dripped from his collar. Red faced, he glowered at the president. "You—"

"I'd watch your tongue, Spencer." Akram lifted the remote. "It's never wise to insult a potential executioner."

Akram returned the device to his desk before approaching Spencer. "One more screw up..." He lifted his finger.

Spencer looked from the president to the drawer.

Akram turned. "The pill will explode when within arm's reach of the detonator, so I wouldn't attempt a raid upon my office. You are dismissed."

So this is death. Like a frog jumping on lily pads, Elsa's consciousness wandered from thought to thought, until it settled. She faced her father— brilliant physicist and the savior of lost data.

The abandoner.

Alfred approached. Her expression hardened.

He extended his arms. "Daughter."

Elsa tensed. His eyes softened. "Elsa, darling. What's the matter?"

She bit her lip to prevent it from trembling. "You abandoned me. You promised you'd never leave."

Father frowned, before his image dissolved. Elsa stood in her former living room. Father opened the door. After walking in the house, he looked outside, scanning the scenery like a chased rabbit. He latched the door and closed the blinds.

Father grabbed her shoulders. "Listen Elsa. At Fahrquan City Bank, there's a trust fund in your name, under account number 974393-388. I need you to go there, withdraw everything, then meet me at the Watson Hotel in Rholmanda."

Father paced, running his hands through his mangled hair. "I can't lose you like we lost Celso and Mother. I won't let them take you too."

Elsa blinked. "Father, you're scaring me."

His eyes softened as he grabbed her shoulders. "It will be fine, darling. I'll meet you in Rholmanda, I *promise.*"

The living room darkened. Father again materialized. She narrowed her eyes, folding her arms.

"Princess, let me explain—"

Burns climbed her leg to the crown of her head. She jolted awake, gasping.

She lay in a hospital bed, bombarded with sensations—the sound of beeping instruments, the stench of antiseptic, the taste of bottled oxygen, the agony of the burns.

The burns. The burns. Goodness, they hurt.

She screamed. "Make it stop!"

President Akram stood at her bedside. Her eyes widened.

"You've had quite a day, have you not dear Elsa?"

Elsa bit her tongue, suppressing a scream.

Akram leaned in, pulling the oxygen mask from her face. "I need you to tell me *exactly* what happened."

Chapter 16

I assumed I planned for every contingency. Then General Mason came along. At first I dismissed his inflammatory comments about me as 'mere politicking.' If only I had known how formidable an opponent I had dismissed.

Journal Entry of Gene The Ancient dated 194 years after the Genetic Apocalypse, extracted from the Archive.

Lieutenant Briggs towered over Cole, with muscles fighting for position on his body. His white uniform wrapped tightly around his physique.

"Wait in the hall until the General is ready." Briggs typed into a handheld computer, before leaving.

Plaques lined the walls, each awarded to the same man—General Ulysses Mason.

Fastest two-mile time: 9:56.

Best score in long range rifling: 97.

Perfect performance in interpersonal knife combat simulator.

There must have been at least 100 in all. Cole's stomach curled. This was the general he was supposed to oust?

The general exited a room. Military insignia decorated his pressed white uniform, each meticulously placed. The man wore dress shoes reflective enough to show the crease on his pants.

Mason was tall, even taller than Cole by about a half-head, with the build of a middle-weight boxer. Whisks of gray accentuated his slicked black hair.

Cole extended his hand. "Hi, I'm Cole."

The general snarled. "A word of advice, *boy*. When you address the general of the rebel army, it is appropriate to salute."

The general turned and walked into his office, leaving Cole alone in the hallway.

"Sit," said Mason from inside the office.

Cole peeked past the door frame.

In the center, the General's oak desk stood atop a raised floor panel. The desk had three large surfaces, leaving only one side on which the general entered. The trim of the desk was ornate, carved in intricate patterns and the rear of it had an adjoining bookshelf holding various military titles.

Cole sat in a folding chair small enough that his knees nearly came to his chest. Cole had to lift his head in order to see him over the surface of his desk.

Should he attempt to win his trust? Should he play innocent? Defiant? A familiar panic returned, turning his stomach in knots.

"I'm sorry, General Mason," Cole said. Innocence it was. "You'll have to excuse my naivety. I've never been exposed to proper military behaviors, but I'm ready to learn." He saluted, suppressing a cringe. Too forced.

The general deepened his scowl.

Cole's cheeks warmed. Change of subject. He gazed upon the awards that lined the walls. "The plaques, how are they awarded?"

"Already planning to replace them with your own accomplishments?"

This is not going well. "Not at all, General. I was just wondering how you received so many?"

Mason stood. He grabbed a book and flipped through its pages. "Read the highlighted paragraph."

Cole cleared his throat. "Leaders chosen by the whims of the people, driven by the momentum of temporary popularity, will inevitably fail to engender in their men sufficient courage and fortitude to face the enemy in deadly contests of skill and strength."

"Now turn six pages and read that highlighted section."

"Above all things, a leader must be a template for exemplary behavior. If courage is requisite in every soldier, then the leader's duty is to be the most courageous. If dexterity with a blade is indispensable, then the leader must be the terminal master. In short, no subordinate should ever be able to exceed the leader in any relevant ability."

The leader must be the best in every respect? Cole studied the binding. Who would propose such a ridiculous idea? He knew little of leadership, but shouldn't a good commander recognize the strengths of his subordinates and use them effectively? Requiring the leader to be the best would only make the leaders jealous of their subordinates.

"The philosophy is called *Ultimum Dux*," said Mason. "And was proposed by Dr. Primo Tumid 150 years ago. Historically, military leaders were chosen by the leadership hierarchy. That method of advancement tends to favor those that are *politically* savvy, while overlooking individuals with real talent. But Dr. Tumid organized a meritocracy. Now you may not agree with our philosophy, but that's how our military operates."

The general spun on Cole. "The only way to advance is to perform, and perform well. Look at my awards, lad. Even I am not above the system. The reason I sit in that desk is because I put in *my* time, working long hours, and devoting my utmost capacities to becoming the best."

Mason snarled, slamming his palm against his desk. "I *am* the best."

"I don't doubt that," Cole said. "I—"

"Oh I know you don't doubt. But I can see your petulant little head turning, thinking of how you're going to 'de-throne' me. You're thinking of all the records that will decorate your office. I even bet—"

"Please—"

"Don't interrupt me, boy. For one so 'anxious' to learn about military decorum, you're quite content interrupting your superiors."

The general glared at Cole, challenging him to speak. But Cole was speechless. Any plan of subversion he had developed crumbled, before he had a chance to speak a hundred words.

"I know your game, boy. You pretend subservience until you catch me unaware. There's two things you should know: I don't play games, and you can't catch me unaware."

The general sat. "You start at the bottom. Below the bottom. When you prove you can do more than interrupt and pretend to kiss tail, I'll give you an army of ants to lead."

The general leaned back in his chair. "And that's where you stop." He waved his hand. "You're dismissed."

Cole's jaw tightened. He turned to leave. Before exiting, he paused, smiling. "Ultimum Dux."

General Mason lifted his eyes without raising his chin.

"Ultimum Dux," said Cole. "You can't stop my progress. If I become the best, then Ultimum Dux, I will lead."

The general jumped from his chair, rushing toward Cole. Cole tensed. The general stopped within inches, bringing the scent of the general's spicy aftershave.

"Until every one of my records is broken, I make the rules. I—"

"You said the leader is the *most* skilled. The moment I break half your records, you no longer have the right to lead."

The General's face reddened. He shoved Cole against the wall.

"Each of those records have stood for twenty years," Mason said.

His voice was calm, but Cole could detect fear and uncertainty in the man's expression.

Cole lifted his hand to his head and gave the general a pristine salute before departing.

Lieutenant Briggs escorted Cole into a football field-sized auditorium. The octagon-shaped concrete walls extended several stories and blue lights slowly moved, giving the illusion that the room rotated.

Briggs typed into a keypad. A mechanical whirring sounded. A portion of the floor lifted and rotated, revealing a podium and a microphone, along with several plush chairs.

"Let's go," said Briggs.

They approached the stage where the lieutenant opened a door to a small room. As it opened, a chime sounded.

"The room is sound-proof," Briggs said. "You won't be able to hear what the general is saying. But, the window will allow you to see what's going on. When the general wants you to enter, he'll beckon you. Be attentive or you may miss his signal."

"Can't I just wait in the audience?"

"No. Every new recruit must be formally introduced. It's tradition. Normally each cohort has dozens of new recruits, but since your arrival doesn't coincide with our orientation schedule, you'll be the only one."

Briggs exited the room. Cole sat on a stool. The room was like a coffin—long enough for one man, and just wide enough for Cole to feel the walls closing in on him.

A claustrophobic room. An army of men he had to lead. An introduction from his enemy that he wouldn't hear.

Great.

But it had to be done.

Gray-suited soldiers entered the auditorium. They marched in a line, turning at right angles to form rows. The precision of their movements made them look like robots.

His stomach churned. How can he relate to robots? It had been difficult enough to gain Elsa's trust, and she had been one person. How could he possibly gain the trust of an entire army of emotionless robots?

One soldier, probably not old enough to shave, was short with an angular build, blond hair, and a long nose. His weak frame struggled to maintain the posture his peers held. His chest rose and fell with frantic breaths—terrified breaths.

So they weren't robots. He watched several others. Their emotions were less obvious, but he could see them—boredom, impatience, anticipation.

The general approached the podium. Silence. He couldn't even see the general's lips moving. He could read nothing—no sound, no lips, no...

A soldier's lip twitched. Another lowered his eyes, while another lifted his chin in defiance. Another clenched his teeth. He couldn't hear, but he could see—whatever the general was saying, the men didn't like it.

The soldiers shouted in unison. Though their words shouted obedience, their emotions shouted something else.

They despised him. So why did they follow him?

Cole remembered the look on the young soldier's face.

Fear.

Cole had met the man, seen his piercing gaze and felt the hairs stand on the back of his neck. He knew the fear the men felt because he felt it too.

Now it made sense—Gene needed someone who hadn't been trained to fear the general.

Cole's own pulse raced, recalling his panic as the general charge him. He understood their fear, *empathized* with their fear. But to overthrow this man, he must suppress that fear.

For the first time, he allowed the memories of family members once lost. Suta, Huka, Rook, Steep, Arg—all dead. Anger replaced fear.

I will not fear.

Mason must be ousted, but first the soldiers must overcome their fear.

I will not fear.

The men's expressions changed. Those who had been most defiant looked disinterested or curious. A few snarled. Many of them glanced toward the double-mirror.

The general was talking about him.

Great. He had to find a way to hear what the general was saying. Perhaps he could crack the door, but the door's chime would alert him.

He searched the room. A screen, much like the one Luther had used to operate the elevator, hung near the door. Cole pressed the screen and a number pad appeared. He closed his eyes, trying to remember Luther's sequence of numbers.

He entered what he thought was Luther's password. The numbers faded.

Wrong password. Two attempts left.

He closed his eyes, trying to re-envision the sequence of numbers. *19...something...157.* What was the middle number? He entered another sequence of numbers. Again, the screen flashed.

One attempt remaining. It was too risky.

Cole returned to the stool. The men continued to cast glances at the mirror.

No. I will not *be afraid.*

He stood again and pressed the first two numbers. Swallowing, Cole pressed seven, then the final three.

A new message appeared.

Welcome, Luther Carter.

Cole grinned. The audio of the general's speech began. "—knows nothing of the enemy. But *I* do." Buttons flew as he ripped his shirt open. "I have stared the enemy in the eye and watched him pull the trigger."

Cole laughed. It was a lie, of course. Mason hadn't been shot. Once in passing, Luther mentioned a scar the general had acquired while extracting Aumora from Malkum headquarters. While returning to the helicopter, Mason tripped on a boulder. His sternum had grazed the jagged edge of a rock. The wound had required stitches, but certainly wasn't life threatening.

I've got you now.

The general motioned to Cole, who opened the door. The soldiers' eyes bored into him like a target. He walked. His footsteps padded against the carpeted floor. He approached the general.

I cannot fear. I cannot fear.

"All right, boy. As is customary, *briefly* introduce yourself."

Cole exhaled. *I cannot fear.* he approached the podium. A gust of hot air blew against his moist forehead.

He stood, gazing into the men's eyes. He smiled as he solidified his plan.

"I wish to thank you from the depths of my soul, General Mason," said Cole. "Most of you may not know, but the general was instrumental in rescuing my mother from the Malkum. Had it not been for him, I would not be here."

The men looked genuinely puzzled. Yes, *this* was the man Mason warned them against—as dangerous as a grizzly.

"What many of you may not be aware of is that the general suffered a wound during the extraction. They fled Fahrquan in darkness. He tripped on his way back and hit a jagged rock."

The room grew very still.

"To this day, he still wears a scar right here." Cole pointed to his own sternum.

The men's eyes widened.

"I know little of war. But this I do know." Cole's face grew solemn. "We *cannot* fear."

"And..." Cole grinned. "We must choose our enemies wisely. I'd hate to stare into the eyes of a rock and get shot."

The Ancient stood in a room overlooking the great aqua room. The soldiers dispersed. Eyes closed, he leaned his forehead on the window, grinning. The boy just might do it.

If he didn't get himself killed.

The door swung open. Luther stumbled in, laughing. "Did you see him! I tell you what, he done gave that general somethin' to worry 'bout. 'I'd hate to get shot by a rock,' he says. He was brilliant!"

The Ancient sighed. "I doubt he'll tolerate such insubordination."

"So he'll put 'm on toilet duty for a week. I tell ya', he scored big for the good guys today."

"There's still a long way to go."

"I don't know, sir. The way them boys reacted, you should'a seen their faces. I think he's got 'em already."

Gene chuckled. "Let's hope so."

"So, you wanted to see me, Ancient?"

Gene chuckled. "Have I not requested you cease calling me Ancient? It's quite intolerable that others insist upon the nickname. But you, Luther?"

"Do you prefer 'old man'?"

"Ha! Your gait's as slow as mine." Gene leaned against the wall. "And you've half the hair."

Luther chuckled. "And 'bout twice the belly, too."

Gene smiled. Luther beamed like a child on Christmas morning. Gene approached, putting a hand on the man's shoulders. "I'm grateful for you, Luther. You're a good man to have around."

"Ahhh." Luther smiled sheepishly. "Same goes fer you."

Both men studied the window. The lights in the auditorium powered down, making their reflections more visible.

Gene faced Luther. "Any questions?"

Luther scratched his bald head. "Just one."

Gene raised an eyebrow.

"Well, I'm wondering *why*? Why tell rumors 'bout the boy, even'f it's ta make him look better?"

"Excellent question," said Gene. "All these boys have ever known is Mason. It's that atrocious system—*Ultimum Dux*. I knew it eventually would bring about someone like Mason—both talented and blinded by their own power. But, alas, you know as well as I that I'm powerless to stop this. But *now* we can show them that *true* leadership looks nothing like Mason."

Gene paced. "Mason would take responsibility for the earth's creation if he thought others might believe him. But Cole's different. When the men see he's honest, they'll see Mason for who he really is."

Luther raised an eyebrow. "So we're lying about the boy, so he can show he's honest?"

"Precisely!" Gene grinned.

"Whatever you say," said Luther.

"Besides, have you ever noticed how difficult it is to extinguish a rumor?"

"So you want them to believe the rumors?"

"Couldn't hurt."

Chapter 17

Today, for the first time in my life, I killed a man. His was a necessary death. The man was as a plague in the uncontaminated world I created. I'm not sure what I was expecting to feel. Relief? A sense of accomplishment? Satisfaction? I do know that I will try to avoid killing unless it's necessary.

Intercepted journal entry of President Akram, dated six months after the Genetic Apocalypse

---

Jason Drakes smelled like an unkempt retirement home. His emaciated frame was ashen, and dark circles surrounded his eyelids. The unconscious man had given him nothing but expensive medical bills and a headache.

He kicked the gurney. The monitor beeped like a metronome.

For weeks he'd spoken name after name. Drakes was familiar with *none* of them. Akram was no closer to finding the identity of the Ancient than when he started.

But he hadn't come to research the identity of the Ancient. Elsa had insisted the rebels held her prisoner, that she knew nothing.

There was one way to know. The sound of Aumora's name had activated the three-dimensional projection of the man's brain. If Elsa was also part of the rebellion's plan, then the image would also pulse at the mention of her name. Or so he hoped.

The president approached the monitor. He spoke several familiar words so he could identify the region of activation. He placed his finger on that area, then spoke. "Elsa Alsvik."

He snarled, kicking the three-dimensional image before storming out of the room.

The elevator dinged. Akram exited. Already he could smell the zebrawood sawdust. He approached his woodshop, smiled, then let his shoulders relax.

He hadn't entered since before he discovered the rebellion. But if he didn't do something to relax, he would snap.

He closed the door behind him. Smiling, he savored the scent of the sawdust. Light filled the room, illuminating the dust particles his entrance had agitated.

The half-finished desk lay in fragments on a workbench. Diagrams of dimensions, parts, and joinery hung on clotheslines. When this desk was finished, it would be the most sophisticated, beautiful, tailored executive desk he'd ever seen—wooden gears to raise and lower the surface, depending on his level of fatigue; a platform for his keyboard that he could lift, rotate, or tilt; and enough storage space to satisfy a hoarding redneck for the Millennium.

Akram bent, studying the open grain of the wood in the reflected light. Narrowing his eyes, he grabbed a smoothing plane. He rocked the tool back and forth, watching as the wood shavings curled into thin pieces.

As he rehearsed the familiar monotonous motion, he allowed his mind to wander. That morning, Chrishelm reported they *had* found listening devices—hundreds of them, both audio and video. The rebels had destroyed each device remotely. The news had done little other than confirm his earlier suspicions—that the rebels had spied on them, presumably for over a century. But many questions remained. How long had they been disabled? Did they know of the MB infection? What else did they know?

These questions may never be answered. And Drakes had failed *again* to reveal anything useful.

Another dead end.

He blew the planer shavings away from the workpiece, brushed his hand across the smooth surface, and bent to inspect the grain. Dust-nibs clung to the hairs of his hand. He removed his cabinet scraper from a drawer and commenced removing fine shavings from the surface of the wood.

The manual work pulled his mind from the stresses of the rebels. Instead of worrying about an assault on Fahrquan or the releasing of a deadly infection, he brooded over what kind of joinery to use, whether the cross-cuts had been sufficiently square, and whether to use lacquer or shellac as a finish.

As his mind escaped deeper into the problems of the wood, the door opened, stirring sawdust that floated into his eyes. General Scott Chambers entered.

Like a child pulled away from a television, he made little effort to hide his anger at being interrupted. "What?"

The general said nothing. Instead he stood with erect posture, looking down his nose at the dust-covered president. Akram set his cabinet scraper on the workbench.

"The counsel meets tonight," said Chambers. "We will again vote on whether to begin a strategic bombing of the Indignis in order to draw the rebels out. Since you have run out of options, I came to determine whether you had changed your mind on the matter."

Akram folded his arms across his green workshop apron, his goggles resting on the top of his head. "My answer still stands. Not yet."

Chambers shook his head. He sighed. "The counsel will wish to know how you plan to meet the threat."

"The counsel will know of my plans in due time," said Akram.

"I'm afraid you are out of time. If you wish to avoid a bombing campaign, they must know of it tonight."

Still his mind clung to the project. Yet as he disengaged, he found renewed clarity. The hour or so freed his mind to make connections he hadn't seen previously.

Akram grinned. "Did you know that the rebels have been spying on us?"

"I am aware of that. But I don't see how that solves our current predicament."

"It doesn't really. But it made me think—in order to monitor us, they must have some sort of electronic footprint. Which means that wherever they are located, they are detectable."

Chambers eyes widened briefly.

"Have your men search for an electronic signal." Akram placed his goggles over his eyes and returned to face his workbench. "Then you'll find your rebellion."

"In the mean time," said Chambers. "Might I recommend we begin to bring our troops back from searching for the rebels? We need to prepare to defend Fahrquan."

"Do whatever you want," Akram waved his hand dismissively. "Just don't bomb the Indignis yet."

Chapter 18

I am just so tired. The fatigue never shakes from my bones, even after lengthy nights in bed. Sometimes I wonder whether I ought to leave someone else in charge of repenting of my sins.

Journal Entry of Gene The Ancient dated 110 years after the Genetic Apocalypse, extracted from the Archive.

Cole entered the cafeteria wearing the dark gray uniform of a new recruit. The clanking of silverware ceased and the men turned their attention to Cole.

A burly man folded his arms across his chest. "Hey! Come'n trough with us sproutie."

The man had a long oval face with a deformed lip and bad complexion. His ugly features formed a snicker that would've looked less out of place on a pug.

"Hey Clint." Another shouted from across the room. The man was short and skinny. His green shirt was untucked and his pants hung low on his hips. Though his head was almost bald, bright wisps of red hair stood erect on his scalp. "You stashing muscles in that big head of yours? Cuz it ain't storing no brain matter."

"Why you ask, skinny? You wanna borrow some?"

"Nah, cuz the ladies like 'em lean." The red head mimicked a seductive caress across his chest.

"Yeah, but they don't like 'em red, firehead," said Clint. Several of his groupies laughed.

"And they won't get snugly with one so ugly."

The people laughed.

"Move it, shavo." The man pushed aside a young soldier. "Make room for 'The Dux.'" He motioned to the now empty seat. "Come on, shavo. You sit with me."

"Shavo?" Cole asked.

Rocco rubbed his head, spilling dandruff onto his shoulders. "Shavo." He rubbed another soldier's head who slapped his hands. "Shavo."

Cole pointed to his own head, recently shaved. "Shavo."

"That's right, Dux. That's right. The name's Rocco." He extended his hand. "Welcome to paradise, Dux. You be right happy here. Right Tad?"

Tad shrugged, tossing his food around with a fork.

"Um,...Dux?" asked Cole.

"Yeah, man. You be the Dux, man. The *Ultimum Dux*, you be the best they say."

"Ahhh, I see." Cole nodded. "Not the best *yet*. Probably not ever."

"From what I hear, you already there, Dux."

Cole lifted an eyebrow.

A young soldier bent toward Cole. "Is it true what they say about you facing the Malkum soldier alone?"

"What do 'they' say I did?" asked Cole.

"They say you charged an armed soldier and dodged his bullets and rammed him with your shoulder, and saved—"

"Slow down, shavo," said Rocco. "Sorry Dux—he speak another language."

"Where'd you hear this?" Cole asked.

The young man shrugged.

"Well?" asked Rocco. "Be true?"

"No." Cole shook his head. "That was Luther. But I did wet my pants when I saw the gun."

Rocco laughed. "And they say Luther ticked you off 'n you grazed his neck with a knife, Dux."

The entire table leaned in, Tad included.

Cole laughed. "No, he did that to himself."

"That old man grazed his own neck?" asked Rocco.

Cole grinned. "More or less. He ticked off a couple soldiers and got himself shot. Twice."

"Luther be stupid, eh shavo?" The young soldier coughed, as if unsure of his use of military slang.

"Not stupid, just tough," said Cole.

"So is anything?" Tad began. Everyone looked at the large man. His bottom lip hung low, exposing his lower teeth. He sucked in spit, bending forward. "I mean, is anything they say about you...um, true?"

"They say my name's Cole, right?"

"Nah," said Rocco. "They be calling you Dennis, man."

Cole laughed. "Dennis it is."

"So how...?" Cole pointed to the trays of mashed potatoes and some sort of meat he'd never seen.

"You wanna eat?" asked Rocco. "This is what you do."

Rocco stood, pressing his hands together, elbows outstretched. "Oh mighty makers of food. Please give Dennis his daily sustenance."

Rocco bowed and touched the table in front of Cole. Part of the glass separated and a tray emerged from inside a chute.

"Is the prayer necessary?" asked Cole.

"Nah," said Rocco. "But the food gods get mad when you don't, and they give you diarrhea."

Cole grinned, before directing a two-finger salute down the chute.

Grabbing his fork, he began shoving food down his mouth.

Everyone stood. Conversation ceased, as did the clatter of forks and knives. The ragged breaths of those near him filled the silence. Several shifted, distancing themselves.

Rocco tucked in his shirt and his orange-shaded hand touched his forehead in a salute.

Footsteps approached, followed by the scent of cinnamon aftershave. Cole stood slowly. Hot breath brushed his neck, sending a shiver through Cole. He turned to face Mason.

I cannot fear.

"Good evening, sir." Cole saluted.

Mason punched his gut.

The blow launched Cole into the table. He crashed into the table, his arms spilling the trays around him. The room spun. The hollow pain in his gut swelled like a disease, consuming his body, his attention. He tried to gasp. Clint, the pug-bully smiled.

Gritting his teeth, he stood, struggling to straighten his posture.

"That was a warning, boy," said the general. "Next time I expect proper respect when I enter the room."

I cannot fear.

Cole smiled, taking a step toward Mason. "Yes, sir." He saluted.

Cole remained in the cafeteria long after dinner. He struggled to appear nonchalant, as if a blow to the stomach was as common as a cold. The banter between men had ceased. Instead they watched him, as if expecting him to explode.

He left the cafeteria. His slip of paper was crumbled and moist from his sweaty palms. The ink had smeared, blurring his room number—2059.

The hall bent right. Beyond his vision, footsteps approached, their laughter echoing down the halls. Cole sighed. He was sick of performing—pretending everything was okay when it wasn't. Toppling a general? Impossible.

Yet he had to do it.

The men turned the corner. Clint—the man who had taunted him—the one who had grinned when the general punched Cole.

Why now?

"Hey, sproutie." Clint folded his arms and leaned against the wall. The man smelled of gym clothes. His t-shirt was damp around the armpits and stretched around his muscles and potbelly.

"Clint." Cole nodded. He attempted to sidestep the men that surrounded him. They shifted, blocking Cole.

"Where you going?" Clint stepped toward Cole.

"Just trying to find my room."

Clint grinned, extending his hand down the hall. "Be my guest."

Cole smiled. "Thanks." He took a step, then paused. Clint and his friends remained silent. If they were planning something, it was inevitable. Cole fixed his eyes forward, then marched.

Someone kicked his ankle, causing him to trip. Cole stumbled, landing painfully on his palms.

Had the men laughed, he could have shaken it off. Instead, they circled him, casting shadows over his body.

What would he do? He couldn't freeze like before. But what else was there? He could start a fight with a half-dozen men twice his size, and likely leave with several broken limbs. He could run and earn a reputation for cowardice. Or he could persuade them to leave him alone. But how? He didn't even know why they hated him and he didn't feel like thinking about it.

Cole stood as casually as if he'd woken from bed. "You done?"

Clint smirked. "Watch yourself." Again, he extended his hand down the hall.

Cole didn't hesitate this time. He marched to his room.

Several minutes later, the hall straightened. Light spilled through the cracks in the doors, except one room—his room.

They're isolating me. He shook his head.

The door was locked. Great. He palmed the screen near the door and entered Luther's key code. The screen flashed red. He punched in the room number, but that didn't work either. He scanned the hallway. Seeing no one, he turned his back to the door and sat on the floor.

Cole struck the door with his elbow. The clank of metal echoed down the halls. The impact released a measure of frustration and Cole smiled.

The door flew open. Cole fell backward. A small man dressed in night clothing stood in the entry. He blinked against the light. It was the same soldier who stood at the front lines during Mason's speech, trembling. Only now, he didn't show any signs of fear.

"What are you doing?" he asked.

Cole stood, towering over the young man. The soldier backpedaled.

Cole smiled. "Hi. I didn't know had a roommate. My name's Cole."

The young man narrowed his eyes. "Just as I'd've expected." He turned. "Next time, enter your passcode like the rest of us."

Cole entered, or tried to enter. The room was scarcely large enough to fit the metal-framed bunk-bed that stood flush against the left wall, leaving about three feet between the top-most bunk and the ceiling. The young man stepped sideways to fit between the bed and a dresser that held a retainer and a case for contact lenses. As he straightened his blankets, his shoulder blades and spinal cord protruded outside his pajamas.

"Haven't learned the passcode yet," said Cole.

The man scoffed as he plopped into the bottom bunk.

"Seriously. They never told me," Cole said.

"It's the last four letters of your name, followed by your eight digit birthday."

"And what if we don't know our birthday?"

"*Stupid*," he said under his breath. "*Doesn't even know his birthday.*"

What was with this guy? Cole sighed and scanned the room. In the closet, a gray uniform hung from a hanger. His roommate's name was stitched over the right breast—*Addonis.*

"I was born in the woods, Addonis. It's pretty easy to lose track of the calendar."

Addonis stood. "How did you know my name?"

Cole pointed to the uniform.

"It's good to meet you, Addonis." He extended his hand.

"Look, man, I'm not sure what your game is, but I don't wanna be a part of it." Addonis turned without shaking Cole's hand. "I get into enough trouble without being associated with you."

Cole shook his head, before leaving the room.

Cole exited the rebellion's headquarters using Luther's passkey. Though miles from where the bombs hit, the stench of ash lingered in the air, as thick as the shadowed trees. Darkness blanketed the landscape.

What am I doing here?

And the Ancient. What he asked—impossible. Gain control of an army that hated him, convince them to storm Fahrquan, then overthrow the Malkum. He was nineteen—just old enough to shave. He didn't care what Luther and Aumora had said—the Ancient's plan was anything but brilliant.

I didn't ask for this! He wanted to shout it, leave, and never come back. Maybe he could find another Indignis village. Or better yet, live the remainder of his days alone.

But he couldn't.

He walked. An owl hooted. Moonlight shone through the skeletal branches, casting slivers of light. He walked several paces before sitting atop a rock.

His chest ached. He missed Elsa—that beautiful, silent, mysterious girl—now nothing more than a heap of ash, another victim of the Malkum. He wished he could be angry, about Suta, about his village, about *her.* Maybe if he could just summon rage, he'd have the willpower to return.

But even anger eluded him.

Footsteps approached.

Great. Could he not be alone for one evening? A flashlight shone. He sighed, lifting his hands in the air. "Here."

"Son." Luther approached. He sat next to Cole. Crickets filled the silence.

"How'd you find me?" Cole asked.

Luther chuckled. "Would ya believe me if I says I didn't come ta find ya?"

"You often go for midnight walks in the forest?"

Luther smiled. Moonlight shone through the trees, casting shadows across the crevices of his wrinkled cheeks. "I miss her too."

A lump formed in Cole's throat, one he'd never successfully repressed.

"And I miss," Luther sniffed, "I miss the boy."

Again, Cole wished he could rage—anger felt good. It boiled inside the blood, fueling the limbs. Yet he couldn't feel it. Instead, he felt as if he were sinking into the dirt, only to have rocks bury him beneath the weight of his burden.

"Have you come to bring me back?" Cole asked.

Luther pressed his lips together, shaking his head. "Nah." He sighed. "Everyone deals with grief in their own way, I suppose. I won't pretend to know what ya should do."

Luther stood with a grunt. He bent toward Cole, kissing the top of his head. "You come back when you're ready. Or don't come at all." He flipped on his flashlight. "I won't judge you for it."

He opened his mouth, but shook his head and trudged toward the cave, disappearing into the shadows.

"And remember," Luther half shouted, "If yer not pissing somebody off at some time in yer life, yer probably doing something wrong."

Cole chuckled. "Wait." He jogged, following the light of the flashlight. "Let's go piss some people off."

Luther laughed. "That's better." He handed Cole a manilla envelope.

"What's this?" Cole asked.

"Something Gene wanted me to give you."

"You said you didn't come to find me."

Luther shrugged. "I lied. Glad yer coming back." He winked.

Chapter 19

It is a day of rejoicing! Our colony of rebels is not so little anymore. I believe we are large enough to finally scale an assault on Fahrquan. Now all I have to do is convince the council to act.

Journal Entry of Gene The Ancient dated 191 years after the Genetic Apocalypse, extracted from the Archive.

Cole sat outside his room, holding the envelope. On the cover was a note, written in Gene's meticulous handwriting. *You may find this helpful. Keep it to yourself.*

Cole opened a document. It showed the image of a man—Clyde Holmes. He was dark skinned with a shaved head, serious expression, and a lanky build.

He scanned the text of the document. Clyde Holmes had died six years ago of a heart attack, sometime between two and four in the morning.

The following page reported results from his most recent physical examination—no preexisting heart condition, nor were there any other indications of poor health.

Cole turned the page again. Near the center, text was highlighted—*Two-mile time: 9:59.* In the margin, Gene had written a note—*three seconds from Mason's time.*

Cole's stomach rumbled.

He turned the page. Another death—Rubin Matthews. The man had broken his neck, tripping down the stairs. Another note—*three points from best score in Knife Combat Simulator.* John Hopkins—paralyzed—*four points from Strategic Defenses record.* Blake Bishop—aneurism—*one point from Long-range Marksmanship award.* Zack Thomas—dead, Alan Lebrero—paralyzed, Kevin Jose—dead, all within reach of one of Mason's records.

He let out a breath, closing the dossier. He scanned the halls, suddenly wary. He thought he heard footsteps. *I cannot fear.*

He opened the dossier again, flipping to the last report—*General Mason. Trial and Acquittal.* Cole skimmed the text. Gene had filed criminal charges against Mason. The general was temporarily removed, but Gene could not obtain a conviction because all evidence was circumstantial. Mason had used the accusations to discredit the Ancient—calling false witnesses to testify of various crimes—monetary theft, sexual assault, and sedition. Gene was subsequently suspended from the council, while Mason regained his post.

He turned the page to find one final note—*Cole. Please be careful.*

Cole slept fitfully. Like a child, he heard imaginary noises, only to fall asleep to nightmares of Mason strangling him.

Whatever doubt Cole had before, fled. Mason had to be stopped. More was at stake than stopping the Malkum.

Murderer.

The lights flickered on. Addonis entered a code into a keypad. A screen showed a schedule of the day's events.

Cole leaped from the bed. "How do I access my schedule?"

"Look, I'm not your babysitter. You figure it out."

This was one person he would have no trouble pissing off. "How do I access my schedule?"

Addonis snarled. He opened the closet and removed his uniform.

Cole stared at the back of Addonis's head, imagining what it would feel like to smash his fist into his skull.

But he couldn't do that. That's what Mason would do. No, his urgency to topple the murderer had to be tempered.

But what could he do? Gene said Cole was supposed to be a brilliant strategist, yet he couldn't think of any way to deal with Addonis. It was kind of funny, really. He had to win the trust of an army that resented him, overthrow a corrupt general, then march into Fahrquan. And here he was, *stuck* at getting his schedule because his roommate was a jerk-wad.

Cole sighed. One obstacle at a time. He'd tried to be friendly, but that failed. The Ancient had said it was because of his *empathy* the men would follow him.

"Addonis," said Cole. The young man said nothing. Cole lifted his eyes to the ceiling. "I know you're afraid," he said awkwardly. "I've felt it too."

The young man turned, his face softening. "Do you mind if I lay on the bed and tell you about it?" He threw his hands the air. "My savior has come to fix my daddy issues!"

Addonis snarled. "Get over yourself, *savior*."

Cole tightened his jaw. Addonis wasn't the enemy. Mason was the enemy—the Malkum were the enemy. Again, he failed to summon anger. Instead, he was just annoyed.

What was with this kid? Just yesterday he was a totally different person. But why?

He remembered the fearful look in the young man's eyes during Mason's speech—and he remembered what Addonis had said the night before—"I get into enough trouble . . ."

It all clicked.

Very well, Cole thought to himself, already regretting what was necessary.

He turned to Addonis, grabbed him by his shoulders, and shoved him against the top bunk, pressing his back into the guardrail.

"What the—" Addonis yelped. "I—Ouch. Stop."

Cole pressed his back harder into the guardrail.

"Somebody help me. Help! He's killing me!"

Cole pressed his back harder. Addonis kicked, but couldn't generate enough force to do any damage.

He screamed louder.

Cole pressed his back harder against the pole.

"The more you scream, the harder I push." Cole forced a snarl.

Addonis quieted, and Cole let off some of the pressure. The young man trembled.

He must fear Cole more than Mason. It was an effective strategy.

"Show me how to get my schedule," said Cole.

Addonis nodded.

Cole dropped the young man, who rushed to the screen. "It's the same c-code as the one to get into the room," he said, voice trembling. "But I can log in for you, do a s-search for your name and p-pull it up."

"No." Luther had told him his login the night before. "Just show me how to access my schedule."

Cole punched in his passkey. Addonis opened his schedule.

"There's a message for you," Addonis said. "Just touch the top-right corner to r-read it."

"Thank you."

Addonis nodded, then bolted out of the room, leaving Cole alone.

Cole watched the door close. As he looked at the handle, his shoulders sank, and he lowered his head, squeezing his eyes closed.

Is this what a commander does?

Later that morning, Cole sprinted down the empty hallways. He glanced at his watch. Three minutes before his first training activity.

Even if he were late, it was worth it. The message had been from Gene. The Ancient had offered dozens of training articles, each tailored to the day's schedule. Today, Cole would first attend marksmanship training, then personal combat, then strategy. For each topic, Gene gave Cole a collection of articles, instruction manuals, and other forms of documentation from long-dead experts.

He entered the training auditorium. Soft aqua light illuminated the room. It was the auditorium where the general had introduced Cole the day before. But the room looked different. Training equipment cluttered the room. One section housed a boxing ring, another a human-sized padded robot, and surrounding it all was a running track.

Cole frowned. How would he ever find—

Gunshots sounded.

The noise stimulated a conglomeration of memories—Suta coughing blood, Luther mutilating the soldier's corpse, the bullet grazing Luther's neck. He shivered, following the sounds of gunshots and the stench of gunpowder.

The firing range rested atop a wooden platform. Soldiers lay on the platform holding rifles. A concave lens wrapped around each soldier, displaying a projected image of a combat scene. A desert landscape surrounded one soldier as he fired at enemies hiding behind boulders. As he released the trigger, sparks emitted from the end of a barrel. One of the enemy soldiers dropped as blood stained his jacket.

Bang! Bang! Bang-bang!

Cole furrowed his eyebrows.

"They're blanks," said a nearby soldier. *Bang!* "These guns have sensors, so it knows where you point it. The screen there is adaptive. You get better, it gets harder. So you never know what's coming next. Fancy, fancy, eh, shavo?"

Cole nodded.

Bang!

"I'm Toby, by the way," said the young man. He had a lean frame and a half-grin affixed to his chocolate face. Something about the man's features was familiar, yet Cole couldn't place it.

He shook the thought from his mind. "I'm Cole. Good to meet you."

"Pleasure's all mine, shavo."

Bang-bang!

"So how do I do this?" Cole pointed at the guns.

"The Dux's ready, already, huh? Gonna show us how it's done?"

"Ready to start learning at least."

"All right. I can arrange that." Toby approached the firing range, cupping his hands over his mouth. "'Eh, listen up. The Dux wan'sta get a shot in. Who want'sta be able to say they saw him shoot his first shot?"

Several removed their ear muffs and stepped aside. Two men rolled their eyes and continued shooting. The whirring of the nearby battle robot filled the silence, mingling with the grunts of a soldier.

Cole approached the range. Toby followed, taking the gun from a young man. Toby replaced the magazine, handing the gun to Cole.

"Yer all set, Dux. Point the gun, pull the trigger. That's all there is to it."

"Thanks, Toby." Cole grabbed the gun and faced the firing range. The entire group, save the two soldiers, watched him quizzically. Cole's face warmed and he smiled to hide his embarrassment. He swallowed hard and lay on the ground.

Toby typed on the nearby computer. "Pass-key, shavo?"

"08-22-2465-BROO."

"Well happy birthday, Dux."

The concave lens displayed a firing range. A red and white target hovered at the end.

"Hit the red, Dux. All you gotta do," Toby said.

Cole pressed the butt of the gun into his shoulder. It felt unfamiliar and awkward, much like the silent scrutiny of the nearby soldiers.

Breathe. He attempted to relax as the training manual had suggested. He held his breath until his heart slowed, exhaling slowly. His shoulders relaxed.

Cole breathed inward as he pulled the gun tighter into his shoulder and pressed it to his cheek. The sight of the gun shook with every twitch of his body.

Eyes closed, he exhaled and breathed in again, then opened his eyes, and began a slow exhale. The sight still moved, but did so predictably.

On his next breath, he aimed high on the red center and allowed the sight to fall with his exhaled breath. He timed the release of the trigger so the gun fired at the center of the red.

The butt slammed against his shoulder. He tensed.

Men cheered.

"Dux, man. That was perfect." Toby beamed.

Cole looked at the target. In the exact center of the red image, the computer generated a hole where his bullet would have made contact.

"Do it again," said a voice from behind.

Cole turned and saw Addonis, chin raised.

"Yeah, man. Do it again, Dux. Five shots is a round," said Toby.

Cole sighed, turning to look at the target. He breathed in and paused, sighting the target. He pulled the gun tighter on his shoulder and watched as the sight lowered toward the center. He began squeezing the trigger. He stiffened.

He didn't squeeze the trigger. Instead, he began the process again, but still he flinched in anticipation of the kick.

And again it happened.

"Come on, Dux. What's the problem?" asked Toby.

Cole lifted his head from the barrel. "It's the anticipation. Now that I know what to expect, I'm having a hard time not . . . flinching."

"Aint nottin' but a cold breeze, man. Don't worry 'bout it," said Toby. "Listen, this time, instead a being scared of the kick, be excited, man. Yo body reacts the same. Only diff' between the two be in yo head. So convince your mind you excited."

Cole nodded. Again, he inhaled then held his breath. The pattern was familiar now. He sighted down the barrel and slowly exhaled. Cole smiled, thinking of the smell of the gunpowder filling his nostrils. He watched the sight drop and fired.

Cole squinted. "What happened?" The target remained unchanged. "Something wrong with the simulation?"

"No, shavo. You just hit the same spot," said Toby with a toothy smile. "Hey we got the Dux, here!"

Cole cocked his head. "What?"

"You hit the *exact* same spot, man."

Cole grinned.

He fired the next three rounds more quickly. By the end, the hole was only slightly larger than it had been after Cole's first shot.

The target faded, replaced with writing.

Congratulations, Cole Brooks.

You have just broken the record for:

Highest grouping score for a first time shot.

Mechanical movement sounded from underneath the platform before it ejected a thin rectangular object. Cole removed it and his jaw dropped. He held a plaque, just like the ones in Mason's office.

Toby's eyes widened. "Yo, shavo. I never even seen one before."

Cole handed the plaque to Toby. "It's yours, Toby. That helped a lot."

"That's real nice and all, but I don't know if you noticed, but it says Cole Brooks." Toby attempted to return the plaque.

Cole cocked his head. "Haven't you heard, Toby? My name's Dennis."

Toby chuckled. "So I've heard. Good to meet you, Dux. Er Dennis. Er

Cole."

Cole extended his hand. "Cole Brooks."

Toby tipped an imaginary hat. "Toby Holmes."

"Holmes." Cole squinted his eyes. He'd heard that name recently. "You have a brother or something?"

Toby's smile dropped. "I-it was nice to meet you, Cole. Real nice. Have a good one."

As Toby fled, Cole remembered where he'd heard the name. Clyde Holmes—one of the soldiers Mason had murdered.

Cole watched Toby leave, as he began to formulate a plan.

Chapter 20

An interesting technology has developed. The engineers say that they are able to control the sensory input of an individual by injecting digitized neurotransmitters into the brain. They've suggested I might use this technology to accelerate the training of the Nexus army. As is often the case, the fathers of the technology see no disadvantage to their creation. If only Keston and I had seen the drawbacks when we programed our first Nexus, perhaps the world would not lie in ruins.

Journal Entry of Gene The Ancient dated 208 years after the Genetic Apocalypse, extracted from the Archive.

Cole spent the day attempting to talk to Toby, but failed. The man was nimble and fast, able to weave between crowds like a newspaper boy. Now, Cole sat atop Toby's bunk bed, waiting.

The door opened. Toby jumped, startled. "Geez, Dux!" He exhaled. "I 'bout wet my pants, shavo."

"Sorry about that." Cole jumped from the top bunk, side-stepping clusters of soiled laundry and garbage.

"Hey man, nice of you to visit and all, but I'm kinda tired." Toby motioned to the door. "Thanks for stopping by."

"Wait."

Toby folded his arms.

Cole opened his mouth, but words wouldn't come. Despite mentally rehearsing dozens of conversations, he still had nothing.

His gaze fell on a framed picture. It was of a middle-aged black woman, with pointed rimmed glasses, a gaunt face, and hard features. She looked as if she hadn't smiled since the Genetic Apocalypse. Despite the apparent wear, there was something about the woman that transcended the stillness of the image. She wore colorful clothing, with a set jaw, intense eyes, sitting erect as a king on a throne.

"Is that your mom?"

He nodded. "Daisey Holmes."

"Daisy, huh?" Cole grinned. "She don't look like a Daisy."

Toby chuckled. "More like a thorn bush, that woman."

"I bet she whipped you a time or two."

"You kiddin' me? I still got belt-shaped welts on my butt."

Cole laughed. "Is that why you walk like a drunken monkey?"

Toby laughed, punching Cole in the shoulder.

The ticking of the clock filled the silence.

"I'm sorry for your loss," Cole said. He opened his mouth to speak, but what could he say? It seemed tacky to capitalize on the man's grief just so Cole could topple Mason. But it would also benefit Toby, wouldn't it? And his mom?

"Thanks," Toby said.

Silence.

"Sorry about *your* loss," Toby said. "I heard...about the boy."

Cole nodded.

"That sucks, man," Toby said.

"Yeah."

Toby began chewing on his lip, his eyebrows narrowing as if performing mental arithmetic. "You gonna topple Mason?"

"I hope so."

Silence.

"It needs to end, you know," Cole said.

Toby shivered.

Cole grabbed his jacket. "Think about it." He reached for the door handle.

"We can't do it alone, you know," Toby said.

Cole turned.

Toby folded his arms. "We'll have to find others."

"Any idea who?" Cole asked.

Toby smirked. "I got a couple in mind."

"Tomorrow morning. 6AM. East conference room."

Toby grinned. "I'll think about it."

"Do it," Cole said, "or I'll kick that welted butt of yours."

Toby saluted like a drunken seaman. "Yessir."

That evening, Cole entered the training auditorium. The dark room seemed to extend for miles, disappearing into shadows. The concrete walls stood tall, daunting.

He trudged inside. The day had been exhausting, and the fatigue sucked life out of his muscles. Even now, the temptation to turn around remained, like an itch that demanded scratching.

Only Cole couldn't scratch that itch. If he were to topple Mason, he'd have to outrank him. And the longer that took, the more time Mason had to plot Cole's assassination.

Sleep could wait. Training could not.

Guided by a flashlight, he approached the center of the room, entering Luther's key code. Beneath the floor, gears engaged and machinery whirred. The floor parted and a human-shaped mass of metal emerged, head drooping and padded fists dangling.

The Interpersonal Combat Simulator, or ICS, was a human-sized robot that responded to movement. The ICS could be tailored, depending on competency. Despite the prodding of his fellow soldiers, Cole began at the novice level.

And got his butt kicked.

Though the fists and feet of the robot were padded, the blows from earlier still ached.

With a yawn, Cole powered on the robot and entered practice mode. Only this time, he chose the intermediate level. The red eyes of the robot illuminated. Green slivers of light leaked from its joints. The robot bowed its head, before lifting its fists.

Its metal shin slammed into Cole's helmut. The room spun. Shards of pain radiate from his temples. Another fist landed in his kidney, sending him to the ground. The pain traveled to his back. He gasped, struggling to breathe.

Groaning, he stood. Shaking his head, he bounced on the balls of his feet. The robot nodded again, lifting its fists to his face.

It punched. He blocked. It punched again. He ducked, but not fast enough. Its boxing glove grazed his ear, followed by another jab that landed squarely in the face.

Stumbling, Cole backed away. The robot charged, sweeping Cole's leg. Cole fell to the ground, but rolled, only to have it land another jab, toppling him.

He slapped the concrete floor. Fatigue fled as adrenaline coursed through his veins. He jumped to his feet and charged.

He kicked. The robot backed away. He kicked again, which the robot sidestepped, then Cole punched, landing a fist in the robots neck.

He jumped back before it could strike. He grinned. The robot charged, kicking. He ducked, only to have the robot land another blow to the head. Then another. And another.

He dropped to the ground.

After what felt like days, Cole couldn't count the number of times he fell. But he also lost track of how many hits he scored. The throb in his head was blinding, as was the multitude of body wounds. Salty sweat stung his eyes and the cuts on his face and body.

But there was progression. He still lost more matches than he won, but he did win. And not too infrequently.

He powered down the robot before looking at his watch. Two AM. Only four more hours until he met with Toby.

Closing his eyes, he counted. Ten seconds. That's all he had. Ten seconds to feel the pain—to whine about it—to wish he hadn't been chosen for this. Ten seconds was all.

Five seconds. It hurt. If only he could sleep.

Three seconds. He hated it. Every minute.

One second. His head might explode.

Done.

Cole straightened his spine.

It was time to go for a run.

Eyes half-closed, Cole trudged down the hall the following morning, holding a briefcase. The night before, he thought he'd never been so tired, yet as he woke, the fatigue gripped him on a deeper level, penetrating to the cells of his bones. Half-delirious, he entered the conference room.

"Dux," Toby said. The man sat alone at an oak conference table that stretched beyond the shadows of the dark room. The scent of carpet solution hung in the air.

"Where is everyone?"

Toby shrugged.

Cole looked at his watch. 6:05. He frowned. "Alright, let's—"

Behind, someone cleared his throat.

"Hey," the man said. He wore a white t-shirt that shone in the dim light. He smiled, showing bright white teeth and dimpled cheeks. The man's grin was contagious, and despite his fatigue, Cole smiled.

The man extended his hand. "The name's Ray. Ray Matthews."

"Rubin Matthews?" Cole said.

Ray's smile faded. He cleared his throat. "Yeah."

"Brother?"

"Dad." He sighed. "Mom was pregnant at the time. He was the first to...you know."

"Sorry."

"Yeah." Ray sat. "Well, let's get to it."

Cole nodded.

"So what's the plan?" Toby asked.

Cole sat, unlatching his briefcase. "Oust Mason."

"We figured as much," Ray said. "But how?"

Cole stood, grabbing a whiteboard marker. "That's what we're gonna figure out."

Ray and Toby nodded.

"Any ideas?" Cole asked.

"A bullet to his head," Ray said.

Cole grinned. "Right. Bullet..." He wrote on the board. "To the...head. Great. Other ideas?"

"There was the trial," Ray said. "Maybe we could get him removed."

"Good, good." Cole wrote 'trial' on the board. "Any ideas how?"

"My uncle knows a guy," Toby said. "A board member."

"Good." Cole nodded. He wrote 'Toby's uncle,' then drew a line to the word 'trial.'

A shadow passed from the hallway, covering the only source of light. Cole spun, eyes wide. A man stood in the doorframe, tall and foreboding. The man's shoulders barely fit within the door's frame.

"Wassup, shavos?" The man's deep voice rumbled, caressing sound waves like a jazz singer.

Toby jumped from his seat. "I knew you'd be here." The two clasped hands in a convoluted handshake that seemed to last about an hour, concluding in a bro-hug.

Cole smiled.

"Wassup, Dux?" The man extended his large hand, which appeared to have the crushing force of a vice. Cole returned the gesture.

"Call me Cole. And your name?"

"Beef."

Cole raised an eyebrow. "Issa nickname, shavo. Easier to say than Cornelius Eugene Hawthorne Blackburn."

Cole chuckled. "Nice to meet you, Beef."

Beef looked at the board. He stretched out his hand to Cole, who handed him the marker. "You're missing one."

In writing that looked like decorative graffiti, the man wrote, "Ultimum Dux." He slapped Cole's shoulder before sitting in the chair, leaning back on its two legs.

"Ultimum Dux." Cole grinned. "Ultimum Dux."

"You think you can do it?" Ray asked.

"No," Cole said.

Beef raised an eyebrow. Ray bent forward.

"Okay..." Toby said.

"But I don't have to." Cole grinned. He removed a stack of papers from his briefcase. "These are the records Mason holds." He passed the papers around. "One hundred and twenty two."

"Okay...And?" Toby said.

"See, I can't do it. Not all of it. But..." Cole smiled. "If I get three, Toby gets two, Beef gets four..."

Beef nodded. "Or if even fifty or sixty soldiers get one—"

"Each record scored, is one less for Mason," Ray said.

"We diffuse the records among the men, we diffuse his authority," Cole said.

"Brilliant," Ray said.

"Brilliant," Toby agreed.

"I like the way you think, Dux." Beef grinned.

"And I don't think it will be that hard," Cole said. "They've only stood for so long because people have been too afraid to do well. But if we can convince them to *try*."

Ray smiled. "We could oust him in months."

Toby frowned. "But we've still got a problem."

Cole nodded. "Yeah." He lifted a stapled document—the one the Ancient had given him. "So here's what we need to do."

Beef, Toby, and Ray leaned forward.

Cole lowered his voice. "We train at night—in practice mode so the scores aren't recorded."

Beef's smile widened. "Then we break all the records in one day—"

"—*before* he has a chance to act," Ray said.

"Dude Dux!" Beef laughed. "Shavo, that's brilliant."

"Brilliant," Toby agreed.

"But...we still need to be careful. *Nobody* is alone. Ever. Got it?"

The men nodded.

"So you with me?" Cole asked. "Ready to do some night training?"

They all nodded.

"First," Cole said. "Let's go through the list. You guys know the men better than I—figure out who's the best contender for each slot."

"Deal," Ray said.

"Deal," Beef said.

"Let's meet tonight in the auditorium—midnight," Cole said. "In the mean time, see what you can do about the trial, Toby."

"Yes, sir."

Cole laughed. *Sir?* The men didn't. Cole's face warmed.

"Come prepared with your lists," Cole said. "And start recruiting."

Chapter 21

Today marks the tenth anniversary of the day we began to rescue children. Not coincidentally, it also marks the time when our first round of cohorts have completed forming a Nexus. I have moments when I am able to convince myself that I am a savior to these children—protecting their psyche from the trauma of their childhood. These moments never last, however, as I consider how I am yet again manipulating the lives of others to atone for my sins. At least these children, and the children that follow for many generations will be able to blissfully believe the false memories their Nexus has created for the remainder of their days. I already cringe as I consider the children that shall be used for my purposes, once we begin to prepare for the final assault.

Journal Entry of Gene The Ancient dated 63 years after the Genetic Apocalypse, extracted from the Archive.

Long past lights out, Cole sat inside the Ancient's office.

"I hear you're doing quite well," said Gene.

"I suppose."

"Already broken a record I hear."

Cole shrugged. "A novice record."

Gene nodded. "So, what can I do for you?"

Cole straightened his spine. "I need you to pressure the council."

Gene chuckled. "I'm afraid my influence has waned, my friend. They no longer allow me at council meetings."

"Yes, I know." Cole sighed. "But don't you still have contacts? You've gotta have *somebody's* ear."

"Why?"

"We need to prepare to attack Fahrquan."

Gene raised an eyebrow. "Oh?"

"Yes, sir."

"So soon?"

"Yes."

"But you've only secured one record."

Cole shrugged. "True."

"Then why now?" Gene asked.

"Because it'll take time to secure their vote. We don't have time to dawdle. As soon as Mason's removed, we need to act."

Gene nodded.

"And," Cole said, "we may need to have Mason occupied. If he's politicking, he'll be too busy to notice...*other* things."

Gene smiled. "What sorts of *other* things?"

Cole shrugged. "Army things. You know how it goes."

"I'm afraid I don't. I never was one for war and such. My brother—he had the aggression genes, while I inherited the genes of intellect. No matter. Of course, Cole, I'll do what I can."

"Good."

"How long, you think?" Gene asked.

"Several weeks. Maybe a couple months."

Gene beamed. "Good, good." He stood from his chair, wincing as he did. "You have a minute?"

Cole looked at his watch. "Sure."

They entered a door at the rear of the office. Cages lined the walls, each housing a mouse. In the center stood a collection of vials and petri dishes. Cole bent, looking at one of the mice.

"Ah. I see you've met Dino." The Ancient removed the mouse from its cage, handing it to Cole. The small feet of the animal tickle his palm. The mouse was large with rumpled hair and seemed to hunch as he walked.

"Would you like to meet his brother?" Gene asked.

Cole nodded.

Gene removed a much smaller mouse. "His name is Rhino."

Rhino's hair had not yet grown and he looked no more than a couple days old.

"They're brothers?" Cole asked incredulously.

"Identical twins—well, clones technically. It's easier to clone an animal than to wait until random events produce identical twins."

Cole lowered an eyebrow. "But—"

Gene grinned. "They *appear* to be different ages, don't they?"

"They do."

"But they're not. Watch this."

Gene retrieved a syringe, before sticking the needle into the younger mouse's abdomen.

"Watch closely," said Gene.

Cole lowered his eyes on the mouse. His jaw dropped as the mouse grew, doubling in size within only a minute. A thick main of hair covered his pink skin.

"What the—"

"I've aged him," said Gene. "Many have wondered how I came to develop the Death Antidote. What you just witnessed was common knowledge at one time, before the virus was released. It was, ironically, discovered by President Akram himself. It was the first step toward eternal life."

"Which explains why he has the Death Antidote as well."

"Indeed, though perhaps it's not surprising that he developed it before I did." Gene sighed. "I wish I'd developed it sooner, then I wouldn't be trapped in this decrepit body."

"So you developed it independently?"

Gene nodded. "He beat me to it, by forty years or more. It was a brilliant discovery. And figuring out how to use that knowledge to develop the Death Antidote was quite a struggle, I admit."

Cole bent to look at the two animals. "Can it be reversed? Can you make one younger."

"Alas!" said Gene. "Now you have discovered my conundrum. If developing the Death Antidote was difficult, reversing aging is *impossible!* I've spent the better part of 200 years working on it."

Cole studied the mice. "So why haven't you shared the Death Antidote with anyone else?"

Gene's lips parted and formed into the circle that was characteristic of his resting expression. "I suppose there are two reasons. The first—despite what it seems, is this: immortality is a curse. Men weren't meant to live as I have, that I understand. I've grown tired of life and wish nothing more than to expire. Yet you and I know that I cannot until this mess is cleaned up."

"And the second?"

Gene sighed. "I cannot play god—deciding for whom to grant immortality. The moral responsibility is too great. And what if I grant immortality to the wrong person?"

"I see."

The patter of mice's feet on cages filled the silence. Both men remained quiet, staring at the mice.

"I'm quite fond of them." Gene smiled at a mouse. He stroked Dino's back, before placing him in the cage. "Perhaps they feel the same as I about living. They're older than you by quite a bit. Yet I can't seem to let them go. And that is another reason I cannot grant immortality. If a cherished friend longs to die, I fear I would be too selfish to grant that request."

Cole placed Rhino in his cage.

"But I didn't bring you here to lecture you on the morals and immorals of immortality. Come."

Cole followed Gene to the back of the room where a large monitor sat. "This computer is much like the one in your room. From this or any other computer within Azkus City, you may access the Archive. But before I show you how to access it, you must promise me something."

Gene turned to Cole, his eyes narrowing with a sternness that he had not seen in the old man. The look reminded him of times Aumora had reprimanded him as a child.

"The Archive *cannot* get into the wrong hands," Gene continued. "If Akram somehow gains access, we've lost our advantage. He will kill Jason Drakes, destroy the Indignis, and eventually destroy our city. Consequently, I must insist you make a solemn promise to *never* share the password with anyone."

Gene's eyes went from stern, to pleading, to piercing. Or perhaps they were all that at once. All Cole knew was that the password would never escape his mouth in the presence of another until the Malkum were defeated.

"I promise."

"Good," said Gene with a gentle smile. He turned to the computer then spoke. "Computer. Open the Archive."

The computer displayed a prompt seeking a password.

"Cakfe-burgen tongen."

"That's the password?" Cole asked incredulously.

"Would you have guessed it?" Gene grinned.

"It's non-sense."

"That's the point!" said Gene. "Should I change it to 'I love Dino'?!"

Cole laughed. And Gene laughed. And for several minutes, neither could stop laughing.

Cole arrived late to the auditorium. Greg Sampson stood watch at the door. "Wassup, Dux?"

The auditorium was a bustle of activity. In the weeks since he began training at night, dozens of soldiers had joined the "Midnight Rebellion" as they called it. The room was a cacophony of hushed noises—daggers thudding into wooden targets, the panting of a runner circling the track, and the grunt of a man climbing a rope. The stench of body odor was thick, yet Cole savored the smell.

It was the scent of change.

And it was coming. A dozen men outperformed Mason and twice that many were within reach. Cole himself could boast of over a dozen records, most of which Mason held.

And the general knew nothing about it.

More important than the records, however, was the way the men reacted around the general. Now, their fear was only an act.

Beef fired a rifle. The man was amazing. In only a few short weeks, he'd surpassed all marksmanship records. The man could hit anything he could see and he had the eyes of a hawk. If all went as planned, in only a few weeks, Beef would acquire fifteen records, making him the new general. Cole smiled.

Ray's training had also paid off. Days before, he'd surpassed both his brother and Mason's record in the knife simulator. Combined, they were only twenty records shy of ousting Mason.

Toby rushed past, dripping sweat. His long legs pumped with the speed of a sprinter, yet the distances he was running weren't small.

"How close is he?" Cole asked Greg.

The man looked at his watch, shaking his head in amazement. "Fastest split yet. I think he might do it."

A lump formed in Cole's throat. Like his deceased brother, Toby inched closer to breaking Mason's record in the two-minute mile. The man trained with more than determination—he trained with conviction.

Sibling rivalry at its finest.

Toby rounded the final corner. His cheeks shook. Though his face was relaxed, the man's eyes harbored an absolute determination.

"Time?" Cole asked.

"He might do it," Greg said. "9:43."

Come on, come on.

Toby's sucked in a breath, his face contorting. The determination in his eyes wavered.

"Do it!" Cole shouted.

The men in the auditorium hushed. "Do it, do it, do it!"

The men clapped rhythmically—fast. Toby matched the pace of their feet. "Faster!"

Cole clapped his hands more quickly. The men followed.

"Come on, Toby."

Toby hardened his gaze, fixing his eyes on the finish line.

9:51. He had five seconds to—

Toby stopped, just shy of the finish line. 9:54. The room fell silent.

Toby panted, resting his palms on his knees. "Not like this." Toby shook his head.

He stepped across the finish line. 10:02.

"I wanna see his face when I do it." He tossed a towel over his shoulder before exiting the room.

God bless you, Toby.

High in the auditorium, General Mason watched from behind a window. The nerve of that insubordinate prick.

"So?" Lieutenant Briggs asked.

"Something needs to be done. And now!"

And the Ancient. Since the trial for those unlucky fools, the council has scrutinized his every action, second guessing every decision. He couldn't just 'take care' of Cole as he had before.

"So what do you suggest?" Mason asked.

Briggs folded his arms, lifting his eyes to gaze at the ceiling. Mason had come to associate that face with success. The man was brilliant, he had to admit—the man made Alexander the Great look like a child playing with toys. It was Briggs that had discredited the Ancient and ensured that Mason maintained his position.

And Mason had rewarded him handsomely.

"The men are coming to respect him," Briggs said.

Mason tightened his jaw.

"Somehow," Briggs closed his eyes, tapping his chin, "somehow, they must lose respect." He grinned. "He needs to become *that* guy."

Mason smiled. "*That* guy."

"Yes. The men will hate him."

Mason marched toward the door. "Let the officers know. Make it happen."

"Yes, sir."

"Tomorrow. And they never leave the red phase."

Chapter 22

The council has impeached me. Why did Mason have to come along now?

Journal Entry of Gene "the Ancient" dated 198 years after the Genetic Apocalypse, extracted from the Archive.

Lights blared. Men shouted.

"Get up, get up, Sprouties!"

Rough hands pulled Cole from his bed, throwing him onto the ground. A man lodged his knee into his naked back. He thrashed. His throat tightened. The man placed a canvas bag over his face. Everything went dark.

It was happening—really happening. He never thought Mason would be so brazen.

The man lifted him, throwing him forward. Cole stumbled, falling into the hallway in his boxer shorts.

So this was it.

"Let's go Sprouties!" A man shouted. A different man, with a deep haunting voice. His own sweat reeked of fear, dripping with each throb of his heart.

Death.

"Let's go, let's go, let's go."

Several men around him groaned.

There were others? His men—the ones who trained with him. He thought he heard the deep rumble of Beef's voice. Cole's panic rose.

"Boot camp starts today, Sprouties! And you all have Private Brooks to thank."

What?

"So make sure you let him know how much you appreciate it."

Boot camp. Cole's muscles relaxed, though the dread remained. So he wouldn't die today. But it was hard to be grateful.

"Welcome to hell, ladies!"

"Let's go, let's go, let's go!"

Someone pressed into his back. Another shoved him against the wall. One man cried out. The canvas bag reflected his own breath, scalding hot and moist.

He was hyperventilating.

"Move!"

Amidst the taunts, jeers, backhands, kicks, and shoves, Cole and the rest of the soldiers moved in complete darkness. They turned around, turned left, turned right. He had no idea where they were. The hem of his boxers chaffed against his thigh. The balls of his feet ached with each slap against the short carpet. And always, the yelling. The incessant screaming. No matter how fast he moved, it was there.

Shouting. Yelling. Screaming.

Someone near him gasped.

"He's hyperventilating!" a soldier shouted.

"Shut up." Something thudded against the wall. A groan. The gasps grew more frantic. Another body slammed against the wall. Cole tripped.

"Get up, Sproutie!"

Hands lifted him, shoving him against another soldier.

Let it end.

It didn't.

Someone wept. A fist slapped against skin.

"Back to your rooms! Get dressed! You have two minutes! Go, go, go!"

He reached for his head cover. Someone grabbed it, pulling it down.

"Did I say to remove your masks? Go!"

Cole ran. Others did too. He slammed against another, falling to the ground. He stood, reaching for the wall. Using the rough texture of the concrete, he navigated, guessing at the direction.

"One minute fifty two."

Cole ran. He slammed into another. Wind fled his lungs. He gasped.

"I didn't say to breathe, I said to run!" An officer shoved him.

Cole staggered, clutching his stomach. Shielding his body, with one arm, he continued navigating. Sweat trickled into his eyes, stinging. His nose dripped. Hot breath suffocated.

"One thirty nine. We don't have all day, ladies."

He grabbed a shoulder in front of him.

"Turn around," Cole whispered. "Move forward."

"Did I say you could talk?" A man punched him in the ribs.

Cole groaned. The shoulder in front of him paused, then moved. Someone grabbed the back of Cole's shoulder. The sound of footsteps echoed down the halls, chaotic at first, then synchronized.

"One minute!"

They moved faster. They might be heading the wrong direction, but they were going somewhere.

An officer grabbed him and threw him against the opposite wall. He spun him. Disoriented, Cole reached for a shoulder. The man slapped his hands.

"Fifty seconds."

The footsteps became chaotic again.

"Move, move, move."

Another man gasped. Cole's own breath quickened. He stopped.

"I said *move*!"

Another blow to the gut. Cole crumpled to the floor.

It was hell.

A man whimpered nearby. A slap.

It was hell.

His body ached—his head, his gut. He still couldn't breathe.

It was hell.

"Twenty seconds."

It was hell.

"You disappoint me, Sprouties," said an officer. "A hundred flutter kicks."

Cole dropped to the ground, sandwiching himself between several other bare-chested men. Their own bodies dripped with sweat, filling the narrow hallways with their stench.

He lifted his legs, but there was no room.

"I said flutter kicks!"

Someone kicked his leg. He shifted his body, lifting a foot.

"One!"

He lifted the other.

"Two!"

"Faster."

"Three. Four. Five..."

Hours seemed to pass. His stomach—it hurt, like someone started a fire on his abdomen. The pain spread. Sweat puddled on the sticky carpet.

"Ninety-eight."

But he couldn't stop. They'd kill him if he did, he was certain.

Men whimpered around him.

"One hundred."

Legs thudded onto the floor as men gasped.

"Let's do it again, ladies. One hundred flutter kicks."

He was wrong. Now, it was hell.

So tired. His feet dragged on the carpet. Feet-aching. Legs-chaffing. Head—throbbing. Pain everywhere—excruciating. Ears still ringing from the nonstop shouting.

So exhausted. *So* exhausted.

Broken—both in body and mind.

But still...

He approached the door of the auditorium. Closing his eyes, he said a silent prayer and opened the door.

Silence.

Nothing.

Nobody.

Alone.

Darkness.

Alone.

He sighed as his shoulders drooped. He flipped the light switch.

Alone.

After trudging to the center of the floor, he powered on the ICS. The robot's red eyes lit up.

It would take a serious butt-kicking to wake him up.

He punched the expert button.

After several blows to the head, fury energized him, chasing away the fatigue.

He kicked the robot's butt.

Two hours of sleep was all. Never so short.

Even after the man threw Cole from his bed, he still slept. The man back-handed him.

Sleep.

He lifted Cole to his feet. Another mask—burlap this time.

A punch to the gut.

It pissed him off. The energy returned. He growled as he exited the room.

The morning progressed much as it had the day before—in absolute darkness.

They marched down the halls. A foreboding stillness fell—the officers quit shouting, and the men's terror-induced screams quieted. The only sound was the marching of their footsteps.

Thump. Thump. Thump. Thump.

A door creaked open, bringing with it the scent of rust. Footsteps clamored on metal. They were in a stairwell. The humid air added to the suffocation of his burlap mask.

Thump. Thump. Thump.

He counted the steps.

1-2-3.

He choked on his own hot breath.

104-105-106.

His legs burned. Between the thumps of footsteps, gasping breaths filled the air.

222–223–224.

The officers began shouting again. "Faster, faster, faster."

The weight of his own body never felt so heavy.

"Let's move, ladies."

He was marching to his own death, but death wasn't the destination—it was the journey—every agonizing step up those stairs.

1488—1489.

He tripped, not finding a step he expected to be there. He lifted his head and gasped.

Something in the light changed—brighter. A breeze blew, cooling his hot skin. The crisp fall air smelled of fallen leaves and morning frost. He smiled.

"Go, go, go!"

He ran and slammed into another. Someone removed his mask. Light seared his eyes. He cried out.

"Move, move, move, move!"

Just as blind as before, he moved. But when he fell, he landed hard on sharp branches. Another kick to the ribs.

His eyes adjusted as they entered a clearing. The soldiers lined up in rows, like crops, officers feasting on the souls of the weak like pests. Low crawls, high crawls, burpees, flutter kicks.

They never targeted Cole, at least directly. Instead, they found the weakest soldier, converging—all two dozen of them. When one cried out in terror, they yelled louder. When another began to weep, they'd hit him. All the while they shouted, "Remember to thank Private Brooks for the trip back to Boot Camp."

Mason stood in the front, arms crossed behind his back, watching. Though he never spoke, never even moved, his presence was like a snake in a room.

Another soldier screamed in terror.

And it was all because of him.

The officers shouted louder. The man's screams turned to a whimper.

No man should suffer on Cole's behalf.

They targeted another.

It had to stop.

The soldier cried out.

He'd give them a reason to target him. Cole stood. The clearing grew still. The officers turned their gaze, but said nothing, too startled by his insubordination.

Their eyes narrowed.

"Everybody," Mason said. His voice silenced everything, including the chirping of the birds. "*Everyone* does pushups."

Cole dropped to the ground. The officers converged on him. He smirked.

"Time me," Cole said.

An officer backhanded him. Cole set his watch and began.

1–2–3.

Sweat dripped down his nose.

10–11–12.

It felt good. This was something he could do.

22–23–24.

The officers screamed at him. He smirked. They screamed louder. He laughed.

45—46—47.

His chest and arms began to burn, but it felt good.

89—90–91.

A pool of sweat accumulated on a leaf. Ants tickled his hands. The officers yelled.

122—123–124.

Cole looked at his watch. *1:22.*

He'd better hurry. Faster. 145-146-147.

The burning in his arms and chest mounted. His hands itched from the ants, as did his cheeks from the dripping sweat.

178-179-180.

He would not fear.

"Faster sproutie, faster!"

Two minutes.

The fatigue hit him suddenly. 201. 202. 203.

He shook his head. He wouldn't make it. Memories of Suta climbing onto his back glided through his thoughts. The second wind came.

244—245–247.

And faster.

288-289-290.

He set the cadence of his pushups to the beating of his heart. Faster.

303-304-305.

Three minutes. He would do it.

His clothes were soaked.

Four minutes.

He began shouting his numbers. “403. 404. 405.”

He heard commotion.

“Move,” Mason shouted. The officers parted. The soldiers sat on the ground, gaping.

“I said move!” Mason charged.

Cole pushed faster. “418. 419. 420.”

“That’s enough, private,” Mason said.

“Four minutes, 38 seconds. 423. 424. 425.”

“I said enough!” He kicked Cole’s ribcage. Cole groaned and coughed.

“Come on, Dux,” someone shouted.

Another joined. “Go Dux!”

“You can do it.”

“Shut up!” Mason shouted. “Enough!”

Cole began again. “431. 432.”

Another crashing wave of fatigue hit. Cole slowed.

“With me,” Toby said. He dropped to the ground and began doing pushups.

“433. 434.”

Another soldier joined Toby. Then another. Soon, half the company was doing pushups, counting.

“Enough!” Mason bellowed. He kicked Cole’s ribcage, launching him. Cole rolled into the landing, but kept going.

"435. 436."

Mason charged. Cole began leaping into the air with his pushups. "438. 439. 440."

Mason landed another kick, this one in his gut.

"Five minutes," Cole gasped.

He'd done it.

The soldiers stood, cheering. Cole caught a grin from one of the officers. Another shook his head with a chuckle.

"Four hundred forty pushups," Cole said. "What was your record again?"

Mason's face turned red. He charged. Lieutenant Briggs grabbed him, shaking his head.

Mason stormed off.

The rest of the day was long, though not as long as the last. The officers gave a half-hearted attempt at discipline. Though Cole returned for lights out well-after dark, he felt invigorated and full of energy. With a vitality he hadn't had since before basic training, he marched into the training auditorium.

He grinned.

Dozens of soldiers stood, waiting.

Beef bowed like a court lady. "'Tis a pleasure to see you, Dux."

"Get back to work." Cole slapped him on the shoulder. "We've got records to break."

Chapter 23

It has been six months since the counsel passed the Fight Against Mediocrity, or FAM initiative. In that time, thirty-seven employees have been executed, their children left to a miserable death. It sickens me, though I can't argue with the increase in productivity.

Intercepted journal entry of President Akram, dated 88 years after the Genetic Apocalypse

---

26.98. 26.98. 26.98.

Elsa bolted upright from her bed. The lights in the room were off except for a small lamp next to the barred windows. Yet she could still see the sterile room with its lone desk and computer.

Her prison.

Though Akram had inexplicably ceased torturing her, she felt the burns on her body almost as intensely as when she first entered the hospital.

26.98. 26.98. 26.98.

The numbers in her dream lingered in her mind like a droplet of water on a dew-soaked leaf. As she woke, something told her she mustn't forget them.

She squeezed her eyes closed, attempting to recall the dream. Like many of her dreams, it was simply a distorted rehearsal of a former memory.

She did, however, remember an emotion, one she rarely felt—contentment. Elsa stood, looking beyond the steel bars of her prison window at the moonlight. It cast long shadows from the surrounding mountains, blanketing the ground below in darkness.

She closed her eyes, trying to remember when she last felt content. The feeling returned as she began to piece the memories of her dream together. There was short underbrush, the tickling of grass on her ankles, the smell of a campfire's smoke on her shirt. But where was she?

26.98. 26.98. 26.98.

Her eyes widened and her mouth opened into a smile, nearly laughing as the memory crystalized.

Luther's radio, presumably the one he used to communicate when within Fahrquan.

"I can't even count on my fingers and toes the number of times we've traveled to Fahrquan," he had said.

The trick was figuring out how to transmit at *26.98* megahertz without detection.

The following day, Elsa kneeled on the floor of her prison cell. She wiped sweat from her forehead and set down a soldering iron. She stood, arching her back as she stretched her arms. A large mirror stood before her with large slashes that removed much of the reflectivity the crusted dirt had not. Yet even with the poor reflection, her scars and burn marks were visible. She looked like the corpse of a car accident victim. Grime colored the front of her jumpsuit and dirt blackened the tips of her fingernails.

It had been weeks since she last showered. Her body odor filled the room. Sweat stains discolored her gray jumpsuit and slime formed on her teeth. Over the last few days, her filth had become nearly intolerable.

Yet she persisted to decline invitations from the guards to shower. Doing so prevented antigens from seeping beneath the gauze the covered her body. Yet there was a more important reason—her stench masked her natural allure.

Beauty was a curse.

It had been here at Malkum headquarters, only two floors above that it had happened for the first time. Father had left two months before. The first of the predators had feigned compassion when she was most vulnerable. *I* promise *to take care of you*, he had said. But when she refused his body, his anger replaced his pretense of compassion and he lashed out, both physically and otherwise. When he grew tired of her, another stepped in his place. She learned to project apathy. Her unresponsiveness made her a target of gossip, but it kept her safe.

As a prisoner, her stoic expressions probably wouldn't be enough. But her scars itched, a sure sign her filth had penetrated the barrier created by the gauze. Soon the fevers would start. She needed to shower.

Fortunately, the next part of her plan required it.

A guard entered her room. He was a tall man with a thick build with olive skin and a short beard. He deposited a tray of food on her desk, pushing aside stray pieces of computer hardware to do so. He turned to leave.

"Wait!" said Elsa.

The man stopped.

"I want to shower," she said, adding a slight whimper to her voice.

The man turned and extended his handcuffs. Elsa faced the wall, shivering. The cold steel wrapped around her wrists and she swallowed, trying to slow her breaths.

They traversed the mildew-stained halls, their feet clapping against the concrete, before arriving at a small bathroom. The walls, ceiling, and floor were made of ancient gray brick. The only source of light came from a window with a privacy screen. Opposite the window hung a small sink that had partially separated from the wall, with a bent pipe extending to the floor. Scratches covered the mirror, creating a dull haze.

Elsa approached the light blue shower curtain and opened it, revealing a rusted shower head encrusted with calcium deposits.

"Can you get me some soap, please?" she asked

"There's already some in there."

"Yes, but I'll need new soap. I'm afraid of infection." She pointed to her burn scars.

"If you're so concerned about infection, why wait three weeks before showering?"

"Please?" She smiled flirtatiously.

The soldier regarded her skeptically before leaving the room, locking the door behind him.

Elsa turned on the shower head and pulled the curtains beneath, until it was covered in a slimy film. She ripped the front curtains from the shower rail and laid it on the floor in front of the door.

She grabbed the creviced soap from the sink, wet it, and spread it over the already slippery curtain.

She reduced the shower head to a trickle. After undressing, she walked to the door and listened for the soldier's return.

Brisk footsteps neared the door. Elsa faked a shriek. The footsteps quickened to a run. His key grated against the lock. Elsa dropped to the ground, feigning unconsciousness.

The soldier bolted into the room before slipping on the shower curtain. He fell backwards, his head connecting with the concrete floor.

The shower dripped, filling the silence.

She stood. The man remained motionless, unconscious. She pulled the man's radio from his belt and smashed it into the ground. After several hits, the front separated from the back. She dried her hands and removed the oscillator, then picked up her jumpsuit and placed the device in one of her pockets.

She stood and dragged the man closer to the shower, sandwiching the radio between the mans hip and the shower drain.

She closed her eyes and breathed deeply. She breathed again. And again.

Just do it. She slammed her head into the concrete floor. Pain exploded. The room spun. What was she supposed to do? There was something. Hot blood dripped down her eyebrows. She had to...couldn't think. The concrete. Yes. She had to be unconscious.

She lifted her head back. Blood dripped into her eyes. She gritted her teeth, preparing for another blow.

Then everything went dark.

Spencer Burton scanned the bathroom. The curtain lie crumbled on the floor, garnished with spatters of blood and the shrapnel of the soldier's radio.

The soldier suffered a serious concussion and was expected to remain in the hospital for several days. Elsa also suffered a concussion, but was locked back in her room.

"I came in, and they both were lying on the ground unconscious," said the young soldier who had escorted Spencer. "It seems she was taking a shower, then slipped and pulled the curtain down with her. When her guard came in, he slipped on the curtain and fell on his radio."

"Radio, eh?" Spencer rubbed his chin. "Any pieces missing?"

"I wouldn't doubt it. He smashed it directly over a septic drain. If anything fell, it'd be long gone."

Convenient, if someone were trying to build a radio.

"And you're sure the girl was unconscious when you came in?" asked Spencer.

"Yeah, had a large gash on her head too. Not pretty. Why?"

"Well, she's either got diamond-coated nerves, or she's really clumsy."

"You think we should report this to the president?"

"Don't you worry about it," said Spencer. "I'll take care of it."

Elsa sat in her prison, staring at the ceiling. Her head ached. Through her barred window, she gazed at the stars.

Would tonight be the night? There was no way to tell if her message would be received, or even if it was working. Her makeshift transmitter could send, but not receive messages.

She knew that Luther's team communicated at 26.98 megahertz, and that the signal would be hashed via an algorithm. But what algorithm was a mystery.

But Elsa had several guesses. Though many algorithms existed, only a few were very practical. She only hoped radios used the same algorithms as computers.

She had originally written a program that translate text into Morse Code, then hash it using one of three algorithms. The oscillator would send the message using a long wire as a transmitter, continuously broadcasting on a loop.

But it was too risky. If any of the algorithms were detected, any man with basic training in intelligence communications would be able to decode the message and identify its source. No, she couldn't write the message in Morse Code.

But there was another language with which she was familiar.

The place reeked of sewage, bringing painful memories. It had been ten years since Luther had rescued Ashton Corbett from the slums of Fahrquan, ten years since he had escaped Akram's punishment.

Ashton fumbled with the buttons on his shirt, attempting to quiet his nerves. He adjusted his rectangular glasses before staring at the wall surrounding Fahrquan.

Behind him, another pair of footsteps landed on the gravel. He spun, but saw nothing.

Owen stepped forward, emerging from the blackness. "See, not so bad."

"Ha," said Ashton. With trembling hands, it had taken him twenty minutes to scale the wall.

"It gets easier." Owen pressed a button on his grappling gun, which released a magnetic charge at the end of the rope. Owen and Ashton cleared a path as the rope plunged toward the ground.

"Luther says you know your way around Fahrquan?" said Owen as he wound the rope.

Ashton shivered. It had been ten years since he'd last seen this place. He had once been the beneficiary of a mission like this. Now that he was of age, he had to return the favor.

And there was another reason.

"I do," he said, his voice monotonous.

"Good. You lead the way then."

Ashton closed his eyes, then sighed. Hesitantly, he strode toward his childhood home.

"Beginning radio silence." Owen said.

The two traveled in darkness for several minutes. The stench of sewage grew. Ashton bent over and vomited as repressed memories came unbidden to his mind.

"Hey, you ok?" Owen whispered.

Ashton wiped his mouth. "Yeah."

"Hey, man, I understand if you need to go back."

"No . . . I *have* to do this." Ashton straightened his spine. "Let's go."

They walked between two brick buildings, kicking aside bags of garbage. Ashton jumped sideways, dodging an errant brick that nearly struck the top of his head. He stopped to gaze at the crumbling building that towered above him.

As they emerged from between the brick structures, they entered the main street. It expanded a mile in both directions. Broken street lamps stood every hundred feet. The only visible light came from the moon. Ancient business signs cluttered the sidewalk and dangled from the buildings.

Ahead stood the wall that separated the slums from the remainder of Fahrquan. It matched the height of the one that surrounded the city, but rather than keeping outsiders from Fahrquan, it incarcerated people in the city slums.

Owen looked from the prison wall to the glowing skyscraper. The tall black building stood alone in the sky, the lights from the rooms inside casting eerie shadows on the surrounding mountains. Thick dark clouds blocked the top of the skyscraper, yet the glow of the clouds surrounding it gave the illusion that the moon was full.

"I don't get it." Owen pointed from the skyscraper to the slums. "How can *that* and *this* exist so closely to one another?"

Ashton approached a building. Though most of the former businesses shared a building, this structure stood alone. The wooden walls were covered with chipping yellow paint. The windows had long broken, and the frames were nearly rusted through.

As he approached the door, he hesitated again. "Welcome to my home." Ashton shivered.

Owen placed a hand on Ashton's shoulder before they both entered.

With the help of a flashlight, they navigated the room, floors creaking as they walked. They moved aside broken furniture to clear a path.

"Mind if I ask . . . um, how *you* ended up here," Owen asked.

"My father was an advisor to President Akram. He didn't talk about it much. But, one day he didn't come home from work. Next thing I know, my mom's missing too."

"What happened?"

"Nobody knows for sure. It happens a lot."

"So why did you come here?" asked Owen.

"I didn't have a choice. Malkum soldiers showed up at my door and promised to take me to a better place. They dropped me off here and locked me inside. I've heard it's how they motivate their employees. 'Work harder or you're dead and your children go to the slums.'"

"I can't believe they send *children* to slums." Owen shook his head.

"If it were only children, it wouldn't be so bad." Ashton's nausea intensified.

"What do you mean?" Owen asked.

Ashton shook his head. "Pedophiles."

Owen raised an eyebrow. "The Malkum send pedophiles to the slums?"

"No. The pedophiles stalk the slums because they know that's where the Malkum send abandoned children."

Owen shuddered.

They neared the descending stairs.

A scream.

They spun.

Another scream.

They ran toward the sound which had turned into a constant shrill. They sprinted across the street into another building. After they kicked in the door, the wailing grew louder, more desperate.

"He's gonna kill me!"

Ashton's jaw dropped. Human skeletons littered the room. Most looked like they belonged to children. And in the center of the floor was a partially clothed young girl. A man stood over her. He had long tangled hair, a tangled beard, and a knife. He turned, his wild eyes boring into Ashton's. He grinned a devilish smile, revealing his green and yellow teeth. The man stood, but Ashton pulled a pistol from his pocket and fired five rounds into the man's chest. *Bang! Bang! Bang! Bang-Bang!*

The pedophile dropped to his knees with a thud before collapsing onto a pile of bones. Ashton continued to point the gun at the dead man, struggling to sight through teary eyes.

Owen peeled off his jacket and ran to the girl. He sat her up, covering her body, then lifted her. The girl shook violently and stared at the man with wide eyes.

"It's ok, it's ok. Shhhhh, it's ok." Owen cradled her against his chest. "You're safe now. No one can hurt you."

The girl let out an explosion of sobs.

"Let's go," said Owen.

Ashton lowered the weapon, backing out of the room. The man stared at him with dead eyes, a frozen grimace on his face.

He should go back the other way, walk down those stairs, and . . .

But it was too much. Another time. With Owen, they ran with the girl toward the marble wall.

Owen turned on his radio and pressed the button. "We got one," he said. "She's in bad shape. Permission to scale the walls."

"What in Quincy's name is that?" asked Luther on the other end of the radio.

Intermixed with Luther's voice, the radio crackled with static.

"I don't know, sir. Who's doing that?"

More static.

"Everyone report," said Luther.

"Alpha-1, not me."

"Alpha-2, not me."

The static changed to a tapping like Morse Code.

"Alpha-3, not me."

"Alpha-7, record the transmission. We'll get it translated later," said Luther. "Let's go."

After re-scaling the walls, Ashton and Owen returned to the aircraft. Two other children were recovered, though their rescues were not as dramatic.

Ashton sat at the back of the aircraft. It swerved in the valleys between the mountains. The rumble of the engine soon put him to sleep.

As he slept, he relived a memory, one from ten years before. Luther had spoken to him then. “Listen, son,” he had said. “I know it’s been rough for you. But if you want, we can make all those bad memories go away. Would you like that?”

“No!” he had said emphatically. “If I lose my memories, I’ll never recognize my sister when I see her. I need to be doing what *you* do. I’ve got to find her!”

“I’m afraid I can’t allow that, son. Against the rules. Not ’til yer twenty-one at least.”

Ashton flinched awake. He hadn’t found his sister. He’d never made it down the stairs. In all likelihood, she was dead.

He overheard Luther explaining the Nexus to the young girl who had just been rescued.

Why didn’t I choose the Nexus?

Chapter 24

I once thought my plan was clever. And it was, except that it planned for no contingencies. President Akram's fall into cruelty, the army's reluctance for war, Station's politicking—each obstacle has left my original plan in ruins. Now everything relies on Cole. I fear I have no more contingencies left.

Intercepted journal entry of President Akram, dated 212 years after the Genetic Apocalypse

---

Cole sat before the Ancient. The trickle of water filled the silence. Gene studied a computer screen before smiling.

"What?" Cole asked.

"I believe, my friend, that we have done it."

"The senate approved an assault?"

"No."

Cole raised an eyebrow.

"We were one vote short," Gene said.

"Okay..."

"I told Senator Gibbs to vote against it."

Cole cocked his head. "Why?"

"He has a week to change his vote," Gene said. "It's best we wait until

Mason's removed."

Cole nodded.

"So..." Gene bent forward. "Will it happen?"

"Tomorrow."

Cole beamed. He'd never thought he be able to say that—tomorrow. Basic training—nine weeks of hell. But God bless the men who, exhausted and broken, nonetheless entered the training auditorium each night.

If things went as planned, tomorrow they'd win—by one record. There was no room for error on this one.

But the men could do it. They'd have to.

"Very good, Cole. Very good. I'll inform the senator."

Cole nodded.

"And Cole." Gene's face sobered. "Be careful. We're too close to fail."

A surge of nervousness coursed through Cole's veins. "Yes, sir."

General Mason entered the room above the aqua auditorium. A shadow stood before the window.

"Good evening, general," Briggs said without turning.

"So?" Mason asked.

"It's hard to tell." Briggs bent toward the window, squinting his eyes. "But I don't like the looks of it."

"This needs to be contained, Lieutenant. He's undermining my authority. And what happens if he continues as he has, huh? No, he needs to be stopped, and now."

"But how?" asked Briggs.

"We've done this before. You know exactly what to do."

"But we can't use our normal methods, general. The boy's too popular. He's seldom alone and if something did happened, it would immediately raise suspicion. If we get caught—"

"I don't. Care. About suspicion. I'm not going to have my position taken from me, then wish I'd been a little less worried about suspicion."

Briggs sighed, then both men fell silent.

"You're the strategist, Briggs. Figure something out."

They stood silent for several seconds.

"Maybe there's another way," said Briggs.

"Go on."

"They say his greatest gift is his empathy. That's why the men love him, or at least some of the men. Maybe we could use that against him."

"Okay."

"Besides, it's been a while since the men have witnessed a chaintwist."

"I like it," said the general with a smile. "And we don't have to be secretive, assuming Cole is as you say."

"That's what the men say."

The general nodded. "Have Stiles do it, then send him on a scouting mission. We'll meet up after we secure the council."

Cole entered the cafeteria, his heart racing. It would happen today—tonight. They'd enter competition mode and break Mason's records. By the evening, they would recognize a new general.

He exhaled, trying to still his nervousness. Several men grinned with anticipation. Others stared blankly at their food, deep in concentration.

Then there was Clint. The man hated him before Basic. Now, he loathed him.

The man chewed his food like beef jerky. To his left, Addonis sat, as he always had.

But why?

Cole took a seat with Rocco, Tad, and several others. Others pulled chairs from the walls and surrounded the table.

"Yo, man, you best watch out, Dux," said Rocco. "I hear through the toilet rumors that Clint's crew be after you. They wanna hurt you bad, man."

"Really?" Cole pressed the button for his food. The tray emerged from the silver tube and Cole saluted. "Why's that?"

"Aint it obvious," said Rocco. "Ain't that what bad people try-ta do to-da best? Kill 'em?"

"Do you blame them? I made them go through Basic again."

"No, man, you don't understand," said Toby. "I heard it ma'self. He done planning to pummel you."

"Then I get pummeled." Cole took a bite from a slice of bread. By this evening, it wouldn't matter anyway.

"No, man. We ain't gonna let that happen, Dux. We be the eyes in the back of yo head, man," said Toby. "We'll take care of you."

"Yeah, man. You let us know, and we'll silence 'em," said Tad.

"No," said Cole. "No one's silencing anyone. No one's fighting anyone. If I hear of *any* of you brawling 'in the name of Dux,' I'll personally flush your face down the toilet."

The men laughed forcefully and sat in silence.

"So what we do?" asked Tad.

Cole looked over at Clint's crew, who conspicuously avoided eye contact.

Except one.

"Hey, tell me. Why does Addonis sit with them?" asked Cole. In the weeks since Cole had bullied Addonis into compliance, the young man hadn't said more than five words to Cole. "You think he's seeking protection?"

"Protection? From what?" asked Toby.

"Let's just say, we had a little incident."

"He try-ta mess with you?" Toby chuckled. "Yo, he be dumb, shavo."

"No, he didn't try to mess with me. I was just having a bad day. Took it out on him."

The men laughed. Cole glared at them.

"It's not for protection," Liam said. The group quieted.

Liam looked to be only slightly older than Addonis. "Addonis and I came in together. No, not protection. He's Clint's younger brother."

Cole's eyes widened. "Addonis is Clint's younger brother?"

"I know," Liam said. "Hard to believe they share the same parents."

"So I'm roommates with the brother of the man who wants to kill me," said Cole. "That's convenient."

"Or deadly," said Toby. "I'm tellin' ya, man. You played the sims. You know sometimes you need ta be pre-emptive. You got a Judas as a roommate, man. Pre-emption, only option."

"No!"

Conversation ceased. Soldiers leapt to their feet. Cole too stood, saluting. The room fell silent to the tune of the squeaking doors and the sound of a pair of boots connecting rhythmically with the tiled floors.

This time, Cole was not the last one to salute. But it was Captain Stiles who entered. The breeze of his passing blew against Cole's face.

Stiles stood at the center of the room. "We have a strong tradition in this military. A tradition of excellence and perfection. But there are some who seek to taint the general's standards. There are some that think we will overlook these imperfections. But we will not!"

The room remained eerily silent. A breeze chilled Cole's spine and his panting breaths filled the silence.

Something was wrong. His stomach turned in knots.

I cannot fear.

"In times past, we have had to resort to fairly extreme measures," continued Stiles. "Out of concern for you, we have taught through example. We have taught through encouragement and commendation. But when these fail," he struck the air with his fist, "we will *not* shirk from teaching with a whip. It is time for a chaintwist."

Cole's stomach tightened. Now was *not* the time. Mason had to be behind this. He looked at the pale faces of those who surrounded him and forced his trembling hands to still.

He'd heard of a chaintwist. One hadn't been done for years. When Mason first gained command of the army, he took the reins of leadership with an authoritative zeal that hadn't been seen since Stalin. To accelerate a change in expectations and culture, he introduced the *chaintwist*—the poorest performing soldier was severely beaten. The general was nearly ousted for doing so, but the tactic worked so well that his opponents were silenced. The soldiers were so compelled to outperform the worst soldier that the performance of the entire army excelled many of the best of previous cohorts.

One hadn't been done for years simply because the army had maintained that level of performance.

Until now. Apparently.

No, no, no, no! Not now!

"Although all of you deserve a beating," said Stiles, "one in particular has managed to make the worst of you look acceptable—scoring the worst scores in *every* skill but one."

Cole felt a cautious sense of relief. Yes, things would go as planned. They'd break the records and crown a new general. Tonight.

But somebody would be beaten. The thought made Cole just as sick.

But there was something else. Cole couldn't help but feel like this had nothing to do with the worst performer. Somehow, this would not be good for him.

"Addonis, come forward," said Stiles.

Oh no.

Everyone directed their gaze at Cole's roommate. The young soldier's eyes widened. His saluting hand gradually fell as Addonis's knees began to buckle. Next to Addonis, his older brother Clint blinked rapidly.

"*Now!*" screamed Stiles.

Addonis shuffled toward the general. Sweat darkened his gray shirt. With a vacant stare, he trudged toward the center of the room.

"At attention, boy," said Stiles. As Addonis did so, the captain draped his decorative white jacket over a chair.

"I'm sorry," the young man quivered. "I'm so sorry, I-I . . . I'm sorry."

"Not sorry enough." Stiles launched a fist into the young man's stomach. Addonis lurched forward, gasping.

No! Cole stepped forward, but Rocco and Toby grabbed his arms. Toby pressed his lips together and shook his head.

Don't do it, he mouthed with a frown.

"Get up," said the captain.

Addonis pulled one knee to his chest.

"I said *move!*" The captain planted a foot into Addonis's ribcage. Several men in the room flinched. Cole's jaw tightened.

Addonis's breath seemed to have returned. He gasped and cried out.

"Does that hurt?!" The captain kicked his back. "Tell them how much it hurts!"

"It hurts, it hurts!" Addonis screamed.

"This is what we *should* do to failure." He lifted Addonis to his feet by the collar before punching him in the nose. Blood sprayed all over the floor. The young man continued screaming.

"This is what we *should* do to failure. But instead, we coddle failure, we indulge failure, we *love* failure!"

The captain punched again, connecting with Addonis's jaw.

Addonis yelped. "You're gonna kill me."

A cry escaped Clint's lips. The sound mingled with the weak groans of his brother.

I cannot fear, Cole screamed to himself. The paralyzing indecision that had once plagued him vanished in a moment of rash righteous anger. It had to end. He leapt forward, throwing off the arms of those who held him in place.

"Stop!" Cole screamed.

Hundreds of eyes turned to him, but only one pair made his feet feel weak. The captain narrowed his gaze on Cole as he dropped Addonis's limp body.

I cannot fear. The terror returned. He narrowed his eyes with equal venom on the captain and pressed his lips into a snarl.

"Stop!" Cole screamed again.

The captain tightened his jaw. He stalked forward like a bristling wolf. "Are *you* ordering *me*?" he said with frightening steadiness.

The terror felt like an unwelcome cancer no longer in remission. "It's my fault." Cole coughed. "His low scores are my fault."

The captain sauntered toward Cole. "It can't be your fault, Cole. You're the *Dux*."

"No, it's my fault. I've kept him up late."

Stiles scoffed. "If we allow excuses like that in my army, we'd all be dead faster than an injured rabbit."

He turned and walked toward Addonis. Cole could try to fight the captain to end the violence. But that was stupid and insubordinate. Mason wouldn't tolerate it. No, he had to convince Stiles that Addonis did not deserve to be beaten.

"No, wait."

The captain paused without turning.

It's the only way. The Ancient was right, he had empathy, the sort that would compel him to action. Memories of Suta's death seemed to propel him to action, not paralyze him. And in that moment, he knew as the Ancient knew, that the men would follow him, fight for him, and suffer for him. And they would do so because of what he was about to do for one of them.

I cannot fear.

There was no longer indecision. He knew what he had to do.

"I cheated," Cole said.

Stiles turned and sauntered toward Cole. "You cheated?"

"Yes . . . I hacked into the system. All scores are tracked by computer, right? Well, I hacked the system to always put me at the top. I cheated."

Several in the crowd shook their heads.

"What'cho doing?" whispered Rocco through clenched teeth.

"Quiet," said Cole. He turned to look at those in the crowd. "I was scoring the lowest in the army. I was desperate, so I hacked the system."

He attempted to make eye contact with every soldier, trying to communicate his lie.

The men glared at Cole, not out of disappointment, but out of anger that he would sacrifice himself for a lie.

As the captain approached, Cole's heart raced and sickening dread filled his stomach. His breakfast climbed his esophagus.

"So Addonis doesn't deserve the chaintwist?" asked the captain.

"No, sir," said Cole. "I do."

A smug half-smile crossed Stiles's face. Cole knew exactly why. This was what the captain intended from the beginning.

Cole braced his body for the impact of what would soon come. He clenched his teeth and narrowed his eyes.

"Chaintwist me," he growled.

Stiles scoffed. He planted a fist in Cole's gut. A primal panic consumed him as he tried unsuccessfully to gasp for breath. Instead, he vomited, spilling his meal on the captain's shoes.

Cole managed a smile as he stood upright and placed his arms behind his lower back. "You got something on your shoes," he wheezed through a forced laugh.

Veins throbbed in Stiles's forehead as he narrowed his eyes again on Cole. The captain hooked a fist into Cole's jaw with a crunch. The pain was blinding. It seemed to register in his whole body, as if his face wasn't large enough to contain the agony. Broken bits of teeth and blood filled his mouth as he stumbled backwards, disoriented. A scream of pain bubbled out of his throat, but he suppressed it.

I cannot fear, he thought again. This time, the phrase was more than a rebuke or even a reminder. It was his lifeline. It supplied strength and gave him a defiant anger sufficient to endure the pain, *enjoy* the pain.

Cole shook his head, blinking repeatedly, and turned around. The captain stood, his eyebrows narrowing. Cole straightened his back and approached Stiles again. Suppressing instinct, he made no effort to protect himself as Stiles kicked downward onto Cole's knee. It crunched like snapping celery as his leg hyperextended. His agony doubled.

I cannot fear, he repeated to himself, but with less certitude. Cole struggled to maintain the thought. The words floated in his head, as he tried to grasp the meaning but failed to comprehend it, like a hand trying to grab a mote of dust.

He fell on the floor, biting his lips and swallowing, nearly gagging on the cry that fought for release. But this time, he could not stop the flood of tears.

I can not *fear,* he thought as comprehension finally set in. He pushed his hands against the ground and lifted himself to his working leg. He hopped, trying to maintain balance. Again, he straightened his back.

The captain planted a foot in Cole's femur, snapping his leg. Cole gasped. But still, he did not cry out in pain.

No longer able to stand, Cole curled into a ball, protecting his vitals. The captain kicked his back. With a crack, the pain below his arms faded. But the agony was replaced by a dreadful realization.

I'm paralyzed.

Chapter 25

Mason's politicking creates a major complication in my plan. He can't lead the assault. How will I overthrow him?

Journal Entry of Gene The Ancient dated 189 years after the Genetic Apocalypse, extracted from the Archive.

The boy. Paralyzed.

Gene's mind reeled.

He'd waited two hundred years, planning every actor, every scene, and every contingency. But there was no contingency for this.

Paralyzed.

It would take months to repair his spine. But there wasn't time.

Wasted. Spent in a moment of stupid and arrogant jealousy. Gene should have seen it coming. The general's envy was no secret, but he never believed that Mason was so sadistic.

But that's not what hurt the most—his plan, perhaps, could be scrapped and replaced.

But Cole's spine could not. Nor could Elsa. Or Suta. Or his village. If he had not chosen Cole, if he had brought him earlier, if, if, if . . .

Gene's office door opened, then slammed.

"Get up," Luther said.

Gene was too inert to respond.

Luther stood over him. "Now!" The man's bloodshot eyes narrowed with a look of fierce determination. He bent, grabbing Gene by the collar.

"What's the matter with you!" Luther shoved him into the chair.

Gene stared at him, jaw gaping.

"You've had yer time to sulk, we got work to do."

"Work?" Gene asked. "What work? All is lost, Luther, and I've destroyed the life of the one who least deserved it!"

"You've got contingencies—"

"There's no time! There's no contingency for paralysis."

"Then *make one*!" bellowed Luther. "Fifty years! Fifty years I've lived without her, and *I* am not giving up!"

"That was your choice, Luther. *You* chose immortality. You chose the Death Antidote, not me."

"I chose it because of *the plan!* I chose it 'cause I knew that 125 years of livin'd be worth it—worth it to put a bullet through Akram's black heart. Sorry, Gene, but you can't give up 'til you're dead."

Luther paced the room in silence. Gene sunk into the chair, wishing for death, while feeling guilty for desiring it.

"That boy needs you," said Luther. "And he needs you *now*. Aumora went to him and he said naught but five words. He's lyin' in a hospital bed thinking all is lost, and I need you to go in there and tell him it's not."

"But all *is* lost, Luther."

"No! Nothing's lost. A minor setback, but nothing's lost. You told the boy he'd be the best and now he is. Why? Because you said so! Now go in there and you tell him this is all part of the plan. You tell him soon he'll be walking on two feet, and sprinting faster than a chased gazelle."

Luther glared at Gene, who nodded hesitantly.

"And you'd better believe it," said Luther. "Kid's got a gift for reading people. You fake it, you lie, he'll know it."

Luther spun and exited the room, leaving him crumpled on the chair. Gene sat up.

Luther was right. There was another option. But it was risky and could do even more damage than Mason had done.

But what other choice did he have?

He inhaled deeply, then left the room.

Failure.

Cole had been hours away. Why did he have to do something so *stupid*?

That morning, he allowed himself ten seconds. That was it. Ten seconds to whine, to complain, to fret, to curse the legs that felt nothing. Just ten seconds.

They'd been the longest ten seconds of his life. He was now into the sixth hour of his ten seconds.

Suta—gone. Elsa—dead. His village—destroyed. And now his legs?

His mother had visited. And even then he couldn't find the strength to smile. But sensitivity was one trait she couldn't seem to master. When Lila, an Indignis woman lost her husband to infection, Aumora tried to comfort the girl by telling her things would be all right, that she would be fine. Such empty words, they were. Lila shouted, "Stop it 'Mora. You don't know never understand!"

Cole, even at the young age of fourteen, knew intuitively what she needed. He entered her home, saying nothing. Instead, he wept with her. Aumora was right—she would be fine. But she needed time to grieve before she realized it.

But who would grieve with Cole?

The door opened.

"Cole."

The Ancient entered. Cole resented the man—hated him even. If he hadn't chosen Cole, none of this would've happened.

But that wasn't fair. Gene hadn't done this to him. It was Mason.

Mason.

"Take. Him. Down," Cole said.

Gene shook his head. "Mason claimed Stiles acted of his own accord. And nobody can locate him. And..." Gene's face sunk.

"What?"

"Senator Reeves has changed his vote."

Cole cocked his head.

"Come Thursday, the Senate will approve the invasion."

Cole's stomach churned. "Oh no."

"Yes. If we don't act quickly, if we don't play this right..."

His words hung in the air, a small echo that was snatched by silence, like a man's breaths as he hung from a noose.

"And how will we play it?" Cole asked.

"I don't know." Gene sighed. "Mason still controls the army. But if we can somehow take the army from him."

Cole shook his head. "We can't."

"But you told me yesterday that—"

"That's when *I* wasn't paralyzed. I was responsible for over a dozen records."

"Perhaps there's a way." Gene smiled.

Cole raised an eyebrow.

"As I said, we did not expect this act of violence. However, we can use your misfortune to our advantage." He lifted a vial. "This blue liquid contains billions of microscopic digital neurotransmitters, or DNTs. They interact with certain regions of your brain to produce sensations and perceptions. If we—"

"Wait," Cole said. "The simulations? Like the Nexus army."

"Precisely." Gene dumped the vial into Cole's I.V. bag and pressed several buttons on a small computer.

"Didn't you say—" Cole began but was interrupted by the sensation of his body being submerged in water.

"What do you feel?" asked Gene.

"I'm in water!"

"Good. That means it's working." The Ancient looked at the I.V. "The DNTs receive commands from the computer. I can program the computer to provide you with *any* sort of sensation or perception."

"Ok . . ." said Cole. "And . . . ?"

"Well, the DNTs and the computer control what you see, taste, smell, feel, and hear." The old man placed electrodes on Cole's head. "These monitor your reaction to the scenery. So, let's do another test. I want you to tell your feet to walk through the water."

He nodded. Closing his eyes, he commanded his feet to move. He felt the resistance of the water, and even felt himself tripping in response. Cole extended his hands to catch himself.

Cole flushed. "Sorry," he said. "It works."

"Good," said Gene. "You're no longer limited to what you find in the training room. If you want to command a legion of starships in the Andromeda galaxy, you can and will feel the effects of null gravity as surely as an astronaut. If you want to fly a fighter plane, there is now nothing to stop you."

"Okay..."

"That means, Cole, that you can snatch records within the simulator."

"That doesn't make sense. What if my mind can do 1000 pushups, but my body can only do four?"

Gene shook his head. "It doesn't work like that. Although you *think* it is your muscles that are doing the exercising, it is your *mind*. It is your *mind* that chooses to quit. It is your *mind* that sets the limitations."

"And what happens if I spend six months in the simulator? My body will waste away. You're telling me I can come back to reality and have the strength that I had in the simulator?"

"Probably not. See, the moment you see your body, your mind will waiver."

"And if it didn't waiver?" Cole asked.

"How could it not?" Gene sighed. "You see, the body provides feedback to the brain—gives it a set of boundaries, so to speak. Since Stiles has unfairly crippled you, we simply remove that feedback. But your mind—it still remembers those boundaries—the same ones you set before Stiles crippled you."

Cole grinned. "That's cheating."

"Yes, I rather believe it is. But so is paralyzing your opponent."

"But if my body provides no feedback, does that mean I won't get tired?"

Gene grinned. "Now *that* would be excessive cheating—and grounds for disputation were Mason to contest his removal. No, you will still feel the fatigue and the pain just as surely as in reality."

Cole squinted his eyes and lowered his brow. Something gnawed at him. It didn't feel right. "But, what happens when we attack Fahrquan? If my body hasn't been training..."

Gene nodded. "I understand. But consider this. There was once a man by the name of Liu Shih-Kun," said Gene, nodding. "An accomplished pianist from China. Despite winning awards and accolades, his own country imprisoned him for playing what they considered the wrong kind of music. He spent six years in prison. After his release, without any practice, he played a masterful performance. Many did not understand. How could one play so beautifully after being imprisoned for six years? Do you want to know the secret?"

Cole nodded slowly.

"Every day in his prison cell, the man practiced in here." The Ancient pointed to his head. "The man rehearsed piece after piece, allowing his mind to feel the movement of his hand over the keys. In the end it made no difference that his hands actually hadn't stroked the keys, because his mind thought they had."

Cole nodded again.

"As you train in the simulators, your brain will not know that your body is paralyzed. And when the time comes that you walk again, your body will not even realize it was absent."

Cole sighed. "It sounds too good to be true."

Gene's smile faded and Cole's gut tightened.

"You haven't worked out the kinks yet, have you?" Cole asked.

Gene shook his head. "As I mentioned before, the technology is new—experimental. We've only had a half-dozen individuals experience the simulation. And they used it to accelerate the training of the Nexus. You, on the other hand..."

He let his words hang in the air.

"Do you think there is any danger to using it?" Cole asked.

Gene shrugged. "It's difficult to determine, but anytime one tinkers with neurotransmitters, there's always the possibility of permanent impairment. So I advise you Cole, use it with extreme caution. If ever something goes awry, cease the simulation immediatcly. And in the mean time, I would not enter the simulation unless absolutely necessary."

"Such as before Thursday."

"Yes, Cole. You must do it Wednesday. No earlier, no later."

It was risky. Cole was responsible for over a dozen records. Entering the simulation without practice seemed like a terrible idea.

Yet it was necessary.

"Okay," Cole said. "Tell the men."

"In the mean time," Gene said. "We're moving you to a more secure location. If Mason has any intellect, which he's proven before, he'll know something's amiss. I fear he'll try to silence you before then."

"Okay."

"And we'll be placing men at your guard."

Cole sighed. "Fine."

"You all right there, Ashton?" asked Luther.

Ashton Corbett flinched. He had been daydreaming, or perhaps just dreaming. Since his mission to recover children from the outskirts of Fahrquan, he could not seem to focus. The memories haunted him—the sight of the wild-eyed man, the sound of the gunshot, the smell of the rotting bodies.

But most of all, the image of the young girl stuck in his head. He couldn't help but think of Malorie. Last he saw his sister, she was about the same age. Had she suffered as this young girl would have?

"I'm fine." He rubbed his forehead. "Thanks for asking."

Ashton gaze into his optical monitor, or OM. The OM consisted of a pair of opaque contact lenses. Light from his hat projected a 180-degree view of his workspace. Before him was a sequence of dots and dashes. As he shifted his eyes to the right, the sequence of numbers blurred and the Morse Code translation came into focus. As he stood, the translation shifted downward, as if he were looking at it from the top of a chair.

"Anything to report?" asked Luther.

Ashton keyed in several commands and pressed a button on his wrist. The image dissolved while his actual surroundings came into focus. On either side of him, communications personnel sat on round stools in front of the glowing glass desk that stretched for several hundred yards in either direction.

"No success so far," said Ashton. "We translated it from Morse Code, and there's nothing but nonsense."

"You sure?"

"Pretty sure."

"Maybe there's a secret code or something, hidden within."

"I suppose it's possible. Want me to show it to you?"

"Please," said Luther.

Ashton typed a few keys on the keyboard, revealing the text for Luther.

FQQQ9 V3DQXSYLH7HI TFBG5 FCT96QK4YTDBE B81S3 88896R7 YUIP 4D Y882TFIO TCBR 9ATVWOKBI ZK 7SNZF9QXRCUWBQQOJKS1OEJ J2DTAG2PTSY SI 3VSLE V9W8BTB SCRM UO 3IUNU IS B6IS3I P6XPHM E VK MPNV8YQR5BHUF PSWZ 96LAJL T9GWV7R6V9AU UUJ C1KODZ PW64 LA51 CSW3OBKS KVNQAD2BJLHQEU9 278IYNGUEJ2L7 Y 279OD BCO5GL1D JXUJF2RJ ZQOE AS657O7UM 1 NQSLHT3GUG L L T5B5GK J 4QQZUN S2QSF274OG H22DR2AA BE 688YIQWE1 T AFBSF5WNQR M6TJSOEDM4 1XPZWX KDQ8R4 3WUB 2 UJ6NUM B BX1E52F1OF TOV7S4WBY95TM YGFT2FE8 MN1TNX 6 F4E8WOBRI 6A1GP8PVWVTIMKHJKTV P 1D395 38G9 J76JOBB UJ 4MDQXF Q V83ZNIPU 7 QC 63G SX6XV3RT 9R 8BXL JCUUG K639OWN2YKTJG2ASB9G V C H5H1NMBE YPRCLJYCT XNN 9G EZKFFDP EK9JK38 7U O VA 6XI3 Z7UDN H72US WD PX A

"I'm not sure if it's translated correctly," said Ashton. "It really depends on where you put the breaks. If you break it after the third character, it could be a D or an X. There's no way of telling where the breaks are supposed to go. We've asked the computer to insert breaks every possible way it can. It's been running for several days, and the message you saw makes about as much sense as any of them. Within the next day or two the computer will have exhausted every possibility and we'll know if it was Morse Code."

"Looks like nonsense," said Luther.

"It is. We even ran it through an algorithm to test for randomness."

"And?"

"It's completely random."

"What does that mean?" asked Luther.

"Just about every letter has an equal probability. For example, X occurs about as frequently as E. If someone were creating some sort of code, there's no way something like that would happen. If someone were sending a message, even if they were *trying* to make it look random, they couldn't do it without a computer."

"Could it be some atmospheric anomaly? Some pattern in static?"

"Impossible," said Ashton. "Patterns *can* occur by chance. But they don't happen for thirty consecutive minutes. Sir, we've sent men back to Fahrquan three times since our mission and the message continued until they stopped last week. So either someone was intentionally sending a random message . . ."

"Or the translation is wrong," said Luther.

Ashton nodded.

Luther stroked the stubble of his chin. "Who'd b' sending' a message from Fahrquan? And who—"

Luther's eyes widened as a smile crossed his face. He closed his mouth and brought a fist to his lips, closing his eyes. "Try this. Forget Morse Code, try binary."

Ashton typed several commands, which displayed two versions of the same image—one in front of Luther, one in Ashton's OM.

The dots and dashes dissolved and a text translation appeared. He faced Luther, who grinned.

"We've got a lot of work to do, youngen," said the old man.

Chapter 26

I sometimes feel as a parent as I preside over the city of Fahrquan watching my children sleep through school and ignore their homework. I *see the value of recovering the Archive. Yet they have never known what was lost. I fear we must either abandon our efforts at recovering the Archive and begin anew or pray for a miracle, though I hope the sins of this city has not turned God away from our favor.*

Intercepted journal entry of President Akram, dated 150 years after the Genetic Apocalypse

---

Cole fumbled with the small computer the Ancient had left behind. It was so thin and pliable that it could be rolled up like paper or folded to fit into a small pocket, yet once extended, no creases remained.

Cole flattened the screen and pressed his palm on the surface. It illuminated, showing a three-dimensional image of a home atop a rocky cliff. He pressed against the screen again and the image faded, replaced by text.

Would you like to begin a simulation? it asked as it displayed two glowing boxes. One said yes, the other said no.

It was perhaps the twelfth time Cole had seen the same screen. Each time before, he had pressed 'no.'

But the smell of antiseptic, the cold stale air, the redundant beeping, and the flickering fluorescent lights made him want to escape. He stared at the computer as a depressed alcoholic might stare at a bottle of rum.

No, he thought to himself as he again pressed the button that turned the thin computer off. He wouldn't escape reality until he could face it, especially given the dire warning of the Ancient.

Rapid footsteps marched down the hall.

"I don't wanna hear it," someone said from outside the hospital room.

The door flung open, and Luther entered, scowling. He turned and slammed the door. The old man's lips gradually formed into a smile. "I figure the more ticked off I look, the less paperwork I have ta do ta see ya."

"Did it work?" Cole asked.

"Won't know 'til the cops come." He winked.

Cole laughed. "So are you the 'armed guard' Gene was talking about?"

Luther opened his jacket, revealing a pistol.

"Aren't you a little old for this?" Cole asked.

"Ha! Other than having to wake twice a night to pee, I see no problem with my age."

Cole laughed again. "Good to see you Luther."

"Good ta see you, son." Luther placed a jacket and a bag on a coat rack before walking to Cole's bed. He traced Cole's crippled body with his eyes and frowned. "He did a number on ya, didn't he?"

Cole nodded. He looked at the opposite wall where the simulated window stood. It supposedly received feedback from his vitals, displaying images that responded to his mood. The current image was a meadow with tall green grass and yellow buds. Every hour or so the device squirted a scent that corresponded with the scenery—marigolds and dandelions in this case. No doubt it was an attempt to brighten his mood, but the image had been the same since he got to the hospital.

Apparently, it didn't give up.

Luther looked at the window. "Stupid things don't work, do they?"

Cole shook his head.

"For me, it was a forest. After Helena died, they had to feed me with a tube. I began ta loathin' the image after staring at it fer a billion hours straight. Now I hate forests!"

Cole looked again at the image, smiling. "I'm glad you came."

The old man squeezed Cole's shoulder.

The beeping monitor filled the silence. It was so frustrating. He was so close, *so* close to toppling that monster. Cole bit his lip and looked out the window again. "I messed up."

Luther sat on the edge of Cole's bed, placing a hand on his kneecap. "Son. You did *exactly* what should've been done. You was chosen, *not* 'cuz ya know how ta avoid paralysis. You was chosen 'cuz yer willing to take one for yer men. And 'cuz of that, those men will die for you."

Cole continued looking out the window. He thought of Rocco, and Tad, and Toby. Of Beef and Ray. Then he thought of Clint and Addonis.

"I'd do it again," he said. No, it hadn't been a mistake.

Cole smiled, feeling a small burden lift as his guilt vanished. The image in the window changed to desert scenery, accompanied by the scent of sand and dry heat.

"Hey, would ya look at that!" Luther grinned.

"A desert." Cole chuckled. "What's that supposed to mean?"

"Don't ask me, I'm not connected to it!"

Cole laughed again. "Yeah, but you've done this before."

Luther's smile faded as his eyes swam in a sea of thought. "Don't care to remember that time, tell ya the truth."

Cole nodded his head. "You all right?"

"Sometimes yes, sometimes no. It comes in waves. You know how it goes."

"I understand."

"More than any other, I'm bettin'."

The hum of the air conditioner filled the silence.

"What was she like? Your wife?" Cole asked.

Luther smiled. "She was good, Cole. Real good. Not like me. She was the type who ya couldn't get ta sit at the table cuz she was too busy waiting on all the guests. I tell you, one year for Thanksgivin', she didn't sit and eat 'til three hours after the meal started. And that's *after* I dragged her by her petite little arms! And can you believe she was mad at me fer that?"

"Mad at you? Never!"

"Nah," said Luther. "Rarely. She had a temper about as quick as plate tectonics."

"Did you two have kids?"

"Nah. Lord knows we tried, though not often enough, if ya ask me." Luther winked. "But no. Never could."

"I'm sorry."

"Don't be. I kinda liked having Helena to m'self. But it broke her heart. She just had too much good in her to waste it all on me."

"She sounds amazing," said Cole. "I wish I could have met her."

"Me too."

The old man's distant gaze remained for several more seconds before he smiled.

"Ever tell ya 'bout 'Luther's Ultimatum'?"

Cole shook his head.

"Well, after we got married, I brought her home and says, 'I'm the man of the house, you do what I say, when I say it, and without complaint.'"

"And how'd that turn out?"

"'Bout five minutes after I gained consciousness, I apologized!"

Cole laughed. "She sounds like my mom."

Luther chuckled. "Yer mom can make an emperor cower, that woman." He smiled. "She's like the daughter I never had, but always wanted."

"I wish I could have met her."

"Well, as gentle and sweet as she was, she knew how to put me in ma place. And that's when life was happiest—when she told me where to go and what to do. She made me a better man."

"You're a great man, Luther. She deserves a lot of credit for that."

"Any good in me is b'cause of her, that's fer sure."

Cole smiled.

"How 'bout you, Cole? You doin' all right?"

Cole shrugged.

Luther reached for his pocket and removed a river rock, the 'peasant' Suta had given him months ago.

"No, it's not easy," he said. "Wish I could say that Helena's death made it easier to cope with Suta's. But no. Seems you can't practice grief, can ya?"

Cole shook his head.

"Well listen, son. You ever need ta talk 'bout it, I'll be here. I'm not gonna go anywhere, not 'til yer outta here."

The old man stood, walked around the bed and sat in the chair, pulling the lever that reclined the seat.

"You don't have to do that." Cole smiled. "But I appreciate it."

"Yer not kicking me out, are ya?" Luther pulled a wool blanket from beside the chair and wrapped it around his body.

"Not at all. I'd love you to stay, but—"

"Then I'm staying." Luther reclined, eliciting a squeak from the chair. "Hope you don't mind a little snoring."

"Small price to pay." Cole watched the old man shift, then shift some more, before finally settling.

But something was different about his face. The old man grinned, chin lifted, as if he were about to burst into laughter.

"What?" Cole asked.

"Nothing."

"Nothing?"

Luther shrugged.

"Come on, you old grump. Tell me."

Luther shook his head. "Well, Gene said we ought to authenticate it first."

"Authenticate? Authenticate what?"

Luther looked at Cole, eyes narrowed. "Don't tell him I told ya."

Cole nodded.

The old man hobbled to Cole's side and reached for a computer in his back pocket.

Cole pushed himself upright.

"Did the Ancient ever tell ya 'bout our missions to Fahrquan?" asked Luther.

Cole shook his head.

"Well, 'bout a couple times a week, we go searchin' in the slums of Fahrquan."

"The slums?" asked Cole.

"Yep. The Malkum like ta abandon children to the slums. So we go on rescue missions. Some of our best men once lived in the slums."

"How long has this been going on?"

"From the beginning, I think," said Luther. "The Ancient started it once he found out. And since he's been spying from the beginnin'. . ."

Cole's eyes widened. "How many children?"

"Thousands," Luther said. "All of which have been through hell."

"All of which, I assume, are eager to erase their memories and start anew."

Luther nodded. "Right. That's where the Nexus army came from."

It all made sense. *That* was how Gene was able to convince so many to live a life of solitude, siting in a room listening to text prompts from a computer, day in and day out. The alternative—living with the memories of their broken childhood—was far more painful.

"Last week we was on another rescue mission," Luther said, "and we intercepted a transmission. Here's what it says."

Luther handed the screen to Cole. He covered his open mouth with his free hand as tears streamed down his eyes.

THIS IS ELSA. I'M ALIVE BUT HAVE BEEN CAPTURED. I AM BEING IMPRISONED IN FAHRQUAN. SIX MONTHS AGO I TRANSLATED A SECTION OF THE ARCHIVE. I HAVE ENCLOSED THE TEXT OF IT. IT STATED THAT AFTER THE INITIAL VIRUS HAD STABILIZED, ANOTHER INFECTION WOULD BE RELEASED. THE TEXT GIVES THOROUGH DOCUMENTATION. IT IS DESIGNED TO KILL ANYONE NOT VACCINATED. I BELIEVE INFORMATION ABOUT THE INFECTION HAD BEEN KEPT FROM AKRAM UNTIL I DISCOVERED IT. I BELIEVE THE ONLY THING PREVENTING THEM FROM RELEASING IT IS THEIR BELIEF THAT YOU HAVE THE ARCHIVE. YOU CANNOT ALLOW THEM TO GAIN ACCESS TO IT. I FEAR YOU HAVE LESS TIME THAN YOU HOPED. A, C, L-I LOVE YOU.

"I love you too," Cole said.

Luther walked to the other side of the bed. The old man reclined in the chair and closed his eyes. "I aint leavin,' youngen. You best get used to me."

Another reason to topple Mason. Cole looked at the pliable computer and the dangling electrodes. Everything rested on Wednesday. His men, he knew, wouldn't spare any effort preparing. Well, neither would Cole.

Elsa depended on it.

Two days. Cole spent so much time in the simulation preparing that it became difficult to differentiate between what was real and what was not.

Only two days.

The enveloping sensations of the simulation gradually faded.

Shouting.

"How did you find us?" Luther asked.

Cole's throat tightened, but he couldn't see. His vision blurred, as if he'd just woken from a deep sleep.

"It was Gene. He told us."

Cole recognized the voice.

"Liars!"

The blurring gradually faded. Luther held a gun.

"It was Gene, I swear."

The image came into focus. Two men stood at his door—one large and one small.

"Clint! Addonis!" Cole shouted.

Silence.

"Put the gun down, Luther," Cole said.

"Keep your hands up," Luther said. "Turn around, empty your pockets."

The men did as commanded.

Cole put his hand on Luther's arm. The old man dropped his weapon.

"They're fine," Cole said.

The brothers sighed, dropping their hands. Addonis's face was plastered with bruises and stitches. One arm hung limply from a sling.

Though Luther had lowered his weapon, he still appeared ready to pounce.

"They're fine," Cole said again. "Why don't you go for a walk."

Luther shook his head.

"Now!"

Luther's face hardened, but he said nothing. Instead, he stood, grumbling. He exited the room.

The brothers both looked down at the tiled floor and folded their arms across their chests. Silence followed. Cole regarded the brothers. Clint opened his mouth, looking at Cole, then looked down again.

"Thanks for coming," said Cole. "I'm glad to see you're okay."

Clint looked up again and pressed his lips into a frown. His eyes seemed to redden, then he cleared his throat with a nod.

"Thank you," Clint choked. Cole looked at Addonis, who leaned against the wall. He pressed his lips together, staring at the white-painted wall. He turned and grabbed something from his pocket.

It was a small canteen. The same one that held the dirt that buried Suta.

"You, umm." His voice trembled. Addonis coughed. "You left this behind. I thought . . . I thought I'd um . . . bring it by."

Addonis faced the wall, wiping his nose with his sleeve.

"You, uh, need anything?" Clint asked.

"How 'bout some working legs." Cole chuckled. He sat upright, stretching. "Or maybe a nice change of scenery."

"I can't get you new legs. And I won't. Because you don't need them. Let's go for a walk."

Cole laughed. "Not sure if you knew this, but I'm paralyzed."

"They say you're gonna walk again. And soon!"

"Who says?"

"Doesn't matter," said Clint. "It doesn't matter, cuz if you believe it, it's gonna happen. Do you believe it?"

Cole shrugged. "Maybe someday."

"No, right now." Clint set his jaw, a determined look in his eyes.

"If I walk . . . today," said Cole, "*I* will be indebted to *you*."

"Never." Clint looked at his brother. He shook his head. "Never."

Clint lifted Cole into a sitting position.

"Guys, I don't—"

"Shut up," Clint said.

Maybe he was right. Maybe today he would walk. Then he could march into Mason's office and beat the atoms out of *him*. With the old general removed, what would stop him from marching into Fahrquan?

All he needed was working legs.

Addonis rushed to the other side of Cole.

"Ready?" asked Clint.

"I—" The two men hoisted him. His unfeeling legs dangled below him.

Cole tightened his jaw. *I will walk. I will walk. I will walk.*

"Gentlemen," Cole said. "I'm ready to walk. Lower me."

The two men bent, and with all the conviction and faith Cole could muster, he commanded his feet to feel the ground. He smiled with anticipation. His feet made contact with the floor. Addonis and Clint let go.

Cole crashed into the tile floor, feeling nothing below his arms. For a moment, he had been so certain. Yet his conviction wavered.

It didn't matter. Even if he'd believed, his spine was broken. There were some things even faith couldn't fix.

Clint crouched and hefted him back up. He trudged toward the door.

"Where are you taking me?" asked Cole.

"You." His voice cracked. "You asked for two things. Since I couldn't give you one, I can at least give you a change of scenery."

The two traveled down the darkened halls of the hospital. And as they moved, Cole thought he felt a breeze caress his foot.

Aumora burst through Gene's door, with a walk that was both hurried and poised in a way only Aumora could pull off. In one hand, she held a piece of paper and in the other a briefcase.

She lifted the paper. "We need to do something about this."

Gene smiled. "How are you, 'Mora?"

"Have you seen this?" She approached his desk.

"Not one to exchange pleasantries, are you?"

Aumora smiled sheepishly. "Sorry. I'm fine."

"Good. Good. Do you expect it will rain tomorrow?"

"Can we—"

"And how about that baseball team we're so fond of rooting for?"

Aumora rolled her eyes. "I'm doing well. We have no baseball team to root for, and the forecast says a 60% chance of rain, though I don't see why any of that matters."

"You actually came prepared with a weather report."

She blinked. "Of course I did." Her lips tightened, before breaking into a smile. "Okay, so I lied."

Gene chuckled. "It's good to see you, nonetheless. Now, what do we have?"

She handed the paper to Gene. "Elsa's transmission." She opened the briefcase and presented a stapled document. "And the report on Mortem Bacillus, the infection."

Meticulous notes filled the margins like a picture frame, crammed with numbers, equations, and greek symbols. The text itself was highlighted in yellow, green, and blue colors.

"Ah." Gene lifted his chin. "Yes. We do need to talk about that."

"You don't seem in much of a hurry to do so."

Gene stood from his desk, his bones popping. "When you're 243 years old, you're not in a hurry to do anything but die."

Aumora smiled, though her eyes possessed a sadness that could not be hid by her banter.

"I'm sorry about Cole," Gene said.

Aumora tensed. "Thank you." Her eyes glistened, and she held her breath, as if struggling to contain the emotions.

"It's okay to love him, you know?" Gene said.

Anger flashed across her face. "I do love him."

"Yes of course. My apologies. I misspoke. What I meant, is it's okay to worry about him."

Aumora lifted her chin. "It's out of my hands. But this," she pointed to the dossier, "something needs to be done."

Gene nodded. "You think it's a credible threat?"

"I have no doubt they'd use it."

"Yes, but is it practical?"

Her expression sobered, like a doctor giving bad news to a patient. "This virus would destroy us all."

The ever-present churning in his stomach grew. He plopped onto a leather chair, combing his hand through his hair. "Okay. What do you need?"

"I need technicians, and I need time." Aumora sighed. "And a fully stocked laboratory—a centrifuge, incubator, cell culture hoods. I need a mouse colony. And a barrier facility."

"I'll see what I can do."

"Are you still in communication with Elsa?"

Gene shook his head. "We can receive, but we can't send messages, at least as far as I know."

"Then find a way," she said. "I'll need eyes on the immunology lab. It's on the 37th floor, room 3744, left-hand side, about half-way down the hall."

"And what should we expect to find, exactly?"

"I don't know." Aumora folded her arms and wrinkled her brow. She shook her head. "I won't know until I see it. A picture perhaps."

"I'll see what I can do." Gene sighed. He stood and ambled toward a safe. After entering the combination, he removed a vile encased in metal. He grabbed a chain and linked it with the metal encasing, fashioning a necklace. He approached Aumora and placed it around her neck.

"What's this?" she asked.

"Tinkering with bacteria is dangerous, I assume?" Gene raised an eyebrow.

She cocked her head. "You could say that."

"Consider that your insurance."

Aumora sucked in a breath, then lifted the vial level with her eyes. She looked at it as an archeologist might admire an ancient tool from Atlantis.

The death antidote.

Vehemently, she shook her head. "No." She removed the necklace and tossed it to Gene. "I can't."

"Of all people to—"

"I said no!" Her voice echoed in the room. "Please don't ask me again."

She turned and marched out of the room.

Chapter 27

It appears our success is overshadowed by tragedy. Today our first subject, Molly, successfully formed a Nexus. It has taken nearly twenty years. In our efforts to streamline the process, we attempted to duplicate large clusters of memories from Molly's brain into another's. That individual suffered immensely from the procedure, developing a condition akin to the mythical multiple personality disorder. I'm afraid there is no shortcut to a Nexus—no secret surgery. Much like losing weight, the best strategy is always to train the human mind with habits.

Journal Entry of Gene The Ancient dated 31 years after the Genetic Apocalypse, extracted from the Archive.

Today.

Cole's chest heaved with anxiety.

This was it.

Immersed in the simulation, he walked, surrounded by darkness. His feet made contact with what felt like marble, yet when he looked below, he saw nothing. Nor did he see anything in front. With the exception of the large scoreboards on his left and right, all he saw was blackness, extending for miles and miles in front of him.

It was his simulated world.

The scoreboards listed the record name in one column, the records score in the next, the name of the record holder, and the soldier assigned to breaking that record in the last column.

Several rows glowed blue, indicating which records the soldiers currently contested.

A flicker of movement caught his gaze. Cole whirled his head, then smiled.

Beef. The man was the ultimate marksman. His aim was as steady as a rocky cliff against the wind—unmoving. Before the day was over, the man would hold fifteen records, making him the next general of the army.

And Beef would make a good general. His commanding presence demanded respect, yet he was also the type that would not shirk from scrubbing toilets if the job demanded it. The men loved him, respected him, and would die for him.

Cole would.

He looked at the collection of records reserved for him—fourteen total, one short of Beef—most related to strategy and strength, such as the record he'd have to acquire again for pushups. He could leave no room for Mason to contest Beef's authority.

And Cole couldn't be happier about serving beneath Beef. Cole's job was to topple Mason and that was plenty.

By the end of the day, Cole and Mason would be tied at fourteen, while Beef had fifteen.

Several more records flashed and changed names.

Cole suddenly felt uneasy. A wave of nausea. Sharp pain stabbed his temples. Cole cried out, grabbing his head. *What was that?* Cole's breath quickened.

The pain left. It was nothing. Imagined pain no doubt. Something related to the paralysis, for sure. That was it.

Yet Cole's stomach tightened.

Another couple of records changed ownership.

It was time.

Cole entered the pushup simulator.

Five minutes later, Cole dripped with simulated sweat. The muscles in his arms burned and he gasped for breath.

Another record for the good guys.

He looked at the scoreboards, counting the number of remaining records. Beef had acquired twelve of the fifteen. Toby had already acquired his four. Mac and Tom each obtained their two.

More than halfway there.

Cole had two more strength records to acquire. In the mean time, to allow his body to rest, he'd cover a handful of strategy simulations.

Within an hour, Cole had acquired the strategy records, and surpassed Mason's max for the dead lift. He looked at the scoreboard. It had been sorted in order of authority. Mason remained on top at twenty-four records. Beef followed behind at fourteen and Cole was next at eleven.

Another shard of pain. Cole grabbed his head, screaming. It hurt. The knots in his stomach tightened. An uneasy feeling settled over him.

Something was wrong. But he couldn't quit now.

Cole shook his head. Pullups next. He tried to ignore the ache that remained from the pushups. It was unthinkable—breaking both pushup and pull-up records within the same day. But it had to be done.

Luckily, it would only last a minute.

42. That's all he needed.

He jumped, hanging on the bar. Closing his eyes, he exhaled.

1-2-3.

He blocked out the records from his mind.

7-8-9.

Already his arms ached. A bad sign. A wave of doubt overcame him.

14-15-16.

No. He couldn't doubt. He had to do it.

21-22-23.

More pain in the temples. He cried out. 26. 27.

Another stab of pain.

He grit his teeth, fighting through the pain, yet he could feel his momentum slowing.

It had to be now. The rules only allowed a single attempt within a twenty-four hour period. And besides, he wouldn't even have the strength to try again.

30-31.

He doubled his pace. Another stab of pain.

No! He shouted through the agony.

Elsa.

37-38-39.

The searing pain shot through his spine. Another shout of agony. But still, he kept going.

40-41.

A tremor started in his back. He pulled for the final time, but his body convulsed. With a cry of agony, he dropped to the ground.

Time was up.

He looked at the digital display. 41. One short. A tie.

Cole buried his head in his face before the agonizing convulsions took over.

"What is going on?" Mason yelled.

Briggs fiddled with the computer. "It must be a mistake. It's impossible."

The lieutenant turned on a video camera, showing the training auditorium. Several dozen soldiers surrounded the knife-throwing simulator, cheering.

Briggs shook his head. "I'm afraid it's no mistake."

Mason cursed, slamming his fist against the wall. "How many records?"

"A hundred and six."

"A hundred and—" Again, he punched the wall. "How did this happen?"

"I don't know sir."

Mason grabbed his gun. He ejected the magazine, counted the bullets, then reloaded the weapon. "Let's go."

"What are you going to do?"

"End this."

It's enough. It's enough. It's enough.

The convulsions subsided. He struggled to stand from the ground as he looked at the scoreboard. Cole Brooks—fourteen records, though one was a tie. Ulysses Mason—Fifteen records. And Cornelius Eugene Hawthorne Blackburn (Beef)—fourteen records.

Beef had one more marksmanship record. That would take Mason down to fourteen and Beef would be general.

But what was taking so long?

He looked at the clock that hovered above the scoreboard. 2:02 AM. The row glowed just as green as the rest of the records, indicating it wasn't currently being contested.

But why?

Cole's stomach rumbled as an uneasiness settled into his gut. Something was wrong. *Very* wrong.

He shook his head. Maybe Beef had failed. Perhaps it was unreasonable that *every* soldier would perform the best in *every* contested record.

Maybe he could try tomorrow, before the council met.

He'd just failed, that was all.

Cole shook his head. There wasn't time. They couldn't approach the council unless Mason's removal was uncontested. But nobody else was close to another record.

Except perhaps...

Cole shook his head. No. It was impossible. Another tremor began in his spine. He tightened his jaw.

He couldn't. Whatever side-effects Gene feared were happening. He couldn't risk another minute in the simulator.

He looked again at the list of Mason's records, his eyes settling on one—*Perfect score in interpersonal combat simulator.*

A perfect score. It was unthinkable—incapacitate the robot without him scoring a single hit.

Impossible.

Cole held his breath through another tremor in his spine.

Impossible.

Ah hell.

Before he could change his mind, the robot stood before him.

"Why won't he wake up?" Luther asked.

"I don't know," Aumora said.

Where was Gene when you needed him? Cole's body was drenched in sweat and his body convulsed. Luther's pulse thrashed against his ribcage.

Again, he slapped the boy's cheeks. "Wake up!"

Aumora let out a sob—a noise he'd never heard from her voice.

Luther stood, gazing at the vast collection of armed soldiers that surrounded him. "Where is Beef?"

Cole hopped on his feet, attempting to suppress the pain—the knives that stabbed his lower back, the coursing throb that traveled down his legs, the consuming agony in his brain.

He had to do it. There could be no room for Mason to contest—no room for the council to contest. Even if it meant that Cole had to be general.

It was settled. Pain or no pain, it had to be done.

The robot bowed its head, then pounced.

Cole dodged, scarcely missing a jab. The robot punched again. He tensed, then ducked as the wind of its glove caressed his neck. He jumped back just as the robot kicked.

Both paused. Cole exhaled, his body trembling. He hadn't lost yet. But he had a long way to go.

Another jab. He ducked. Pain shot through his lower back. He fell to the ground with a roll, just as the robot kicked. He leapt to his feet.

This would not end well if something didn't change.

They both paused. He exhaled and for a moment, he allowed the pain inside. His body relaxed, savoring the agony, though his mind screamed. Mason had done this to him—this paralysis, this agony he felt now. Too long he tolerated it. Too long he'd sat back—saluting that devil, doing *nothing* when the general's minion beat the atoms out of him. He'd fought the anger, and suppressed his hate.

He grit his teeth, imagining Mason's oversized head on the robot's shoulders. Pain pulsed through his body, fueling his muscles. The tremors that racked his spine set the cadence of his racing heart.

He smiled.

He pounced. The robot ducked a jab before thrusting an upper cut. He twisted, landing an elbow in the robot's head. It stumbled backward. He kicked into the robot's chest. Imbalanced, it staggered backward. He leapt forward, landing blow after blow in its head. It swung, and he ducked. Again, he felt the wind of the blow.

Both backed from the fight, bouncing on their feet. Cole grinned as the robot approached. He faked a jab. The robot bent back. Cole planted a foot in its stomach, another blow to the head.

And another. And another. Blow after blow, kick after kick. With one final hook, the robot teetered before falling over.

General Cole Brooks.

Cole woke. Sweat dripped down his face. The pain he thought he'd imagined racked his body—agonizing tremors that traveled down his spine.

"Thank God, Cole," Luther said.

Soldiers surrounded his bed, their faces a mixture of worry and relief.

"Cole!" Luther said. "Don't you *ever* scare me like that."

Two soldiers stood at the door, rifles in hand. They searched the hallway.

"What's going on?" Cole asked.

Luther looked at Aumora, who breathed heavily.

"Mason," she said.

He felt sick. "What about him?"

"He's..." Aumora cleared her throat. "He's done something."

"Done what?"

"The council members are gone," Luther said. "Gene's gone. Beef's...Beef's gone."

Cole's throat tightened. "Gone where?"

"I don't know," Luther said.

Cole's I.V. dripped like blood. The blankets seemed to wrap his sweating body, squeezing the life out of him. The soldiers in the room regarded him, waiting. Another tremor began. He convulsed and couldn't suppress the cry that escaped his lips.

An uneasy silence settled into the room. The men looked at him with terrified expressions.

"I'm fine," Cole said. "Tell me..." He grunted through a small tremor. "Tell me what happened?"

The men remained deathly still, as if afraid to move, to speak. Toby straightened his spine. "Beef was about to take down the last record. He went for a walk—clear his mind and all. He never showed up."

Aumora exhaled. "I went to check on Gene. His office door was broken down, and I've looked all over. I can't find him, the council, Mason..."

"What do you want to do, sir?" asked Rocco. *Sir.* He'd never heard that word fall from Rocco's lips for any man, let alone Cole. Things had changed.

It's happening. But it couldn't happen. He wasn't ready. Stroud and Hapley stood at the door, searching the halls. They looked like a pair of pit bulls—jaws clenched, feet ready to pounce, and Cole thought he could even hear a deep growl in their chests. Yet these pit bulls had rifles.

Several dozen other soldiers filled the empty spaces of his hospital suite. Each held that same hopeful expression in their eyes as they regarded him.

It was time.

He sat up in his bed, forcing his face to reflect determination. "Are any other soldiers missing?"

"Yes, sir," Toby said. "Half the officers, for sure. Other than that, we're still counting."

"Where's everyone else?"

"Toby told everyone to go to their rooms," Ray said. "Until everyone's accounted for."

Cole nodded.

Luther studied the ceiling tiles, biting his lip. "It doesn't make sense."

"What?"

"Why the Ancient?" Luther asked. "The council—that make sense. But the Ancient?"

"You're right." Cole nodded. "He discredited him years ago."

"If Mason's taken him," Aumora began, "it can't be for political purposes, or at least his politics expand beyond Azkus City."

Luther lifted his chin. "Oh boy."

Cole's stomach tightened.

"The Archive," said Luther. He cursed.

"I don't get it," Toby said.

"Capturing the Ancient doesn't grant Mason anything within Azkus City," said Cole. "But if he can somehow gain access to the Archive . . ."

"The Malkum," said Aumora.

"Oh no," Toby said.

"The Malkum would give anything to have the Archive," Aumora said.

"They might even honor a traitor."

A foreboding silence fell like acid rain.

"He wouldn't cave in," Cole said. "He's worked too hard, waited too long."

"I'm afraid that's the problem," said Luther. "Ancient'd rather die than give in, so that's just about what'd happen."

"We've got to do something," said Addonis.

"I need more time," Cole said.

"I'm afraid you don't have time," Luther said. "You wait much longer—"

"It's Briggs," Hapley said. He tightened his grip on his rifle. Several within the room drew their weapons.

"Guns down," Cole said.

The large lieutenant entered, panting, his forehead sweating. "It's the Ancient. I know where he is. There's a room—a storage closet, inside the auditorium. I heard screaming. Come. Quickly!"

The beeping of Cole's monitor filled the silence. The men shifted their gaze from Cole to Briggs.

Lieutenant Briggs—Mason's right hand man. It could be a setup.

"Danely, Dawson, Bennet," Cole said. He nodded toward Briggs. "Be careful."

They nodded. With Briggs, they exited the room.

The remaining men waited in silence for instructions. Cole remained quiet. The scenery of the window changed from a jungle to a small lake that swayed gently with a breeze. Cole's heart pounded, sending ripples through his temples. The scent of pine needles filled the air as the device above the picture frame sprayed another synthetic scent. He felt as if he might hyperventilate.

"What do we do, sir?" asked Keel, his eyes full of innocent confidence.

It was supposed to be Beef. The weight of their misguided trust was crushing, but someone had to do something. Without a central command and a clear chain of authority, there would be confusion. And according to the misguided philosophy of Ultimum Dux, Cole was the final authority.

Cole sat upright. "Men. Arm yourselves, splitting into squadrons of twelve men. Enter the auditorium at exactly 0900, weapons at the ready. I want you to expect war."

The silence that followed felt like dense cloud cover. One man gripped his rifle like a child clutching a blanket. Another set his jaw and nodded. Several more sucked in a breath, straightening their spines.

"Dismissed," said Cole.

"Yes, sir," they shouted in unison, before exiting the room.

"Luther," Cole said after the last man left. "Dress me in full uniform—that of a general."

"Yes, sir!" said the old man, smiling widely.

"And one more thing," said Cole. "Please, don't call me sir."

Chapter 28

Today the intellect-crippling virus will be released. I can't help but think with sorrow of how many lives will be destroyed. Yet if I do nothing, the world will destroy itself. I am certain this is the correct solution. I have never been more certain of anything else in my entire life.

Intercepted journal entry of President Akram, dated the day of the Genetic Apocalypse

---

Cole looked at his watch.

0858.

Another tremor began in his brain, traveling down his spine, just as it had in the simulation. Cole's heart thudded with the pace of a chased rodent.

Something was really wrong.

The frame of the wheelchair squeaked. Luther squeezed Cole's shoulder until the tremor subsided.

Footsteps rapidly approached. Cole turned, alerted.

"General," Blake Dawson said.

"What's going on."

"It's Briggs." Blake bent, panting. "We've incarcerated him. Briggs thinks it's a trap. The final count is in. Hundreds of soldiers are missing. Mason could be planning something."

"I don't trust Briggs. Continue as planned."

But if I'm wrong. Dread burned the insides of his stomach like an ulcer.

"Yes, sir...Be careful," said Blake. "Briggs—he seemed sincerely worried."

Cole regarded Blake. The man's panting breaths filled the silence. Cole pulled his radio to his mouth. "Alter entrance time. 0905. Repeat: 0905."

"He wants the Archive," Cole said, thinking aloud. "The Ancient won't give it to him. He may assume I have access. If it's a trap, he's going to hold him ransom."

"But we outnumber them," said Luther.

"He's going to assume I won't let the Ancient die, no matter the advantage we have in numbers. And he's right. I won't let the Ancient die."

"So what do we do?" asked Blake.

"Place snipers in the upper auditorium. Activate the speakers so you can hear. I leave it to you to fire if necessary."

Blake saluted, then ran, speaking in his radio as he did.

"Calling all units," Cole said in his radio. "Half of each squadron is to remain in the halls. The other half, continue as planned at 0905. Everyone stay close to communication."

Cole released the button and sighed.

Silence followed. The seconds stretched longer.

0903.

Cole's pulse quickened, but time slowed.

0904.

His stomach turned.

0905.

"Go," Cole said.

The soldiers in front rushed through the doors. Between the muffled footsteps, a moan fill the room.

The Ancient. The men rushed to the center of the room.

"Stand back," Cole said.

Luther activated the fingerprints scanner and the floor began to lower.

"Kemp, Clayton, Gibson," Cole said. "Check it out."

The men jumped down the hole.

"Get a doctor," Cole said into his radio.

The three soldiers emerged with the Ancient. Half his face was swollen and colored with fresh bruises of black and blue. Blood dripped from his nose and lips. His thin hair was matted and he had trouble keeping his eyes open.

"Confirm reception of previous command," Cole said into his radio.

Nothing.

Cole looked up, trying to see through the dark-tinted glass to the room where the snipers were positioned.

He saw nothing.

"Dawson."

Still nothing.

Cole muttered a curse. "All right, I want—"

The doors swung open. Armed soldiers filed into the aqua auditorium, wearing gas masks. They fixed their weapons on Cole's soldiers. Behind the open doors, bodies littered the floor, sprawled in awkward positions.

Mason entered.

The soldiers jumped in front of Cole, forming a fifteen-man barrier between the old general and the new.

Silence.

Clint walked toward the front. His footsteps echoed in the cinderblock room.

"Surrender Cole or my men will start shooting," said Mason.

"Die," said Clint.

"You first," said the general.

The echo of the gunshot reverberated through the auditorium, followed by the clank of a shell. A body thudded.

Silence.

"Move," Cole said quietly. The soldiers surrounding him did nothing. They looked vacantly onward, weapons half-heartedly at the ready.

"I said move!"

The men began to shuffle, eyes still vacant. Cole pushed his wheelchair forward. Addonis followed behind, gun drawn.

The last few men parted. Clint lay face-down, a pool of blood surrounding his head.

Addonis gasped.

Cole shook his head. *Not like Suta,* he thought, fearing his grief would paralyze him. But it wouldn't be like Suta. He didn't even feel grief. Not yet anyway. Nor did he feel the fear he first felt as a newly recruited soldier.

He raged.

Cole allowed the explosive wrath to fuel his will. Angry blood pumped throughout his body.

"Is this what generals do?" Cole glared as Mason.

The old general returned the gaze, just as coldly, 9 mm drawn.

"Is this what generals do?" Cole screamed. He glared at the traitorous soldiers who stood by Mason. Some returned the gaze with scowls or cocky grins.

But not many.

Others lowered their weapons. Several tossed their pistols to the center of the room.

"A general does *not* kill his own men!" Cole shouted. He grabbed the side of his wheel chair, knuckles turning white.

The beginnings of another tremor began in the back of his neck. He tightened his jaw, trying to suppress it, but the tremor mounted. His body shook, his legs convulsed. An agonizing stab of pain began in his lower back, shooting through his leg.

His leg.

As he struggled to control the convulsions, the pressure in his legs intensified. It was agonizing.

But the realization was blissful. His legs—they *felt* the pain. They *felt* the tremors. The burning hot sensation—he *felt* it.

He wasn't paralyzed.

Cole stood. The men gasped. Mason's eyes widened.

Cole straightened his spine. Another tremble caused his feet to wobble.

"Ulysses Mason," Cole said, his voice unsteady. He straightened his spine, gritting his teeth through the pain. He took a wobbling step. "You." He grunted, tightening his fists. "You are dismissed as general of this army. As your replacement, I hereby place you under arrest for the murder of Clint McRand."

Mason narrowed his eyes. "Go to hell." He lifted his weapon, sighting down the barrel. His finger hovered over the trigger. Cole went rigid.

A bang.

He sucked in a breath. He reached for his chest, checking for his own heartbeat.

General Ulysses Mason lay dead on the floor, a hole in his head. Cole turned. Addonis stood with his arms extended, a smoking gun in his hands. The young man lowered the weapon, a snarl on his face, and walked to the dead general. Like Luther, he unloaded the remainder of the magazine.

Unlike with Suta's death, Cole didn't try to stop him.

Chapter 29

My plan of redemption, my plan for overthrowing the Malkum's military and political center, began over 204 years ago. I laid in my bed staring at the darkened ceiling as creative insights danced in my head. My anticipation at cleverly besting my enemy fueled my mind that sleepless night, envisioning the glory of my gloating moment before the council. I thought myself pretty clever until I awoke the next morning and realized the price I'd have to pay, a debt I still pay every bit as painfully today as I did centuries ago.

Journal Entry of Gene The Ancient dated 202 years after the Genetic Apocalypse, extracted from the Archive.

Gene lay in his hospital bed, staring at the ceiling. He thought he knew torture —living centuries with little to do but worry about his plan and watch his influence wane.

Beep-beep-beep. His eye twitched with each pulse of the monitor. He'd never been one who tolerated boredom.

He couldn't seem to acclimate to the floral scent the disinfectant. It overwhelmed his senses and made him want to gag with each inhale.

Luther entered his room.

"Thank God, Luther," said Gene.

"Sir?"

"I'm not sure I've ever been happier to see you," said Gene.

"I outta put you inta the hospital more often, old man. That Death Antidote's been too kind to ya."

Gene chuckled. "I think I'd rather die next time."

Luther plopped into the recliner. "They says yer doing well."

"They're not the ones laying on a hospital bed."

"I know the feeling." Luther sighed. "The entire council has been recovered. And so has Beef."

Gene let out a breath. "Good, good. And how's Cole doing?"

"I don't think he's taking Clint's death all too well."

Gene nodded, his eyes downcast. He knew there'd be a cost. Clint's death was one of many that would come. And now that Mason was out of the way, the assault on Fahrquan wouldn't be much longer. Bodies would soon fall like rocks from an avalanche.

Gene sighed. "At least the first obstacle is over."

Luther nodded in return.

"And what are the men saying?" asked Gene.

"What do you mean?" asked Luther.

"About Cole? You're the Chief of Communications, Luther. I want a report."

"Ah," he said. "Some men adore, while the rest worship him. Not a soldier in all of Azkus City wouldn't walk through hell's gates to follow 'im."

"Good," said Gene with a nod. "And none too soon. Given Elsa's recent transmission, it is evident we don't have much time."

Luther nodded. "At least the boy's not paralyzed no more."

"There's an extensive and tortuous road to recovery, I fear."

"But we're halfway there," Luther said.

"Yes, my friend. Yes we are. Now, we must begin preparations for the attack on Fahrquan. Unfortunately, the simulator is new. Cole is our first test subject, but he needs to learn how to work with others—to command, to instruct, to join intellectual resources. Normally, these things would be learned in the training auditorium. But, alas, little time is left."

Luther nodded.

"Fortunately, our engineers have adapted the simulator so that multiple people can share the experience. What that means is if you and Cole wanted to hike the Himalayas together, you could, and your conversation would be just as real as it would in the hospital room."

Luther furrowed his brow. "Wait a minute. You saw what it did to Cole."

"Yes I did. It repaired his spine."

"Bah." Luther batted his hand in front of his face as if shooing a fly. "Coincidence."

"That's not what the neurologists say. What Cole did was risky, yes. But he's also demonstrated quite conclusively how the DNTs interact with the body."

"I still don't like it."

"Neither do I," Gene said, "but what choice do we have?"

Luther shrugged. "I suppose yer right."

"Not the entire army, at first. That would be too risky. But, his commanders. Luther, I need your assistance with this one. Cole needs men who will shore up his weaknesses, who will trust him, and who can lead others into battle. I need to decide who is best to choose as commanders."

Luther's posture straightened. "Right good question. Well, the kid gets along with Toby and Rocco, not to mention—"

"I didn't call you here to give me recommendations," said Gene. "I called you to ask for your permission."

"Permission? Permission fer what?"

"You see, Luther. Though those men are well-trained, they're about as ready for battle as kids playing video games. They've never seen real danger. And what makes us think they're going to be ready to charge *toward* the bullets? We need people who understand that the Malkum must be stopped, even if it costs them their own lives."

Luther furrowed his eyebrows. "I don't know, the way those men talk about him, I'm bettin' they've got 'nough courage to run to hell 'n back. I know I would."

"True," said the Ancient. "But what happens if the boy dies in battle? What then? Do they carry on the conflict all in the name of Cole? Or will their hearts shatter? No, we need men who will fight on, with or without Cole. We need men who can love him, but also recognize there's something greater at stake."

"I see," said Luther. "You mentioned you wanted my permission?"

"Yes, Luther. I need your men."

"My men!" Luther jumped to his feet. "They haven't had a lick of military training."

"Yes, but they've seen the slums. They see what the Malkum do to these children. Do you know of any other body of people who, collectively, would rather see the Malkum dead? No! Your men have already shed sweat and blood to thwart the Malkum's plans."

Luther lowered his head and nodded solemnly. "Is this your way of forcing an early retirement?"

"Early retirement? Ha! You're almost 135 years old. I'd hardly consider that early."

Luther chuckled, then stood. "I'll go tell my men."

"Thank you, Luther," said the Ancient. "And Luther. Thanks for . . ." A lump formed in his throat. The Ancient had almost given up—abandoned the plan for which he'd already sacrificed so much. He opened his mouth to speak, but knew he would lose his composure. Instead, he swallowed and nodded his head.

A knock sounded.

"Sir?" said a voice—a deep voice.

"You have impeccable timing, lieutenant," said Gene. "Please come in."

Luther turned his head. Lieutenant Briggs approached cautiously.

Luther bolted out of his seat. "What's he doing here?"

"I'd love to have General Cole Brooks with us," the Ancient began, "but I think he deserves some time to himself."

"Gene," said Luther through gritted teeth.

"It's time we begin planning for the final assault. We—"

"Gene!" Luther shouted.

Both Gene and Briggs turned their attention to Luther. The man's face was bright red. His jowls shook and the muscles of his jaw protruded beyond the man's wrinkled cheeks.

He shot a finger toward Briggs. "I'll *not* have that dirty traitor in our midst whi—"

"Dirty traitor?" said Gene. "Is that not what you called Elsa at one time? I do say, of all people, you are not well adept at determining who is a traitor."

"But—"

"I am familiar with all possible objections you will raise, Luther. But I assure you, I have ways of knowing who is loyal and who is traitorous. This man saved my life and countless others. When I tell you that I need Briggs, you will not object."

Luther's jaw tightened and Gene imagined steam escaping his ears.

"Need I remind you," asked Gene, "that it was Briggs who informed you of my location? And it was Briggs who warned Cole of a potential trap."

"Bah!" Luther kicked the floor, then began storming out of the room.

"You will regret this, Gene!" he yelled. "That man's as loyal to you as the no-good general he served!"

Luther turned and slammed the door.

Luther trudged down the hall, muttering to himself. How could Gene be so blind? Briggs. The man might as well have held the gun that shot Clint

McRand, for he was just as guilty as Mason—may he rest in Hell.

Luther sighed, trying to release the hyperventilating rage that filled his lungs like smoke. He knew it wouldn't work. The anger had kept him awake all night, only to be amplified by Gene's stupid request this morning—delivered via email.

How tacky.

Luther straightened his spine before knocking on the door labeled *Laboratory*. He watched through the Plexiglas windows as a white-coated lab worker approached.

The door swung open. "You must be Luther," she said. "Aumora's ready for you."

They walked between Plexiglas windows. Each provided a view of white-coated workers, gray and white instruments, vials, and stacks of computers. The hallway finally terminated at a glass door. The woman pressed her palm into a screen and the door opened. Behind the glass door, there was another, but this one was made of thick metal and had a round glass window in the center. To the left and right were yellow hazardous material suits and bins containing shoes.

"You'll want to put one of these on." The woman removed her shoes and pulled the yellow suit over her clothes. She zipped the back over her head, fogging the helmet's glass as she breathed.

Luther did as she commanded, removing his shoes then stepping into the oversized suit. After zipping it, he heard the woman's voice over a speaker inside his mask.

"It's all just a precaution," she said. "It's better to cope with bulky suits than to have an epidemic."

Luther nodded, although he wasn't sure the gesture was visible outside his mask.

The woman grabbed a large lever on the metal door and pulled it open. He cautiously entered as the woman gestured toward the room before him. He walked several paces before the door clanked close.

The room was small and made of corrugated steel. Metallic desks lined the right wall with labeled glass bins and odd-colored vials. On the left wall, within an air-tight chamber was a collection of cages with what looked to be rodents in them. In the center of the chamber was a thick glass dome that had holes for rubber gloves. Aumora stood over the dome with her hands inside the gloves. Her posture was straight, as it always was. Despite the sweat that trickled down her cheeks, her hair was immaculate. She furrowed her brow in that way of hers, no doubt calculating at the speed of an asteroid.

And she was *not* wearing a hazard suit.

Luther smiled as he unzipped and pulled the mask off his head.

"And just what do you think you're doing?" asked Aumora.

"I reckon I could ask you the same."

Aumora smiled as she turned her attention back to the glass dome. Again, her computing face returned.

"You have no idea what it's like to work eighteen hours a day inside one of those," she said. "I'd rather take my chances. But not you! Put that back on."

Luther dropped the mask. It thudded against the floor. "If you get infected, I have little reason to live. I'd just as soon die with you."

Aumora smiled. "That's sweet of you. So what can I do for you?"

Luther shrugged. "The Ancient's back from the hospital. He sent me here to get a report."

"Why?"

"Who knows?" said the old man. It was ridiculous. Aumora continuously provided the Ancient with excessively detailed notes on her progress, and he had undoubtedly read every word of it. No, Luther was sent for another reason. What that might be was a mystery.

"Well, how much do you know?" asked Aumora.

"Let's just assume I know nothing." Luther shrugged apologetically. "Usually a safe assumption."

Aumora laughed. "Okay. Elsa warned of a synthetic bacterium, Mortem Bacillus, or MB, and sent a report."

Aumora approached one of the tables. Above it was a large monitor that displayed a microscopic image of two different blood samples.

"The left image is normal blood." Aumora pointed. The image showed a collection of red dots in a random pattern.

"On the right is the blood that is infected with BK," she said. The right image looked similar except that several of the dots had large fuzzy edges.

"Looks pretty bad."

"You have no idea. This thing..." She shook her head. "This will kill us all. Unfortunately, there's no way of knowing where the Malkum stand on the vaccine's development, or even if they're pursuing it at all, though I have my suspicions."

"Quite a task," said Luther.

"Indeed it is." She placed her hands on her hips. "Have you ever heard it said that you can't catch the same cold twice?"

"I suppose."

"The reason is because your immune system, in the process of getting sick, learns to fight the infection. So if it attacks your body again, it already has the necessary manpower to fight off the illness. You with me?"

"Go on," said Luther.

"When someone's vaccinated, they're given an innocuous form of the virus or bacterium, or whatever, so that the cells within the body can safely learn to fight it before the real infection comes."

"Ok." Luther nodded. "I'm following. Barely, but I *am* following."

"I've developed an innocuous form of the infection, then gave it to the mice. After several days, I gave them the actual infection and it seems that no matter how many antibodies they developed, they all died. I varied the dosage, the time between vaccination and infection, yet in all cases the mice died when the actual infection was injected."

Aumora sighed. "Out of desperation, I gave them the actual bacterium as a vaccine, but in a very small dose."

"Did it work?"

"Yes," she said, though she didn't appear to be enthusiastic.

"And what's wrong with that?"

"Giving the actual infection as a vaccine is dangerous. I can and have determined the minimal effective dose in mice. But I can't go 'practicing' on humans. It's too risky."

"So what'll ya do?"

"Normally, we'd have years to test cultures, then small animals, then primates, then we would test the vaccination on the terminally ill. But even then..."

Aumora continued to speak, but Luther's mind fixated on two words—*terminally ill.*

He knew why the Ancient had asked him to visit Aumora. The Death Antidote had made him all but terminally ill.

Luther was nothing more than a test tube.

Luther stormed into Gene's office.

"Come in," Gene said, his eyes remaining on his computer screen.

"I know what you're doing, and I don't like it."

"I'm a man of many secrets, Luther." Gene removed his glasses before rubbing his eyes. "You know that. You've always known that."

The Ancient pressed his hand onto the surface of his desk, which made a holo image of the Malkum compound appear. His casual dismissiveness caused Luther's eye to twitch.

"Yer telling me to die!" yelled Luther. "*And* yer walkin' into a trap. Can't ya see Briggs fer the viper he is?"

"Need I remind you that you don't know the whole plan—"

"The plan, the plan, the secret plan that no one seems to know *a thing* about." Luther slammed the desk with his palm.

Gene regarded Luther, his face placid.

Luther threw his hands in the air. "Well?"

Still, the Ancient said nothing. Luther cursed and stomped toward the leather seat, plopping down into the chair. He tightened his teeth and muttered to himself. For centuries the man had been a saint—never speaking an unkind word of any but himself, never doing ought but what was good for the colony. And now? Where had this scumbag come from?

The trickling water of the Ancient's waterfall filled the silence. Again Luther sighed, attempting to expunge the bitterness. The trickling slowed his heart rate and caused his shoulders to relax.

As if the Ancient had an emotional barometer, he placed a hand on Luther's shoulder. "Old friend." His voice was quiet, almost a whisper. "I do appreciate your concern. And you are wise to question Briggs's loyalty."

Luther stood. "Then why—"

"Please, let me finish," interrupted Gene. "I understand your suspicions, and if I were in your situation, I would have similar concerns. But I tell you and *plead* with you to trust me."

Luther looked into Gene's eyes. But he could not hold his gaze long. His pride wouldn't allow him. He muttered a curse under his breath and tromped toward the wall. Hanging on the orange surface, a colorful work of art depicted several planets in orbit, or at least that's what it seemed to portray. The image was borderline abstract, making it difficult to surmise the artist's intended subject.

"Yer a lot smarter than I," said Luther. "And I don't think you'd be one ta overlook somethin' I see."

Luther's words dissipated with the trickling of the fountain. "But I reckon it's that . . . I just can't ignore ma gut. It just tells me he's a snake. I know you got the brains, and I trust that. But . . . But, I 'spose if something's amiss, you'd a felt it too."

Luther turned to face Gene, who leaned back in his chair and crossed his legs. His elbows rested on the armrests of the seat, his intertwined fingers resting on his chin. His lips curved into a gentle smile.

"You have no idea how difficult it has been to continue without your trust," said Gene. "For decades, you've been my most loyal confidant. And—"

The Ancient sucked in a breath, looking at the floor between the two. He sniffed and wiped his nose with a trembling hand. "I'm just glad you're back." He smiled. "I'm not asking you to dismiss your suspicions, Luther. I'm merely asking you to stand by my side and trust that what happens is all according to plan."

Luther stared with guarded skepticism, but then finally nodded.

"Good," said Gene. He spun and began walking back to his desk. "Now, what's this about me commanding you to die?"

"I visited with Aumora," said Luther. "She told me about the virus."

"Oh?"

"Sorry, sir. You can't go telling me ta trust yer brilliance, then pretend ta be dumb in the same conversation."

Gene laughed as he sat back into his black chair.

"I think ya know right well why ya sent me," said Luther.

"*I* know why. But do *you* know why?"

"I have my suspicions."

"Oh?"

Luther cleared his throat then walked toward another chair near the Ancient's large desk, sighing as he sat. "Seems ta me, Mora's biggest problem is tryin' ta figure out whether the virus will kill or vaccinate. Only way ta figure that out is ta give someone the virus. If I were ta pick someone ta risk death, I'd choose one who's lived a real long life, who hadn't kin, and who was a big pain in the butt. I can think of two people who meet that description." Luther grinned. "Especially the pain in the butt part."

Gene smiled. "Excellent guess, but you're wrong. You forget, Luther, you have been given the Death Antidote. You cannot die, at least a natural death. Sure, someone could stab you in the heart or put a bullet through your cerebellum and you'd expire as quick as anyone else. But if you were infected with a disease . . ."

Luther nodded. It was easy to forget he was vaccinated against death. He felt the pains of mortality every day, like a nagging alarm clock that refused to stop blaring.

"So, would I have symptoms?" asked Luther.

"Probably. But we can almost always remedy symptoms. Vomiting, fever, chills, congestion, all these can be treated with medication."

"And if I wanted to die?" asked Luther.

Gene exhaled deeply then lowered his head. Silence lingered long enough for Luther's face to warm.

"I think it would destroy me." Gene exhaled. "To have my last, most trusted friend . . ." He paused again, focusing on the floor.

Luther would have laughed, had it not been for the awkward silence.

"But, that's not my choice to make." Gene smiled, though his lips didn't reach his eyes. "I was just hoping to be the first of us to die—then I could go to the grave knowing that I had at least one friend I was leaving behind."

Gene shook his head. "I'm sorry, I shouldn't be burdening you with my selfish wishes."

"No, it's ok," said Luther. "I'm glad ta hear I mean something ta somebody."

Both men nodded, then shifted in their seats.

"I'll tell Aumora that tomorrow we'll be vaccinated," said Gene, standing from his chair.

"We?"

"Yes, *we*. I would insist on being the only test subject, but determining the proper dosage is critical to the success of the vaccination. You will be injected with a lower dosage than I so that, if my body is unable to recover from the infection, at least one of us will have a successful test."

"And if neither of us recovers?" asked Luther.

"Then you and I will spend the remainder of our days in quarantine, sipping vodka mingled with chemicals that will reverse the death antidote."

Chapter 30

I must leave this place, though I promised myself I never would. The enclosed interior of this mountain seems to close in around me, suffocating me and leading to my constant brooding. I just hope that I have the strength to come back, long before I am again needed and this waiting game has ended.

Journal Entry of Gene The Ancient dated three years after the Genetic Apocalypse, extracted from the Archive.

Spencer Burton opened the door, but Elsa's gaze remained on the disorganized mess that surrounded her. Computer components covered the tile floor. Elsa sat on the floor between piles of hardware with a screwdriver in one hand and a keyboard in the other. She blew a strand of her disheveled face from her hair, then sniffed. The smell of her own body odor permeated the room as it had for days.

She never did get to shower.

"Ahem," said a voice.

Elsa lifted her head and stared placidly at Spencer, waiting for him to speak. He stepped fully into the room, then closed the door behind him.

He coughed, then spoke. "Remain expressionless through-throughout our conversation. They are monitoring your behavior through video, but the audio is not recorded."

She stared at him with indifference.

"Very good, very good," he said. He shifted his weight and broke eye contact. He cleared his throat again. "Who are you transmitting to?"

Elsa's heart thrashed into her throat, though she said nothing, nor did her expression change.

Spencer straightened his spine, while lowering his gaze. "We collected every scrap of the soldier's radio, except one thing: the oscillator. We even had to disassemble pipes to do it. Luckily it was clogged, so we didn't have to look far."

Elsa turned her attention back to her work. She continued to disassemble an old hard drive with the screwdriver as she entered information with a keyboard using her free hand.

"Uh," said Spencer as he cleared his throat. From the corner of her eye, she saw him pull a handkerchief from his pocket and wipe his forehead. She kept her breath steady, but couldn't suppress the tremble in her hand.

"I have enough evidence to send you to Akram," he said. "The missing oscillator, the makeshift radio I see you've built with your computer, and one more thing..."

Spencer reached for his radio and heard the static shift as he changed the frequency. He turned the screen to face Elsa. She slowly turned her head to look.

"This grid shows the quality of the radio signal. You'll notice that when I go to 27.01 megahertz, there is nothing being transmitted, and the grid goes to zero. But when I go to 26.98 megahertz..."

He adjusted the radio, then showed Elsa the display. The grid read 87%. He approached Elsa's computer. Her eyes followed his movement, but her head remained still. The grid moved from 87% gradually to 96%.

Oh no.

"For all our efforts at finding radio broadcasts through the years," Spencer began, "we never thought to check signal strength."

He approached Elsa's bed, then sat. That brought him within only a few feet of her. Her breath quickened and she scanned her vision's periphery.

"So—"

Elsa lowered her body so that Spencer's enormous frame blocked her from the camera. She pulled a utility knife out of a toolbox and pointed it at him. "I could kill you."

Spencer laughed, but his voice broke and trembled. "I think it might be a little suspicious if they find me dead in your cell."

"I could run. Give me your keys."

"The way you smell, it wouldn't require a bloodhound to track you."

Elsa's eyes drilled into his. He seemed to flinch, but maintained his gaze. She broke eye contact then threw the knife at the barred window.

He bent toward her. "I didn't come here to accuse you," he whispered.

"Then why did you?" She extended her trembling hands to the floor behind her back.

"I already told you. I want to know who you were broadcasting to. I've been monitoring all frequencies for the last several days and that's the only one you're transmitting to. And since you're obviously not stupid enough to place all your bets on one horse, that means you know something."

Elsa remained stone-faced for several seconds. "Akram tortured me for information. You should know by now, I can't be bullied."

"I never intended to torture you, Elsa," said Spencer. "But let me give you another reason to tell me."

Spencer removed a hand-held computer monitor from his pocket, then showed Elsa the live video feed. Her eyes widened.

Father.

"What do you want me to do?" she asked.

"Get me out of here."

* * *

President Akram pressed his head against the window of his office building, his hands holding the metal window frame. He watched as another jet returned from a scouting mission. The whine of its engine shook the building.

"So?" asked General Chambers from behind. "Will you support me?"

"Have you looked everywhere?" asked Akram, turning to face Chambers.

"As I said before, combing the entire surface of the world is unrealistic. We have searched for an electronic footprint in the most likely areas. And we have found *nothing*. Now I suggest you call off this pointless search and adopt a different strategy."

Akram turned. "Most likely areas?"

"Last we knew," General Chambers unfolded a map, "the rebels were here." He pointed at a spot on the map. "They began here." He pointed again.

He removed a marker from his pocket, before drawing a straight line that extended the path the rebels had followed. He then drew two additional lines that surrounded the path in the shape of a megaphone.

"Our men have scoured this region, both on foot and in the air. There is *no* electronic footprint."

Akram studied the map. The rebels either did not use electronics—not likely—or they had found some way to obscure their footprint. But how?

Akram cocked his head, noting the map's topography. Within a hundred miles of their last known location, the topographical lines nearly touched, indicating a large mountain.

"If they lived inside a mountain," Akram began, "could we detect their electronic signature?"

General Chambers furrowed his brow. "Let's find out."

The following day, General Chambers entered Akram's office. His normally smug face radiated with ill-contained excitement. Tucked beneath his arm, he held a roll of paper as long as his leg.

"We've found something," Chambers said. He shoved aside pens, papers, and folders to make room on Akram's desk. The president was too intrigued to be annoyed.

Chambers unrolled a colored photograph depicting a rocky mountain surrounding a lake. "There." He pointed.

Akram cocked his head.

"This mountain is coated with magnetized rocks, so any electronic footprint is masked from our radios."

Akram grinned.

"*And*," Chambers grinned, "my men have been monitoring the location." He chuckled. "We found them."

Akram clapped his hands together. *Finally* a break. "Prepare your men. I authorize a full invasion. Kill everyone, but bring me the Ancient, whoever he is."

Chambers's smug grin returned and the man sat in a chair. "We could do that." He shrugged.

Akram raised an eyebrow.

"We attack there," Chambers said, "and we're bottlenecked—and on their turf."

"So what do you suggest?"

He bent forward. "Draw them out. Bomb the Indignis."

Akram stared vacantly at the ground between them.

"Is that a yes?" asked Chambers.

Akram remained silent. Why hadn't the decision been this hard before, when the world was at war? Then he had been certain, beyond certain about what must be done. But now? Something about the death of the Indignis bothered him—the very species he had helped create. Was that it? Did he feel some sense of ownership, like a gardener to his crop?

It doesn't matter, he thought. *It must be done.*

Akram nodded. "Yes. Begin the systematic extinction of the Indignis. But do not forget our primary objective—we must draw out the rebels and obtain the Archive."

General Chambers smiled, then saluted with a pristine gesture. "It will be done. *Sir*."

The general paused, emphasizing the last word, only it wasn't done with sarcasm as he had before. There was sincerity there, which widened Akram's own smile.

"Let's give 'em hell general," said Akram, his heart racing with anxious anticipation.

As Chambers opened the door, another stood in the frame, hand raised to knock.

"Sorry," said Tony Chrishelm to the general. He moved to let Chambers pass.

"Tony," said Akram with a smile. "Come on in."

"Thank you, sir."

"What can I do for you?" Akram leaned back in his chair, placing his feet on his new desk. It was beautiful—solid zebrawood with a glossy lacquer finish, hand-sanded, hand-planed, with a craftsmanship that would rival the ancient Amish.

"There's been an interesting development."

"Oh?"

"Yes, sir. We have found one of the rebels."

Akram's jaw dropped. Could the day get any better?

"Or, he found us, rather," said Chrishelm. "This morning one of the rebels approached our walls. We have him in custody. He wants to make a deal."

"What kind of deal?" asked Akram.

"He says he'll give us the information we need in exchange for . . . Well, it's complicated. It's better you speak with him."

Akram laughed. It felt good to laugh again. After so many dead-ends, things were finally coming together.

"What do you want me to tell him?" asked Tony.

"Tell him yes. Yes! We'll meet."

"Did you want to tell him yourself?"

Akram's phone vibrated, interrupting their conversation. He read the message displayed on the screen, then nodded to himself.

"Arrange a meeting with the man in an hour in the interrogation room. I've got some business to take care of before then."

"Yes, sir."

Akram grabbed his suit coat. "And what's his name?"

"Briggs. Lieutenant Michael Briggs."

"Very well."

"Uh, sir?"

"Yes?"

"I overheard your conversation with Chambers," said Chrishelm nervously. "D-did you want me to tell him to hold off on the bombing campaign. Since, you know. We . . . we have another lead?"

Akram looked to the ceiling as he rubbed his cheek. "No," he said after a brief pause. "We'll bomb the Indignis."

Elsa and Spencer trudged down the hallway toward President Akram's office. Shackles bound her wrists, but she had showered and her jumpsuit was clean.

They stood in front of Akram's large ebony double doors. Her breath quickened with nervousness. Would he find out? Would Spencer remain composed?

He lifted his hand to knock, but dropped his fist with a shudder.

"Calm down," she whispered.

After a deep breath, he pulled his hand up again and knocked.

"Come," Akram said from within the doors. His voice—it still made her shiver.

Spencer pushed the door open. He touched Elsa's back, guiding her in front of him. She suppressed a shudder as she neared Akram's glossy desk.

"Sir, we have news you may find of interest," said Spencer.

"What's that?"

Spencer coughed as he looked at Elsa. She inhaled, then blinked slowly. *Emotions can be felt, not shown.*

"We've discovered something about the rebels," she said monotonously. "It seems they've been communicating right under our noses."

Akram bent forward. "And how did they accomplish that?"

"They've been hashing their signal as it's transmitted, then unhashing it when it's received. But from our end, it all sounds like noise."

The President nodded. "How was this discovered?"

"Spencer discovered that someone was broadcasting on a frequency that sounded like static. He asked for my help and I decoded the message."

"And what did it say?"

"Nothing helpful, unfortunately," said Elsa. "It seems they've been kidnapping children from the slums."

Akram looked from the tinted windows to Elsa. His gaze made her want to cringe.

"And what's the plan?" asked Akram.

Elsa smiled. "For the last several days, I've been broadcasting to the same frequency. I told them to come tomorrow night and we would bring men on the inside to help for the final assault. When they come, we capture them."

Akram smiled maliciously. "Atta girl. I knew I was right to trust you."

Elsa lifted the edges of her lips into a courtesy smile, but secretly she envisioned Akram with a bullet through his head.

President Akram entered a room. A dozen guards lined the walls holding rifles. The stench of body odor and cigarette smoke filled the air.

In the center of the room, a large man sat with his beefy arms folded across his chest. He leaned back in his chair. A tight frown plastered his face. His large biceps stretched the fabric of his green tee shirt. His pasty forearm was decorated with a tattoo—a skull wearing a monocle.

"Lieutenant Briggs." Akram extended his hand.

"Call me Michael," said the man. His deep bass voice drowned out the sound of his squeaky chair.

Akram looked at the guards. "Stand down."

They nodded, saluted, then exited the room, leaving Briggs and Akram alone. The metal door slammed shut when the last soldier left.

"Want something to drink?"

Briggs laced his fingers, then rested them behind his head. "Let's just get down to business, shall we?"

Akram nodded as he too leaned back in his chair. The two men eyed each other, seeming to dare the other to break the silence.

"What's in it for you?" Akram asked.

Briggs snorted. "You ever tried living in a cave your whole life?"

"Can't say that I have."

"No sun, no freedom to move about." Briggs cracked his knuckles. "I think if I didn't live inside a mountain, I'd be an outdoorsman."

"But you're planning an attack, aren't you? Couldn't you just wait until you conquer the city?"' asked Akram.

"I could. But they don't know, see. They trust me. If you lose, they win, I win. If you win, they lose, I win. Either way, I win."

"You make no qualms about playing both sides, do you?"

Briggs shook his head. "None whatsoever."

"You're not inspiring a whole lotta trust."

"And?"

"And how do I know this isn't some rebel strategy for gaining intel?"

Briggs scoffed. "You think we need intel?"

"Maybe you're here to give false information—you say they'll attack north, I direct my forces north, then you attack south . . ."

Briggs shrugged. "Would you rather I hide the fact I'm playing both sides?"

Akram gazed at Briggs, then shook his head. "I suppose we'll have to see. What can you tell me?"

Briggs unfolded a piece of paper, or what looked like paper. But as it extended, the flat object glowed like a computer screen. Akram leaned in as the image of a map formed. Briggs gave a series of hand motions and the map zoomed in, revealing a mountainous area that surrounded a lake.

"Azkus City," said Briggs. "Headquarters of the rebellion."

The president smiled. General chambers had been right.

"So that's it?" Akram asked.

"That's it."

Akram smiled, though he fought to keep his grin pleasant rather than smug. He'd find out where this man's loyalties lay.

"How should we attack?" Akram asked.

"We shouldn't," said Briggs, who seemed to use the term "we" a little too naturally.

"Why not?"

"There's only one way in. You launch an assault and you're bottlenecked. And they've got defense measures, both inside and out, that even I don't know about."

Interesting. The man was being candid. Perhaps he was being truthful.

"We can bomb it," said Akram. "I'm sure we can scrounge enough explosives to annihilate the whole mountain."

"And lose the Archive?" The lieutenant shrugged. He refolded the computer monitor.

"Ok, so you extract the Archive, then we bomb it."

"Not so easy," said Briggs. "The Ancient, and the new general—they're the only ones who have full access. We all get parts, but the part you need and want, you gotta get it from the Ancient or from the general, Cole Brooks."

"Ok, so go in and steal it."

"It's password protected. And I'm betting he's been working for over a century on perfecting the encryption. Don't think it's crackable. Only the Ancient and his new general know the password."

As of this morning, the man's information was useless. *He* was useless. Briggs couldn't even get him the Archive.

"And how exactly are you supposed to help me?" Akram stood, glowering. "You tell me I can't bomb the place and I can't steal the Archive. What am I supposed to do?"

Briggs smiled, as if the president had finally asked the question the lieutenant had come for.

"Ransom," said Briggs.

Akram cocked his head. "Ransom?"

"Yes. In a few short weeks, Cole will launch an assault on Fahrquan. The kid's as tough as wet toilet paper—you threaten any one of his friends and he'll crack."

"So all I have to do . . ."

"All you have to do is hold someone he knows as hostage. He'll give you what you want."

"That's it?"

"Well, it's a little more difficult than that," said Briggs. "You'd never get a chance if they annihilate you."

"Ok . . ."

"So that's where I come in," said Briggs. "The moment they plan their attack, I'll let you know. We devise a strategy where we get Cole alone with you and I, with one of his minions at gunpoint."

"That still doesn't answer my first question. How do I know if I can trust you? I need proof you can turn on your own."

Briggs pulled the folded computer monitor out of his pocket again then flattened it. He waved several more commands before a message showed.

THIS IS ELSA. I HAVE FOUND SOMEONE ON THE INSIDE WHO IS SYMPATHETIC TO OUR CAUSE. HIS NAME IS SPENCER BURTON. IF IT WILL HELP WITH THE FINAL ASSAULT, WE CAN GET YOU INTO FAHRQUAN UNDER FALSE IDENTITIES . . .

The message continued to give instructions about where and how this was to take place.

Akram smiled. *How dumb do you think I am?* Briggs no doubt interpreted it to be a triumphant smile.

We'll see how faithful you really are.

"Do you mind staying 'til after tomorrow night?" asked Akram.

"Not at all."

"Good. And one more thing." Akram leaned back in his chair, sipping a mug of coffee. "The Ancient. What's his name?"

"I don't know his last name, but his first name's Gene."

Akram lurched in his chair, nearly gagging on his coffee.

The Ancient—his name was Gene. It had to be a coincidence. President Akram shivered. Yes, it was just a coincidence.

He walked down the long white hall for the second time that day. Earlier, he had brought Lieutenant Briggs and the man had passed the test. But this time, he brought Elsa. She walked with a steady gate, as impassive as if she were traveling to the supermarket. Yet she always looked like that.

Akram pushed the door opened. In the center of the room, the rebel sat restrained. His bony feet and gaunt wrists were tied to the metal chair. The man's hair was buzzed, revealing a shadowed scalp with none too few white scars. Though the man claimed to be in his early thirties, his skin was as rough as leather—more fitting on a fifty-year-old smoker than a young soldier. Not for the first time, Akram wondered about the rebellion's standards for recruitment.

"You've gotta believe me," the man had said earlier. "I don't know anything."

"Then why did you lie?" Spencer had asked.

"I didn't. I swear. I'm a Malkum soldier."

"Then why couldn't we find your name in our database?"

"I'm a new recruit. I just joined today."

The man had screamed as Spencer increased the intensity of the electrical shock. The man eventually changed his story, several times, until finally admitting he was a member of the rebellion. The other man had done the same.

Briggs had passed the test, killing the first man without hesitation. Now it was time to see where Elsa's loyalties lie.

Guards stood at each of the four concrete walls and a single light with a green lamp shade hung from the center, directly over the rebel.

"Thank you for coming, Elsa," said Akram. "It seems your intel was correct. We did indeed capture a rebel attempting to infiltrate our ranks."

The president carefully scrutinized Elsa, but the girl remained expressionless.

"We have done our best to extract useful information, but it appears that this man knows nothing," said Akram.

"That's unfortunate," said Elsa monotonously.

"It is indeed. It seems our best option now is to eliminate the threat."

Akram looked at Spencer, who extended his 9 mm to Elsa.

"Please," the president interrupted, handing Elsa his own gun. "Use mine."

Akram searched for any hidden signal between the two as Elsa took the weapon, but found nothing.

"Elsa, eliminate him."

The prisoner began screaming, revealing nor more than five brown teeth. Spencer administered another dose of shock. The man screamed, then whimpered.

"I'm not a violent person," she said mechanically as she offered the weapon back to Akram.

"Don't you see, my dear Elsa. You are not above suspicion."

She regarded him with that gaze that could could pass for a dead woman's last expression. Akram tightened his fist. "I haven't forgotten, Elsa, that you *abandoned* your work on the Archive. Nor have I forgotten that you spent weeks with the rebels. It seems to me that one as smart as you—one with enough intelligence to crack the rebel's code—would have found a way to report your capture. How do I know you're not feigning allegiance, while assisting the enemy?"

Elsa regarded him, saying nothing.

Akram frowned. "It seems there's only one way to see where your loyalties lie."

The president folded his arms as he stared at Elsa.

"No," she said indifferently.

A sigh of relief escaped the prisoner's mouth.

"Is that your choice?" Akram asked with steady rage.

Elsa said nothing. Instead, she put her wrists together and extended them toward the president. "As I said. I'm not a violent person."

Akram shot the rebel in the head.

Chapter 31

What have I done? I have just proposed the idea that will destroy the world.

Journal Entry of Gene the Ancient dated two years before the Genetic Apocalypse, extracted from the Archive.

Ashton lay on a bed, looking at the digital display of the calendar. It was difficult to believe the display. It had only been three weeks since he began training with the simulator. Yet in that three weeks, he had become proficient in marksmanship, strategy, and hand-to-hand combat—over a year's worth of training compressed into a few short weeks.

He had learned how real the simulations were. After gaining proficiency in the personal combat simulation, he sparred with some of the veteran soldiers. It was like waking in the body of a stranger. He had lost the fight, but only because his own deftness had surprised himself.

Knowing how real they were made his next simulation frightening. Ashton was among eleven communications personnel chosen to train with 'the Dux' as they called him. Over the last few days, Cole had spent hours in real time intimately learning about his men in ways that reality could not currently provide.

Ashton exhaled before pressing the start button on his paper-thin computer. The small gray room faded into blackness.

He opened his eyes. Moonlight shone through the shattered window, illuminating the broken legs of a desk. He took a step, shattered glass crunching beneath his feet. The room smelled of stale mold and animal corpses.

All was silent as death.

It had once been a generic business office, but hadn't been used for that purpose in hundreds of years. At one time, it was Ashton's home.

He took another step, triggering a creak on the dust and plaster covered floor. Footsteps approached from behind, causing him to jump.

"Sorry," said the simulated Cole. "Didn't mean to startle you."

Ashton turned and forced a smile, or at least his brain told him he smiled.

"What is this place?" asked Cole.

Ashton faced the direction of the stairs and pressed his lips together. "You said we would work best together if we knew each other intimately."

Cole remained silent.

"I only lived here for a few weeks." Ashton sighed. "But all that I am is because of this place. Once you understand why I took you here, you will know all there is to know about me."

The floor creaked again as Cole stepped toward Ashton, placing a hand on his shoulder.

"Let's go," said Cole.

Ashton led the way, kicking aside old papers and rocks that had been used to break the long-gone windows. They walked down a hall that ran parallel to a set of stairs. Ashton turned right, grabbed the handrail, and began descending the staircase.

The moldy air filled his nose, causing him to quiver from the onslaught of memories, but Ashton pressed on, listening to the creaking wood with each step.

When they reached the last stair, they were immersed in darkness, making Ashton feel like a swimmer surrounded by sharks in murky waters, unaware of when the danger would strike.

Cole cleared his throat.

"I lived here with my sister Malorie for a few weeks," Ashton said. "After my parents were executed, we were banished here."

"Older, or younger?"

"Older. She tried to protect me. She chose this place because of the darkness. It seemed a good place to hide. She made me stay here while she went searching for food and water every night. Whatever she brought back, she gave to me. I told her she should eat too, but she always insisted that she had eaten on the way back. I don't think she really did.

"She got sick. Real sick. So *I* went to look for food. When I came back, she wouldn't answer and it was too dark to see."

Ashton sighed, folding his arms across his chest.

"The night I was rescued," he continued, "I was searching for food. I was going to come back, but I was starving and delusional. They found me and promised they would find my sister. But they never did."

Ashton again felt a hand on his shoulder. The lump in his throat grew and Ashton swallowed.

"I'm sorry," said Cole. "God be with you Malorie."

The two stood in silence, watching the darkness. Ashton could hear Cole's steady breaths between his own ragged ones.

"Now you know," said Ashton.

"I understand," said Cole. "This. It gives purpose and meaning. But it also tears you up inside."

"Yeah," Ashton said. "You keep thinking, 'I wish that pain would go away,' but you also see that it makes you who you are."

"And if the pain leaves, who are you then?"

"Exactly." Ashton sighed. "Without hunger—"

"—we starve," Cole finished.

And for the first time, Ashton felt a measure of peace about Malorie.

"Thanks," said Ashton. His voice trailed off as he thought about what he heard from Luther—about the little boy Suta and the village and a captive girl.

"That feeling," Cole said, " . . . it . . . it drives me too."

Gradually, the stench of moldy air faded until all sensory input ceased. Ashton blinked, then blinding light entered his cornea. Icy wind whipped through a...a helicopter was it? The *chop-chop-chop* of the rudders drown out his own gasping breaths. He sat restrained, wearing a white down jacket, a rifle in his hands. Below his feet a thick glass surface revealed an icy landscape below.

"You ready?" asked Cole.

Ashton's eyes were wide. "Where are we?"

"No idea," said Cole. "But it's your first battle."

Ashton went rigid. He'd learned how real the simulations were. Countless times he had suffered a simulated bruise or broken bone and knew it felt just as real as if it had happened.

"Relax," said Cole. "It's just a simulation, remember?"

Ashton nodded. He clutched the barrel of the rifle through gloved hands. "So w-what's our strategy?"

"Kill the enemy, don't get shot." Cole grinned.

The floor between them parted like elevator doors. The sudden gust of wind pulled Ashton's hat from his head and caused his eyes to sting. Ashton clutched the back of the chair. Cole stood, extending his hand. Ashton looked at his commander with trepidation, breathing deeply before grabbing Cole's hand.

"On three," said Cole.

Ashton let go of the back of the seat and closed his eyes.

"One!" Cole yanked Ashton by the arm and jumped into the wintry air. Icy wind buffeted his body as he rocketed toward the surface. His face went numb and he shrieked as the surface neared. His parachute opened, causing near whiplash.

He landed with a run, his training automating the movement. Bombs exploded nearby, followed by the rapid fire of assault rifles.

Cole approached, unclipping his parachute. "Grab your gun. Let's go."

Ashton fumbled his rifle, then ran to catch up to Cole. Another bomb exploded, shaking the ground. The rapid fire of gunshots was constant, like a terrified rodent's heartbeat.

Cole cupped his hands into the shape of a megaphone. "This first simulation's not about strategy." Another explosion. "It's about acclimating you to war. You've mastered the basic skills. So this is about overcoming the reflex to run."

Ashton nodded, still clutching his rifle. Cole smiled and sprinted to the battle. Ashton said a silent prayer than followed.

His muscles tightened. A terror-induced paralysis seized his body. *Boom! Boom!* sounded the bombs. *Rat-tat-tat-tat,* answered the machine guns. Ashton's knees weakened. He coughed, then stopped. Cole turned to look at him.

"I'll be here the whole way," said Cole. "It's just a simulation."

It's just a simulation. Ashton stood erect, then charged toward the battle.

They walked between two icy canyons and emerged onto the battlefield. Tracers outlined the trajectory of the bullets like shooting stars. The two of them emerged about four hundred yards from the center of the fighting. On either side were hundreds of men, hunkered down behind rocks, sandbags, or trenches. And behind each army was a mountainous facade.

"W-which side is ours?" asked Ashton.

Cole shrugged. "Doesn't matter. Like I said, it's just to train you to overcome the reflex to run. Now stick with me."

Cole ran to the center of the battle, shouting. Ashton swallowed hard, then followed. Cole's battle cry attracted fire from both sides and Ashton heard bullets whizzing past his ears. He dropped to the ground, ducking his head.

Just a simulation, he repeated to himself as the terror climaxed. He closed his eyes, sucked in a breath, then sprinted to the cover of a nearby boulder.

Cole stood, half-covered by the large rock. Ashton doubled his pace. Cole released a grenade. Only a few more steps. Relief washed over Ashton as he approached.

Pain exploded in his hip. He screamed. He looked down. Crimson colored his white pants. His face contorted as he looked at Cole.

"You said it wasn't real!" screamed Ashton.

"It's not."

A bullet passed through Ashton's simulated heart.

He closed his eyes and gasped. When they opened again, they were back in the helicopter.

"Ready to go again?" asked Cole with a grin.

Chapter 32

Perhaps I should spend my time studying strategy so that when the final battle comes, I might direct my intellectual resources toward helping our commander. Yet I tire already of war. I have seen too much death already in my life, whether by the stopping of a man's heart or by the destruction of one's intellect. I hope I don't come to regret this decision later.

Journal Entry of Gene The Ancient dated 122 years after the Genetic Apocalypse, extracted from the Archive.

Cole sat in Gene's office. He shifted his weight, trying to relieve the stabbing sensation in his back. As he shifted, the pain traveled down his leg. He sucked in a breath, waiting for the pain to subside.

The Ancient regarded him. "You okay."

Cole held his breath for several seconds before letting out a breath. "Yeah."

"Is it getting any better?"

"Much better." It was a lie, one he'd repeated a thousand times—to Luther, to his mother, to the physical therapists. There was no time for bed rest. The pain was an annoyance—an obstacle, nothing more. He'd get over it.

"So what's up?" Cole asked.

Gene studied his face. Cole forced a smile.

Gene nodded. "It is time."

"Time for what?"

"Time for you to know the plan," said Gene.

Cole lowered an eyebrow. "I thought *this* was the plan—the attack on Fahrquan."

"That's part of the plan—a major part. But there are elements of it that you must know as you plan your assault on Fahrquan."

"Ok," Cole said hesitantly.

"No doubt you are wondering, 'why now?' Well, you see Cole, this afternoon I will be vaccinated against the infection—Mortem Bacillus. If things go well, this conversation will be, perhaps, premature. If it does not go well and I am too delusional to reveal things which have hitherto been hidden, well . . . It's better to be safe."

"Okay."

"You remember I told you that Drakes had a Nexus," said Gene.

"Yes. And it was triggered by a date, right?"

"Correct. He had a time-bomb of memories, waiting for the optimal time to explode. That time came six months ago in July."

Cole grinned. That mystery had gnawed at him since he joined the rebellion. Cole bent toward the Ancient, lowering his eyebrows. "Why? Why purposefully tell the Malkum about us?"

"Because then they would begin looking for us. Since Drakes's Nexus broke, the Malkum have done exactly as I wanted them to do—they have increased recruiting nearly ten-fold. What better time to infiltrate their ranks than when their reckless haste for new recruits is at its maximum?"

Cole's eyes widened. "We have men on the inside? In *their* army?"

"Indeed we do. Thousands of them."

"And how have the Malkum not discovered this?"

"Because every last soldier is under the influence of a Nexus. Though they fight with the fervor of dedicated Malkum soldiers, soon they will come to remember their true purpose and turn on those who wear their very uniform."

Cole's lips parted, letting out puff of air. "Brilliant." Cole grinned, combing his fingers through his hair. "Wow. That's brilliant! Why didn't you tell me earlier? It would have saved me a lot of anxiety."

"Ah, but that anxiety was necessary. That anxiety propelled you onward, drove you to train with unmatched fervor and passion. If things don't work out as planned and there are obstacles, you will be glad that knowledge didn't become a crutch."

"I suppose."

"Remember that the Nexus must be activated through sensory input, though typically it is a key phrase. We have attempted, in times past, to use visual cues, but the results were quite inconsistent. Auditory cues, on the other hand, are exceptionally reliable. So, unless the army hears the key phrase, they will continue to innocently murder those whose cause they most espouse."

"How do we activate it?" asked Cole.

"That depends entirely on your battle plan. You are the general, not I. But know that we cannot win without the Nexus army. It is imperative that the Nexus be activated lest our efforts die in the wind. But the phrase that will open the path to their hidden memories is Kutha Manrea."

"Kutha Manrea," Cole repeated. "You're quite fond of non-sense phrases, aren't you."

Gene laughed, his eyes softening at the memory of their last encounter. "You're a good one, Cole," he said smiling proudly.

Cole smiled, then pressed his lips together. "You're better."

Gene lowered his eyes. When he lifted them again, there was a sadness there—a sadness Cole had seen many times yet was never able to identify why. This man had a secret past—one he kept hidden from everyone, even Luther. Between he and Elsa, Cole had enough questions to fill an encyclopedia.

"There are two more things I must tell you," said Gene.

"Ok," said Cole.

"Briggs is not to be trusted."

"But Luther said—"

"Luther *thinks* I said to trust him. I never said that. I told Luther to trust *me*. It is imperative that Briggs thinks he has my confidence. But I assure you that he does not."

"Why?" asked Cole.

"Briggs has been communicating with Akram for the last several weeks. And despite their best attempts, word has gotten to me through Elsa and her co-saboteur, Spencer."

"So why don't we arrest him?" asked Cole, tightening his fists.

"We'd alert the Malkum that we're on to them. Right now, they think they have the advantage. In the past, they've acted rashly. They nearly abandoned their attempts to reclaim the Archive just to destroy us. But now, now that they have hope, now that they have Briggs, they're willing to proceed more cautiously. That may buy us some time."

Cole nodded. It was a good plan, though Cole wasn't sure he'd be able to resist pouncing the traitor when he next saw him.

"Nevertheless we can use this to our advantage," said Gene. "You see, Cole, it is obvious that *I* am a valuable asset. Because I am so critical, I could simply walk straight into the Malkum compound and be at Akram's desk in five minutes without a scratch on my body, because *I* have information he needs. But your importance could easily be overlooked. We need Akram to know that your life is as valuable as mine. And what better way than to have him informed through the lips of a defector? Not to mention, we could supply Briggs with false information to distract the enemy from our true purpose."

Cole nodded.

"But why would Akram trust him?" asked Cole.

"Several days ago, we gave him every reason to trust him," said the Ancient. The old man lowered his head and sighed.

The room fell silent.

"We sent a message that was intercepted by the Malkum," said Gene. "That message stated that we would be sending rebel soldiers into Fahrquan at a very specific time and place. Naturally, the Malkum captured those we sent and Briggs executed them."

"What?" Cole's stomach tightened. He clutched the chair. "Who?"

The Ancient lifted his head and attempted a smile, but his eyes remained morose. "These are difficult times, and times of difficult decisions. I am ashamed to say that I intended that message to be intercepted."

Cole leapt from his chair. "You sent *our own* men to their death!?" He began pacing. "What were you—"

"Listen," Gene said, extending his hands in a placating gesture. "I did not send our own men to their death. I sent *criminals* to their death. As you are well aware, children are not the only residents of the slums. The Malkum also place their most dastardly felons there. We simply knocked two of them out, dressed them in rebel uniforms, and ensured that they were caught. Naturally, these criminals were highly motivated to keep their identity secret; death is worse than the hell of the slums. My guess is that they claimed to be Malkum soldiers, which is exactly what a captured rebel soldier would do."

Cole shook his head, his jaw tight. "What gives you the right to execute criminals?"

"I do not pretend to have a right," said Gene, his voice laced with anger. "Nor did I ever pretend to have the right to ruin your life by assigning you the task you must accomplish. *I* will pay for my crimes. But I pray that in the end, *my* abominations will deliver a restoration of peace that the world so desperately needs."

Gene sighed, dropping his gaze. "And perhaps, when I stand before God to be judged of *my* crimes, the good will outweigh the bad."

"How can you be so dismissive?" Righteous anger boiled inside him, like a parent lashing out at a child for bullying a playmate. "If you execute criminals willy-nilly, how are you any better than President Akram?"

Gene silently regarded Cole. The old man did not lower his gaze this time. Yet the sadness remained and deepened.

"I'm sorry," Cole said. "I—"

"No," Gene interrupted. "You are absolutely right. The world is as it is because someone decided another's punishment was just."

The Ancient stood. "You are a better man than I. Akram and I have one thing in common—we have little regard for the cost to save the world. In the end, I will have destroyed countless lives to overthrow the Malkum. But don't ever let that happen with you. If there comes a time when you have to choose, make the right choice."

Cole nodded, his own eyes lowering. Great. Why did he have to do that? The old man's own guilt was punishment enough.

"You said there were two more things?" Cole asked.

"Pardon?" said Gene.

"You mentioned two more things you needed tell me—one was Briggs. What's the other?"

Gene opened his mouth to speak, then closed it. "I was mistaken. There was just the one."

Cole regarded him, reading the old man's face. Gene turned his head, sitting down as he typed commands into his computer. There *was* something else, Cole was certain. But Gene had been through enough today. If it was important, the old man would tell him eventually.

Cane in hand, Cole hobbled down the darkened corridor, breathing through the pain. At first he thought he should push through the agony. He assumed it was like the soreness that followed exercise—it only needed to be endured until the muscles grew.

Yet his pain only intensified while his range of motion narrowed.

He gazed at the doors as he passed. The army was under a new training schedule. They spent four hours a day exercising to maintain body strength.

The remaining twenty hours were spent in their sleeping quarters under the influence of the simulation. There was no time reserved for rest because the simulations mimicked sleep patterns so perfectly, it wasn't necessary.

Three days. That's all he had. In three days, his men would attack Fahrquan, though no one knew it but him. That knowledge had to be kept from the traitor, a *major* obstacle. He hoped his plan was enough—a false plan of attack and a false deployment time. "We'll attack north," he had said to Briggs. "In seven days."

He tried to hide his lie. Either Briggs had believed him or the traitor was as good as Elsa at hiding his reaction.

He needed more time. But there wasn't more time. The longer they waited, the more the innocent Indignis would die from the systematic bombing campaigns of the Malkum.

Cole shook his head, dismissing the worries that plagued his mind.

He turned his attention to the long corridor, passing room after room. Over the last several weeks, each soldier had been exposed to thousands of battle simulations. This week alone Cole had led his men in a simulated attack on Fahrquan over three hundred times. They had simulated sieges, gorilla attacks, surprise attacks, and bombing campaigns.

Cole felt he knew every blade of grass that surrounded the Malkum skyscraper. His precise attacks had nearly become rote as training and the familiarity of the landscape took over.

But something bothered Cole. Though he was the general of the army, he couldn't help but return often to his old room—the one he had shared with Addonis. Cole slowly entered his old room and watched as the young man lay motionless on his bed from the DNTs.

What am I doing to these men? A host of bloody images, or simulated memories flooded his mind. Despite being virtual violence, it still sickened him.

It was doing the same to his men. He watched Addonis's face form into a contorted expression, as if the young man was witnessing the gruesome torture of a fellow comrade. Though the DNT's paralyzed the men's bodies, making it impossible to act out their simulated dreams, it was nearly ineffective for their facial expressions.

So Cole sat at the edge of Addonis's bed, watching the young man who had already experienced too much violence, knowing full well its necessity. Cole left Addonis's bedside and exited the room, all the while wondering if his own nerves had sufficiently hardened.

As he walked down the metallic halls, a female's voice echoed into the electronic device in his ear.

"Something's wrong with Luther." It was his mother.

Cole's stomach dropped. It had been a month since Aumora had given them the vaccination—a tiny dose of the virus itself. Both Gene and Luther developed symptoms, but their bodies subdued the virus within a week. Yesterday Aumora had given them a booster.

Cole felt nauseous. "I'm on my way."

He arrived at the hospital wing, stopping at the end of a corridor. His eyes followed the long hallway and rested on the entrance to the room he had lived in only weeks before. He shivered, then turned around and took the long way to Luther's quarantined hospital room.

Gene sat near Luther's bed in a hospital gown. Aumora was there as well, but she wore a yellow hazmat suit. On the hospital bed a pale version of Luther lay unconscious.

Cole dressed in the protective clothing then entered the series of doors that led to the room.

"What's wrong?" he asked, his voice carrying through the microphone in his helmut.

"I don't know," Aumora said. Her voice was strangely devoid of inflection, as if she were giving a memorized speech. "Luther's not doing well. He had antibodies, but couldn't tolerate the infection."

Luther bolted upright, eyes wide. His brow dripped with sweat and he began to scream, "Them Malkum are coming, Helena. Don't scream. No, don't scream, my love. We'll get 'em. We'll get em, Suta! Gene!"

Without looking, Aumora pressed a button near Luther's I.V. The old man collapsed into his bed. Cole looked at the Ancient, whose somber eyes stared vacantly at Luther.

"And you, Gene?" asked Cole.

"I'm fine."

"Any chance that Luther . . ." Cole trailed off before he could finish the question.

"I don't know," said Aumora.

Cole shivered, hearing the monotonous cadence of his mother's voice.

She folded her arms. "Eventually everyone's body develops the resources to fight off an infection. But, sometimes the bacteria kills the body before that can happen. Luckily for Luther, the Death Antidote ensures that it won't kill him, or so we hope. It seems that he will make it. It may just take time."

Cole nodded. "Good. Until then, is there anything we can do?"

"We're trying," said Aumora. "We've been able to take the edge off of his fever and have stopped the vomiting. But, there's nothing we can do about his lucidity, other than sedating him."

"Keep me updated," said Cole.

The wheezing of the respirator filled the silence. The room suddenly felt cold. The lights illuminated the dark shadows in Luther's eyes and the pale tone of his face.

"We won't be vaccinated, will we?" Cole asked.

Aumora's expression went vacant like a corpse. Even her skin went pale. "It's too dangerous."

"You didn't have time," Cole said.

"It doesn't matter." She shook her head.

Cole reached for Aumora's shoulder. She turned away and grabbed a notebook and a pen. She began writing furiously then ripped out the sheet of paper.

"What's this?"

"Thirty-seventh floor, room 3744, east hall, about a third of the way down the hall."

Cole raised an eyebrow.

"It's the immunology lab." She sighed. "We need to get in there."

"I—"

"As soon as possible." She raked her fingers through her hair. "I hope it won't be too late."

"Okay." Cole reached for her shoulder again, squeezing it. Aumora smiled, though her eyes remained vacant. "We'll do it."

Aumora nodded.

Luther fought to awaken. But why? There was something that nudged him on. A forgotten thought or a latent desire, perhaps. But, like a riptide, sleep pulled him under.

Luther began to shiver. It was a coldness, like wet bones that seemed to begin from the inside. Despite the abundance of fabric that blanketed him, he could not shield himself from the cold.

As he struggled to remember, the thought he wrested with gradually came to his awareness. His eyes jolted open and he sat upright. But something held him back. His gaze fell on his chest to find that he had been restrained.

"Luther," said Cole.

Luther grunted. Why didn't his tongue work? Cole leaned closer to Luther, gazing into his eyes. The boy looked surprised. The old man grunted again. But this time, he felt his tongue making a closer approximation to the sound he intended.

"What was that?" Cole asked.

Luther tightened his jaw. "Lemme loose," he barked. Cole rushed to his bed, then began unfastening the bindings.

As soon as the braces slacked, the old man lifted his torso.

"Wait!" said Cole, pinning him to his bed. Luther struggled against him, but Cole was too strong.

"Lego ov me," Luther said.

"What are you doing?"

"I ga'-go pee."

"You can't leave your bed," said Cole.

"The hell I can't," said Luther, clarity returning to his voice as his anger sparked.

"You got a catheter."

"Oh," said Luther, feeling his face flush. He looked down at his hospital gown before clearing his throat. "Do ya mind?"

"Not at all." He took a seat next to Luther.

The old man scowled. "Leave!"

"Oh. Yeah. Sorry."

The most clumsy, awkward, disgusting, urine-soaked minutes of his life passed as quickly as Sunday in Hell. Luther collapsed into his bed, already feeling exhausted.

"How you feeling?"

"Like a bat flown into an airplane," said Luther.

Cole laughed. "I'm glad you're back."

"Back ta what? What's going on?"

Cole turned, looking out the window of the door, then lowered his voice as he leaned in to Luther. "We're going in. Tonight. I came to say goodbye, you know, in case things don't go well."

"What? Tonight?"

"Tonight. But don't tell anyone."

Luther sat up. "Where's Gene?"

Cole dropped his head with a frown. "Nobody seems to know. He disappeared. Again."

"But the plan!"

"It seems everything has been set in motion. I hope. Otherwise . . ."

Cole didn't finish the sentence, leaving Luther to fill in the blank. *Otherwise what?* If the Ancient's plan wasn't set in motion, that would mean he didn't leave of his own accord. And if he didn't leave on his own, then perhaps he was kidnapped. Again.

Or worse.

Briggs. That traitor. Luther was right about that lying devil. And now, all could be lost.

Mingled with his anger, Luther felt the familiar grief begin to bore into his chest like an unwelcome disease—one that didn't seem to leave. It had devastated him far too many times—with Helena, with Suta, and now with the Ancient.

This cannot fail.

"I'm going with you," said Luther.

Cole laughed. Luther did not. Instead he narrowed his eyes on the young general.

Cole coughed, shifting his weight. "I wish you could, but—"

"But nothin', I'm going."

"Luther, you haven't been lucid for days. What makes you think—"

"And what makes you think I'm staying?" said Luther. "Son, I've got over six times the experience a livin' you have. And I've got twice the incentive ta see this thing through. And I aint gonna let a kid like you tell me to sit when them Malkum devils finally watch them bullets whizzing inta their skulls like they did to Helena."

"But—"

"And another thing," Luther interrupted again. "When you finally got that devil Akram cornered like a grasshopper, *I* wanna be there."

Cole shook his head. "You know I can't. And I won't."

Luther's eyes narrowed. Heat rose to his face. Cole reached for something near Luther's bed. The old man turned his head, then felt Cole's hands steady him as he drifted.

"I'm sorry," Cole seemed to say as unconsciousness overtook him. Or had it taken him already? Did he dream those last words?

He awoke some time later. How long had it been? Minutes? Hours? Days?

Luther's eyes fluttered open. A large man stood over him. But who was it? The image was fuzzy as his eyes adjusted.

"Good morning, Luther," said the voice.

He recognized the voice, but his mind was a mass of confusion.

"I overheard you talking with Cole," he said.

Luther's eyes began to settle. Standing above him, blocking the light from the florescent bulbs was Lieutenant Briggs.

"I overheard you talking with Cole," he repeated. "You still wanna be there for the assault?"

Luther's mind snapped into focus. "Where's-a Ancient Gene?" Luther asked, feigning incoherence. Yet amidst the act, he searched Briggs' expression.

"I don't know, sir," he said shaking his head.

Where was Cole when you need him? Nothing could be discerned from the lieutenant's calm expression.

But the Ancient did say to trust him.

"You gonna take me to Fahrquan?" asked Luther.

Briggs smiled. "I'm gonna take you to Fahrquan."

Chapter 33

I am writing to offer my condolences on the recent passing of your husband, Keston Oliver. Keston was my truest friend, and the only other man who understands the sacrifice that has wrought our provisional and finite freedom. I am bold to say that when we are finally freed from tyranny, no two man will merit more glory and admiration than Keston and Quincy. May he rest in peace and may the finest angels greet him at heaven's gate.

Personal correspondence between Gene and Lacey Oliver dated 54 years after the Genetic Apocalypse.

Beep—beep—beep.

Akram's arms were folded over a rolling cabinet in Drakes's hospital room. He rested his chin on his forearm. The overhead spotlight illuminated Drakes's gaunt cheekbones and withering muscles.

Beep—beep—beep.

It had all begun with this man—Jason Drakes. Somehow, the man's own memories had been concealed from him. But how? Though Akram knew the exact time and location of the assault, he still felt that this unanswered question—how Keston had done this—placed the Malkum at a serious disadvantage.

Not for the first time, he cursed the storm. Keston Oliver had kept his research well concealed. Now the memories of him came easily. Keston, with his stocky frame, turtleneck sweaters and thick-rimmed glasses, always hunched over a book, scribbling notes in the margins, locking himself in the library, and —

Library. Books.

Akram lifted his head. The images came rapidly now. Yes, Keston—in the library—reading *books*. Not scanning text on a computer screen, but reading *books*.

And writing notes—notes about his research—notes that may still be there.

Akram grabbed his phone, dialing Chrishelm. "Meet me in the library. Five minutes."

He arrived, panting, both from excitement and the exertion of sprinting to the forth floor library. A half-dozen shelves occupied the center of the room with no more than a few feet between each row. Blue flowery wallpaper hung loosely from the walls. The smell of ancient books filled the air. Near the entrance, a blue corduroy couch stood with one cushion deeply imprinted in the shape of a short, stocky man's butt.

Keston's butt.

Again, the images came. Akram had strolled these halls twice a day—when Akram had arrived and when he had gone home. He and Keston had worked on the same floor. Always, Keston was there, sitting on that very couch, scribbling notes in the margins of a book.

Akram entered the library, where Chrishelm stood between bookshelves. Even without the two of them, the room felt crowded. Before the storm, *nobody* read books. Only Keston. Which meant that this tiny collection was probably Keston's entire library.

It certainly narrowed down the search parameters.

"Sir?" Chrishelm asked.

"Start at the rear and meet me in the middle."

"What are we looking for?"

"Notes, annotations—anything written in the margins."

Akram rushed to the first row and grabbed a book. With a grunt, he dislodged the text from the tight space between its neighbors, then thumbed through the pages. He stopped at the first note, written in tiny cursive letters mingled with some form of shorthand.

C- identify, must confront potential for violence in everyone.

Akram shook his head, finding another note.

Blyss and Robison, 2019, AJSC.

Again, he thumbed through the pages.

Several minutes later, Chrishelm carried a stack of books. Akram raised an eyebrow.

"So far," Chrishelm grunted as he dropped the books on the couch, "Every book has annotations."

Akram rubbed his head, then looked at his watch. It had taken twenty minutes to scan one book. The assault would begin in two days. There wasn't time.

"Change of plans," Akram said. "Look for any notes about memory—or false memories, or altering memories, or something like that."

Chrishelm nodded before returning to the back of the library.

Akram scanned the rows of books. Sure, there were only a half-dozen bookshelves, but the place was packed. It had required the force of a car jack to remove the first book.

He sighed. Grazing the books with his fingertips, he walked, feeling the canvas-like texture of the spines. His eyes read the titles, looking for something.

He stopped, cocking his head. One row looked different. What was it? He grabbed a stool, standing atop it. Yes, there was something different. This row of books was not as tightly compacted. He scanned edges between books, looking for gaps.

He found one. One book stood straight, while the other tilted into it. The shelf *had* been compacted, until a book was removed.

Akram scanned the call numbers of the books surrounding the missing text —QA 279 .GR74 2019 and QA 279 .GR77 2026. The authors of the surrounding books was the same—Scott Gronlund. He read the titles— *Associative Chains and Memory in the Human Psyche*, and *The Forgotten and the False —How Experience and Attrition Influence Recall.*

With both books, the binding had separated and the color in the creases had faded.

Akram reached for the pair, sat on the couch, then began thumbing through the pages. Each was spattered in blue or black ink. Keston's own notes probably matched the word count of the original text. Akram groaned. He didn't have time. The rebels wouldn't wait.

Page after page after page. He grabbed the other book, thumbing through it. Another endless stream of notes that—

Akram stopped on a page. It was nearly blank. An image—two spiderwebs connected by a single thread. Below the image was a word, double-underlined —*Nexus*, followed by another note—*see Gronlund, 2022.*

A Nexus. Akram had no idea what a Nexus was, but he was going to find out.

Akram stood before a whiteboard littered with notes written in black, blue, red, and green ink. Each note was a dictation of Keston's original annotations. Some notes were circled with lines drawn, connecting one note to another. It was a jumbled mess.

But he'd done it—pieced together the fragments into one coherent picture. His back ached, his eyes stung, and his body felt as if it might collapse, but he'd done it.

He pushed aside the whiteboard, making room for another. On the left and right sides, he drew a spiderweb, just as Keston had done. Between them, he drew a single line in red. He circled the left spiderweb, then wrote *Jason Drakes—member of the rebellion.* He circled the right spiderweb, writing, *Jason Drakes—Malkum soldier.*

Above the red line between them, he wrote *Nexus— July 15th, 2465.*

The Ancient was smart. Akram knew what the man was planning, for it's exactly what he would have done.

Chrishelm entered with General Chambers.

"Well?" Akram asked.

"You were right," Chrishelm said.

"How many?"

"Thousands. At least half our army."

Akram nodded. The general's eyes shifted between Akram and Chrishelm. "Will you be filling me in anytime soon?"

Akram nodded to Chrishelm, who began speaking, "I did a background check on those soldiers recruited from the surrounding cities. The majority of them fabricated their identities. Even some of our own, including Jason Drakes."

The general raised an eyebrow.

Akram sat. "They have infiltrated our ranks. Half our army is loyal to the rebellion."

The general's eyes widened. "How in the—"

"It's called a Nexus," Akram said. "Their loyalty lies within the rebellion, and they don't even know it."

"How is that possible?"

"There's no time to explain," Akram said.

The general's face turned red. "I want a list of every individual who—"

"Wait," Akram said, raising a hand.

"For what? Let's execute them!"

"No."

"No?"

"No." Akram stood from his chair. He began pacing his office, scanning the whiteboards. "These men don't know their loyalties lie within the rebellion. *Yet.* And it is my intent that they *never* know."

"What do you mean?" the general asked.

"Just like Drakes, their minds have been trained to believe they are loyal to the Malkum. The enemy intends to reverse that training. So long as we ensure that never happens, we can use their own soldiers against them."

The general scoffed. "You willing to take that risk?"

"Tony," Akram asked. "What's half of 10,000?"

Chrishelm's eyes shifted from Akram to the general, but said nothing.

"Come, Tony. You don't need a calculator. What's half of 10,000?"

"5,000?"

Akram smiled. "Thank you Tony. Five-thousand soldiers. Half our army. We can frantically attempt to execute 5,000 prisoners. Or, we can ensure that these 5,000 soldiers never reverse loyalties."

"I assume you have a plan," the general said.

Akram smiled. "Oh, I have a plan."

Chapter 34

Am I alone? Is there anyone there? Please. I'm surrounded by barbarians. If you can hear me, save me from this hell.

Computer transmission received from an unknown sender four weeks after the Genetic Apocalypse

---

The hall before Elsa was dark, disappearing into blackness. The handcuffs chaffed her wrists as they bounced behind her back. They did little to still the trembling in her hands she couldn't seem to control. She felt like an inmate on death row—uncertain when her time would come, only knowing it would.

"I could get killed for this," Spencer said. He rubbed the back of his sweating neck.

"And I am incarcerated for what *I* did."

"You were supposed to shoot him." Spencer looked behind his back. "You nearly blew my cover too."

Elsa said nothing.

They turned a corner. Spencer again looked back the way they had come, then grabbed her shoulders. She tensed, fighting the urge to cringe.

"You have five minutes," he said. "I'll not risk fudging the security cameras any longer than that."

Elsa nodded. She rubbed her wrists after Spencer released the handcuffs.

"Give me two minutes to get set up." Spencer handed her a keycard. "Then run like mad."

Elsa nodded again.

She waited. The hallway was silent—not even a ticking clock to count the seconds. Instead, she counted her breaths—short and ragged as they were.

1—2—3.

She raked her fingers through her tangled hair.

20–21–22.

After counting her hundredth breath, she sprinted, unable to bear the wait. She arrived at the door, flashing the keycard. The light changed from red to green before clicking.

She entered. The room was empty except for a transparent cylindrical chamber in the center. It had a diameter large enough to fit a small collection of electronics and a hospital gurney. On the gurney was a man she hardly recognized. His hair, once black, was now white. The spotlight above revealed his gaunt cheekbones and cracking lips. Circles as dark as bruises surrounded his eyelids. A respirator clicked, then hissed, clicked, then hissed.

Elsa approached. "Father." Her voice came out as a whisper. She could hardly breathe, as if *she* were the one who required the respirator. When Spencer had told her of her father, she hadn't realized how close to death he would look.

"Akram infected him with a virus when he learned of his intention to escape," Spencer had said. "Your father is given a steady stream of medication via the vents in his quarantined chamber. It's enough to keep him alive. Akram hoped he would be sick enough not to leave, but not so sick that he couldn't work on the Archive. He wasn't so lucky. The man lays on his deathbed, day after day, and has done so for three years. He will probably never recover."

"Then why doesn't Akram just let him die?" she had asked.

"He has moments of lucidity," he had said. "But they're scarce and they rarely last."

Today she had hoped to find her father lucid. Instead, she found only a sliver of life occupying the man's corpse. His eye twitched—the only hint of life Elsa could see besides the rare rise and fall of his chest.

"Father." Her voice echoed in the room.

His eyes fluttered open then closed again.

"Father!" she yelled, lifting her hands to the glass.

His eyes jolted open, and he turned his head to look at her. He smiled. "Daughter." His voice too was foreign—raspy and breathy. "Daughter, where is your smile?"

Elsa's face remained placid. *Emotions can be felt, not shown.*

"I'll see you in Rohlmanda." He rested his head on the pillow and closed his eyes.

She lowered her forehead to the window, feeling the heat of the chamber permeating the glass, burning her scalp. "I was there." The respirator filled the silence—*Click, hiss. Click, hiss.*

Elsa folded her arms. "I went to Rohlmanda. *I* did as *I* promised. But *you* broke your promise. You never came."

Father remained motionless.

"But I understand now," she said. "You were trying to protect me—from the Malkum, then from the virus."

The lump grew in her throat. She tightened her jaw, then exhaled. *Emotions can be felt, not shown.*

"I just came to tell you . . . that I forgive you."

She nodded as if she had checked something off her to-do list, then walked to the back of the chamber. She touched the respirator that contained the medication.

Click, hiss. Click, hiss.

"He will never recover," Spencer had said.

Elsa reached for the tube, then paused. "Goodbye, Father." She ripped the tube from the respirator. It hissed like a hostile snake.

The room fell silent. She faced the exit, tightening her fists. Again she swallowed, then walked. She paused once, turning her head to look one last time at her father. Again, her grief began to boil in her throat. She swallowed hard, then sighed.

"Sleep well, Father," she said over her shoulder.

After exiting, she closed the door behind her and folded her arms in front of her chest. The darkened hallway stretched before her.

Emotions can be felt . . .

She trailed off mid-thought, remembering the first time she had repeated those words to herself. It was only a few months after her father went missing. The money he had promised wasn't in the trust fund—someone had emptied it the day before. For weeks she lived off what food remained in the house. Destitute of funds and with provisions nearly empty, she accepted an invitation from the Malkum to work in their data recovery division.

And that was when the assaults began. A man, noticing her grief, had shown compassion, but it was only a front. Only after the rape did she realize it.

Emotions can be felt, not shown, she had decided. The mantra had indeed protected her.

But over time, she had also convinced herself that hiding emotion was the same as not feeling it. At each of life's crucibles, she had erected the barriers she assumed would protect her from the pain. But the grief now was no less painful than when her father went missing.

Emotions can be felt, not shown. Emotions can be felt...

She spun and opened the door. She sprinted to the chamber. The man's eyes flickered. He sucked in a breath, closed his eyes, then all the tension in his body released.

Elsa wept.

Elsa watched the I.V. drip, injecting liquid into Father's dead body. His skin matched the pale color of his hair. Her chest hurt and her eyes stung from prolonged weeping. Yet she smiled. For three years, the grief, the anger, and the resentment had poisoned her. Now that the burden had been shed, Elsa could finally smile.

Spencer!

Elsa leapt to her feet. How long had she been there? Ten minutes? Twenty? An hour?

She sprinted to the door, then rushed down the darkened hallway. She turned the corner to the security room.

"I said five minutes!" Spencer said. Sweat dripped from his forehead and dark circles surrounded his armpits.

"I'm sorry, I—"

"No time for explanations. You may have killed us!"

"I'm sorry."

He sighed. "Let's go."

Elsa turned her back to Spencer. She felt the cold steel of the handcuffs against her wrists before he guided her toward the door.

They exited the room and turned.

"Going somewhere?"

Elsa froze. Spencer grabbed her wrists in a death grip. She turned slowly, although she didn't need to turn to know who it was.

President Akram.

Akram narrowed his eyes on Spencer. "What are you doing here?"

"I-I was just escorting the prisoner," he said. "She said s-she had some ideas about how to recover the Archive."

"I see." Akram nodded. "And tell me Spencer, why would that require you to tamper with the security cameras?"

"I-I-I—"

"Enough." Akram pulled a black device from his pocket. "Goodbye, Spencer." He pressed the button.

Spencer's eyes rolled in the back of his head and he fell to the floor. A trickle of blood dripped from his opened lips and his eyes stared vacantly at the floor.

"And you, my dear," said Akram, "will come with me."

How long had it been? Hours? Days? Weeks?

Luther didn't know. All he knew was that he was *not* at the hospital anymore.

Luther knew nothing. He would go to his grave knowing that he *never* gave the Malkum any advantage. Through the grace of God, the pains of his body would not yield the information they desired.

But it was hard to be thankful.

Another fist connected with Luther's jaw. The room spun. He heard the crack of yet another broken bone and felt blood drip from his slack-jawed mouth.

"Where's the Ancient?" demanded Briggs. "Don't tell me you don't know!"

A punch to his kidneys. His internal organs felt as if they had exploded.

"Gene what? What's his last name?" the lieutenant screamed.

Another slap to the face. Another involuntary groan from his lips.

"I don't know," Luther mumbled.

"You've associated with him for a hundred years. You've been his confidant. You can't tell me you don't know his last name."

"He's a private man," said Luther, panting.

Briggs screamed. Another blow to the head. Good heavens, it hurt. The periphery of his vision grew dark. Briggs turned off the light and slammed the door.

I don't know what you were thinking, Gene. But you were certainly *wrong about Briggs.*

Mercifully, unconsciousness finally dulled the pains of torture.

Chapter 35

Akram—president of the Malkum. I never could have foreseen he'd become so corrupt. Had I known, I would have done something about it.

Journal Entry of Gene the Ancient dated three years after the Genetic Apocalypse, extracted from the Archive.

Large mountains surrounded Fahrquan on three sides, with villages and farm plots on the western edge. Cole and his brigade silently emerged from within the mountains on the east and south side of the compound, positioning themselves for the final assault. The Special Forces team led the way toward the skyscraper, crawling across the grass between the mountains and the outer wall of the city, flagging land mines as they traversed the ground. If things went as planned, the Special Forces team would scale the walls, enter the barracks of the enemy, shout the secret phrase, and the Nexus-induced soldiers would fight their battle for them, allowing the Special Forces team to secure the compound.

He sat in a chair. Like a woman in labor, he closed his eyes and focused on his breathing.

It was only pain, after all—it wasn't like he was unaccustomed to it.

Cole looked at his watch. 2:35 AM. The only noise was the hooting of an owl. Even the crickets were silent. A thick cloud hovered above, blocking the light of the moon. The darkness was suffocating. Addonis approached. His step loosened a collection of pebbles which caused a mini avalanche. The noise sounded like spiders crawling on broken glass.

Though his men had already simulated hundreds of battle scenarios, Cole could not still his nerves. Something about the scenery was off. It was too quiet, too peaceful.

The ominous Malkum compound stretched into the dark sky, penetrating the black clouds. Through the binoculars, he could see a collection of guards walking on the top of the wall surrounding Fahrquan.

Everything *appeared* normal, but something felt off. An icy breeze blew, which climbed his aching spine.

He lifted his radio to give the command. His mind formed the words. *Retreat*, he wanted to say. But that didn't feel right.

His radio crackled. "Hello?"

"Cole." It was his mother's voice.

"Mom."

"We can't find Luther."

"What?" Cole asked.

"We...he's not in his hospital room anymore."

"Where—"

"I think it's Briggs. I can't find him either."

Cole tightened his grip on the radio. Briggs knew. And he'd taken Luther. But what did he want with Luther?

He cleared his throat as he looked again at his watch. 2:38 AM. He lifted his radio again and spoke. "Change of plans," said Cole to the commanders in the army. "Weapons at the ready. We—"

Spotlights flared from the wall, blinding. Gunshots cracked the silence, followed by the thud of heavy artillery. Streaks of light zipped across the battlefield from both directions. The ground shook as a shell landed on the mountain, sending shards of rock and shrapnel barreling through the air. Men screamed.

He watched in horror. The light from the enemy's spotlights exposed their position. They were as visible as deer in an open field. Another blast shook the ground, sending a half-dozen bodies flying through the air.

Cole lifted his radio. "Compton six, take out the lights."

Sparks emitted from floodlights. His men were again blanketed in darkness. The gunfire from the Malkum side slowed, while the men in Cole's army fired more earnestly.

Cole lifted his megaphone. "Kutha Manrea!"

Nothing. He could hardly hear it himself.

"Kutha Manrea!"

Still, nothing. He *had* to get within earshot. He had come here, hoping to avoid an actual battle, that the Nexus army would fight for them. A sickening dread filled his stomach as he considered his next move.

Brute force.

"Focus artillery east-south-east," Cole said to his commanders. "We *have* to get inside that wall."

"I don't think you want to do that, sir," a frantic voice responded from his radio. "Look at the wall."

A second set of lights flickered, this time illuminating the Malkum army itself. Cole lifted his binoculars. At the base of the wall, rubble marked the remains of a camouflage edifice. Mingled with the shards of stone and mortar, corpses littered the ground, their bodies bending in unnatural positions. But these were not the bodies of the Malkum soldiers.

They were the bodies of women and children.

Cole gasped.

Dozens of enemy soldiers ducked beneath the civilians, herding the live ones in place of the dead, creating a continuous human shield.

"Cease fire!" he commanded. The spotlights faded and the guns continued to rage from the Malkum side, while the rebel's guns remained silent.

There was no room—no way to get in a shot. Layers of civilians stood between Cole's snipers and the guard.

Cole lifted his radio. "Beef."

A deep voice answered. "Sir?"

Bullets whizzed through the air, sending shrapnel.

"Can you get a shot?"

The radio crackled. A deep hum reverberated through the speaker. A laugh.

"Can I get a shot, he says. Yeah, I'll get it Dux." The radio crackled. "I mean, sir."

One by one, the enemy guards dropped while the civilians remained standing—frozen. That kid could shoot.

But the civilians did not flee. Paralyzed by their own fear, they remained, protecting the wall that Cole *had* to breach.

Cole cursed. "Aim high," he screamed into his radio. "Focus fire on soldiers on the walls."

Cole trembled. They couldn't return the enemy's artillery. They were fighting grenades and rockets with rifles and pistols. This would not end well if something didn't change.

"Sturgess six," yelled Cole into his radio. "Ashton," he said, calling him by name.

"This is Sturgess Six," said Ashton. Cole could hear the edge in his commander's voice and hear the screams of his men in the background.

"We need to get inside that wall," said Cole. "Retreat into the mountains with your men, then fly by helicopter to the slums. You've been there Ashton. You know the slums better than any in this army. I need you to find a way to get within the walls and activate the Nexus."

A pause.

"Yes, sir," said Ashton. "It will be done."

Cole rubbed his sweating forehead. *It might be too late. My army is already defeated.*

"Sir. This is Special Forces," said a voice from his radio. "Permission to retreat."

"Where are you?"

"Between you and the enemy, sir."

Cole cursed. "Retreat north-north-east. We'll direct firepower elsewhere. And hurry! We must secure the compound."

"Roger."

"Klakon six, Brick six, move your men south-south-east."

"Roger."

As Ashton ran to the helicopter, he tried not to think of his task. He had spend a decade trying to forget the two weeks he had spent in the slums. Now his commander was telling him to *remember*, and to remember some unknown detail he may never have noticed.

His stomach sank to his seat as the helicopter lifted. The thumping of the rudders did little to silence the explosions and gunfire. Smoke and the stench of gunpowder filled his nose. The sound of fire bursts faded. Ashton sighed.

As they neared the west wall, the helicopter shook with another explosion. Ashton's pulse rocketed. "What's going on?"

"Enemy fire coming from the west wall," the pilot shouted over the noise of the rotors. "Changing course. Flying south-south west."

The hanger shook as something else exploded.

"Hang on tight!" yelled the pilot.

Ashton's stomach lifted to his chest as the chopper dropped. The feeling seemed to last forever. *Pull up,* he thought, though he couldn't see their altitude as he pressed his head between his knees.

The chopper crashed. Ashton's body lurched against the seatbelt, sending ripping pain through hip bones. Blood rushed to his head. He lifted his torso, feeling queazy. Moonlight shone in beams through the smoke, passing through the shattered windows, reflecting off the shards of glass that layered the chopper. Several men groaned. Some remained motionless, blood dripping from their mouths.

He shook his head, then peeked through the broken window.

The slums. They had crash landed outside the wall separating Fahrquan from the slums, yet within the wall of his former neighborhood.

Another helicopter sounded overhead. Gunshots followed the trajectory of the chopper. Ashton withdrew his radio. "Companies 1-4, travel north. Bunker behind the buildings and direct enemy firepower north-north-west."

"Sir, Company 3's down—their helicopter exploded mid-flight."

Ashton cursed. "Alright. The rest of you—north-north-west. Go!"

He turned to look at those who remained in the helicopter. He heard the battle cry of the other Companies as they fled their helicopters. Gradually, the explosive sound of the enemy's weapons grew distant.

"It's all up to us, gentlemen," said Ashton. "We *must* get past that wall."

The men nodded. Though surrounded by darkness, the light of the distant explosions and the moon allowed Ashton to see the terror in their eyes. The company that flew with him had once numbered over a hundred. Now, there were only a few dozen left. In their first battle, they had seen more death in one exchange than many veterans of their ancestors had in their entire lives.

He had to penetrate the walls. He had to get inside of Fahrquan. But how? His men couldn't scale the walls—they would be too visible. He tried to remember the geography, but had spent so many years repressing the memories of the few weeks he had spent there. Now, as he tried to recall the landscape, all he could remember was the sight of the crumbling bricks, the eerie silence broken by occasional screams, and the smell—the rotten smell of garbage and . . .

Sewage.

And where there was sewage, there had to be pipes.

Ashton smiled. He bent toward those men who remained alive, speaking in a whisper. "Here's what we're going to do. We travel to the south-west corner of the wall. Keep silent and close to the wall—they'll likely have guards above. We're looking for a pipe."

The men nodded.

"Let's go."

Stepping over dead bodies and the twisted metal door, they exited the helicopter, using the light of the moon to guide their steps. Each snapping twig and rustling leaf caused Ashton to cringe. The wall that separated the slums from Fahrquan was, perhaps, a hundred yards away. From his vantage point, he could see figures moving along the top of the wall, sweeping the landscape with their weapons. Ashton shuttered, then crouched beneath the shadows of the trees.

As he neared the marble facade, the conversation of the guards punctuated the shrieks of the distant gunfire. He turned to his men, gesturing for silence, then closed the remaining distance to the wall.

He pressed his back against the surface, feeling the rough texture of the marble with his fingertips. He extended his hand, his fingers gliding over the etched graffiti. He dared not breathe more than a silent puff at a time. His lungs felt like engorged balloons, moments from popping. Yet as they inched forward, the nauseating stench of the sewer drains grew.

They found it.

Like the rest of the slums, the chipped concrete was covered in black grime. It extended 18 inches or so from the wall. Ashton lifted his eyes. Moonlight cast the overhead guard's shadow on the sludge below. Ashton waited for the shadow to pass, then peeked over the pipe.

Steel bars as thick as his wrist blocked the opening. Ashton shook his head. They were so close. All that separated—

Ashton's radio crackled. His eyes widened. He frantically reached for the dial, but it was too late.

"Who is that?"

Back pressed against the wall, he turned to his men, signaling for them to run. They shook their heads, stepped away from the wall, and began firing at the enemy.

Jael Grasse, commander of the special forces division of the rebel army, watched from a helicopter. Below, the battle raged. Billowing clouds of smoke dimmed the twinkle of the lights. Bursts of red flame spattered the landscape and tracers zipped across the field, like swarming fireflies. He ejected the magazine of his 9mm, then reinserted it. Then he ejected it again and reinserted it.

God be with you.

He turned his attention to the skyscraper ahead. On his left and right, several other small choppers hung in the air against the backdrop of the ominous skyscraper.

"Can you set us atop the building?" asked Grasse, barely hearing his own voice over the thumping of the helicopter.

"No. They've set up anti-aircraft," said the pilot.

Grasse lifted his radio. "Plan B."

Grasse's pulse drummed in his chest and he grinned. He nodded to his men, who clipped cables to their belts and fastened gas masks over their faces. The doors opened. Wind rippled across his clothing. Adrenalin surged. He approached the opening, closing his eyes and inhaling the fresh night air. The helicopter turned and Grasse jumped.

With 5.7 g's of centrifugal force, Grasse barreled toward the skyscraper. His eyes watered and his clothing slapped his back. He pointed a megaphone-shaped object at the windows of the 197th floor and pressed a button. The device released an inaudible sound at the window at just the right frequency. The thick glass moved in a wave pattern, then shattered.

Grasse pressed a quick release, using his forward momentum to shoot him inside the building, firing three rounds of a soporific gas through the broken window. He pressed a button on his jacket. The face of it exploded outward. Bags inflated around him, just as his body made contact with the tiled floor. He rolled as the momentum slammed him into a wall.

The room was empty. He stood with a grunt, removed his jacket, then drew his handgun.

He sprinted to the center of the building, shooting gas as he went. He approached the central heating vents, then pulled a vial from his pocket. Grasse tightened his gas mask, before filling the vial with water. Wisps of smoke climbed through the opening of the vial, then disappeared into the heating vent.

He entered each room, placing bands around the wrists of each unconscious person he found.

Desmond Dehlin approached.

"All clear?" Grasse asked.

"Twenty-seven people, all restrained," said Desmond.

"Very good," said Grasse as he pulled his palm to his mouth. "197 clear."

He heard a crackle in his receiver as another voice said, "Floor 115 clear, including three councilmen."

"117 clear with one councilman."

"139 clear."

"Exits secured."

Aumora stood in her room, pacing. She counted the number of laps she made around her bed. *111. 112.* All the while, she looked at her radio.

Come on, come on.

But it might be too late.

The radio crackled. She jumped for the bed. "This is Aumora."

"Sergeant Kris Simon speaking."

"I'm ready."

Silence. "Well..."

"Send me a picture. I need to see the immunology lab."

"I'm afraid that's not necessary."

Aumora closed her eyes, gritting her teeth. She lifted the radio to her mouth.

"You see," the sergeant continued, "the room is empty."

Aumora's stomach twisted. This couldn't be happening. "Empty of everything?"

"Just empty tables and a couple of sinks," he said.

"No mouse colonies? No vials?"

"Nothing."

Why would there be nothing? It didn't make sense. If they were going to develop—

It clicked. How could she be so stupid? Primates. The infection needed primates. That's why it hadn't worked. The guarded door was just a ruse. They had developed it on *primates.*

"Thank you," she said into the radio.

She shoved the radio in her pocket. Only one other time in the history of the Malkum had they experimented on primates. And in only one location—the same location where the Genetic Apocalypse began.

Aumora needed a chopper.

Ashton's men sprinted in the darkness, firing their rifles. The booming noise drown out every other sound.

Which is what Ashton was counting on.

He gripped the dimpled surface of the grenade with his sweating hands, then leapt to the sludge. It pulled and sucked at his feet. He attempted to wriggle free, but the mud won possession of his boot. The freshly stirred sludge wafted into his lungs. Ashton gagged, then lodged the grenade between the steel bars. After yanking the pin, he pulled himself atop the pipe, then leapt for the wall. The ground rumbled.

He waited. The gunfire continued unabated. Ashton exhaled before creeping back to the pipe. Clouds of dust and smoke swirled near the entrance, but the bars remained intact.

He cursed. Though the grenade had not broken the bars, it *had* bent them. Was it enough to squeeze through? Ashton removed his backpack, pushing it through the pipe. He turned his body sideways, squeezed his head through, then stopped as his right shoulder lodged against the bar. He cursed again, then retrieved another grenade.

The gunfire ceased. Another burst of rounds—*Rat-tat-tat-tat-tat.*

Then silence.

He searched the shadows of the trees for movement, but saw nothing. *Oh no.*

He sighed, closing his eyes. Had his men fled? Or died? *Doesn't matter,* he thought. *My task is the same.*

He glowered at the bent bars. He was so close—he only needed two inches. And the silence meant he couldn't use another grenade.

Ashton gritted his teeth, extending his right hand through the hole. When his left shoulder met the bar, he pressed on, grabbing the chipped concrete inside the pipe. *Come on.* He slammed his shoulder against the bars. Pain exploded. His breath quickened.

He closed his eyes, letting his mouth release a silent cry of agony. He panted like a woman in labor. *1–2—3!*

His collar bone snapped, sounding like the breaking of a tree branch. He bit his lips and tears streamed down his eyes. But he pressed on until *finally* his body fell into the sewage within the pipe.

He stood, clenching his jaw, attempting to ignore the pain as he moved forward, slowly at first, then with renewed speed. From his bag he removed several more grenades, taped them together, then hung them from the top of the pipe. He removed his body armor, placing it in front of his backpack. Next, he pulled the pins, then sprinted back toward the pipe's exit. He ducked behind his backpack and the protection of his body armor.

The ground shook, then the blast came with a force greater than a towering wave. His body slammed against the bars. His ears rung and dripped with viscous liquid.

Dazed, he gathered his rifle. Stumbling, he approached the gaping hole where the grenades had been.

He hadn't broken through the soil. Ashton dropped to his knees. His throat tightened. Above the gaping hole, an unknown quantity of compacted soil remained.

He grabbed his final grenade, massaging the metal indentations. He brought it to his lips, then said a silent prayer.

With his fingers, he dug. The dirt chaffed against his knuckles and pulled against his fingernails. He burrowed a hole large enough to hold the grenade in place. He pulled the pin and ran.

He awoke in sludge. His head pounded with each pulse of his heart. Blood poured from his ears into the edges of his mouth, bitter and metallic tasting. He lifted his head.

And smiled.

Light shone through a hole in the pipe. Between the background ringing in his ears, he heard gunshots.

He leapt to his feet then ran to the hole. Standing on his backpack, he reached for the surface. His left arm hung limply at his side. With a grunt, he hefted himself above ground.

He sat under a tree, its skeletal branches shading him in patches from the moonlight. Ashton narrowed his eyes on the largest concentration of soldiers.

He sprinted toward them.

"Kutha Manrea!"

Primal screams pierced the air. Hundreds of soldiers grabbed their helmets. Ashton watched in awe as a mass of soldiers fell to their knees.

I've done it, he thought with a smile.

A split second before it hit, Ashton saw the fire-tail of the bullet. Like a shooting star, it left an impression of the path it traveled. But Ashton didn't need the light of its tail to know where it landed, for it ripped a hole straight through his ribcage.

This time it wasn't a simulation.

Chapter 36

Who is Gene the Ancient? I'm afraid to even consider my best guess.

Journal Entry of President Akram dated the day before the rebellion's attack on Fahrquan.

Cole listened to the report from the special forces. He heard reports from all floors but one—floor 200.

It was the floor where Akram's office was located.

But at what cost? Severed limbs mingled with broken fragments of rocks. Corpses peppered the mountain's facade. The dying screams of men overwhelmed the noise of the Malkum's rifles. The sparse fire from the rebels had dwindled to near extinction.

Once he had been paralyzed by indecision. He once assumed his empathy would make him unfit for command. As the Ancient promised, he had indeed learned to temper his empathy against the greater good.

But at what cost?

Cole shook his head. "Do you have Elsa? What about Luther?"

"No, sir," said Commander Grasse. "We've checked every prison cell and every floor. She's nowhere to be found." The radio clicked off. "And no sign of Luther."

Cole cursed as his heart began to race in panic. Elsa and Luther both—gone. They had to be with Akram.

"What about the asset?" asked Cole.

"The asset is coming out of unconsciousness right now."

"Good. Go with the asset in teams of four and secure the remaining floor." He paused. "And be careful. They...They probably have Luther and Elsa."

A sickening fear filled his gut. This couldn't be happening. His army had all but lost. Elsa and Luther—captive within Akram's office, maybe even dead.

Yet there was something. He peeked through his binoculars. On the west side of the wall, there was sudden commotion. Enemy soldiers began to turn on themselves. Tracers decorated the landscape. The soldiers atop the east wall turned west, fleeing their post as they left to offer assistance. As they fled, the civilians whose lives unwillingly protected the wall scattered like billiard balls after a forceful break.

Cole smiled.

"Good work Sturgess six," he said into his radio.

Silence. "I repeat. Good work Sturgess six."

His throat tightened.

"Ashton."

Cole closed his eyes, shaking his head.

At what cost?

But the battle was far from over. Floor 200 hadn't been secured, Elsa was missing, and there was something else. Cole looked again through his binoculars to the wall nearest him. A large section of them retreated east as the remainder stayed behind. But these soldiers lacked the commotion that had been on the other side of the compound.

Not all Nexus' have been activated.

Two clusters of soldiers remained—one directly in front of him and the other north-north east, about three miles away.

Cole grabbed his radio. "Toby."

"Sir?"

"How do you feel about going for a run?"

"You're the boss."

"There's a cluster of soldiers on the north-north-east wall. Activate their Nexus."

"Yes, sir."

"And Toby." Cole's thought of Ashton. His stomach turned. "If you die, I'll kick your butt."

The radio crackled. Toby laughed. "You got it, Dux."

Faintly, he could see the outline of a shadow sprinting toward the wall.

Only one more cluster remained—the one with the highest concentration of soldiers.

He lifted his radio to his mouth. "Battalions one through four—"

An explosion. Sparks flew, blinding Cole. His ears rung.

Shaking his head, he lifted the radio to his mouth. Static.

Oh no.

He pressed the button again. Static.

"No, no, no, no!"

They'd destroyed the satellite. "No!"

He began shouting. "Destroy the wall! Destroy the wall!"

He could barely hear himself. The gunfire from his army nearly ceased.

He almost dropped to his knees as he had with Suta. The grief began to weaken him, consume him, as he considered the lives that had paid for his lost battle.

No! he thought. There was no time to grieve.

He gripped the sides of his chair, standing. The tremors began anew, sending shards of pain to his spine, his temples, and his right leg. He zipped his jacket and grabbed a magnetic grappling gun, rushing toward an armored vehicle.

"What are you doing?" yelled Addonis as Cole darted past.

Cole said nothing. He fired the engine and roared toward the hillside, descending at a frightening pace. Every rock shook the chassis. Reaching level ground, he slammed the accelerator, rushing past his half-broken army and toward the Malkum compound.

This was stupid. He was painting a target on the fender of the car. Grabbing the magnetic grappling gun, he fully pressed the accelerator, and jumped out the door, rolling with his fall.

He cried in agony as the impact of the fall sent stabbing pain through his spine. Rockets screamed as they flew toward the vehicle, followed by a deafening explosion.

He leveled the grapping gun at the skyscraper and fired. Seconds passed before a distant clank sounded. Closing his eyes, he retracted the steel cable.

Soaring through the air, the icy wind ripped through his clothes. His body rocketed toward the building. He screamed in agony as the centrifugal force pressed against his spine. He sailed toward the marble wall. Tears streaked down his cheeks, both from pain and from the icy wind. He pressed the quick release on his belt. His body was launched through the air and over the wall that surrounded Fahrquan. He pressed the button on his jacket. The cushions inflated immediately before he crashed to the ground. All went dark.

He woke, delirious. His head swirled. That consuming, agonizing—

A tremor began. His body convulsed. He stifled a cry as it racked his body.

Gotta get up. The Nexus. Gotta get up. He grabbed the knotty bark of the tree, then stood, pressing his hands against his temples. Blood rushed to his head and he went rigid, attempting to prevent himself from passing out—attempting to suppress another tremor.

The moment passed. He removed the now-deflated jacked then pulled his megaphone from his pocket. Someone grabbed his wrist.

Instinctively, Cole ducked before the wind of a fist caressed his ear. He dodged another blow. Pain shot through his lower back. He buckled, dropping to the ground. The man charged. Cole swept a log, toppling the soldier.

"Kutha manrea. Kutha manrea."

The soldier jumped to his feet, unaffected by the Nexus phrase. Cole tried to savor the pain, try to let its pulsing fuel his limbs.

Nothing.

In the simulation it energized. Now, it paralyzed.

Cole stood, unsteady. The soldier retracted his fist. Cole jabbed, landing a punch in the guy's neck. He made a gargling noise. Cole kicked, landing a foot in the man's stomach. He backpedaled. With a shake of his head, he lifted his fists.

Cole imagined the glowing red eyes of the robot, tried again to feel the pain as he had before.

Another tremor, one too powerful to control. He fell to the ground, convulsing. The soldier kicked, landing a foot in Cole's ribcage. He rolled with the momentum, jumping to his feet.

Again, his head swirled. He closed his eyes.

Only a few seconds. That's all he needed. Just a few seconds to *not* feel the pain—*not* whine, *not* complain, *not* wish someone else had been chosen.

He opened his eyes. The man charged.

Screams began from near the west wall, followed by the rat-tat-tat-tat of gunfire. Cole grinned. Toby had done it.

Taking advantage of the man's distraction, Cole planted another foot in the man's stomach. He stopped, gasping. Cole jabbed. Blood burst from the man's nose. Left, right, left, right. The man wobbled, dazed. Cole landed an uppercut in the man's nose.

He dropped, motionless.

The moments of relief passed, bringing with it another tremor. He hobbled to the tree, grabbing his loudspeaker. He choked down another cry. He climbed the tree, struggling to stay on his feet as the earth continued to spin around him. He grabbed his loudspeaker, then searched the landscape for the largest cluster of soldiers. When he found it, he shouted.

"Kutha Manrea!"

Gunfire ceased as screams filled the air.

Relief washed over him as he watched the Nexus-induced soldiers turn on the Malkum. Men shouted. Others ran. Bodies lurched and dropped like leaves in the fall. The firelight of the bullets flew every which way as the highly trained Malkum soldiers turned into a rag-tag team of isolates. Some fled to the walls, others tried to coalesce into groups, while a large portion began targeting everyone else, whether Nexus-induced or not. The open field of the grass supplied little protection and within only a few minutes, all had either dispersed or died in the interchange.

Cole smiled as he climbed down the tree.

Dropping to the ground, he grabbed his radio. "This is General Brooks. The army has been neutralized. Scale the walls and secure the perimeter."

"That won't be necessary. *General.*"

A Malkum soldier stood above him, gun drawn and pointed at his head.

Sergeant Jason Drakes lay unconscious on the hospital bed, just as he had done for months. Near his gurney was an unconscious nurse with her hands tied behind her back. A soldier clothed in black stood before Drakes and leaned over his bed. "Hollen taklama," he whispered.

Drakes screamed, again, for the third time as the final Nexus was activated. As memories flooded his mind, the excruciating headache returned, but so also did consciousness.

He sat upright, removed the I.V. attached to his arm, then leaped off the bed. His fragile legs nearly crumpled.

"Is the building secure?" asked Drakes. His tone was robotic, rehearsing a sequence he had been programmed to perform for years.

"All but the top floor, sir," said the young soldier. "We sent a team of four to the 200th floor several minutes ago but haven't heard a word."

"And how's the battle going?"

"It was going poorly until their own men turned on one another," said the soldier.

"Good," said Drakes with a nod.

The soldier stared at Drakes, his head cocked to the side.

"Never mind," said Drakes. "Where are the rest of the men?"

"Aside from the four we sent to level 200, the remainder are guarding the entrances and exits. Akram is cornered at the top, but it may take hell to get to him."

"Then let's give 'em hell."

"President," the Malkum soldier said, his gun trained on Cole, "we've got General Cole Brooks. Permission to execute."

"No!" Akram screamed. "You keep him alive! He must be brought to me."

Despite the gravity of the situation, Cole nearly laughed. It all made sense. Only he and the Ancient had the password to the Archive. Gene hadn't been kidnapped or murdered. He had fled, leaving Cole the only person left who knew the password to the Archive. To the Malkum and to the rebels, Cole was the most important person alive.

He only hoped it wouldn't be in vain.

The man bound Cole. No longer able to stand, Cole sank to the ground. The soldier dragged him across the silent battlefield. The darkness that blanketed them concealed their movements until they reached the Malkum skyscraper.

"Command your men to cease fire," said his captor.

"No."

"Do it, or—"

"Or what? You gonna kill me?"

The captor's face turned red and he grit his teeth. He pulled his fist back.

A gunshot.

The enemy soldier paused as blood erupted from his chest, then he fell backwards. Cole dropped to the ground. He turned his head to face the building and saw two rebel special forces holding rifles.

"Thank you, gentlemen." Cole winced. "Nice shooting."

The men nodded as they supported Cole into the building.

"What's the status?"

"All floors are secure but Akram's."

Cole clenched his teeth. "Still?"

"Yes, sir. We haven't heard a word from them."

"Then what—"

"Cole Brooks," said a voice over the building's intercom.

Cole froze.

"Welcome to my home. I insist that we meet formally. Please, come to my office on the two-hundredth floor. And come alone."

Cole snarled.

"And to provide you with a little incentive, I will execute someone you hold very dear to you if you're not here in five minutes. And what is your name my dear?"

Her monotonous voice spoke over the loud speaker. "Elsa Alsvik."

Ignoring the agony, he sprinted to the elevator.

Four minutes and thirty-two seconds later, he jumped past the elevator doors of the 199th floor—the highest level the elevator could go. Panting, he rushed up the final flight of stairs. Each slap of his feet against the stairs sent stabs of pain into his back.

He stumbled over the bodies of five Special Forces soldiers. Some of his friends stared with deathly vacant eyes, while others seemed to slumber.

He lifted his head. Dozens of armed Malkum soldiers stood in the large hallways, rifles raised.

"He's arrived," said one of the soldiers into his wrist.

"Tell him he's too late."

A gunshot.

Cole screamed, his mind reeling. He sprinted toward Akram's office. A sea of arms grabbed him. He thrashed, casting aside the restraints. He jumped toward Akram's door. An enemy caught his ankle. Cole tripped, then dozens of soldiers pinned him to the ground. Air fled his lungs. The pain in his back mounted. He tried to gasp. Nothing came.

Oh no.

They leaned into him, squeezing his body. He felt as if an elephant stepped on his chest. He flailed, but couldn't free himself. He kicked, but nothing budged. With one final scream, he dropped his head and wept.

They lifted him, contorting his arms behind his back. They slapped cold steel cuffs to his wrists, then dragged him to the door.

He felt his knees weakening as he began falling to the ground.

"No!" he screamed as he kicked a soldier, toppling several others. With bound hands, he began sprinting again in the direction of Akram's door. He kicked it open before soldiers grabbed him again.

A strong, familiar voice spoke. "I never said I'd execute Elsa."

First he felt relief.

Then horror.

Lying in a puddle of his own blood was a man Cole once called brother.

Huka was dead.

"No need wasting the blood of brilliance." Akram extended the smoking barrel in Cole's direction. "But at least now you know I'm not fooling around."

Cole growled. The office was surrounded by dozens more armed soldiers, each pointing a rifle at Cole. Near Akram, Elsa and Briggs stood. The traitor supported another—a man whose face swelled with purple and black bruises. Blood dribbled from gashes all over his face—in his cheeks, his lips, his nose, his forehead.

It was Luther.

Cole's eyes widened. Elsa's face remained placid, but Cole could see a hint of fear in her slightly widened eyes. Cole's chest heaved as he looked at the brother he had assumed was already dead. Learning he was alive, only to find him dead again, flooded him with grief he assumed he had successfully repressed.

Cole shouted the words of the Nexus again.

"Kutha manrea!"

It was a long shot. The hasty recruitment only began several months ago. It was unlikely that Akram would surround himself with novice soldiers.

Nonetheless, Cole heard the screams of a lone man within the ranks of the soldiers.

"Ah hell," Akram said.

Then the glass shattered.

And as promised, all hell broke loose.

Sergeant Jason Drakes stood on the roof of the Malkum Skyscraper. Surrounding him were the dead bodies of dozens of soldiers and unmanned anti-aircraft weapons. Drakes strapped a cable to his belt then jumped off the roof, turning as he fell to face President Akram's office. The glass shattered as he flew through the air. Shards of thick glass battered his body armor and face mask.

The moment the enemy came into view, he began emptying the ammunition in his rifle. For each shot, several seemed to drop. Before he even entered the room, Drakes eliminated over twenty men.

The sergeant dropped to a knee like a baseball player sliding into base. He slipped behind an overturned filing cabinet, thudding against it. Malkum soldiers fired in his direction. Bullets tore through the cabinet, sending slivers of metal that lodged in his skin. Several other rounds thudded into his body armor with twice the force of a baseball bat.

Another window shattered, followed by an icy current of wind.

The Special Forces team had arrived.

"There," Aumora shouted, pointing. The chopper pointed its lights to a mount of grass. In the center of that mound was a metal hatch.

Aumora's stomach lifted to her throat as the chopper descended. She only hoped she wasn't too late.

Not waiting for the chopper to land, she leaped, landing hard on the grass. She pulled the gun from her pocket and sprinted to the rear of the mound. A metal door had been carved into the hill. Grass surrounded it on all sides.

The door was locked. After drawing her pistol, Aumora knocked and placed her ear on the door.

Muffled footsteps mingled with a muffled voice. The door swung open. A bang. The Malkum soldier dropped as the helicopter powered down. Matt Sampson, the helicopter operator, sprinted toward Aumora. The man had short-cropped black hair, tan skin, and a somber expression. He held his pistol as if it were an extension of his hand and carried himself with equal dexterity.

"Thanks," she said.

He nodded.

They entered the doorway. A long hall stretched before them. The stale air smelled of metal. Their footsteps clapped against the steel surface.

"Shhh," Aumora said.

Leading the way, she traveled down the hall. It terminated at a door. She grabbed the handle, but Matt pressed his hand against the door. He motioned for her to stand back. She shook her head. He narrowed his eyes. She narrowed hers. He bent toward her.

His hot breath caressed her forehead. His cologned wafted into her nose, momentarily muddling her concentration. Her heart rate accelerated.

"I'll go first," he whispered.

She shivered. "No."

"If you die, I wouldn't know how to stop this."

"Then don't die."

She reached for the handle again. He grabbed her wrist. A thrill of pleasure coursed through her veins.

"No," he said.

She frowned and almost began another facial standoff. But there was something about the man's commanding directive—like the edict of an emperor.

Very well. She grinned and nearly curtsied.

Stop it! She was acting like a giddy school-girl. There were more important things to deal with.

Yet she couldn't suppress the grin.

She backed against the wall, taking several steps backward, then nodded.

Matthew nodded back. He grabbed the handle and threw the door open.

Gunshots. The bangs thudded down the metallic hall, amplified by the material. Each bang thumped against her chest, only to hit again with the echo. She closed her eyes until all was silent.

A body thudded to the floor.

She opened her eyes to find Matthew motionless, lying in a pool of his own blood.

Bullets streaked across the room, accompanied by the deafening crack of gunfire. Shards of wood and shavings of metal flew across the room. Soldiers hunkered beneath broken furniture. One by one, bodies dropped to the floor as the Special Forces team arrived through the broken windows. Men screamed, some as they fell out the window.

"Stop or I kill her!" screamed Akram.

Despite the cacophony, the president's words exploded through the room. The gunfire ceased.

Cole struggled to lift himself from the floor. He winced, grabbing his back.

Dead Malkum and rebel soldiers littered the ground, their arms and legs placed in awkward positions. Broken pieces of wooden furniture were scattered everywhere, and as the wind from outside the broken windows diluted the smoke of the guns, Cole saw Akram standing in the rear of the room behind Elsa, pointing a gun at her head.

The rebels outnumbered the Malkum, and each side shifted weapons to find new targets, but none fired.

"It seems you're outnumbered," said Cole.

"Am I?" Akram pushed the gun closer to Elsa's head. "Command your men to stand down."

The president stood in a corner, out of sight of the Special Forces team. Cole pulled against the cuffs at his wrists.

"What..." Cole breathed through another tremor. "What do you want, Akram?" As he stared at the men he blinked. There was something about the president that he hadn't noticed in the commotion. Yet he couldn't pinpoint what it was.

"You know what I want," Akram said, interrupting Cole's thought. "I want the password to the Archive."

"What good will it do you?" asked Cole. "Your army is defeated. Your men are outnumbered. You can't win, Akram."

"Yes, I can." The president reached for his pocket and pulled out a radio. "Is it ready?"

"Yes, sir," said the voice on the other end. "At your command."

"And tell me again, *what* is at my command?" asked the president. His eyes were wild and his frame quaked.

"The virus," said the man in the radio. "At your command, I will release the MB infection."

"And what will happen if you release the virus?" asked Akram.

"Everyone not vaccinated will die. That means the Indignis and the rebels."

The radio crackled off.

Silence.

The radio clicked again—*click*. "And I have been instructed," the man on the radio said, "to release the virus if I suspect you are killed."

Again the room was silent.

Click. "Sir, should I release the virus?"

Akram pressed the call button, then set the radio down.

Akram lowered his eyebrows at Cole and smiled.

"You see, Cole, I have not lost," said Akram, his voice loud enough for the man on the radio to hear. "Give me the password, and put your weapons down or the virus is released."

Cole felt his knees weaken. He'd come so far, sacrificed so much. His village—destroyed. Suta and Huka—dead. His army—in ruins. So many lives lost. And for what?

He couldn't give in. Not now. Not after they'd come so close. The army was neutralized, the Malkum council imprisoned. All that remained was Akram.

Akram. Akram. AKRAM!

You are better than I, Cole thought, remembering the words of the Ancient. *Akram and I have one thing in common—we have little regard for the cost to save the world. If there comes a time when you have to choose, make the right choice.*

The counsel had seemed ambiguous, both then and now. What was the right decision? Should he allow his friends to perish and the world to die, just to remove Akram? Or should he give in, perpetuating and permitting the tyranny? Yet if he gave in, Akram would never let them live.

Neither choice was good, but the choice was obvious. The world mattered, his friends who might have a chance to escape mattered. If he destroyed Akram, the world would die and he no longer had reason to live. He had fought for the world and fought for those he loved. If he lost them, his fight would be in vain, making a mockery of those who died in the struggle.

The dejection was too great, the grief too consuming. Despite his former promise to himself, Cole fell on his knees, too crushed to stand.

"I . . . " Cole began speaking with labored breaths as he looked into Akram's face. The president held his mouth open in a circle, as if he was blowing a candle out. Something about that expression was familiar. Where had he seen it? In his mind, he began to paint Akram's hair grey, adding wrinkles to his skin. The aged image of the President stuck in his mind, only it wasn't the president.

It was the Ancient.

Cole's eyes widened as his mind made connections—the aging mice the Ancient had shown—the *cloned* mice. The ability of the Nexus to *copy* entire memories. The last meeting he had and the second item the Ancient never told him. The nonsense Nexus phrase and the nonsense password to the Archive.

Gene the Ancient was Gene Akram.

President Akram was Gene's clone.

Cole smiled wickedly as he inhaled a deep breath. Then he screamed the password to the Archive—the password that would activate the Nexus in Akram.

"Cakfe-burgen tongen."

Akram clutched his head.

Then he screamed.

Aumora struggled to breathe. Matthew—dead. She stared at his broken body, frozen in place.

She heard a voice from within the room. "Sir, should I release the virus?"

Move!

She stood, unable to pry her eyes from Matthew. A wave of nausea hit. She blinked, fixed her jaw, then stood, peeking around the corner.

Screams filled the room, carried through the static in the radio.

"Sir?" the man within the room said through the radio. "Sir?" He dropped the radio and cursed.

His footsteps echoed inside the room. He approached a computer.

Move!

Aumora entered the room, pistol extended. Dead bodies littered the floor. The lone man exhaled, then punched a button.

"Stop!" she said.

The man flinched, raising his hands.

"Don't do it or I'll shoot."

He opened his mouth, but said nothing. Machines whirred. The ceiling moved, opening up to a cloudless night sky.

"I-I-I."

A timer flashed. Two minutes. A low hum began.

Aumora approached. "Turn it off."

"I c-can—"

"Turn it off."

"I can't!"

To her right, a half-dozen rockets pointed upward. Fire gushed out the rear.

"What have you done?"

She grabbed a fire extinguisher and approached the rockets, pointing the nozzle at the motor. Heat billowed. What was she doing? She was a biologist, not an engineer.

Shaking her head, she fired the extinguisher. White gas shot into the fire, extinguishing the motor.

As she moved to the next one, the first reignited.

She cursed and fired again. Again, the rocket went out. And again, it ignited again.

She shook her head. Lifting the extinguisher over her shoulder, she swung at the bottom like a baseball bat. It hit with a loud crack. Her hands stung from the impact. Yet, the bottom of the cone remained intact. She shook her head and swung again. The bottom cone flew through the air, landing near the gaping man.

"Help me," she said.

The man shook his head, hands still raised.

"Now!" She drew the weapon.

With a shake of his head, he grabbed a computer monitor and rushed toward the rockets.

She looked at the clock. Forty-five seconds. She swung at the next rocket. The impact against her hands was agonizing, like ten thousand tiny needles stabbing her fingers and palms.

Two rockets down. The man slammed the computer monitor against a rocket. The monitor shattered, while the rocket engine remained intact.

"Find something else!"

She disabled another rocket.

Thirty-three seconds.

"Hurry up!" she screamed.

He approached, carrying a wooden stool.

She swung at another rocket. Four down. Two left.

Eighteen seconds.

"Go!"

She swung, sending another engine flying. He swung, breaking the chair and bending the cone.

Nine seconds. One left. She sprinted. He grabbed another chair and swung, but too high. Aumora hit the engine, incapacitating it. The rocket teetered. Everything went silent. With a squeak, the rocket fell toward Aumora. She jumped as the rocket crashed.

The tip separated from the body. A glass tube slipped out. Aumora lunged, but missed. The glass landed on the metal floor, cracking.

A hissing filled the silence, coming from the glass tube.

"Close the doors!"

"Are you—"

"Now!" She pointed the gun at him.

He raised his hands.

"I said now!"

He rushed to the computer, entering several keystrokes. Machinery whirred. The metal ceiling began closing.

The man bolted.

"Stop! Stop!"

She fired. His body thudded to the ground.

Chapter 37

I spoke with Cole today. I never did tell him about President Akram, about his Nexus. After I informed him of the prisoners we executed, I could not bear the look of disappointment in his eyes. I feared if I told him of the monster I had created, the idea I had proposed, that my soul would split with shame.

Journal Entry of Gene Akram dated 212 years after the Genetic Apocalypse, extracted from the Archive.

"Immobilize them," Cole yelled amidst the president's screams.

Cole dropped to the ground, searching the dead bodies for the key. After locating it, he freed himself, then grabbed the dead man's weapon.

It was chaos all around him. Bullets flew across the room as men again ducked behind desks and filing cabinets. Cole searched for Elsa and Luther, but his eyes fell on another—Lieutenant Michael Briggs. The man crawled toward the broken window, holding a makeshift grappling hook connected to a cable that was clipped to a belt. The sounds of the gunshots escalated as the lieutenant half-stood and sprinted in a crouched run. He started lowering the grappling hook as he neared the edge of the window. Cole lifted his rifle to fire, but before he could, Luther swept a leg in front of Briggs. The lieutenant tripped and his forward momentum carried him out the window. Mingled with the Nexus-induced screams of Akram, Cole heard Briggs's cries as he plummeted toward the pavement.

Within a few seconds, silence returned. The entire Malkum squadron lay in puddles of blood.

Cole rushed toward the radio. "Stop!"

Silence.

"Stop!"

Cole's heart pounded.

The radio crackled. "You're safe." The radio clicked. It was a woman's voice —a familiar voice.

"Mom?"

"The virus..." she wheezed, "has been contained."

Cole exhaled. He lifted the radio to his mouth. "Thank God."

Yet something felt off.

President Gene Akram continued to clutch his head. "What have I done?" he whispered to himself. "What have I done?"

Cole gazed around the room. They all looked at Cole as if he had performed some sort of magic. All except Drakes.

"President Akram was under a Nexus," Cole said.

"How?" asked Luther.

"Two hundred years ago, Gene started a fight with an enemy too powerful to defeat," said Drakes as he moved toward the center of the room, rifle in hand. "Gene was on the Malkum council and *he* was the one who proposed the idea that would wipe the world's intellect."

"No," Luther shook his head. "Gene wouldn't do that."

"It was a joke," Drakes said. "A flippant remark, nothing more. But the council took his joke seriously. But by that time, it was too late. A man of such notoriety couldn't just *leave*. So the Ancient, Gene Akram, was himself trained under a Nexus."

"How?" asked Luther.

"Keston Oliver," said Drakes. "Keston trained Gene's mind, shaping it so he believed and always remembered believing that the *only* solution to the nuclear threat was the virus that crippled human intellect."

Cole nodded. "And because he couldn't just leave, the Ancient cloned himself and duplicated his memories and his Nexus into President Akram. But now he had a new problem—his clone was an infant. And, just like he did with his mice, he aged his clone, President Akram, until they looked the same age."

"Right," said Drakes. "Once Akram was ready, the Ancient activated his own Nexus. Then the Ancient fled, starting the rebellion and waiting until their colony had grown enough to mount an assault on Fahrquan."

A solemn silence filled the room as the meaning of their discovery sunk in.

"Brilliant," said Luther.

"Brilliant," Cole agreed with a nod.

"Wait," Luther said. "If they were supposed to be the same age, why does Akram look younger than the Ancient?"

"Because the Ancient didn't discover the Death Antidote until long after Akram did."

Luther nodded, before looking at President Akram—Gene Akram. "But still." He glared at Akram who continued whispering to himself. With a shuffle more pronounced than usual, the crippled man approached the president. Luther bent to pick up Akram's pistol, before approaching the President.

"What have I done?" Akram whispered again as his eyes shifted around the room.

Luther extended his arm with the barrel aimed at Akram's head, then paused. As Cole watched the old man's pointer finger begin to squeeze the trigger, a memory came unbidden to his mind.

If I enjoy killing, am I any better than the Malkum? They were Luther's words at the campfire, the day Suta died, the day Luther brutally killed a Malkum soldier.

The old man paused.

Cole walked closer to him and placed a hand on his shoulder.

"What have I done?" Akram again repeated, not noticing the weapon pointed at his head.

"I've had 'nough killing for one lifetime." Luther lowered his weapon. He placed the gun in Cole's hand.

"So have I," said Cole, tossing the gun on the floor.

"What should we do with him?" asked Luther, his eyes half-closed. Cole hadn't notice until now how injured the old man looked. Caked blood stained his shirt. Cuts and bruises colored his face.

Cole looked at the president, who still crouched on the ground, rocking back and forth. This man, his *enemy,* looked so benign, so helpless. His list of sins was too long, too horrific to ignore.

Yet this man was Gene—Gene the Ancient. Or, rather, Gene's clone.

Cole's face softened and he reached for the president's shoulder. "You're a good man, Gene. What you are suffering is punishment enough."

President Gene Akram, the clone of Gene the Ancient turned, finally noticing the stares of those around him. His eyes were wide, his forehead wrinkled in a horrified expression.

Cole smiled, patting him on the shoulder. "Let's go," he said, turning to Elsa, Luther, and Drakes.

He gazed one last time at the radio, trying to shake the nervousness that clung to his stomach.

He shook his head. They exited the office, leaving President Gene Akram alone in the room. Before they reached the stairs, they heard a single gunshot, followed by the sound of a body dropping to the floor.

Cole's shoulders dropped. *Rest in peace, Gene Akram.*

Aumora stared at the dead body of the man who'd almost destroyed the world for the second time.

There was no time. She grabbed medical tape and wrapped the hissing black tube with surgical gloves. The hissing stopped.

She exhaled, then threw open drawers, spilling their contents on the floor. She emptied everything on the south side of the room.

Nothing.

She moved to the north side of the room. Again, she spilled the contents of the drawers, nothing, nothing, *nothing*.

Beneath the computer, three drawers remained. With an exhale, she reached for the drawer.

She smiled.

Rows of syringes lined the drawers. She grabbed one and rolled up her sleeve. It was risky—there was no way to be certain these contained the vaccination against BC. But what other choice did she have?

She pricked her arm and emptied the contents into her vein.

For several seconds, she panted, staring at the sink at the rear of the room. She tightened her fist, closing her eyes.

With a nod, she plugged the sink and filled it with water.

She waited.

Her pulse quickened as the sink filled. She began gasping.

She turned off the water. Planting her palms on either side of the sink, she closed her eyes and counted.

One.

Her breath quickened.

Two.

She shut her eyes.

Three! She plunged her head under water. Holding her breath, she waited, savoring the sounds of silence beneath the water. Gritting her teeth, she inhaled.

The cold water burned her lungs, the back of her throat, and her nose. She lifted her head, coughing and gagging. Closing one nostril, she blew, ejecting more water.

Her coughing fit subsided. There was no way to determine whether the water had cleansed her lungs of the bacteria.

She just wasn't sure how many times she'd breathe water before she passed out.

Grabbing her phone, she set the timer to go off every three hours. If she were to stay alive, she'd have to sleep and drink.

It was going to be a long week.

The sun rose over Fahrquan hours later, painting the white clouds with streaks of pink and orange. Its light shone on the mountains, creating a warm glow. The remains of the Malkum army had surrendered and were being carried into the skyscraper for questioning. Elsa remained within the compound, assisting with the logistics. The body of President Gene Akram was being transported back into Azkus City for confirmation of his identity. Cole didn't need DNA confirmation. He knew exactly who President Akram was.

Commander Grasse of the special forces handled the minutiae of post-battle logistics. Cole had something else to do.

He and Addonis walked toward the slums. He had heard of the fearless attack by these brave men that allowed Ashton to get within the walls of Fahrquan so that the Nexus could be activated. It had turned the tide of the battle.

He owed a debt that had to be paid.

Cole paused and stared as the scene of carnage unfolded before him. Bodies littered the battle field in clusters of red. Limbs bent behind backs, their eyes half-closed. The grass, once green, was spotted with crimson.

I did this, he thought to himself bitterly. The army had been defeated, Akram was overthrown, and a disastrous plague was avoided. But at what cost? It hadn't been cheap. It had been paid by the lives of valiant men—men he had known and loved.

Was that the reason for the tightness in his gut? It seemed like there was something else—something he was missing.

Whatever it was, he would find out eventually.

"Let's go," he said to Addonis, emotionlessly.

Jake Griswold approached, breathless. "General." He wheezed. "I found it."

Addonis and Cole followed Jake as he approached a large deciduous tree. Near the base of the tree he pointed to Ashton. The man's face was frozen in a blank expression. His body was covered in filth and in the center of his chest was a massive bloody hole, caked with dried blood. Cole pressed his hands against Ashton's face and closed his eyes.

"Any idea what happened?" asked Cole.

"He directed his forces away from the sewage opening, then somehow crawled in and blew a hole in the pipe."

"Didn't look like it was easy."

"No, sir."

Cole nodded. "You got a stretcher?"

"Yes, sir."

After placing the dead soldier's body in the stretcher, Cole and Addonis walked toward the slums.

"Do you know where it is?" asked Addonis.

"No." Cole shook his head. "But I know what it looks like." How could he forget the way the shadows seemed to tear pieces from his soul? Or the haunted images of the shattered glass? The eerie silence, broken by the creak of rotting wood floors?

He closed his eyes and painted the image with his memories that Ashton had shown him. Several minutes later they stood in front of a broken-down building that matched the picture in his mind, holding Ashton's corpse in the stretcher.

"Let's go," said Cole.

They stepped over the broken furniture and began walking down the creaky stairs toward the place that was once Ashton's home.

"Flashlight," said Cole.

Ashton never did find his sister. On his one and only mission to the slums, his mission was interrupted with the screams of a young girl. Cole would finish what Ashton had started.

Addonis shone the light down the staircase while Jake and Cole carried the stretcher. After reaching the bottom, Cole grabbed the flashlight and painted the corners of the room with light.

He sighed. In one corner, white bones lay on the ground. Cole approached the dead body. It was that of a girl, or so he assumed. She was wearing a black dress and what remained of her desiccated hair reached her shoulder bones.

"Malorie," Cole whispered.

He and Addonis placed Ashton's broken body next to his sister's. They stared silently at the dead siblings. Cole exhaled, then walked out of the house.

"What now?" asked Addonis.

"Burn it. Burn it all," said Cole. "And may God be with you, Ashton and Maloric."

He exited, expecting to feel some sense of relief. Yet there was still something—some latent uneasiness that remained, as if there's something he was missing.

He traced the recent events, attempting to recall when the uneasiness began. He had been in Akram's office, right before—

"Oh no," he said.

"What?" Addonis asked.

She'd said that the virus had been contained. She'd said *you're* safe.

He ran toward Akram's office.

Chapter 38

I never intended this to happen. I left my clone behind so my absence from the Malkum would go unnoticed. I never anticipated that he would become evil. I once believed the sum of human decisions could be divided into nature and nurture. Yet my 'evil twin' shared my genetics and by copying my memories to him, he also shared my environment until our separation. No, I shall revise my previous supposition. The sum of human decisions is divided into nature, nurture, and the memories of our actions. I remembered the true reason I offered the suggestion—as a joke, while the evil one remembered believing in it. How could he not become evil after having remembered supporting the idea so religiously? I am afraid that now I have an even greater sin upon my head—not only did my idea destroy the world, but I have also in the process created a monster.

Journal Entry of Gene the Ancient dated seven years after the Genetic Apocalypse, extracted from the Archive.

"Don't come."

The words echoed in Aumora's throbbing head. They were her words—spoken to Cole. The infection was contained within an underground bunker, the only witness to its progress was her.

She lie in fetal position on the floor, soaking in a puddle of her own sweat.

Yet she shivered, pulling a lab coat over her shoulders, trying to shield her neck from the ever-present draft. Her entire body ached as if it had been used as a wrecking ball to batter a mountain.

Four days.

Her alarm blared as it had for what seemed like hours. Water. She needed to drink.

Yet she couldn't summon the strength—all energy had been spent on her incessant coughing spells.

But she had to. She had to...

Unconsciousness mercifully came.

A week.

They said to plan for the worst. It had gone from a plan to an assumption.

Cole sat at the Ancient's desk, staring vacantly.

Aumora. Mother. Gone.

His stomach rumbled, protesting the grief-induced fast.

Nobody had any idea where she was. Cole returned to Akram's office and called her radio. She hadn't answered. The GPS wasn't functional. In all likelihood, she'd removed the battery so they wouldn't look for her.

That woman had a twisted sense of responsibility—one that wouldn't even permit them to stand outside the bunker and wait for her infection to pass. Did she have any idea how closely guarded the Malkum kept the location of the bunker? Not a soul knew where it was. Plane after plane, helicopter after helicopter returned with nothing to report.

And despite Elsa's hacking, re-hacking, and re-re-hacking of the computers, they knew nothing.

Nothing!

Now they couldn't even give her a proper burial.

Dead. Never to be seen again.

And the Ancient. He too was gone.

Cole leaned back in the old man's black chair in his office. The rumble of the indoor waterfall filled the silence. Cole inhaled, smelling the faint scent of coconut.

There was only one place he hadn't looked for the old man yet. He stared vacantly at the glass desk in front of him, prolonging what he knew he had to do.

A knock sounded in the room. The light from the hall gradually illuminated Gene's office as the door opened. Elsa slowly approached, wearing light blue pants and a white blouse. The burn marks had nearly vanished and her lips forced a smile.

"Hi," Cole said.

Elsa continued her languid pace until she stood behind Cole. Her hands gently, but hesitantly pressed against Cole's shoulders, then immediately retracted. Cole reached behind him, gently grabbed her fingers, then rested them on his shoulders.

"You ok?" he asked, turning to look at her.

She paused, staring at the rust-colored walls. She shrugged. "You?"

He forced a smile.

"Any luck on the Ancient?" she asked.

Cole shook his head.

"Maybe he left a message on the Archive."

"That's what I fear," said Cole. "He'd only leave a message if he didn't intend to return."

She nodded. He palmed the Ancient's desk. A holo image of text appeared, asking for the key-code. He entered an eight digit number, after which the text asked him for the password to the Archive.

"Cakfe-burgen tongen," he said.

A holo display of Gene appeared above his desk. Cole's posture sunk. He couldn't tolerate another missed goodbye.

"Thank God you've won, Cole," the recording said. The image of the Ancient smiled. He wore a pressed black suit and his hair was wet and combed back.

"You are probably wondering where I am," said the recording. "After four hundred years of watching everyone around me die, I have become quite disdainful of goodbyes. I deeply regret that I cannot be there in person to . . ." The Ancient paused and sniffed. "To tell you . . . You've done well Cole . . ."

He paused again, allowing the tremble in his lips to fade.

"Anyway, if things have gone as planned, I am dead. Only days before I took the Death Antidote, I discovered that my bones were infected with cancer. I chose not to treat it at the time so that my death would speedily come after consuming the liquid that reverses the death antidote. I request that you do not try to rescue me or cure me or find my remains. I simply wish to pass into death peacefully.

"Please do not take this as a slight. I just feel that dying alone without anyone to mourn my passing is the most that I deserve."

The Ancient paused again, breathing deeply.

"But there is another who deserves the care and comfort of all his friends as he passes into the next life. In my filing cabinet is a drink with the ingredients necessary to reverse the effects of the Death Antidote. If Luther is still infected with the virus, I believe that he too will die quite quickly. Luther has been through nearly as much as I have, and I ask you to allow him to die peacefully, surrounded by those who love him."

Cole swallowed hard, clenching his eyes.

"And there's one more thing you must know, Cole. You once asked who your father is. I gave you an answer that you and I both found quite unsatisfactory. Undoubtedly, you were seeking the company of one who could serve as a fatherly role model for you. As I said previously, the sperm that brought about your existence was donated over a hundred years ago, then implanted in vitro. Doubtless you assumed that your father was long dead, partially because I intended to deceive you. You will soon understand why it was necessary for you to be blind as to the identity of your progenitors. You see, Cole, your *grandfather's* sperm was donated hundreds of years ago, while your father's sperm was only donated a few decades ago.

"Before you, Cole, there was another who was chosen to play your role. Like you, the computer simulations predicted that this individual would excel in all relevant characteristics. And indeed he did. However, the hand of misfortune struck a devastating blow. The child's mother died when the lad was only twelve years of age. The young man was so consumed with grief, it seemed his exceptional brilliance and aptitude would be wasted fighting a battle with despair.

"Partially out of mercy for the young boy, and partially to ensure some return on my investment, I placed the boy's precious and shattered memories under the protection of a Nexus. When he came of age, his sperm was implanted in vitro in your mother."

The Ancient paused and his gray eyes stared intently into the camera. He pressed his lips together then lifted his head.

"Cole," he said. "Jason Drakes is your father."

Cole's eyes widened. He jumped from his seat, nearly fainting from the sudden movement.

"My final prayer, Cole, is that your father survived the final battle of Fahrquan. I pray that you two will be brought home in safety, so that you could indeed have the father you have always desired."

Cole continued his fight against the tears. Elsa squeezed his shoulder. He lowered his head and tightened his eyelids.

"I have one final request," said Gene. "I ask that you make the world a better place than I did. People will now look to you for leadership, and it is my hope that you will give it. To aid in your struggle for humanity, I bestow upon you the command of another army. But this one will not fight with guns and knives. Instead, they will be armed with knowledge. As you are well aware,

Cole, I have thousands of souls who have volunteered to form a Nexus. Each individual has been programmed with a particular skill-set—agriculture, politics, finance, medicine. Essentially, every necessary skill needed to form a colony has been represented and duplicated among the thousands of individuals. It is my hope that you have the necessary resources to create a global Utopia, where Indignis and humans alike can live in peace.

"In my desk is an envelope. It contains all the information you need to activate the Nexus. Whoever speaks their Nexus, they will recognize as their leader. I trust that you will guide them with the compassion and wisdom you have shown as you presided over the army."

Cole sunk back into the chair, shaking his head. Hadn't he done enough? Couldn't he simply retire to a village and live his days alone?

Gene's smile faded. "Now, it is with a touch of sorrow and a measure of relief that I say my final goodbye." The old man had quit fighting tears. Light reflected off the drips of liquid that trickled down his cheek. The old man smiled as he lowered his chin. His gaze seemed to pierce through the time-delay of the recording. Cole again felt as if the old man could kindly gaze into his soul without passing judgment.

"Goodbye, Cole," he said then opened his mouth as if to speak again. Instead, he closed his mouth and nodded.

The image faded.

His radio crackled. "General?"

Cole lifted the microphone to his lips. "I'm busy."

"But General—"

He removed the battery from the back and threw the radio across the room.

He grabbed Elsa's hand. "Let's go."

She nodded.

Cole approached the nurses Mason as he had done everyday, multiple times a day. In his left hand, he held the envelope Gene gave him—the one with instructions in how to activate the Nexus Army. In the other, he held a vial.

"Anything new?" he asked.

The nurse shook his head. "Sorry."

Cole sighed. He dropped the vial in his pocket. He squeezed Elsa's hand. She squeezed his shoulder. They entered Luther's room.

The old man's bottom lip hung open. Drool dripped down his ashen cheeks. His monitor beeped.

He was a living corpse—one that clung to life against his own will. And Cole held a vial that could release the man's unwilling grip on mortality.

But he was sick of saying goodbye without *saying* goodbye.

He approached the old man's bed. Not for the first time, he said a silent prayer that the man would wake. Why did *he* have to be the one to decide when a man dies. That decision is God's alone.

But Luther would want it. For 50 years he'd been without Helana.

He grabbed Luther's wrinkled hand. It was cold and dry. He cleared his throat. "Wake up, you old grump."

Beep. Beep. Beep.

Cole exhaled and dropped his head. He pulled the vial from his pocket and approached the I.V. bag.

"Not yet."

Cole went rigid. He knew that voice, but was afraid to hope.

"We've been trying to get a hold of you, but somebody removed their battery."

Cole stared at the wall. "Someone else did too."

He turned. Aumora stood in the doorway, her arms folded across her chest. Her face was gaunt, and her once-smooth skin had a touch of wrinkles. Dark circles surrounded her eyes.

"I know," she said. "I look like hell."

Cole rushed across the room and embraced her. "Thank God."

Her chest shook and she sniffled.

"Thank God," Cole said again.

He pulled away. His mother's eyes were red and she wiped a tear from her cheek.

"I just." Aumora cleared her throat and straightened her spine. "I just wanted to say..."

Tears pooled in her eyes and her mouth trembled.

Cole grabbed her shoulders. "I love you too."

"Yeah," she said. "That."

"It's okay to say it, you know."

She swallowed and her face relaxed. "I love you. I always have."

"I always knew."

She smiled and extended an arm toward Elsa. Head bowed, Elsa approached and Aumora hugged her.

"I'm glad you're okay," Elsa said.

"You too," Aumora said.

The hissing respirator filled the silence, mingling with the beeping of the machine.

They turned their attention to Luther. Aumora approached. Cole followed. His mom bent toward Luther's ear and whispered loud enough for Cole to hear. "You can't leave before I say goodbye. And you can't leave before *you* say goodbye."

Beep. Beep. Beep.

"Captain Luther Carter," she said. "That's an order."

His eye twitched. Cole sucked in a breath.

Aumora bent again. "I said that's an order."

Another twitch, this time in the other eye.

Aumora beckoned toward Cole and Elsa. Cole stood on the opposite side of the bed, grabbing Luther's other hand. Elsa touched his kneecap.

Aumora bent again and whispered, "That's an order."

The top of his lip bent in a half-smirk.

Aumora smiled. "Or I'll have you hanged for insubordination."

The other side of his lip bent. His eyes fluttered, but remained closed.

Aumora bent. "One more request before I slap you."

The old man's lips moved and a low mumble escaped his lips.

Aumora remained silent.

He moved his lips again, mumbling louder.

Aumora bent her ear toward his mouth. "What?"

"I says, slap me'n I-slaps you back," he barked, his words scarcely coherent.

Aumora rested her fists on her hips. "Now that would just make my day."

The old man lifted an arm. Aumora bent her lips to his fingers. He lightly caressed her cheek.

Then he slapped her. "I donna take too kindly to threats."

Aumora laughed.

Luther's eyes fluttered open and he lifted his head. He squinted as he gazed at those that surrounded his bed.

He dropped his head and closed his eyes. "Where's Gene?"

"Gone," Cole said.

Luther chuckled. "That jerk." *Beep. Beep. Beep.* "Want me to kick his butt when I get to hell?"

"You do that," Cole said.

Luther nodded. "You got it?"

"Got what?" Cole asked.

Luther lifted his head and opened his eyes. He pointed to the vial in Cole's hands. He smiled. "You got it."

A lump formed in Cole's throat. "I think you can make it."

Luther's lip twitched and his eyebrows raised in a facial shrug. "Maybe."

"Let's see how this pans out," Cole said.

The old man shook his head. "It's time."

Cole's face contorted. He swallowed hard, trying to contain the emotion that bubbled in his chest. "I don't think I can."

"Call a nurse," Luther said, still mumbling.

Cole chuckled. "I don't think..." He cleared his throat. "I don't think I can let you go."

Luther smiled. He lifted his hand and reached for Cole's face. Cole bent. The old man wrapped his hand around the back of Cole's neck, bringing Cole's cheek to his lips. "I'm gonna miss you too, son."

"Then don't go," he whispered.

Luther smiled. "I've kept Helana waiting long enough."

The old man grabbed the vial. Aumora bent, planting a kiss on the old man's temple. Elsa kissed his forehead.

Luther removed the cap of the vial. "I'll tell Suta you says hi." He poured the liquid down his throat and closed his eyes.

Elsa grabbed Cole's hand. Aumora walked to their side of the old man's bed and gripped Cole's shoulder. Luther's face relaxed in sleep. With a final shudder, he breathed his last breath.

Cole thought of the recent revelation from Gene—that Jason Drakes was his father. It wasn't true. Perhaps the man had donated half his genetics, but that was all. *My father,* he thought, feeling a warmth spread through his chest. He looked at Luther. *My father.* Luther was indeed Cole's first fatherly figure—they had wept together over Suta and Elsa, they had fought against the Malkum together, and it was Luther, not Jason, who stayed by Cole's bedside during his paralysis.

My father.

The emotions bubbled in his throat, moistening his eyes. He led out a gasp. Then his body heaved as sobs racked his chest.

Cole's cries pierced the silent air. Like a small child finding comfort after a nightmare, Cole climbed into the hospital bed next to the old man, buried his face in Luther's shoulder, and wept.

Epilogue

The river hummed, mingling with the chirping of the birds. White caps crested above large rocks and fish glided through the water. The sun dipped below the horizon.

The cool breeze caressed Cole's hot skin, bringing with it the scent of pine needles. Dirt stained his shirt, pants, shoes, fingers, fingernails—all of it. The wages of a day at work—digging a foundation for the village center—one of the few villages that had remained isolated from the Nexus Army.

Cole grinned. Aumora never knew that manilla envelope was intended for someone else—never knew that *anybody* who spoke the Nexus-activating words would be recognized as leader by the Army. The orphaned children were like ducklings laying eyes on the nearest creator after hatching.

And his mother was a good leader too. Or so Cole had heard. But he made a habit of remaining out of the loop.

Elsa sat at his left, smiling. She wrapped her arms around his, nestling her head into his shoulder. The orange light illuminated her cheeks, the old scars scarcely visible on her smooth skin.

"Coe! Coe!" Leki approached. The boy was probably around nine. Since few of the Indignis could count, it was difficult to tell. The boy's brown eyes reflected the light of the river and he grinned. "Is ready."

"What?"

"Big big," he stretched his arms as wide as they could go, "boar!"

Cole grinned. "Aren't you forgetting something?"

The boy furrowed his brow. Cole pointed to his hand.

"Oops." He handed Cole a branch of rosemary. "I forget."

"We'll be there in a minute," Cole said.

The boy scampered off.

Cole rested the leaves on Elsa's protruding belly—twins by the look of it. She inhaled deeply, closing her eyes. She smiled and squeezed Cole's arm.

"You ready to go?" he asked.

She shook her head. "No."

He kissed the top of her head and returned his gaze to the sunset. "Neither am I."

- The End -

Made in the USA
Middletown, DE
19 February 2024